Copyright 1999 and 2018

Laurence E Dahners

ISBN: 9781517725181
ASIN: B003ODI7Z0

Bonesetter 1

—cast out—

Laurence E Dahners

Author's Note

This is the first book of the "Bonesetter" series.

This book is licensed for your personal enjoyment only.

Other Books and Series
by Laurence E Dahners

Series

The Hyllis Family series
The Vaz series
The Bonesetter series
The Blindspot series
The Proton Field series

Single books (not in series)

The Transmuter's Daughter
Six Bits
Shy Kids Can Make Friends Too

For the most up to date information go to

Laury.Dahners.com/stories.html

Table of Contents

Prologue

The boy who would one day be known as the "Bonesetter" had a humble childhood.

He was born on a cold and bitter winter night to a woman called Donte. She gathered and cooked for the Aldans tribe.

His father, Garen, was a flint worker. Garen named his son Pell, a term in their language for a flake of flint.

During Pell's seventh winter, before Garen taught his son more than the bare rudiments of flint working, Garen developed pains in his stomach, then fevers and agony. Though no one knew what it was, he nonetheless died of his appendicitis a few days later.

When Garen felt death approaching, he called Pell to his side. A little delirious, Garen gritted his teeth against the pain and said, "I've seen my death spirit Pell... it comes for me soon." Garen gasped a moment, then continued, "I *hope* you'll become a great hunter someday. But I've watched you playing with the other boys and... I fear you won't have the hunting skill. I didn't, and sons often take after their fathers. Though, thank the spirits, at least you don't have a clubbed foot like I did.

"If you *are* like me, your 'skill' will be in the making of tools and in being able to see better ways to do things. The others of the tribe may not recognize such abilities as worthy skills. But Pell, whether the others recognize your value or not, where they are strong and quick, you must make and use tools..." Garen's thoughts slipped away for a moment, then returned. He whispered, "I'm sorry... sorry I didn't teach you how to work flint." The boy sobbed as Garen's consciousness lapsed.

Pell's father woke a few more times but only incoherently babbled.

Pell's father'd been dead for many years before Pell understood what Garen's last words had meant. His father was wrong in the long run, at least about peoples' recognition of Pell's abilities. Pell himself didn't recognize the truth of his father's assertion that his "great skill" would be in the making of tools and in the vision of better ways to do things. Not until after many others had already recognized the deep currents of power held in Pell's great skill.

Chapter One

The first joint Pell relocated was on his own finger.

~~~

It was a bitterly cold day, nearing the end of winter. Sharp winds and densely overcast skies made it even more unpleasant. He and his friend Boro, both scrawny, undernourished boys of thirteen summers, were returning from yet another unsuccessful hunt. Hunger pangs gnawed their guts and weariness steeped their bones as they plodded homeward. As usual, by this late in the cold moons of the year, the sparse winter game near the cave had been hunted out. Most of the big game had migrated away, and many of the animals that did stay nearby were hibernating.

The stores of grain and roots put up in the cave during the previous summer were mostly eaten or spoiled. Meat killed at the beginning of winter and placed under rock cairns to freeze had almost all been eaten or else found by industrious scavengers.

Roley, the headman, harshly rationed what food was left. The Aldans had used up the thick layers of fat they'd built up gorging themselves during the plentiful kills of summer. They desperately needed to move away from their winter cave to a hunting ground that hadn't been exhausted, at least until the plentiful game of the warmer moons returned.

Unfortunately, the weather was still too cold for the tribe to live without a cave for shelter. They lived in grass huts in the summers, but even trying to build such huts could be life-threatening in the present cold weather.

There was talk of trying to do it anyway, but their summer hunting grounds were a two-day trek away. Pell shook his head. Traveling to those grounds, carrying their possessions, in this frigid weather, in their current poorly nourished state, was unthinkable. It'd kill some of the weaker members of the Aldans, especially the children. Then they'd still have to try to build huts—which wouldn't be warm enough...

***

On the fateful day of his injury, Pell and Boro had gone out for an entire day's hunt up on the sere plateau above the cave to the north. The tribe's better hunters had taken the more desirable southerly directions into the forests and meadows downstream, nearer to the great river. Down south the trees broke the cold winds.

Pell and Boro had walked half a day northward on the blustery plateau and then looped back. Pell had only seen a single scrawny snow hare on this hunt. His and Boro's stones had both missed; in fact, neither had come close. But that was normal; the two friends were clumsy adolescents and wide of their marks much more often than not.

As daylight faded, they walked carefully back down the steep path above the cave, but Pell's right foot slipped on a small patch of ice in a shaded area of the worn path. Later his toppling would replay in his mind over and over—as if in slow motion. His right hand flailed back to break his fall, his cold, numb fingers catching on one of the boulders at the edge of the path.

His right buttock and elbow struck the rocky path simultaneously, sending shock waves through him. His head cracked down onto stone with a "whock" that resonated through his skull. A few seconds passed in the sure knowledge that something would soon be agonizingly painful.

Then the pain arrived. His elbow wracked with torment. His head and buttock simply ached. The full magnitude of the disaster hadn't struck home until the moment he reached up to rub his head... his fingers weren't working correctly! He shook the furs back from his arm to look at his hand.

With dismay, he saw his pointer finger was crooked! It had been disjointed at the second knuckle from the tip so that the distal part bent backward from his palm. Because of the angulation, the backwardly bent tip of the finger hadn't touched his head. As he stared at the deformed finger, the pain from it finally arrived at his brain, despite the numbing effect of the cold. However, the pain held a distant second place to the gibbering terror shouting through his system at the thought of being a useless cripple or "ginja."

Memories ripped through Pell:

Durr with his broken arm—broken in a fall during one of the hunts that were Durr's great skill.

The hushed clan staring at Durr as he returned with the other hunters, clutching his swollen, deformed arm—grossly twisted and angled midway between the wrist and elbow.

The grimace of pain and terror on his face.

The wracked agony of Durr's cries as the Aldans' healer, Pont, tried over and over to straighten his arm.

The elation on Durr's face when Roley agreed to let him stay the summer because, that summer at least, the hunting was good.

The growing despair as hands of days passed and the arm remained crooked and useless. Each day Pont had tried anew to straighten the arm but, despite the agony it brought Durr, the limb remained deformed and barely functional.

The arrival of Fall with Durr still unable to cast a spear or throw a stone.

His pitiful attempts to do so with his left hand.

The horrific day that Roley declared Durr ginja and sent him away.

The stoop of Durr's shoulders as he trudged slowly away—to his certain death.

Durr had only had the one "great skill"—hunting. He hadn't had any "small skills" he could perform with one good arm and one crippled arm. He didn't have any important knowledge to teach the young because, after all, there were many other hunters. And, so Roley said, he must be exiled.

He had to go forth and remove his burden from the clan.

Pell had been the one who discovered Durr's ragged remains at the bottom of the cliff two days after Durr'd been exiled. Pell had heard jackals coughing and grunting at the base of the cliff. There were only a few and Pell had frightened them away with a few stones, hoping to steal some of the jackals' meal for himself and the clan. As Pell had come closer he'd recognized Durr's spear and some of his furs.

Durr's corpse reeked of rot.

Pell wept for hours that day. The tears came back over and over as he pictured the once proud Durr leaping from the cliff.

Choosing a quick death rather than slow starvation.

~~~

A great tremor ran across Pell's shoulders as he stared at his finger. With a cry, he grasped the finger in his left hand and pulled as hard he could in an effort to straighten it. A grating, grinding sensation emanated from the finger and agony shot through his hand and arm.

He stared at the finger. It remained just as crooked as before. He thought to himself, *it's just a finger*, recalling others in the clan who'd prospered despite a missing finger.

But, Pell knew with certainty that he hadn't been among the good spear-casters or stone-throwers even when his hand had been normal! What were his chances of success with a bad finger? Though he thought of hunting as his "great skill" he knew in his heart that he wasn't really much of a hunter. Though he'd hoped and prayed for one of the older men to take him under their wing, no one had even tried to teach him a "lesser skill" since his father died.

Now the finger was turning a dusky blue color! He felt a roiling in his stomach. Kana's finger had turned blue, then black, after being crushed under a boulder she and Tando'd been trying to move. Soon after that, the rest of her hand had begun to swell and turn red. This was followed by swelling of the whole arm. High fevers came next, with Kana going out of her head.

Shortly before she died, her hand burst open, oozing fluids with horrible odors.

Tando's finger had gotten caught under the same rock, but at a sharp corner that cut his finger completely off. It'd taken a while, but the wound healed and Tando remained a respected hunter. It'd only been the small finger on his lesser left hand after all.

Connecting these two facts in his mind, Pell quickly decided that, if the finger was turning blue, he'd be better off without it. He heard a gagging sound and looked up to see Boro staring at Pell's finger with enormous round eyes. Boro's hand was over his mouth. Boro turned and retched. Pell felt his own gorge rising, but knowing he was far too hungry to spare anything that might be left in his stomach he choked it back. Pell scrabbled out his flint knife and laid it against the finger, directly over the most deformed part.

He paused as, in his mind; he saw a scene from the previous summer. Pell had been told to gather trophies from the body of a man the Aldans had killed while fighting with the Kinto tribe over a rich hunting area. Pell had been surprised to learn just how difficult it was to saw through a dead man's fingers. Nonetheless, Pell steeled his nerve to chop off his own finger. He repositioned the blade several times, but finally dropped the knife to his side in disgust at his inability to even *begin* cutting through the useless finger.

Maybe if he walked back to the cave Pont would be able to put his finger back in place? Pont was, after all, the Aldans' "healer," though it usually seemed to Pell there was little enough that Pont could do. Or would do. Maybe Pont could cut Pell's finger off for him? Pell struggled slowly to his feet and limped on down the path to the cave.

Boro had run ahead, so by the time Pell arrived, Pell's mother Donte was already outside the cave. Hair in disarray, she hysterically wrung her hands, tears streaming down her face. "Oh, Pell…" she began.

Determined to be brave, Pell marched past her into the cave to find the healer. With disgust, he saw the bandy-legged Pont sitting in his healer's corner, a glazed expression on his face. He'd been chewing his own herbs again! Roley had once demanded that the healer stop taking his own medicines, but Pont insisted, claiming a good healer must use his medicines himself in order to understand and guide their powers.

It seemed, however, that Pell mostly chewed the hemp leaves that made you glow inside. Some of the adults joked that Pont had the powers of the hemp completely mastered.

However, they only said such things well outside of Pont's hearing. Even the massive Roley quailed before the healer's potential anger. You *never* knew when you might need the healer's powers for your *own* benefit, so no one wanted to get on Pont's bad side.

Pont peered owlishly at Pell's finger. The healer rocked back and forth and it seemed he could hardly focus his close-set eyes. He pulled on Pell's finger perfunctorily. The tug stung like the bite of an angry child but did nothing to restore the form of the finger. Pont squinted at it a moment longer then dropped to his knees and began to rummage through his baskets.

"What are you looking for?" Pell heard himself asking in a querulous voice.

"Dried hemp and other herbs to help ease the pain, boy!" was the slurred answer as Pont held out a handful.

Pell didn't see any "other herbs" in the handful of hemp he was given. He stuffed it in his mouth anyway, beginning to chew. "The finger's so cold I can hardly feel it," Pell mumbled around a mouthful. "What now?"

"Give the medicine time to work! Come back when your head sways." With dismay, Pell saw Pont put even more hemp in his own mouth!

Pell wandered about the camp chewing his mouthful until his head began to swim. He returned to Pont.

"You're gonna have to wait a bit!" Pont said crossly, "Even a healer has to piss once in a while." He heaved himself to his feet and made his way unsteadily out of the cave.

Pell stood, swaying uncertainly until Pont returned. "Let me see it," Pont said reaching out.

Pell tendered his finger and Pont grasped it, pulling savagely. Despite the cold and the effects of the hemp, it hurt fiercely and Pell bent over, howling in agony. Nonetheless, when Pont released the finger, Pell held it up and looked hopefully at it. His finger was unchanged! He looked accusingly at Pont, but the healer'd already turned and begun rummaging through his herbs. "What now?" Pell asked with some trepidation.

"A poultice to stop the swelling."

"No! That's what you did for Kana! She died! *Cut off* my finger... like Tando's!"

"I *can't* cut off your finger, you ginja fool!" Pont ducked his head a little in embarrassment at his slip of the tongue.

Pell stared at him, aghast. Ginja (useless) was a common enough swear word or insult, but not one you'd ever use on someone who might actually *be* ginja! Pell felt the hemp making his world slow down. Rather than making everything feel better as it had on the other occasions when Pell had given him hemp, a black rage built from deep inside him.

Pell felt his face flush with heat. "I'll rip it off myself!" he shouted, his voice breaking to a squeak at the end. He gripped his finger with his left hand and bent it even farther backward, as if to break a green stick by wrenching it back and forth. As he bent it back, he pulled as hard as he could in order to tear the offending digit from his hand.

Pell's hands flew apart with a violent jerk. For a moment he thought he'd succeeded in pulling off the finger. He peered blearily at his left hand, but to his disappointment there was no dismembered fingertip resting in his left palm.

His eyes wandered unhappily to his other hand.

He stared in shock at his injured finger. Though it remained swollen, it had a normal shape! He tried to move it and it wiggled! As he watched, its dusky color flushed pink—then brighter red than his other fingers. He worked it some more in growing amazement.

A foul odor bit his nose and he noticed the healer standing in front of him with one of his poultices of half-rotted leaves. Pont stared at the relocated finger, eyes wide with surprise. Then Pont's expression quickly turned to calculation. "See, boy, I *told* you the herbs'd work!"

Wide-eyed Pell stepped back. He shouted, "Your cursed hemp didn't fix my finger! *I* fixed my finger!" Pell could hardly believe he was hemped enough to scream at any adult, much less the tribe's healer. But he was doing it nonetheless.

Pont brutally cuffed Pell to the ground.

His shout brought other members of the tribe crowding around. They'd all uncomfortably looked aside earlier when Pell first entered the cave with his deformed finger. Now they stared in excitement and amazement at his finger. Pont boomed, "My mixture of special herbs put his finger back in place! But does he offer his gratitude? No!"

Pell opened his mouth to protest again, but Tando, the well-respected hunter who'd lost his own small finger under a rock, grasped Pell by the shoulder. "Don't argue with your healer, boy. Just be glad your finger's better. It might still turn out badly, look how swollen it is."

Pell stumbled back, holding his finger in his other hand and slurring. "It wasn't the hemp! *I* fixed it! I don't want your ginja poultice either!" As the finger warmed up, its feeling came back with a vengeance. The finger throbbed and tingled, but somehow Pell thought that was good.

A minute or two later Pell stumbled over to the pile of leaves and furs where he and his mother usually slept.

There he collapsed and darkness overtook him.

***

When Pell awoke the next morning, only the urgency of his bladder dimmed the pain in his finger. It throbbed with each beat of his heart as if he were striking the knuckle with a knapping stone. After he'd stumbled out of the cave to relieve himself, he quickly began to want more hemp. Unfortunately, he didn't think he'd better ask the healer for more of the mind-addling leaves.

Pell sat a while cradling his injured digit. Eventually, he resolved to beg the healer's forgiveness when he awakened.

However, Pont awakened in a surly mood. He beat his mate Lessa for some offense even before he went out to relieve himself. When he returned, he immediately began rummaging in his baskets and chewing on a mixture of his herbs.

Pell considered this a good omen. Pont chewing on herbs usually became Pont in a good mood. After some time passed, Pell sidled over and, in a timid voice, asked if he could have some more of the hemp.

"Ha, what's this? Is this the young ginja who proclaimed my medicines useless last night? Get away from me! *You'll* get no more of the blessed hemp!"

Pont had spoken in the booming voice he cultivated for important ceremonies. Everyone in the cave heard. There was scattered laughter, which brought a flush to Pell's face, but as he looked around he saw horror on the faces of many in the tribe. Pell realized with dismay that the healer may have just sealed Pell's fate as an outcast. He'd been worried because he threw badly. He knew they considered him a third-rate hunter. His own father'd predicted he'd have inferior hunting skills. Now, he not only had all those same deficits, but he was injured and the tribe's healer had declared him ginja!

When he'd been younger, Pell's mother'd consoled him with stories about how Roley himself had been clumsy until after his adolescent growth spurt. However, a gnawing fear that he'd never prove to be an adequate hunter had always yammered in the back of Pell's skull.

Pell's long-dead father couldn't teach him the secrets of flint knapping, a skill Garen had been so good at that the tribe had gladly supported him. Supported him despite the small, twisted foot which, in addition to his natural lack of hunting skill, had left him useful only as a beater on hunts. Pell had tried working some flint in hopes that his father's gift had somehow passed to him naturally and would blossom without training. Unfortunately, the points Pell had made so far were no better than the untrained efforts of any of the other tribe members.

And worse than most.

To get good points the Aldans had been forced to trade with other tribes at the summer gatherings.

Other than his mother, Boro was Pell's only friend. It often seemed as if their friendship was only a result of the fact that Boro's social standing was just as low as Pell's. Both clumsy social-outcast, pre-adolescents, they were bound together by their unspoken fear of being declared ginja. In a fit of emotion, Boro and Pell had once pledged to leave the tribe together if either of them were ever cast out.

Pell looked over at Boro. Boro avoided Pell's eyes by staring into his own lap. Pretty much everyone in the cave avoided Pell's eyes—except Donte, his mother. Pell returned to his bedding and collapsed to nurse his misery.

Pell found that if he kept his finger high in the air it didn't throb as much. He could move it, as he proved to himself over and over, despite the pain involved. He found himself holding it next to his middle finger so the good finger could protect it. There was nothing but a thin gruel of roots to eat that day. The way people had been looking at him, Pell didn't have the courage to get any of the soup himself, but his mother brought him a bowl of it and sat behind him, grooming his hair while he ate.

He felt comforted by her actions, but his stomach sank again when he saw the way a couple of the hunters looked at him. He could tell that some of them were already thinking of him as ginja. They didn't want to waste their food on him if he'd soon be cast out to die anyway.

***

The next day, having tired of holding the injured pointer finger and its neighboring middle finger together with his other hand, he bound them together with a thong. At first he wrapped the two fingers together, but had difficulty tying off the thong with only the one other hand to work with. Finally, he managed to tie a small noose in a thong and slipped the loop around the base of the fingers. Then he wrapped enough turns to use up the thong, cinching a few half hitches about the fingers out near the tip. A revision of the wrap a little later that morning taught him his hand could function almost normally with a short wrap of thong between each of the joints.

Pell decided he should go out on a hunt so that the Aldans would see him *trying* to contribute. He looked about for Boro, but couldn't find his friend. Eventually, he embarked on a hunt by himself.

As he trudged up a little side valley toward the plateau above he knew in his heart that this hunting trip would be a farce, but he waited until he was far out of sight of the cave to try throwing a rock with his injured hand. As he'd feared, the pain in his bound finger made him even clumsier than usual. He practiced throwing for a while but soon realized that there was less chance than ever that he might hit anything that day. Nonetheless, he trudged on.

It was a clear, windless, cold day without a cloud in the sky. In his tired and hungry state, he had no appreciation for the day's placid beauty. Instead, he cringed away from its cold bite, drawing deeper into his furs.

A rabbit exploded from under his feet! Daydreaming, he hadn't noticed it until he'd almost stepped on it! Pell was so frightened he dropped the stone he held in his injured hand and nearly fell again. The rabbit shot across the floor of the little ravine and vanished. Pell followed it half-heartedly to the spot where it'd disappeared and stood, looking around disconsolately.

After a moment he noticed he was standing next to a hole in the ground! The rabbit had its *own* little cave! He crouched down and reached into the burrow as far as he could—no rabbit. He sat by the hole and pondered. If he waited long enough, would it have to come back out? Might he catch it then?

Who was he kidding? He wasn't fast enough to catch a rabbit!

Perhaps if he covered the hole with a fur? No, then the rabbit just wouldn't come out at all. As Pell sat contemplating the problem, he unwound one of the thongs from his finger—the finger remained swollen but pink. He could still wiggle it. Daydreaming, he played with the thong a bit, tying the knots he'd learned. While practicing the slip knot he'd used to start the wrap on his finger, he fumbled and dropped the thong. When he picked it up, the loop at the end caught on a small stump next to the rabbit hole. When he jerked on the thong the little noose he'd formed cinched tight around the stump. He had to sit down next to the stump and work it loose.

An idea came to him that he might be able to make a similar loop catch around the rabbit somehow, thereby slowing it enough that he could capture or club it. He tied one end of the thong to the little stump next to the hole. He propped the slip loop about the opening of the rabbit's hole with bits of brush and twigs so that the opening in the noose was somewhat bigger than a rabbit's head.

As he got up and walked away from the hole, he got out another thong and rewrapping his fingers. He stepped behind a boulder about fifteen paces from the rabbit hole. Picking up a broken branch he could use to club the rabbit, he knelt down in a sprinter's crouch to watch. He envisioned the rabbit's coming out and briefly getting entangled in the loop. While it was freeing itself, he'd make a mad dash with his club.

He waited almost an hour. His excitement had faded and he was leaning one haunch against the boulder when he saw several vultures circling to the east. With a sigh, he got up and started that way, hoping that whatever held the vultures' interest still had some meat on it.

When he got to the area where the vultures had been circling, he found nothing. Either the vultures had been deceived or some other scavenger had already dragged it away.

He thought disgustedly that the rabbit hole was out of his way back home. Pell debated a minute, but decided that he should at least salvage the thong he'd left there. There probably remained enough daylight. He trudged back that way.

As he came around the corner he saw a puff of white about two feet from the hole! He picked up a stone and crept closer—the rabbit!

He threw, but missed as usual. The rabbit didn't move though! As he came closer he saw the thong biting deeply into its neck. It'd gotten caught, then the rabbit's own violent thrashing had apparently broken its own neck, or perhaps strangled it.

Pell was beside himself with excitement. He'd never successfully hunted before. He'd contributed to group kills, sure, but he'd never killed an animal by himself.

When he brought home this rabbit he'd gain status in the tribe!

Status he desperately needed.

Pell never even considered eating the rabbit himself. No matter how hungry he was, the value of the nutrition in the rabbit couldn't even *compare* to the value of being recognized as someone with the potential to become a hunter.

Pell threw the rabbit over his shoulder and started back jauntily. He contemplated his reception back at the cave and how he'd describe his hunt. An unerring stone that struck the rabbit dead in its tracks? Pell stopped abruptly when he realized that the rabbit's carcass showed no sign of being struck by a stone.

He took it down from his shoulder and looked at it for a moment, then ran his fingers over it, pondering his story. For an instant, he considered describing how he'd actually ensnared the animal. But, no one would believe such a story. Besides, the prestige of his "perfectly cast stone" story would be lost forever. After more thought, he lay the animal down, backed up a few paces and cast a stone at its prostrate form.

He missed!

Disgusted, he threw several more times. He was about to walk over and manually strike the rabbit with a rock when a throw finally struck its hindquarters. He reexamined the carcass.

The portion of the hind limb just below the knee was deformed, with the lower leg sticking out at an angle. It reminded him of his deformed finger after his fall. He pondered this for a while, then tugged on it. He couldn't get it to come back out to normal length. He pulled as hard as he could. Still, when he let go, it remained shortened and angulated. With his eyes narrowed, he thought back to how he'd bent his finger even farther back when he'd tried to rip it from his hand. Only when he'd bent it backward had his finger slipped back into place.

He bent the rabbit's leg in the same direction it was already angled, like he'd bent his finger, angling it even beyond ninety degrees. Then, rather than pulling on it to make it longer, he "pushed" the apex of the angle out, as he had when trying to rip off his finger. To his delight the rabbit's bone crunched slightly, then it felt as if something slipped back into place. When he straightened out the angulation in the limb, it held its length and lay nearly straight! With a little push, he straightened it the rest of the way.

Pell pulled the leg back out to the side and it fell apart again. He felt it carefully. He could tell the bones weren't in contact the way they should be because when he pushed on them the limb shortened. In addition, it was floppy and tended to lie in a bent position. He reduced the fracture again using his trick of bending it more before trying to push it back out to length. It worked again!

He put the bone back out of place again and tried straightening it in a number of other ways. None of them worked! No matter how he pulled and tugged, it wouldn't go back into place unless he first bent it back at an angle. He was very puzzled by the whole thing, not understanding that he'd discovered a "bonesetting" principle—a principle that would still be in use many thousands of years later.

He wanted to cut the leg open to try to find out *why* it worked. However, Pell knew that if he brought the rabbit back to the cave and it'd been cut open, someone would think he'd eaten part of it—without sharing. After a moment's consideration, he shook the leg back out of place, put the rabbit back over his shoulder and resumed his way home.

***

When he arrived back at the cave, Pell's mother Donte was the first to see him. Initially, she greeted him with a little wave, but shortly thereafter with a loud cry as she recognized that he had a rabbit draped over his shoulder.

Donte appeared to be even more excited than Pell about the kill. In an instant, he realized his mother was also worried her son might be declared "ginja" if he didn't develop hunting skills soon. Such being the case, she intended to broadcast his success hunting rabbit to the rest of their little community as strongly as possible.

Pell felt grateful for her efforts, as the questions her excitement generated provided him a ready opportunity for a little bragging. He soon found himself repeating the details of his "throw" which, though a little off, broke the rabbit's leg so that Pell readily caught it and broke its neck.

The rabbit's pelt, intermediate between winter white and summer gray-brown, had soon been removed. The carcass itself was gutted, broken up and thrown into one of Lenta's pots with some water, grain and the bowl full of blood that'd been drained from the animal. The clay pot was set into the fire. The guts were split, washed, chopped and dropped back into the pot. The bones were broken and dropped in as well.

Though the brains would normally be used to cure the hide, they were also scooped out into the pot. At this time of year, nothing that was potentially edible missed its opportunity to become part of the soup.

Though one rabbit among the twenty-two of them living in the cave wasn't much, it was better than they'd had in several days, so everyone felt excited.

Just as it was getting dark Gontra and Bonat came in with a hare Gontra'd killed. Everyone's spirits rose even further. To his disappointment, the spotlight shifted away from Pell when Gontra arrived. However, later when Tando came in and heard of Pell's kill, the respected hunter congratulated Pell warmly. Tando's reputation as a hunter freighted his kind words with even more meaning. Pell sat down to eat his share of the soup feeling an intensely happy glow.

Pell managed to retrieve the broken leg bone from the stewpot and covertly examined it between sucking any remaining marrow from it. With most of the flesh gone, he could see the fracture just above the knee. It could be moved in and out of place with ease. Funny maneuvers were no longer required to reduce it. After pondering these phenomena for a while, he decided that it must be the overlying flesh that constrained the "bonesetting" so that it required he bend it first.

Perhaps later, during the fat part of summer, he could break a rabbit's leg and cut into the flesh to understand better what happened.

That night, drifting off to sleep without his stomach growling in hunger, Pell had a period of nagging doubt regarding his deceit in claiming to have killed the rabbit with a thrown stone. How could he maintain the lie? A few witnessed throws would quickly bring questions about his ability to throw well enough to be a hunter.

To his dismay, it came to a head the very next day. Belk and Lenta's new baby died during the night. Everyone had been expecting it because, with little to eat herself, Lenta's breasts produced scant milk. Expecting it or not, the tribe's mood hung bleak about the cave and Roley decided to dispatch the hunters in small groups.

Roley assigned his son Denit to take Pell and Boro with him on a hunt. Denit had fifteen summers and was bigger and stronger than Pell and Boro at thirteen summers each. Denit considered himself a man and he deeply resented being sent out to hunt with boys. Fuming, he strode ahead. Once out of earshot of the cave he turned angrily. "You *boys* had better be absolutely silent. If you spoil my hunt, I'll bring your ears home for the dinner pot." Pell and Boro nodded meekly. Denit turned on his heel and strode on.

Pell tried to walk quietly, but to his dismay, both he and Boro frequently broke twigs in the wooded areas and sent pebbles tumbling on the rocky spots. He expected Denit to turn and explode at all the noise they made, but Denit didn't seem to notice. After a while, Pell recognized that Denit was making as much, or perhaps even more, noise than he and Boro! Maybe Denit *wasn't* the great hunter he made himself out to be? In fact, as Pell thought back on it, he realized that, even though Denit was always bragging to the younger boys about his hunting skills, as best Pell could remember, it had been many moons since Denit had brought home any game. Pell frowned, *Has Denit ever had a kill of his own?*

Denit wasn't looking around much either. Roley and Tando were always telling the boys that a good hunter constantly surveyed his surroundings. Game frequently froze in plain sight and could be hard to see if you didn't carefully scan the entire area you were passing through. With a guilty twitch, Pell realized he wasn't scanning either—he swept his eyes to the left and right. He stared! There, not thirty feet from where they were passing, was a hare. It was standing absolutely still at the base of a bush. Nearly invisible due to its smudgy brownish-whitish color, it just sat there! Denit still hadn't noticed it so Pell whirled and threw the stone he had in his hand.

As he'd feared the night before, his throw went wide. Way wide! It hit so far away that for a second he thought the hare wouldn't bolt, but then it exploded up the hill away from them before he could throw again. Pell was still staring disconsolately after it when Denit struck him a powerful blow to the side of his head. For a second Pell didn't know what'd happened. When his mind cleared, Denit was astride his chest, angrily waving his flint knife and demanding to know why he shouldn't take Pell's ear. Boro was standing wide-eyed three paces away.

Boro showed no evidence that he might try to physically stop Denit.

Pell sobbed apologies.

Denit finally rose to his feet in disgust and stalked off in the same direction they'd been going.

Pell stumbled to his feet and staggered after him. Soon his wooziness disappeared, but the throbbing ache in his head persisted. A sullen anger developed as well. What had Denit expected him to do, call out to him, "Hey, Denit, you missed a hare—did you want to throw first?" The animal would've been long gone.

They trudged on through the rest of the day without sighting any more game within range of a throw, though it gratified Pell when they saw a few larger animals in the distance. Winter might truly be drawing to a close!

When they got back to the cave a celebration was in progress. Roley, Belk, Gontra, and Tando had driven a small pack of wolves away from a deer the wolves had killed. The men had managed to steal most of the carcass for the tribe. The cookpots were truly full for the first time in nearly a moon. Gontra was drumming on his hollow log using one hand and a knobbed stick he'd picked up on the way back from the hunt. The different tone produced by the stick allowed him to produce an entirely new and interesting set of rhythms that Pell found fascinating. Lessa was chanting a counterpoint to the rhythm that had everyone clapping and shuffling their feet.

The men were bragging that Roley had nearly killed a wolf for the pots as well. Pell was intensely relieved when, in their celebratory mood, the adults took little notice of Denit as he described how Pell had ruined his hunt.

The next morning, however, Denit pursued the subject again when Roley was making up the hunting parties. "Don't send me out with Pell again. He makes too much noise. And he throws so badly he couldn't hit the wall of this cave standing inside it."

Speculatively, Roley looked his son in the eye, "Don't forget he's had a kill since your last one."

Denit's face went white with a mixture of fear and rage. Pell abruptly realized Denit was worried about his own lack of kills and therefore actually felt *jealous* of Pell. That insight helped little when Denit whirled to stomp out of the cave and, finding Pell between himself and the entrance, knocked Pell to the ground on his way out.

Pell hunted with Boro that day. Predictably, they had no luck. It was a clear and bright day, cold in the morning but almost pleasant by afternoon. They saw some animal sign in keeping with the better weather. A few wolves trotted past far away. Boro even thought he saw an antelope in the distance, which would be great news if it truly indicated the herds were returning.

In the late afternoon, as they walked down a ravine toward the cave they came to a narrow choke point where a flash flood had washed up a large assemblage of sticks, brush and other debris. It'd caught on a couple of small trees to form what appeared to be impenetrably entangled disarray. For a while, they thought they'd have to climb out of the ravine because the brush was too dense to navigate.

Then they saw—from the way all the tracks came together at one point—that animals had found or created a small passage through one area. The two boys crouched down to follow the passage themselves. Pell was pushing through a tight spot when a strand of vine got caught around his neck. A little claustrophobic, he struggled somewhat frantically to get it loose in the tight little space. Afterward, he mused that what he'd just gone through must have been something like what'd happened to the rabbit he'd trapped with his thong.

When they got to the other side of the tangle of brush, they smelled blood. Looking about, they saw an area off to the side where a big hole had been torn in the brush pile. It looked like some kind of animal had gotten trapped there and been killed. To their disappointment, there wasn't anything left except a little blood splattered here and there. The ground was so rocky they couldn't even tell what'd made the kill, much less track it to try to steal its prey.

When Pell and Boro arrived back at the cave, they found Denit strutting about proudly. A small boar hung roasting on a spit in the center of the cooking fire while Denit bragged to Exen and Odran about his hunt. The two boys listened raptly, chins in their hands and eyes shining. Pell and Boro sat down to listen too as Denit described his chase. "So I just kept trotting after it and trotting after it. I felt so tired it hurt to breathe, but I could tell the boar was getting worn out.

Then it started up a little ravine. I thought I'd die going upslope, but the boar came to a spot where the ravine was choked off with brush. For a little bit, it cast about looking for an exit. When it didn't find one, it turned and charged right at me! Its head lowered, tusks swinging side to side, its beady little eyes glowing red, it attacked! I knew how much we needed food, so I didn't give an inch. I dropped to one knee, my spear butted into the ground behind me. That boar spitted itself right below the breastbone and dropped in its tracks."

Pell was musing to himself about the fact that it must have been the same brush clogged ravine he and Boro came through earlier and must have been the kill they saw the blood from when he heard Denit continue…

"Yeah, good thing Pell wasn't there. He probably would've thrown a couple of wild pebbles and frightened the boar away."

Pell startled. A sick feeling came over him. Everyone was going to think he couldn't hunt—and maybe he couldn't. Inwardly he raged at Denit. Suddenly his rage broke through to the surface, "Yeah, how come when Boro and I were in that same ravine on the way home from our hunt it looked like a pig got stuck in the brush and some great hunter just walked up and stuck his spear up its ass? Charging? Ha! Hey, did anyone see a wound in the front of that pig?" Pell looked around. "Where's the skin?"

Pell found himself on the floor of the cave with Denit astride his chest, pounding him. His arms were trapped under Denit' knees, but he convulsed one knee up to strike Denit in the back and knock him forward. Denit fell almost off Pell for a moment, but quickly sat back and resumed flailing at Pell's head. Pell had turned his head and was trying to bite Denit on the thigh when Roley walked over and broke up the fight with two well-placed blows.

***

Later Pell cowered in the corner, in more pain from Roley's single blow to his side than the many rained on him by Denit. Dazed, he thought to himself that it was little wonder no one challenged the massive Roley for leadership of the Aldans.

~~~

Laurence E Dahners

That night developed into a joyous celebration. They feasted on the leftover deer from the day before and the roast pig from Denit's hunt. Pell sat by the cooking fire, sucking the marrow out of a couple of ribs. He didn't feel the celebratory mood of the others; though he thought to himself that life probably couldn't get much better. After all, he had a full stomach and the warm fire made for a pleasant feeling all over.

Still, he felt uneasy and worried about his status in the tribe. Though gratified, he was amazed that Roley'd cuffed Denit, his own son, as well as Pell when he stopped their fight. Donte said Roley'd respected Pell's father Garen. Perhaps that led Roley to have a relatively soft spot for Pell—if Roley could be said to have a soft spot. He thought to himself that the most you could say was that he had a "not so hard spot."

Nonetheless, Pell doubted Roley would make even a pretense of fairness if it came to something really important. After all, Roley'd never really singled Pell out for special treatment. He hadn't even tried to teach him to hunt. What if Pell *never* got to be a better throw? He resolved to try flint-knapping again. *I've got to find another skill!* he thought. *Somehow I've got to become a productive member of the tribe!*

Having made that resolution, he sat back, feeling contented. He saw that the healer squatted near him, brewing one of his concoctions. It seemed, once again, to consist mostly of hemp leaves. "Who's sick?" Pell asked.

Pont glared over at him. "None of your business, ginja boy!"

Pell started back. The healer's answer was practically dripping vitriol. It was a bad portent to be on poor terms with the tribe's healer, since even the seemingly invincible Roley carefully stayed on the healer's good side.

Pell'd often wondered why? It seemed to him that Pont could do little enough when someone got sick. However, his hemp concoctions eased pain and dulled worry. Also, his chanting rituals had some kind of calming effect on everyone, not just the victim of the illness.

Now Pell found himself in need of some calm. He'd barely relaxed from worrying about his finger and now he felt a gibbering terror run through his stomach at being on the outs with the healer. "Pont…" he mumbled, trying desperately to think of a way to apologize, but the healer turned his back and shuffled toward his furs.

Pell watched him wide-eyed, wondering what he could do to salvage this mess. After a moment he realized the healer was simply partaking of his own medicine once again.

Pell wondered for a while whether Pont might actually be sick and treating himself. Or was he only taking the hemp because he liked the way it made him feel? Pell resolved to collect some hemp for Pont when the leaves began to grow again. Perhaps that'd soften Pont's attitude toward him.

Pell fell asleep that night with a persistently gnawing feeling of sick dread. Something terrible was going to happen…

***

Despite Pell's fears, the next day passed uneventfully. The tribe rested, gorged on meat and generally laid about. The day after that broke clear and

Laurence E Dahners

cold with a few high clouds, but little wind. Pell was set
to building up the fire and soon the tribe gathered to
warm themselves around it. They breakfasted on the
remains of the deer and pig, but there really wasn't
enough to gorge.

Roley looked about outside and proclaimed it a fine
day for a "great hunt." Soon the men and older boys
had set about sharpening their wooden "char" tipped
spears. The good flint-tipped spears were checked and
their bindings tightened. Pell and Boro practiced
throwing with some spear shafts. Pell spent some time
trying to get a better point on his two hunting spears,
rolling their tips in the fire, then rubbing the charred
wood off on a stone to bring them to hard, sharp points.

He longed for a good flint point and once again
wished his mother had somehow saved him some of his
father's good flint spear tips. She'd used the last of
them in trades long ago; trades that'd helped the two of
them out of difficult situations.

Sometimes now, she had sex with one of the hunters
when she needed something she couldn't get any other
way. It seemed like the men always wanted sex, though
none of them sought a long-term mating with her.

Pell worried about what would happen if she got
with child again. If she had no mate, it would be Pell's
responsibility to be the man of their pitiful little family;
something for which he was far from ready.

Pell felt embarrassed to be grateful that, though
she'd swelled with child three times since Garen died,
none of the babies had lived. It made Donte sad, but he
thought they'd be much worse off with another mouth
to feed.

The band of hunters set out down their little valley
and into the big basin surrounding the great river to the

south. When they broke out of the forest to reach one of the big open areas of the basin they saw it dotted here and there with animals grazing on the sere grass.

Roley took out his "far-seer" and held it up to his eye. It consisted of an elaborately carved stick with a flattened area at the tip. Someone had bored a small hole in the flat area. Peering through the hole apparently improved the vision of many people, producing a sharp image from a blurred one. Pell had heard some of the hunters discussing it one night. Tando said that it only helped the vision of those whose vision wasn't good to begin with. He claimed that, using the "far-seer," Roley only saw things that Tando'd already seen. Tando even claimed that he'd looked through the far-seer and could see no better with it than without it.

On the other hand, Pont said it held great magic. He chanted over it before each hunt.

Pell had bored holes in several small wood chips and found they improved his distance vision without any magic chanting. He wondered if it worked like "squinting." Members of the tribe who didn't see well in the distance could often be seen squinting at things that were far away. Pell thought they were looking through small slits between their eyelids like the little hole in his chips and the small hole in the far-seer. Maybe the "far-seer" just formed a better slit than squinting did?

Pell carefully told no one of such thoughts.

The hunters passed the "far-seer" around and discussed the animals that they saw. They were nothing like the big herds that would arrive later to consume the rich forage of summer, but they were infinitely better than the empty dry fields of winter. Pell wanted to look through the "far-seer" himself, especially to settle his curiosity regarding whether it worked better than his little chips of wood, but the hunters never saw any need for boys to survey the plain before a hunt.

Roley outlined a plan to encircle some antelope and trap them between the hunters. The men formed into a wide, crescent moon shaped skirmish line with the points forward. This plan would take tremendous coordination from the group. While the circle was large and the hunters were far apart, hunters in the section of the circle an animal broke toward were to make a great deal of noise in order to drive the animal back toward the center of the circle. Once the circle closed to a point where they were within a few paces of one another, the boys were to continue making noise so that the antelope would shy toward one of the men who would spear it. "Remember, don't *throw* your spear unless the animal's already broken out of the circle!" Roley reminded the younger hunters. "Stab yes, but if you throw and you miss, you might hit another hunter."

"That especially means *you*, Pell," Denit jeered. Many of the group snickered and Pell felt his face flush.

Roley muttered, "That means all you ginja fools."

Denit brightened, "*Ginja* fools? That'd be Pell and... maybe Boro?" He laughed again while Pell and Boro flushed with angry embarrassment. However, neither of the two friends was brave enough to make a retort.

~~~

Roley stayed in the center of the line and they walked toward the animals. He'd occasionally wave someone into place, but led entirely through silent gestures. Pell tried to watch his own step and cringed inwardly whenever he stepped on a twig or otherwise made some noise. The sun had moved almost a fist across the sky before they started to surround three antelope. There were more in the distance, but these three were grazing away from the main herd.

Roley stopped and began waving the points of their party out around the three animals. As he'd been taught, Pell didn't get any nearer the antelope, instead trying to walk around them in a circle, maintaining the same distance. The antelope seemed nervous, but continued to graze while looking up repeatedly. As the circle began to close, one of them made a quick dash toward the closing space, but Denit, who was on the right point, dashed into the opening, yelling and waving. It skittered nervously away and back to the center of the hunters' circle.

With a great deal of slow pointing and gesturing, Roley dressed their ranks and got them moving slowly toward the center. The animals were obviously alert now and prancing nervously about, skittering this way and that. When the antelope got too far from center, the hunters on that part of the circumference shouted and dashed about, driving them back into the center.

One of the antelope bolted towards the gap between Pell and Tando. Pell shouted, waved his spear and dashed toward the gap. Tando charged in from the other side of the gap, but then Pell found himself skidding face first into the grasses when he tripped over a stump or rock.

Panicked Pell leaped back to his feet, but the animal was already passing behind him. He dashed back into the gap that'd formed between himself and Bonat during this fiasco. Another animal was bounding for that gap! Pell shouted and ran, but realized that this antelope was also going to escape!

In desperation, he cast his spear after it had crossed the circle on its way out. To Pell's dismay, his throw was so wide that it came within a pace or two of Bonat! Cringing inwardly, he looked to the center of their circle. Yes, the last antelope remained! But as Pell's spirits surged he saw the animal gather itself and dash for a gap on the other side of the circle. It flew between Boro and Gontra despite their attempts to frighten it back to the center.

Dejected, they gathered for a postmortem on the hunt. As Pell had feared Denit had a few choice words for Pell, "Can't you even stay on your feet for a *hunt*, you ginja fool? Are you really so clumsy or did you just lie down to take a nap?"

Pell hung his head. He had no spirit to argue. Even though he knew Denit was simply using the term "ginja" as an oath, it still struck terror in Pell's heart.

Roley tried to cheer them up. "This encirclement plan *is* going to work. We just need to try it again." With a start, Pell realized Roley wasn't confident in this hunting method. He wondered who Roley'd learned it from, not considering the possibility that Roley might be trying to invent something new.

Soon they were spread out in their skirmish line again and advancing across the plain. It was another hour or so before they came on a large boar and a couple of sows. Pell was nervous, boars could be dangerous and this one was huge, nearly chest high and so dark it was almost black. Its tusks looked as long as Pell's foot.

At least the boars let the circle close considerably before becoming agitated. When they did take notice of the hunters, it was with a belligerent attitude, heaving their heads up and down and slashing the air with their tusks. Then they began making short charges directly at members of the hunting party. To Pell's relief, none of the charges came toward him.

The circle got smaller and smaller. The big boar took a full charge on Boro. Though he appeared to be terrified, Boro nonetheless did as he'd been taught and dropped to one knee. He planted the butt of his spear in the ground and held the point out at the charging beast. The boar spitted itself on Boro's spear, bowling Pell's young friend over.

The two sows exploded out of the circle on either side of Boro and the insanely thrashing boar. Gontra appeared out of the dust and began stabbing the boar with his spear. Others quickly joined the melee. Pell turned from the excitement and checked on Boro. His friend was limping a little, but so excited he could hardly hold still. "I did it! It was my spear that killed it, wasn't it?" He hopped up and down with delight.

Other hunters came over to congratulate Boro as well. Pell, initially excited for Boro, now found himself mired in jealousy and dismay. Until now, when he worried about his own inadequacies, at least he'd felt superior to Boro. Now Boro had a *major* kill—of a charging boar no less! Pell's pride over his rabbit kill seemed a petty thing now, especially since he knew that it was a trick with a thong, rather than true hunting skill or courage that brought his rabbit down.

As Pell stood scuffing his toe and worrying about his own predicament, he slowly became aware that a silence had fallen over the group. He looked quickly about for a cause. Exen's face was ashen. Pell followed Exen's eyes. Exen was focused on his father Gontra.

As Pell took in the scene he saw Gontra was grimacing and holding one hand with his other. The veins were standing out on his usually pleasant face and no trace remained of his customary grin. "I fell," he said, as if that explained it all.

Everyone gathered around to gawk, so it was a while before Pell could get a look. When he could see, it was evident that Gontra'd injured his finger. Pell saw that it was bent back the same way Pell's own pointer finger had been! Pont looked at it briefly, and rummaged in his pouch. "You've done the same thing that that ginja fool Pell did to his finger. Don't worry, I fixed that worthless piece of boar droppings, I'll fix your finger too. Here, chew on this."

Pell choked on his rage. He wanted to shout that he'd fixed his own finger! Pont hadn't done it! How could Pont's hemp possibly fix a finger? However, when he looked at the others they all appeared relieved the healer'd taken charge of the situation. Other than Pell, no one appeared to doubt the healer's ability to fix Gontra's finger. With dismay, Pell recognized that, tenuous as his situation was, he'd best not express any of his opinions regarding Pont's abilities.

The hunters fell to hacking the boar up into pieces small enough to carry back. Pell wasn't surprised to be assigned to carry the intestines. Everyone else was packed up and had started back before he'd finished squeezing out their contents and coiling them into something he could carry.

He thought to himself that it was a good thing summer wasn't here; he'd be covered with flies. Of course, during the good hunting of summer, they usually didn't bother with intestines. He set out, up into the little valley leading back to the Aldans' cave, hiking rapidly to catch up with the others.

When the hunters came in sight of the cave the women saw them carrying haunches of boar and began to celebrate. Then Tonday cried out and came running toward the group.

She'd seen Gontra wasn't carrying anything.

Gontra shambled along, holding one hand in the other. She took in Gontra's drugged look and began wailing even before she saw his finger. Gontra tried to console her in his own gruff way, but even in his glazed over state, his own apprehension was readily evident.

In a few minutes, Tonday's hysterics had degenerated. She half lay, half sat at Gontra's feet, tearing at her hair. The other women and children came out to the group and soon Tila, Gontra, and Tonday's little daughter, added her own hysteria to the mix. Though Tila was too little to actually understand what was wrong, she readily picked up her mother's distress.

Pont's woman, Lessa, sat down with Tonday and tried to comfort her, stroking her hair and crooning one of her soothing chants. Soon thereafter, Pont marched Gontra up to the cave and laid him out on the furs he and Lessa shared. Lessa brought a still sobbing Tonday up a little later. Pell found himself assigned to slicing up the intestines he'd carried back. This was a tedious job, but he managed to situate himself so that he could watch what the healer did with Gontra.

When Gontra seemed deeply under the influence of Pont's hemp concoction, the healer began to examine the man's finger. Pell was relieved to see that the finger was maintaining a good color. Pont wiggled it around a little, looking at it from different angles; then he grasped it and pulled vigorously. Gontra woke immediately from his sleep, incoherent eyes wide with agony. He flailed around, striking the healer repeatedly on the back and finally shoved Pont violently aside. All eyes, attracted by the commotion, now focused on Gontra's finger.

The deformity hadn't changed!

Pell felt a sick feeling rising in his throat. He thought to himself that Pont had just pulled straight. With Pell's finger and with the rabbit's leg, Pell had first had to bend the member even farther in the direction of its deformity before being able to slip it back into place. "Pont..." he ventured.

Pont looked up at Pell with a murderous expression in his beady eyes. Pell found his words dying in his throat. Sheepishly he went back to cutting up the intestines.

Pont sat back down next to Gontra who'd dozed off again. Pell realized Pont had been careful to position himself between Pell and Gontra's hand in order to obstruct Pell's view. Pont began to chant and took some of his hemp mixture himself. Pell continued to work on the boar's guts while he contemplated the strange paradox that required that the deformity be made worse before it could be made better.

He wondered whether the healer might know about the phenomenon and would therefore try that maneuver next. His reveries were interrupted by another episode of flailing and screaming from Gontra. This episode again ended with the healer bowled over, but this time Gontra stood on his feet staring wide-eyed at his own finger. Pell could see the finger was just as crooked as ever. With a cry, Gontra bolted out of the cave and into the night. Pont lay cursing on the floor of the cave, holding grimly to the small of his own back.

Roley got to his feet, took his good spear and followed Gontra out into the darkness. Tonday collapsed to the floor, sobbing hysterically. Pell thought in dismay that Gontra, injured, weaponless and drugged, would make an easy victim for the big felines that roamed the night. Hopefully, Roley would bring him back soon.

They began to eat the pig, but the normally happy mood that accompanied feasting after a big kill had clouded with a somber pall. Before they finished, Roley came back, a shambling Gontra in tow. Moods improved, but Gontra's deformed finger and Tonday's persistent sobbing damped any festivities for the rest of the night. No one entertained them with any stories.

Certainly, no one was going to try to drum Gontra's log on this night.

After they'd eaten, Gontra, who'd sobered considerably, went to speak to the healer. An argument erupted and it became apparent from Pont's shouting that the healer attributed the persistent deformity of Gontra's finger to poor patient cooperation. Pell expected Gontra to be angry, but Gontra soon took another dose of hemp and lay down again on the healer's furs. Several times during the evening, bellows of agony erupted from that part of the cave, the last episode waking Pell from a sound sleep, heart pounding in his chest.

Chapter Two

The next morning broke on a persistently somber mood. Gontra's finger remained deformed. Now it was even more swollen and angry looking. Tonday, intermittently sobbing, refused to even rise from her bedding. Pont denounced Gontra's lack of cooperation to Roley in a stage whisper everyone could hear. Lessa tried to counter the bleak mood with tea and soup she brewed in two of Lenta's big pots, chanting a pleasant tune while she did it.

The tea didn't help much, though the chronically hungry tribe gathered readily enough to eat the soup.

Soon after downing some of the soup and tea, Roley announced that everyone could hunt as they liked, he wasn't organizing anything—then stalked from the cave, alone but for a couple of spears. Pell thought about trying to join him, but before he could, Denit scrambled to his feet and ran out after his father. Pell certainly didn't intend to go anywhere Denit was going, so he settled back down, hoping someone else would ask him to hunt with them.

With little ceremony, the hunters left in ones and twos. As he might have expected, it soon became evident no one was going to ask Pell to go with them. He unwrapped his fingers and flexed the pointer finger he'd dislocated. Still somewhat swollen, it hurt much less and seemed to be moving pretty well. He bound it to his long finger again, gathered his two char-tipped spears and went out to hunt by himself.

The sky was dotted with small clouds, but brisk winds cut under Pell's furs with a cold bite. He stopped down at the little stream running below the cave and filled his water skin. The water was so frigid he could hardly stand to put his hand in to fill the skin. When he brought the icy water skin back out of the water he hung it outside his furs so it wouldn't suck out all his warmth. He meandered down toward the flats a while, but when the flats came into view, their greening grasses were empty of game. *Besides*, he thought to himself, *the big game on the flats isn't something I could hunt by myself.*

He found himself walking up the small gulch where Denit killed the little boar. He walked up into it and came to the area where it was choked with brush. He contemplated the little hole in the brush he thought the pig had run into, becoming trapped so Denit could kill it. It looked much like the small tunnel in the brush that did go through to the other side.

If only he could drive an animal up this ravine and have it try to get through that same dead end that *looked* like a passage. In fact, as he looked at it, he realized it looked even more like a passage because many animals had wandered into it and back out, leaving tracks looking as if they'd passed in both directions. He went over to the tunnel that actually made a complete passage and crouched down to start through. He'd gone in a few feet when he heard someone shout his name!

Pell's first thought was that someone was calling a warning! He was crouched over in the narrow passage and when he heard the call he jerked upright, or tried to. He panicked and tried to back out, but immediately stuck himself on one of the spears he'd been trailing behind himself. The butt of the spear had caught in a root and the point stabbed him painfully in the back of the thigh. Losing control, he thrashed about for a few moments.

Finally understanding he wasn't in any immediate danger he calmed down, but it still took several minutes to disentangle himself and back his way out of the tunnel. Thank the spirits he hadn't encountered some fierce predator in there!

As Pell carefully backed out, he thought to himself, *I'll never climb into a tight passage like that again!* When he finally got all the way out, he found Exen and Gontra waiting for him.

They seemed uncomfortable. Exen scuffed his foot and asked what Pell had been doing in the pile of brush.

"Trying to get through to the other side."

"Why'd you make so much noise?"

"Um, I caught myself on some thorns."

An uncomfortable silence stretched, Gontra ventured, "Exen says he saw you straighten out your own finger—that Pont didn't do it."

"No! Pont *didn't* do it!" Pell exclaimed. "All he did was give me hemp!" Pell was surprised at his own vehemence.

Another long gap in the conversation ensued. Gontra looked up into the sky and Pell found himself scuffing his own feet as well. Gontra asked, "Do you think you can straighten *my* finger?"

Later Pell would wonder why he was surprised at the question. In retrospect, it seemed obvious they'd followed him out of sight of the rest of the tribe to ask that very question—certainly a question Pell would have been asking if he'd been in their place. Nonetheless, caught off guard, he said nothing for a few moments. Later, he'd also be angry they hadn't asked him in front of other members of the tribe, but at *that* moment he actually felt glad they hadn't asked in front of the healer. Pont would surely have raised a fury.

"I could try," Pell said tentatively.

Gontra's shoulders dropped in relief. "Good!" he said. He held his hand out to Pell.

Pell started back. The finger was still swollen and angled back, the same as Pell's had been. It looked hideous. Pell reached out to touch it, then remembered how Gontra'd flailed at Pont the night before, knocking the healer away several times and completely over on one occasion. He drew his hands back.

"Come on boy!" Gontra almost shouted. He shook the hand in Pell's face. "Do it… Now!"

Pell abruptly recognized Gontra's fear! Frightened of the pain that would surely come, but even more terrified that the finger might remain the way it was. Understanding Gontra's state of mind didn't keep Pell from shying away. "No! You'll knock me down like you did Pont!"

Gontra shrunk in on himself. "No, I won't… Come on, you've *got* to do it for me," he whined in a petulant tone. Gontra sounded like a child denied a treat, Pell thought, feeling some surprise.

"No! You've got to at least chew some hemp first, so it doesn't hurt so badly. Before I fixed my own finger, I chewed some of Pont's hemp."

"Oh, yeah," Gontra mumbled. He scrabbled about in his pouch with his good hand. "Pont gave me some for the pain."

Pell saw Gontra grimace when he bumped his bad finger trying to hold the pouch open with that hand. Pell's own finger hadn't seemed that sensitive, even before Pont gave him the hemp leaves. Was it because of all the times the healer'd pulled on Gontra's finger the previous night? It could be, but then Pell remembered how his own finger had been so numb from the cold he could hardly feel it anyway. Should he wait till nighttime and send Gontra out into the cold?

His hand bumped the skin full of cold water hanging at his side, just outside his furs. Maybe he could numb Gontra's hand with cold water from the skin? When he poured some out of the water skin and onto his own hand, he found that the water had warmed up considerably, at least as compared to how cold it'd felt while it was still in the creek.

He looked up to find Gontra stuffing his mouth with hemp leaves. "Wait! Spit those back out. We're not ready yet."

Gontra spat them back into his good hand with a look of puzzlement and anger. "What now?!"

"We need to go back to the stream."

"The stream? Why?"

"Your hand needs to be cold. You can hold it in the water a while."

Gontra didn't want his hand cold, certainly not as cold as it would get in the stream. Nonetheless, while he argued they started walking back toward the cave. Having resigned himself to putting his hand in the cold water, he began to argue for going to a section of the stream some distance below the cave. He and Exen were glancing about.

Pell realized that they didn't want to be seen with him. Pell felt a little disturbed by Gontra and Exen's unwillingness to lower their status by associating with him, but on the other hand, he didn't want the healer to see him with Gontra. Or other members of the tribe either. What if he failed to "set" Gontra's finger? After a few moments consideration, he agreed to go to the little swimming hole downstream from the cave.

Some distance before they arrived at the hole, Pell had Gontra start chewing the wad of hemp he still held in his good hand. When they got to the hole Gontra was shambling and slurring his speech. Pell had him crouch at the edge of the hole and immerse his hand to the wrist. He was surprised how readily Gontra acquiesced but attributed it to the hemp.

Shortly, Gontra began to complain about holding his hand in the cold water. Pell didn't blame him, but insisted that he keep it in anyway. After another minute or so Gontra pulled it out of the water of his own accord, complaining loudly and incoherently about how he could hardly feel his hand.

Pell saw the whole hand had blanched white, but made him put it back in the water anyway. He sat down next to Gontra and wiped sweaty palms on his furs. He wondered why his hands would be sweaty on a cold day like this one. He saw Gontra trembling and thought he was about to pull his hand back out again. "Okay, take it out and give it to me."

Gontra jerked his hand out of the water and extended the white, trembling member to Pell.

Pell grasped the deformed part of the finger in his fist, bending it *way* back, like he had his own finger and the rabbit's leg.

He pulled mightily.

Gontra bellowed and jerked his hand out of Pell's grasp, rolling back onto his buttocks. He gripped the offended member in his other fist and curled over it in agony, though he didn't seem as miserable as he had during the healer's attempts the night before. Pell scrambled away fearfully, thinking that Gontra might strike him when he recovered.

But Gontra slowly opened his good hand to look tremblingly at his injured digit. Pell could see, even from where he stood, that the finger was straight again! Massively swollen still, but by the Spirits, straight! Exen let out a whoop of joy and knelt to throw his arms around his father. He and Gontra swayed about in each other's grasp, sobbing in relief.

Gontra, seemingly sobered by the event, reached in his pouch and pulled out a flint knife he tossed to Pell. "Thanks," he said, and with that, he and Exen started back up the trail with as jaunty a step as they could manage in Gontra's drunken state.

Pell stood looking at the knife, wondering at his tumultuous emotions. He felt elated that he'd straightened Gontra's finger, but somehow it seemed the celebration was far too short. Or that it hadn't included him the way he felt it should've.

They'd hugged each other and he'd thought they'd turn to hug Pell as well.

But they hadn't.

He could see that Gontra's gift was an old knife he didn't use much anymore. It had several chips out of the blade and, though bigger, wasn't even as good as Pell's primary knife. At first, surprised that Gontra had given him anything for what he'd done; Pell now found himself disappointed by the shoddiness of the gift. Pont would have demanded, and received, a much better reward from Gontra if he'd successfully reduced the finger.

Of course, Pont was a real healer and Pell wasn't.

Pell contemplated what had happened for a little longer, then set out again on his interrupted hunt. As he traveled, his thoughts returned over and over to the incident just past.

He was hurt that Exen and Gontra hadn't invited him to hunt with them.

He wished he'd insisted on some sort of public recognition from them.

He wished he'd thought to accompany them back to the cave where they were probably celebrating—he could've been the hero of the moment.

Maybe there would be a hero's welcome for him anyway, when he got back later. The Aldans would surely recognize the value of having one in their midst who could perform such bonesettings. While he was lost in these thoughts, he wandered back up to the same ravine he'd been in earlier. When he got to the brush barrier, he remembered that he didn't want to try to go through it again. Rather than go back down the ravine he resolved to climb up the side and thus go around the barrier.

The side of the ravine was steep and hard to climb, but, pulling himself up on various tough, scraggly plants, he scrambled up onto the rocks directly east of the brushy barrier. The afternoon sun had warmed the rocks somewhat and so he sat puffing at the top for a minute. His eye caught some motion on the north side of the brushy barrier. A group of small pigs like the one Denit had killed were snuffling around in a small patch of rotting vegetation.

Pell threw the spear in his hand, but it clattered off the rocks three or four paces from the pig he'd aimed for. His second spear bounced into the legs of a running pig and tangled in its feet a moment. It fell, but quickly regained its feet, apparently unharmed. Pell scrambled down the side of the ravine, but to his dismay, the pigs kept scattering back up to the north. By the time Pell got down to the ground on the north side of the brush pile, the pigs were far out of reach of any more throws of his spears.

He collected his spears and examined them. *Of course, the point of my best spear broke!* Cursing, he sat down to re-sharpen it. He tried out the knife Gontra had given him. He noted that at least it had a better handle for such scraping than his old one. He was still working away when a small boar burst out of the tunnel in the brush and rocketed up the west side of the ravine to join its fellows. Startled, Pell dropped the spear and the knife.

He scrabbled around to get his second spear and launched another miserable throw, again missing widely. Cursing even more vehemently he walked over to pick up the spear, noted that *its* point was now ruined as well. He walked back to pick up the other spear and his new knife. The flint knife lay beside the spear, shattered into three large pieces and several smaller ones.

With hot tears running down his cheeks Pell sat, got out his other knife, and jerkily brought both spears to points.

After the tears ran down, he gathered up the fragments of his new knife and put them in his pouch. Dragging his spears, he went back to the brush tunnel. Too dejected to consider climbing over, he crouched down and started through the tunnel. When he got to the area where he'd been trapped the day before, he took it in with new eyes. During his struggle, he'd broken off a couple of sticks and branches, which had then protruded into the tunnel on a slant. *They* were what had been poking into him when he tried to back out the other way, not a spear.

He noticed some blood on one of them; he couldn't remember being stuck badly enough to start bleeding though. He smelled it—it was fresh boar's blood! The little boar, the one that'd just escaped him, it must have been trapped in here too!

He wondered if he could just wait a while. Perhaps some other animal would come along and get trapped as well? Well, they wouldn't come in here if he was here; his scent would keep them away. But, could he get back in here before they got free? If he did, would he be able to take on a boar in such close quarters? Maybe if the sticks were sharper they'd kill the boar for him? While contemplating it he began scraping the one that had gore on it, thinking to diminish the scent of the blood. As he did so he realized that he was bringing it to a point like a spear. With sudden insight, he began to do so purposefully. It was made of a springy wood that made it easy to push aside but tended to hold the point out in the center of the tunnel. It would be easy to get past it going one direction, but not the other!

Inspiration struck and he began finding similar branches, sharpening one end and wedging them into the surrounding branches so they sloped into the center of the tunnel. He moved a few paces the other way and did the same thing, this time making the little spears so that they faced the opposite direction.

This created a small section of the tunnel that was easy to get into by brushing the spears aside, but once within that section, the spears faced you from both directions. Pell'd be able to get out by careful use of his hands, but he thought a boar might get stuck in the section for quite a while. He climbed out of the little tunnel, intending to sit up on the side of the ravine and wait for an animal to try to go through the tunnel. Then he'd dash in to kill it before it could get loose.

Unfortunately, he realized the sun was getting low. He didn't want to be out after dark with the big night predators, so he headed back to the Aldans' cave. He resolved to come back out and sit by the ravine in the morning.

When Pell got back to the cave there was a celebration in progress. Hoping it had to do with Pell's reduction of Gontra's finger, he trotted up to his mother and asked her what'd happened.

Donte said, "Another kill of a small boar, this time by Belk. Even better—Gontra popped his own finger back in!"

"*Gontra* popped his finger back in?!"

Donte didn't notice Pell's dismay at the news. "Yes, yes, isn't it wonderful? He fell into a bush and when he pulled his hand back out the finger was straight! He was chasing a boar at the time; you know one of the same kind he'd been hunting when his finger was hurt to begin with. Pont says he'd been praying to the spirit of the big boars all day today. So, the spirit must have heard the healer's call and decided to give Gontra his finger back... Pell are you okay?"

Pell felt as if he'd been poleaxed. "Gontra, put... his own, finger back?" he repeated stupidly.

"Yes, yes. Well actually, the Boar Spirit did it. What's the matter with you?"

Pell looked up and saw Gontra staring at him. Gontra looked nervously over at Pont who was all dressed up in his ceremonial finest. Gontra looked back at Pell and quickly shook his head. He lightly put fingers over his lips, shaking his head again. Feeling lightheaded, Pell sat down where he stood. *So much for my hopes of being recognized upon my return this evening!* The most important thing he'd ever done in his life—and all he'd get out of it would be one shoddy knife, already broken? Not even a real "thank you" from Gontra? *Is no one to even know I did it?*

For a moment, Pell thought to announce to the camp what'd really happened. Then he recognized, with even more dismay, that any such claim, contradicted by both Gontra and Pont, would make him a laughingstock.

Getting no response to her query, Donte said, "Rest a moment Pell, I'll get you some tea." She scurried off toward the cook fire.

Before they ate dinner they sat through one of Pont's interminable ceremonies, this one to "Thank the Spirit Boar for restoring Gontra's finger." Gontra even did the drumming, holding his new "knobby stick" in his poulticed hand. Pont danced about, chanting monotonously while Lessa keened a tune that wove through Pont's monotone. Pont and Lessa together did sound haunting.

Pell sat against the back wall of the cave, covertly sipping the tea Donte brought him and wondering whether the healer had ever *actually* made anyone better. *Or, does he just take credit when people get well for some other reason?* Pell realized with a start that Pont certainly spread the blame when people got worse under his ministrations. Someone else had always "angered the Spirits" when the healer failed to make one of his patients better.

After they ate, Roley announced that they'd have another big hunt in the morning. While the hunters were out, the women were to pack for the move to the summer hunting area. If the hunt was successful, they should have enough meat to tide them over during the move. They'd begin their transit the day after the hunt.

Pell had great difficulty sleeping that night. He lay awake thinking of how he should have made Gontra and Exen march past the cave with him to the upper stream before reducing the finger. He should have insisted on better payment than that old knife. He should have insisted on accompanying them back to the cave after he put Gontra's finger back in place. He should have said something when he got back to the cave and found the celebration in progress—though he knew no one would've believed him.

But maybe Gontra would have admitted it.

I should've... I should... I shou...

***

The next morning Pell woke thinking of the brush tunnel. He'd been going to go sit beside it today. The more he thought about it, the more certain he felt that some passing animal would get stuck in there long enough for him to spear it! He'd have to go by himself so he could claim to have killed it in a real hunt. He snorted—the way people had been turning against him, going hunting by himself wasn't going to be a problem.

Roley was already organizing his big hunt though. As per Roley's usual, this involved a lot of bellowing at other hunters, shouting at the women and children, stamping of his feet and cuffing those who moved too slowly for his taste. When he got in this kind of mood it made everyone anxious. Pell resigned himself to trying to visit the brush tunnel later in the day, *after* Roley's big hunt. Roley soon had all the hunters out on the trail down toward the great river, most of them still gnawing on a remnant of yesterday's kill.

It was overcast, but not particularly cold. Pell's stomach wasn't growling because he'd had some leftovers from last night's feast before setting out. He'd even gotten over some of his dismay at Gontra's betrayal and was looking forward to an opportunity to prove himself in the day's hunt.

Then Denit turned to Exen and said, "Don't you think Pell should have stayed back with the rest of the women to pack?"

Pell's stomach lurched.

Exen looked at Pell out of the corner of his eye and quickly glanced away. But after a little pause, he said to Denit, "Yeah, you should let your dad know we've accidentally brought one of the girls with us on the hunt."

Pell's heart sank to be so betrayed by Exen after fixing Gontra's finger. *I probably saved his father's life and he's agreeing with Denit?!*

Denit laughed. He shouted ahead, "Roley, one of the girls came along on the hunt. Do you want to send her back?"

Roley turned in anger, scanning up and down the line. "Where is she?" he demanded.

Denit laughed and pointed at Pell, "Can't throw, send her back, can't throw, send her back."

Several other hunters laughed as well. Pell's face turned red. He saw even his supposed friend Boro was laughing! Gontra stared off into the distance, seemingly embarrassed, but evidently not about to intercede.

Roley strode back to where the three boys were standing and stared at Denit until even his son's insolent grin had faded. "Hunting is serious business, for men—not for boys who play games! Do I need to send *you* back to the cave to play with the children?"

Denit stared down at the ground and scuffed his feet. "No Father."

Roley turned on his heel and strode back to the front without another word. They started off again. Denit and Exen continued to put their heads together and giggle, but no more loud taunts ensued. Pell wished Roley'd said something positive about Pell instead of just coming down on Denit. The last time, when Roley reminded Denit of his kill, Pell had felt a lot better.

Once they came out of the forest and onto the open flats near the great river, Roley spread them out in a wide, crescent-shaped skirmish line like he had several days before. They moved forward at a steady walk and soon came on a pair of the large boars. Pell was at the left end of their line and began to surge ahead to swing their line around the boars into an encirclement. The boars didn't seem to have noticed anything, but then a great deal of shouting came from near the center of their line and the boars were spooked into trotting away.

Pell thought surely someone must have been hurt and trotted toward the disturbance. So did most of the rest of the hunters, but when they got close it was evident that Roley was trying to put them back out into their line again. No one seemed hurt. Pell asked Belk, who was next to him in the rearranged line, what'd happened.

Belk said the healer claimed to have promised the Spirit Boar to spare the next boar they hunted in return for mending Gontra's finger. Apparently, it'd been Pont who'd shouted to spook them away. Roley'd been angry at first but then acknowledged that it was worth the loss of those two boars to have the spirits on their side.

Pell's mind was in turmoil. *Was* Pell's putting Gontra's finger back in place due to the healer's ceremonies? How could that be? Why hadn't Pont been able to put the finger back himself the first night if that was the case?

Why hadn't Exen stood up to Denit for Pell after Pell fixed his father's finger? Just because Denit was Exen's best friend and Denit hated Pell? For that matter, why did Gontra come up with the story about falling into a bush and pulling his finger out okay?! He looked over to check his position relative to Belk.

He cursed. While he'd been daydreaming, the line of hunters had come on a couple of horses. The center of the line had halted and the ends had started to curl around. Pell had missed Roley's signals and had continued straight rather than curving around like he was supposed to. Since he was at the end of the line, no one had curved around in front of him to cause him to pay attention.

Pell was way out of position! Roley'd be furious! Pell was tempted to run to get back into position but, of course, running attracted attention and would almost certainly spook the horses. As quickly as he thought he could possibly get away with, Pell slinked back toward his assigned position. If this hunt went poorly, Roley would probably beat him for his stupidity.

He'd beaten Bonat for shouting at Boro during a hunt last fall. Beaten him so badly that Bonat had limped for days afterward. Bonat's shout had spooked their intended prey at a time when everyone was hungry and irritable after several hands of days of poor hunting. At least this time they'd had good hunting for several days now. Perhaps Roley wouldn't be quite so angry. The sinking feeling in Pell's stomach said otherwise though. He found himself trembling at a time when he needed all his coordination to move quickly and quietly.

The circle was closing more slowly as they neared the horses, though the horses didn't seem very skittish yet. Pell continued trying to catch up to his position, trying to walk quietly, but feeling as if the horses would surely be spooked soon.

If by nothing else, simply by the sound of Pell's pounding heart.

Suddenly one of the horses looked up! The hunters stopped raggedly. The other horse looked up as well. The larger one swung its head about nervously, but all the hunters had become stationary. After a bit, the horses resumed their grazing. A small hand wave from Roley started everyone slowly moving in again. The horses looked up again—the larger one pranced around the smaller horse in a little circle. They both bolted toward the opening between Roley and Denit. The two hunters began shouting and waving their arms.

Pell ran for his position. He *had* to close the circle. His absence was making the normally weaker section where the two points came together gape even more. Roley and Denit successfully turned the horses back. But, as if it were a nightmare come true, they headed for the hole Pell should've already closed!

Pell ran faster than he thought he'd ever run before, but it obviously wasn't going to be fast enough! He felt terror detonate in his bowels, as if he were running away from one of the night cats, rather than toward his own prey. The horses were going to get away and they were going to do it through the hole he'd left when he'd been daydreaming! In desperation, he skipped a step and hurled his spear. It was wide! With a sick sensation he saw his spear fly straight and true toward Tando, no it was going to be short!

No! The spear skipped off the ground and flew into Tando's running feet. Pell saw as in slow motion, Tando's arms flying out as he fell.

Tando struck the ground, hard.

The horses pounded away.

Pell stumbled to a stop.

With great dread and a pounding heart, he walked toward where Tando lay, praying to all the spirits that Tando would bounce back to his feet and say he was okay.

But Pell could already tell *that* wasn't going to happen. Pell noticed his own hands trembling; in fact, his whole body was shaking like an animal in its death throes. Instantly, Pell's bladder was full. He *had* to urinate—there was a spasm in his crotch and a warm feeling spread down the inside of his thigh.

As Pell neared the group around Tando, he felt as if he were walking in a dream. He saw the hunters turning intermittently to look at him as he approached. Their countenances looked to Pell much like the Evil Spirit masks that some of the healers wore at summer gatherings. He heard his name repeatedly spoken as if it were a curse. However, he couldn't seem to understand what else was being said. Pell's ears rang, his head felt light and his knees felt weak. He looked at Tando's legs and, with relief, saw no blood or other sign of injury— then he realized that Tando was holding his left wrist...

It was deformed.

Bent back at an angle.

Tando was white as the chalk of the cliff.

Pell swayed, wondering momentarily if he was going to be able to keep to his feet. Roley solved that problem by taking one quick stride and knocking him to the ground. The offhandedly delivered blow once again demonstrated the frightening physical power that made Roley their leader.

Roley stood furiously over the semiconscious, but nonetheless cowering, Pell, "First you daydream and get out of position! Then you rush to get back into position and frighten the horses! Then... then, you break the most important rule of the hunt. Over and over I say 'Don't throw your spear towards other hunters!' Of course, you miss! Everyone knows you can't hit anything! But somehow you *do* manage to hit Tando!" He took a deep breath, standing straighter, "I declare you ginja! Ginja forever! We've kept you in the tribe out of respect for your mother and your dead father. But, now you've proved yourself worse than useless, you're *dangerous*. We cast you out. We cast you out. We cast you out!"

The others took up the chant. Pell was not surprised to see Denit and Pont shouting the curse louder than any of the others. He thought of appealing to Gontra for support against this death sentence. Gontra surely owed Pell something, but as Pell searched for Gontra's eyes, he found them downcast. Gontra was chanting, same as the others, not as loud perhaps, but still the same death sentence, "We cast you out."

Exen too, eyes on the horizon, not meeting Pell's.

Boro chanted as well, his old pledge to follow Pell from the tribe if Pell was cast out appeared to have been forgotten.

Pell looked pleadingly at Roley, but Roley's face hardened and he raised his spear. Pell scrabbled back a few paces on his buttocks, then rose to his feet and began to run. Out of habit, he curved around back toward the cave, running homeward the way he always had before. He'd probably covered a mile or two before he slowed, realizing the cave was no longer his home. He stumbled to a walk, tears streaming down his face as he tried to consider his options.

People just didn't survive outside their tribes. If they were cast out, they died if they couldn't join another tribe. Pell had sometimes heard tales of a few who'd lived for a season alone. Good hunters, cast out for fighting or some other crime. Even excellent hunters eventually died if no tribe took them in. A few hands of days of bad hunts; a minor injury with no one to help you; an encounter with a night cat.

There were just too many things that could go wrong if you were alone.

However, Pell knew he wasn't even a marginal hunter who *might* survive a season through good hunting and later be taken back in. His pitiful hunting was, after all, the primary reason he'd been cast out of his tribe. He knew, if it hadn't been brought to a head by his stupidity today, he might have been cast out some winter anyway. But perhaps with a few more years of maturity, he would've outgrown his clumsiness. Maybe, in a year or two, he'd have been able to hit something when he threw.

He'd never get those years.

How can I possibly survive?

He considered jumping off the cliff the way Durr had. At least it'd be a quick death, not a slow starvation. What kept him going was the possibility that, if he survived for a few days, Roley might reconsider. Pell would need fire to keep away the night cats though. If he had to sleep outside the cave he'd also need more furs to keep himself warm. And he'd have to find shelter somewhere, not necessarily a cave, but at least a defensible windbreak

When Pell thought about how he needed a coal to start a fire, he realized that the women back at the cave didn't know he was cast out... yet. Perhaps he could get some supplies? He continued back to the cave. His mother saw him coming alone. With an exclamation, she ran out to ask if he'd been hurt.

"No Momma, Roley cast me out."

Donte staggered and turned white as a sheet. "No!" was all she could say.

Pell grasped her arm to hold her up, but she sank slowly to the ground anyway. "I'm hoping to get a coal from the fire and a few sleeping furs before the men come back and tell the rest of the women. Without supplies, there's no way I'll survive." He shrugged, tears beginning to run down his face, "Maybe I don't deserve to live. Perhaps there's no chance I can make it. But..." he croaked out, "I want to try."

Donte just sat there, staring unseeingly up at her son.

Pell shook her shoulder a little, "Momma! *Please!* If you won't get me a few supplies before the hunters come back and tell everyone, I won't have *any* chance at all."

Donte's face took on a look of resolve. "I'll come with you; we'll form our own tribe of two."

Pell stared at her with joy. It would be so good to have some company in exile. Even, he thought guiltily, in death. He realized that half the terror of being cast out was the thought of being alone. Later in the spring when the plants began to green and the roots fattened up Donte would be invaluable. She knew the woman's art of gathering.

Pell came back to reality. Partly because taking Donte into a situation that would likely kill both of them wasn't fair to her. But, also because, right now it was early spring when they depended on the hunt for all their food. Donte, being a woman, would only be a burden for a terrible hunter such as himself. Pell never considered the possibility that Donte might help with hunting. The concept of women hunting wasn't within the pale of his experience. Finally, he said, "Oh Momma, we can't form a tribe without hunters. You'd just die with me."

"Better to die with you." Donte's face sagged, "All my other children are dead… so many years now… It's no use going on if I lose you too."

Pell thought a moment longer, "No! You've got to stay with the tribe, at least for now. You might be able to sneak me a few supplies. You won't be able to help me if you're an exile too!" Pell paused, thinking, "Later this summer, if I'm still alive, you can join me and help me gather for the winter. We could try to form our own tribe. Besides, what I'm really hoping is that Roley'll change his mind and let me back in the tribe. If you stayed, you'd be able to beg him to have mercy toward me. You can't do that if you're an outcast too."

Tears brimming in her eyes, Donte sat staring into the distance awhile. She finally nodded, then simply said, "Wait."

She turned and walked back up the path to the cave. A few minutes later she came out with a bundle and walked back to where the forlorn Pell stood, somewhat out of sight behind several small trees.

"Here," she said handing him the bundle, "Two furs, one of Lenta's old firepots with a couple of good coals, some flint, some sinew and thongs, a big piece of leather and a chunk of meat from yesterday's kill. I've been thinking about where you should set up your camp. You need to be a day's walk from here so you'll be out of Roley's regular hunting areas. It'd be good if it was towards the Aldans' usual summer hunting areas so I'll be able to find you when the gathering gets better."

They talked a while and Pell agreed to try to set up his camp in a ravine much of a day's walk toward the summer gathering place. The tribe normally summered at the edge of a large grassland almost two days walk away. The summer tribal gathering and trading area was south of that. Thus, he'd be about half way between the tribe's winter and summer areas, but at a day's walk, still outside the usual hunting areas for either. The ravine they agreed upon was easy enough to identify because it had a spring-fed stream. The water of the stream was known for running ice cold, even in the heat of summer.

Donte clasped Pell to her bosom. Grasping bemusedly that he'd grown to be almost as tall as she was, Pell hugged her back.

When she let go he turned and trudged away.

***

Initially, Pell started directly for the ravine with the cold springs. He hadn't gone far when he realized he wouldn't be passing too far from the brush-choked gulch where he'd wanted to lie in wait, hoping an animal would get stuck in his trap. He'd intended to go there later that day anyway. On the one hand, he didn't want to go, because he needed to set up a shelter as soon as possible against the fear of the big night cats. On the other hand, that thicket of brush might be a safe refuge from the cats. They'd have difficulty insinuating their bulk into the brushy tunnel. It didn't look like rain that night anyway and the dead brush would provide plenty of material for a fire.

So, instead of passing by it, he turned into the mouth of the little gulch.

When he arrived at the brushy wall, he immediately smelled blood. Something had made a fresh kill nearby. Whatever it was it wasn't on his side of the brush wall. Perhaps it was on the other side? Trembling with excitement, he crouched down and began to crawl through. A few paces into the mess of sticks and brush he saw some motion ahead. He realized that it was coming from the area he'd worked on. There was a boar in there!

And a wolf!

He backed up warily, holding his spear ready to ward off the wolf if it came his way. His heart was throbbing, but the wolf didn't pursue him. In fact, it appeared that there were only a few abortive motions coming from the wolf. The boar lay still.

Pell waited quite a while. When nothing more happened, he eventually advanced again. Approaching the wolf and boar, he held his spear rigidly in front of himself.

When he got close again, he saw that both animals had become thoroughly trapped in the little area that he'd set up between his sharpened stakes. He suspected the pig had been trapped first. The wolf had likely come to investigate, hoping to make a meal.

In any case, they'd gotten wedged into the small area with one another. It looked to Pell as if the young wolf had eventually killed the boar, but the boar had battered the wolf up against Pell's stakes and caused some serious injuries of its own. The wolf lay weakly on its side, lapping at blood still dripping from the boar's carcass. It looked up at Pell's approach and he could see the fear in its eyes.

The wolf was rather small but had a beautiful pelt of silvery brown fur. Pell braced himself to plunge his spear into the wolf's chest, thinking that the pelt would be valuable. He slid the spear through the stakes that blocked the exit and put the tip almost on the wolf's chest so that he couldn't miss.

The wolf looked into his eyes piteously—in those eyes Pell saw a reflection of himself, begging Roley for his life.

It licked at his spear.

Pell cursed and pulled the spear back. The wolf was no threat in its current condition. Harvesting its pelt while he was traveling would be a waste anyway, he wouldn't be able to stretch or work it. He had more pig than he could eat before it rotted and in any case, wolf meat was tough and stringy.

So he told himself.

He started disengaging the stakes that blocked the passage. Once he'd removed them so they no longer formed their one-way blockage of the passage, he reached in and grabbed the front limb of the dead boar. He heaved hard and began hauling it slowly back out of the narrow passage that'd been its deathtrap. The wolf lay unmoving. Pell pulled the boar back out to the end of the passage and over to where he'd left the bundle Donte had made for him.

To his dismay, he saw his bundle had fallen over! In horror, he untied it and felt the little firepot inside. It was barely warm! Desperately, he got out his good flint knife and made some shavings from one of the dry pieces of wood. He broke off some small dry twigs and laid them close to hand. He opened the firepot and put the shavings on the coal that lay within. He blew gently. It didn't raise a glow! Frantic, he shook the little vessel, nudged the coals and blew some more. Spirits!

His coals were dead!

He couldn't possibly survive without the tribe, without a cave, *and* without fire! He'd have to go back and get another coal. But by now the hunters must've returned and everyone would know he'd been cast out. Perhaps he could trade the pelt of the wolf for a coal?

He turned and looked back into the tunnel. The wolf stood swaying in the entrance, barely able to stand. Pell took his knife and walked over to it. *It should be easy to kill,* he thought. He planned to grasp its snout and cut its throat, but as Pell reached for its nose the wolf licked his hand. He jerked his hand back but then recognized it for the friendly gesture it was. Once again Pell found himself unable to look into the wolf's sorrowful eyes and kill it. He backed away and began cutting up the boar's carcass—after a minute he threw the boar's head to the wolf. The animal lay down and began gnawing on it.

Pell skinned and cut up the boar while he worried about what to do.

Done, he wrapped one haunch of the pig, with a chunk of the liver in the large leather skin his mother had brought him. That was all he thought he could possibly eat before it rotted. He carried this bundle back into the tunnel in the brush. He collected the downhill set of sharpened stakes that had trapped the two animals and worked his way past the uphill set.

There he laid his bundle and the pig haunch in its leather. He used the sharpened stakes to make another one-way block facing uphill. Now the tunnel was again doubly blocked, but this time to keep animals away from his food, rather than trapping them in a zone. He took his little firepot and made his way back out of the tunnel. There he wrapped as much of the pig meat in the pig's own skin as he could carry and set off back to the Aldan's cave.

He got back just before sunset and stopped on the path below the cave where he called for his mother. A crowd gathered at the ledge outside the cave and gawked at the doomed young man. Donte hurried down the path to him.

"Are you okay Pell? What's all the blood?"

"Yes, I'm okay. The blood's from a boar I killed, but my firepot tipped over and my coal went out."

"Oh no, Pell! I don't think they'll let me get another coal. They're in a foul mood. Pont hasn't been able to do anything for Tando's wrist and the hunting remained terrible after you left. *All* of the last kill is gone, so they're looking forward to a hungry night."

"I've brought most of my pig. I'll trade it for the coal. I could even try to fix Tando's wrist if he'd like."

"What? You have a pig? Where did you get it?"

"Remember? That's why I'm bloody—I killed a pig." Pell wondered for a moment how bad this lie was, but decided that, after all, he'd built the trap that killed the boar and he couldn't help the fact that she'd assume that he'd killed it in a hunt.

Donte stared at him in stunned amazement. "What do you mean you could try to fix Tando's wrist?" she asked in a near whisper, looking at her son as though he'd lost his senses.

"I fixed my finger when Pont couldn't." He reflected that he'd only let the healer try once on his own finger. "I *also* fixed Gontra's finger. It wasn't any 'bush' or 'Boar Spirit'. I've found a trick for doing it. I tried to tell Pont about it once, but he won't even listen to me."

Donte's eyes narrowed. Pell thought with dismay that even his own mother didn't believe him. Finally, she said, "Give me some of the boar and the firepot. I'll see whether they'll trade... I don't think I'd better bring up Tando's wrist."

Pell gave her the haunch from the boar. "I'll give them the rest of the boar I brought if they let you bring me a coal. All I'm keeping is one haunch." He handed her the little firepot and she started up the hill.

More of the tribe had crowded out onto the ledge to stare and Pell felt quite self-conscious. He shifted from foot to foot and looked away at the horizon. He worried dark would fall before he'd be able to get back to the brush-choked ravine he now thought of as his safe haven.

There was some shouting from up at the cave. Pell recognized Roley, Pont, and Donte's voices but couldn't understand what was said. After a bit, Donte came back down the hill. With mixed feelings, he saw that she was carefully carrying the little firepot. So it must have a coal in it, meaning she'd made his deal. Why did he feel so disappointed?

He realized he'd been hoping that somehow, in view of his kill, Roley'd change his mind and let him come back.

Donte stopped in front of him with a sad look in her eyes. "I asked them to let you stay. I think Roley was feeling guilty about exiling you, but Pont reminded him about Tando's wrist. Pont even tried to claim that you've been bringing bad luck to the tribe. Pont told Roley to just have the hunters come down here and *take* your meat, 'because you were going to die anyway.' Pont's... he's just... just *evil* sometimes! Anyhow, the best I could get them to agree to was to let you have some coals."

"'*Let* me have some coals?' This meat's worth a lot more than a few lousy coals!" Then Pell thought of Tando's wrist—actually, probably Tando's life he'd cost them. Embarrassed, he said, "Oh well, you did what you could, thanks, Here's the rest of the meat." Pell loaded her down with the remainder of the boar, gave her another hug and hurried off with his firepot. "I've got to go before it gets dark," he called over his shoulder.

The sun had set and it was nearly dark by the time he got back to the little brush-choked gulch. He quickly found the little pile of shavings he'd made earlier and this time successfully started them on fire with the little firepot. Adding twigs, he soon had a fire going. To his surprise, he saw the young wolf was still there. It lay on its side gnawing on the boar's head. He'd been sure that the wolf would have dragged itself away by now. Or, would've died. He thought again about killing it for its fur—then he looked the wolf in the eye again.

It wasn't going to happen.

Using a brand from the fire for light, he relocated up into the little tunnel in the brush. He moved into the area he'd blocked off. He enlarged that little area by breaking and tearing out branches, chiefly to make the roof higher, piling the extra wood in the uphill part of the tunnel. Once he was sure a small fire wouldn't catch the entire brush pile he started a little fire from his brand. He unrolled his bundle and laid out his sleeping furs on the downhill side of the fire. This left him with a path for escape if the brush pile did catch fire.

Finally, he sliced strips off the pig haunch he'd kept and roasted them over his little fire. For some reason, the meal tasted better than any he'd ever had before. Unfortunately, even as he gorged on pig, his fear and dread of a life alone returned.

He stoked his fire and lay down to sleep. Tossing and turning, he couldn't stop thinking about how he didn't deserve to live after what he'd done to Tando. This alternated with brooding over his burning hatred of Denit, sick betrayal over his lack of support from Boro, Gontra, and Exen and wondering how it'd ever be possible to feed himself.

Maybe he'd gain coordination soon. Maybe he'd get better at throwing.

He briefly pictured himself returning to the Aldans, triumphant, having become a mighty hunter. A hunter they desperately needed. Eventually, he drifted into a sleep tormented by visions of Tando and his deformed arm. These shifted seamlessly into visions of Durr's even worse deformity. Then of Tando/Durr lying broken at the bottom of the cliff. He woke repeatedly in cold sweats, often imagining he could see the eyes of enormous night cats reflected in the light from his fire. He built up his little fire after each run of nightmares and struggled to get back to sleep.

The next day dawned cold and clear again. Pell woke exhausted but felt relieved to see no evidence of impending rain. Bad weather would've made his journey to the ravine with the cold springs even more difficult.

First, he worked on the bundle his mother'd given him. Using some of the thongs and leather straps in it, he fashioned a shoulder sling so he could carry it easily. He spent time putting some good coals from the night's fire into his little firepot. He collected his meat, picked up his spear and made his way out of the little tunnel.

To his amazement, the young wolf was still there. She was sitting up and appeared to be waiting for Pell's next move. When he set out on his journey she laboriously got to her feet and limped along behind him. She was almost carrying one hind paw but, after they'd been traveling a while, she seemed to warm up.

After they'd gone a little farther she had little difficulty keeping up. By late morning, limping less, she occasionally ranged ahead a bit. When Pell's course turned out to be different than where the wolf'd gone, she'd swing around and follow behind him a little way. Once sure of his direction, she'd take the lead again. Pell thought somehow she'd gotten confused. It was as if she thought she and Pell were their own little wolf pack.

The day passed slowly as Pell followed a route the tribe had taken every spring and fall since before he could remember. He thought he was making better time than the Aldans did in their semiannual treks. After some consideration, he realized that with few possessions, he wasn't burdened the way the Aldans normally were when they made the trip.

Rather than good news, that seemed grim.

This thought again led him to worry about how he could possibly survive without the equipment and tools that the tribe had built up over the years. This was to say nothing of all the skills that different members of the tribe had. Skills he didn't have. He wished he'd paid more attention to how the women cooked the Aldans' meals.

But at least he had vague ideas of how they cooked from being present while it was done. He hadn't gone on gathering trips with the women since he was a toddler, so his knowledge of the gathering of plants, roots, and berries was abysmal. When the plants began to green up later in the spring he'd have virtually no idea which ones were edible and which ones weren't. Of course, he'd be able to recognize many of the edible berries and some of the grains.

How to separate the grains from their stalks and hulls and how to recognize plants which had edible parts underground—now that was another matter altogether.

He thought of the other hunters taunting him about women's work. If only he actually *did* know how to do a woman's work! Why *hadn't* he let his mother join him in exile? To augment his despair, his thoughts returned to how poorly he performed at the man's work of hunting!

He trudged on, head down, heart heavy, nearly oblivious to his surroundings. Abruptly the wolf began growling behind him. *What? Is the damned beast going to attack me now?!* For the Spirit's sake, Pell wondered, why didn't I *kill* it when I had the chance? He turned, swinging his spear about, to confront the wolf, but the wolf was staring fixedly off to the north. She was snarling viciously now, lips wrinkled up, tail low.

Pell glanced in the direction that the wolf was glaring. He saw a flicker of a tail and then a rippling, tawny body bounded into view. It was a big cat that'd been lying in ambush. Now, ambush ruined, it was accelerating his way! Pell's bundle fell unnoticed as he vaulted into a nearby tree, grasping its lower branches and swinging up. He scrambled up until the branches got too dense for him to make any more progress; then looked down. The big cat stood on its hind paws at the base of the tree, reaching up with outstretched claws. Shuddering, Pell realized that, absent the wolf's warning, he'd have already been in the cat's jaws!

He looked around and saw to his amazement that the wolf was fifteen paces back, hackles up, her hair raised on end. She continued snarling, lips still curled back to show her teeth. Even more unbelievably, she was making little dashing movements toward the big cat as if contemplating an attack. Pell didn't believe his eyes. The wolf couldn't possibly think that she could defeat one of the big cats, could she?

To Pell's dismay, the cat began trying to climb the tree. Cookfire discussions back at the cave had taught Pell that smaller cats could climb trees after prey, but there'd been arguments about whether big cats like this one could. It appeared as if Pell might find out who'd been right in those arguments—in the hardest way. The big cat pulled up a little and looked like it was about to reach for a higher grip with its front paws! The wolf dashed in and nipped at the cat's hindquarters! Snarling and snapping, the cat dropped out of the tree, knocking the wolf end over end. The big cat twisted after the wolf, but the wolf skittered out of its path. The cat pursued halfheartedly, seemingly recognizing a futile chase. Moments later it returned to the base of the tree. Pell looked frantically about, considering his chances of leaping from this tree to a neighboring one.

As the cat began to rise up at the base of the tree, the wolf returned! Again it took up station fifteen paces back, growling and snapping. The big cat regarded it warily, looking up at Pell a moment longer. Then, to Pell's complete astonishment, the cat slowly turned and moved off into the woods.

Pell regarded this turn of events with complete bewilderment. The wolf had now saved his life twice. First by giving warning of the cat when he'd been daydreaming, and second by attacking its hindquarters when it attempted to climb after him. Still clinging to the tree, trembling, he offered up a few prayers to the Spirit Wolf.

When Pell's nerves steadied and the shaking faded, he slowly climbed back down out of the tree, watching tremulously for any evidence that the cat might be returning. When Pell picked up his pack he smelled the meat in it and realized that the smell might have attracted the cat.

Amazingly enough, with the wolf pestering it, the animal hadn't even gotten around to stealing his meat. Suddenly fear swept through Pell again—what if the coals in his firepot had gone out *again* when he dropped the pack? He unpacked the little pot with trembling hands and checked the embers inside. To his relief, they seemed undisturbed, glowing readily when he blew on them. He considered building a fire with the embers in order to start new coals, just in case these were about to go out. However, it'd be hours before a fire produced good coals again—he'd have to spend the night here.

Where one of the big cats was hunting.

Loath to stay in that location without good shelter; especially after the experience he'd just been through, he started walking again. He began worrying that he might not find shelter in Cold Spring Ravine either. After considering the options and thinking about his recollection of the ravine's rough, rocky walls, he decided his chances were better there.

Pell continued on his way in a hyper-alert state. Now, whenever he looked around and saw the wolf, the sight relieved him. On impulse, he got out his pig haunch, carved off a chunk and tossed it to the young wolf. She bolted the meat down in a few ravenous gulps, then resumed her scouting position.

***

It was midafternoon when Pell and the wolf reached the ravine. Waters running down out of the mountain had cut the ragged cleft. High mountain streams disappeared into the plateau above the ravine, reappearing as several springs near the beginning of the cleft. Snow runoff from the mountains made up most of the water and was the reason it ran icy cold year round. Pell began to explore for a natural shelter. After spending an hour searching up and down the ravine, a deep limestone overhang, just a little way up from where he'd first entered still looked best. Not great, but better than any other locations.

The stream had deeply undercut the area thousands of years ago, then diverted away as it shifted to the other side of the ravine. The overhang would block some of the wind and rain and protect his back, but it left three sides exposed. In addition, he could tell that when it rained, the water ran back under the overhang and would drip into any proposed campsite. There was an overlying cutout in the depths of the overhang where the floor and roof were higher than elsewhere. The water wouldn't wet that area, but it was only a little bigger than his bedding and pack. Any protective fire would be located right where he expected rainwater to drip.

He placed his pack up on the shelf, quickly collected a little firewood, made shavings and got out his firepot. To his immense relief, he found the coals still glowed. He started a fire easily enough. With the fire to protect his pack, he took his leather and began making trips down to the stream to collect mud mixed with broken reeds. He brought the mud back and, as he'd seen the women do at the mouth of the Aldan's cave where there'd been a similar problem, he began forming a "drip-lip" at the periphery of the ceiling of the overhang. He placed it far enough out to provide an area where he could store dry firewood and sleep down beside it.

Smoke from his fire had risen into the area over the little shelf and he could tell it'd be nearly impossible to sleep up in there. Just inside the area where water would fall from his "drip lip," he made another ridge of mud on the floor. This would divert any water that ran over the floor away from his new living area. When he finished, he still had time to collect a small pile of deadfall for firewood before it got dark.

As he roasted some of his pig for dinner he saw the wolf slinking closer and closer. She was obviously spooked by the fire. Despite her fear, she crept nearer until she was well under the overhang with him. With some surprise, he found himself relieved rather than disturbed at the prospect of having a wolf in his shelter. He shrugged; she *had* saved him from the cat. After a while, he threw the wolf another chunk of meat. He considered this. It seemed a dull-witted thing to have done when he was certainly going to run out of food soon. On the other hand, perhaps it was a worthy offering to the Spirit Wolf. A Spirit Wolf to whom, after all, he'd found himself praying earlier that day.

As he settled down for the night he considered a plan for the next day. He had to hunt, he decided. The tribe only hunted when it needed meat, because, with no way to store it, having too much in reserve simply meant a lot of spoiled meat. They hunted daily during the winter when hunting was poor and meat froze and therefore kept longer. However, the way he threw, Pell knew he'd have to hunt all day, every day, to have any hope of surviving—even in the summer.

Spirits alone knew how he might survive the winter.

***

True to his plan, the next day Pell banked his fire to keep animals out of the cave and set out to hunt. He put his haunch of pig meat and the meager contents of his pack up on the smoky shelf in the back of the cave, thinking the smoke might keep scavengers away.

As he'd expected, his hunt was a complete failure. The wolf followed him faithfully throughout the day. Pell initially thought the animal would spoil his hunt, but soon could tell she was much quieter than he was. In addition, she recognized game before he did. He found himself watching for cues from Gimpy, as he was thinking of the animal because of her limp. In the early afternoon, they came upon a deer.

Pell quietly and slowly moved closer with his spear. The wolf slunk along a few paces to Pell's side. They were moving upwind and the deer appeared unsuspecting, but Pell stepped on a pebble that crunched. The deer's head came up with a start and it looked right at Pell. He cast his spear, but it whistled harmlessly over the deer's head.

The wolf took off after the deer, but the deer bounded away unharmed. Pell was sitting on a fallen tree whittling a point back on his spear when Gimpy came back, tongue lolling, limping even more than before. He considered the possibility of killing and eating the wolf if the hunting went as badly as he feared. He wasn't sure he could bring himself to do it, but he decided he could if he got hungry enough. He realized that the animal could serve as a kind of walking larder.

The remainder of the day passed without the two hunters drawing any closer to success than they had with the deer. As they followed an animal trail back to their campsite, Pell found himself thinking wistfully about the brush-choked ravine with its little tunnel. He wondered if he should have stayed there. He could have rebuilt his trap in the tunnel and perhaps more pigs would have gotten stuck in it. At the end of this fruitless day, he despaired of his ability to stalk close enough to make a kill with his fire-hardened spear points. *Why didn't I ask Donte to steal some flint spearheads? Though the tribe has few enough, and, the way I throw, they'd break as soon as I missed my first throws!*

Pell thought back to his exploration of Cold Springs Ravine the previous afternoon. There was a narrow point in the ravine. Could he choke it with brush? He shook his head as he considered the sheer volume of material it'd require. He only had one poorly knapped hand axe!

As they neared the campsite, the wolf went off to the side to explore a scent. Watching Gimpy, Pell almost stepped on a rabbit that'd been frozen right in plain sight. It rocketed away into the brush. He and Gimpy gave short pursuit, though to no avail. The rabbit disappeared into dense brambles where they couldn't follow. Pell peered into the brambles. He mused that the little tunnel in the brambles where the rabbit had vanished resembled, though on a smaller scale, the tunnel where he and Wolf had captured their boar.

As they completed their journey back to the camp, Pell's thoughts drifted repeatedly back to the little tunnel in the brambles. His mind envisioned blocking the tunnel in the brambles at arms depth and rigging a one-way passage into the tunnel with sharpened twigs—a miniature version of his boar trap. He thought of the rabbit he'd caught with the noose. He became more and more excited over the prospect of getting more meat in such a manner. He resolved to try making both kinds of traps the next morning.

Back at the camp, he steeled himself to eat the spoiling meat. He built up the banked, smoldering fire first, then got the boar haunch down from its shelf in the back. He came out coughing and hacking from all the smoke up in the shelf area. To his dismay, the meat was dark from exposure to the smoke! He wouldn't even have spoiled meat to eat; the smoke had ruined it!

Chagrined, he stared at the blackened haunch. His stomach rumbled in anticipation of the first of what would likely be many days of hunger. Perhaps only the outer layers had been ruined? He cut into it. The outer layers had a hard, crusty, almost-cooked consistency. The deepest parts of the meat looked bad, but he thought they might still be edible. He cut off a strip and sat down to eat. As he expected the spoiling deeper meat tasted bad, but to his immense surprise the more superficial meat tasted a lot better—despite the taste of the smoke! In fact, as he chewed, he recognized with some surprise that he *liked* the flavor the smoke gave the meat. He thought it was probably still rotten, but the taste of the smoke just covered the taste of the decay.

In any case, if the meat near the surface tasted better because the smoke had gotten to it, he realized he could create more surface. He cut the rest of the haunch up into strips and took it up to the smoky little shelf in the back of the overhang. He laid the strips of meat out over some sticks so the smoke could get to all sides of it.

Pleased with himself, he tossed some of the worst of the meat to the wolf who happily bolted it down.

***

The next morning Pell ate more of the smoky meat and set out to build the traps he'd been excitedly thinking about until late in the evening. As he walked, he kept an eye out for edible vegetables. He craved something besides meat. He found some young onions sprouting and pulled them up. The bulbs were small this early in the season, but he ate the bulbs and much of the green part as well. Soon his mouth tasted foul, but the onions were a welcome change from the all meat diet he'd been eating. Besides, everyone knew people got sick if they ate only meat. He picked more onion sprouts for his evening meal.

Bushes of many types looked like they might soon begin to flower. Pell thought that some of the flowering bushes might have berries eventually, but that didn't help much at present. He pulled up a variety of other plants as he walked along, looking for edible roots. He did find one that had a small bulbous portion. He wiped it clean and took a bite.

It was tough, but chewing it released some sweet fluids. He decided that if it was sweet, it must be edible. He found a few more of the same type and chewed on them as well. He wasn't sure whether they were different root vegetables than the women gathered at home, or whether it was simply too early in the season for them to have developed good sized mature bulbs such as he was familiar with. Perhaps if he boiled them? He collected some of the bulbs to take back to his shelter.

Pell stopped at several thickets. Searching around their bases, he found passages where tracks in the dirt showed small animals traveled in and out of the dense undergrowth. When he found a hole in the brambles that seemed to have impenetrably thick walls, he blocked it off with a stone that he placed as deep in the little tunnel as he could reach. He sat down with his knife and sharpened sticks. These he worked into the opening so that the points aimed inward, allowing passage into the tunnel, but blocking passage back out. When his own hand got stuck reaching in to adjust the sticks he got excited about the trap's potential.

When he found openings that didn't have tight walls—and most of them didn't—he made a noose from one of his thongs and tied the other end firmly to a stout branch. He carefully suspended the loop within the opening. The top of the noose went at the top of the opening. He suspended the bottom of the loop across the opening about halfway up. This, he envisioned, would catch below the animal's neck.

After installing the first couple he sat back to look at one. He worried the animals would stop when they saw the thong hanging across the opening. Or if they stopped to smell it and smelled Pell's scent they might not enter or exit at all. If only he could be chasing them so that they'd run into their tunnels too hastily to investigate! But, he realized with disappointment, he wouldn't be able to chase a rabbit into its tunnel very often.

Working on placing his next thong, he got it tangled in the vegetation. When he pulled it out, it had a vine tendril twisted on it.

Aha! Pell twisted grass leaves about the most visible part of the thong where it hung across the entrance. As he got up to leave he saw some rabbit droppings and had another idea. To hide their scent, hunters often smeared themselves with herbivore dung. He'd seen wolves rolling in droppings to do the same thing.

Pell found some fresh rabbit pellets and took them back to the trap. He smeared dung on the thong and rewrapped it with grass. As he walked he smeared dung on the rest of his thongs.

***

He placed about ten traps that morning, then headed back to work on improving his shelter. As he neared his campsite Gimpy began a rumbling growl. *Oh no!* Pell thought, *Another cat?*

To his consternation, when Pell had carefully reached a spot where he could see the little outcropping he thought of as his, he saw people squatting in front of his fire! They'd even built up the flame. His stomach sank as he thought that surely they'd found and appropriated his meager possessions. He didn't even consider the possibility of driving them away. After losing so many fights to Denit, he never envisioned winning a physical contest. Especially against more than one opponent and he saw at least two people near his fire. He stole closer, hoping to observe without being seen. Lifting his far-seer, he saw with great dismay that the brawny, hairy individual nearest the fire was Tando. Tando's arm, still deformed, hung out over his knee in front of him, as if to taunt Pell, saying, "Look what you've done!"

Have they come to take revenge on me?

Then Pell recognized that the person further back under the overhang was his mother Donte. She seemed to have heard something and she moved out into the light, peering around. Seeing Pell, she called out to him. "Pell, come down here. Tando wants to see if you can fix his arm."

Pell slowly walked down to the campsite. Distantly he noted the wolf slinking away into the forest. Pell began trembling with reaction. Might he be able to right his wrong? Conversely, the likelihood of his being able to fix Tando's arm had to be low. It was, after all, *much* larger than a finger or a rabbit bone.

The pall of the situation subdued Pell's reunion with Donte. Pell had the feeling his mother clearly foresaw his impending doom. Though she saw no realistic chance of avoiding her son's demise, she was willingly grasping at straws. *Bringing Tando here was a desperate but hopeless gamble,* Pell thought. At least she hadn't made a huge investment in grasping at this particular straw, since the tribe was probably on its way to the summer campsite. Coming to see Pell would've required only a minor detour.

One bright point in a litany of bad omens came when Tando told Pell that Gontra'd admitted Pell had been the one who fixed Gontra's finger. Tando had come to Donte asking if she knew where Pell had gone. When he realized it was close to their route, he'd asked if she'd take him to find Pell.

Though she didn't come out and say it, Pell could tell his own mother doubted Pell's claim that he'd reduced Gontra's finger.

This, even after Gontra's admission. His own mother's doubt helped Pell understand just how preposterous the claim must seem. He himself found it surprising Tando'd decided to seek him out. *But,* Pell thought, *Tando must be desperate as well.* Donte and Tando had brought a little meat for Pell but, in fear of infuriating Pont, hadn't told the rest of the tribe where they were going.

One look at Tando's face told Pell that Tando felt torn between viewing Pell as evil incarnate for having destroyed his life and wondering frantically whether the boy could possibly be his savior as well. Pell'd been staring at Tando's arm from across the campfire. Finally, Tando held it out and exclaimed, "Spirits! What're you waiting for? Come on, try it!"

Pell swallowed, "Let me look at it first." He moved around the fire to examine Tando's wrist. The break was a little proximal to the wrist and bent the arm back away from his palm. There was considerable swelling around the break, but Pell had a sense that the bones were shifted or displaced toward the back of the hand and that they were overlapped to make the arm shorter.

He gently probed it with his fingertips and Tando immediately reacted, pulling away, "Just fix it, you ginja fool, I don't need you to *poke* it!"

Pell realized with surprise that Tando was even more frightened than Pell. "Tando," he said, as calmly as he could, "I've got to feel it so I can understand how it's broken and how I might try to put it back in place. I've fixed two fingers with my trick, but *I* don't know whether it'll work for a wrist. I'll try if you want, but just fixing fingers caused a lot of pain, it's bound to hurt even more trying to fix your arm."

Tando looked surprised. However, he seemed reassured by Pell's calm demeanor. "Yeah, well Pont's jerking on it felt like it was going to kill me... so I suppose I already know it's going to hurt." He paused, studying Pell for a moment, then held his arm out again, "Okay, do what you can." He turned his eyes away, tensely gritting his teeth.

"Wait. Do you have any hemp to chew for the pain?"

"No."

Donte stood up. "I saw some hemp growing on the sunny side of the ravine. It's down a way. I'll get some and be right back." She started off down the canyon.

Pell thought his mother looked relieved to have something constructive to do.

Far from whatever her son was about to attempt.

Pell sat down and surreptitiously palpated his own arm in the area of the wrist where Tando's was deformed. As opposed to the two dislocated fingers Pell had reduced so far, he soon recognized Tando's arm was deformed in an area where there didn't seem to be a joint. At least when he felt his own arm in that area, just proximal to the wrist, it felt solid without even a hint of the flexibility provided by a joint.

There must be bone in the area, he thought, not a joint. *Tando must have broken the bone, whereas I just put the joint in my finger out of place.* Pell wondered a moment whether the same trick of bending it back would work for a broken bone the way it did for a dislocated joint—then he remembered that it worked on the rabbit's broken leg. But were rabbits different than people?

He decided he'd just as well try it.

It didn't seem that things could get much worse.

Not for Pell, *nor* for Tando.

Donte arrived back with some hemp while Pell was still contemplating the problem. Pell's mind whipsawed, from the excited hope that he might be able to relieve Tando's condition, to fear of the overwhelming chance that nothing he did would make any difference.

Except that it'll make Tando hate me even more!

Tando began chewing. After a while he started looking glassy-eyed. Pell got him to walk over to the stream, lie down and put his arm in the icy water. Tando immediately pulled it back out of the water, protesting bitterly about the cold. Thinking of the effect that his calm tone of voice had before, Pell kept speaking in a soothing tone and reminded Tando of how cold makes it hard to feel your fingers. He told Tando he was sure the cold had helped with the pain when he reduced his own and Gontra's fingers. Pell continued calmly reassuring him and Tando eventually put the arm back in the stream, lying on his stomach with his head resting on his other arm.

Pell waited until Tando had resumed his drunken expression then lifted the arm out of the water to look at it. It was pale and cool. Pell put it back in the water and, taking a deep breath, stepped into the icy water himself, positioning himself over Tando's arm and trying to picture how best to grasp the wrist. He lifted it out of the water and bent it back, like he'd bent the fingers and the rabbit leg back. It was too big and the water made it too slippery! He couldn't pull it out to length!

Tando started to struggle and the arm slipped out of Pell's grasp. In a slurred tone Tando began berating him—for breaking his arm in the first place; for putting it in the cold water; for jerking painfully on it; for not getting it straight; for ruining his life; for killing him slowly; for being a worthless ginja; outcast, lowlife...

Pell cringed, heart pounding, wanting nothing more than to jump up and run away.

Once he got himself in control, Pell climbed out of the water and backed away a few paces. He turned and struggled to speak calmly again. Despite the effort, Pell couldn't keep the tremor out of his voice, however, in his drugged state Tando didn't seem to notice. "Sorry Tando, your wrist was just too big and slippery for me; I need something to help me get a better grip. You settle down, I'll look for something to help me get that grip and we'll try it again."

Tando looked blearily at Pell for a moment, considering. "Okay," he slurred.

Donte gave Tando some more hemp to chew.

Pell walked back up to the campsite thinking furiously. Easily said, but *how could* he get a better grip? For a moment he envisioned tying a slipknot around the wrist with a leather strap. How would he bend the bone back while he pulled on it though?

He pawed through his meager possessions and looked around the campsite. His eye fixed on a piece of driftwood left from an old flood in the ravine. It lay near some leather straps he'd made earlier while cutting out thongs for his "traps." It was about half a hand wide and the length of a forearm. He picked up the driftwood and the straps and went back down to look at Tando's wrist.

Tando snored loudly, oblivious to the world as Pell looped straps about his own arm in different directions and held the piece of driftwood up to his own wrist, cocking his head to look at it from different angles. Finally, Pell used his crappy hand axe to split the driftwood lengthwise. He hacked and scraped away at it until he had a fairly straight little board. It had a flat surface that was relatively smooth, but was contoured a little to fit comfortably against Pell's own forearm, wrist, palm, and fingers.

Pell pulled Tando's arm up and laid the board against Tando's palm to ponder the possibilities. Because of the angulation at Tando's wrist, the portion of the board which should lie against the forearm stood away at least a handspan. Pell scratched his head, contemplating the problem. He tied the board to Tando's palm with a couple of leather straps. With a shock of excitement, he saw that the portion of the board that would eventually lie against the palmar surface of the forearm gave him a handle such that, when he pulled on it, it'd bend the bone back! This would increase the deformity the way he'd had to do when he reduced the fingers and the rabbit's broken leg!

Pell wrapped the board into place with even more straps, extending from the hand, back up across the wrist and just onto the forearm bones, but only on the hand side of the break. Tando tolerated all this fairly well, with only an occasional moan. The hemp—and maybe the cold—must be working its magic even without Pont's other herbal ingredients.

Pell inspected the apparatus a moment more; then put Tando's arm, board and all, back into the cold water. Tando moaned and struggled a bit, but bore it better this time. When Pell thought the wrist should be numb, he pulled it out and checked the straps, snugging up a few tighter than he'd had them before. He put Tando's arm back in the stream again and once more stepped out into the icy water to stand over the arm.

As the submerged limb cooled again, Pell carefully considered how to exert the greatest possible force during this next try. He was fairly certain that Tando wouldn't give him a third chance if he failed this time. He'd pulled really hard on the two fingers he'd reduced. *How much harder would I have to pull on an arm?*

Pell climbed out of the water and rolled Tando onto his back, bending Tando's arm up to a right angle at the elbow. He grabbed the proximal part of the board with his right hand, just below the fracture, bending the wrist and hand back. He grasped the other end of the board with Tando's strapped fingers in his left hand; then put his foot on Tando's biceps just above the bent elbow.

With a surge, Pell pulled mightily. The board bent the bone even farther back at the fracture site.

Even through the board, Pell could feel the bones grinding together as they slipped around.

Tando flailed up, striking Pell on the back, though Pell hardly noticed.

Pell used his left hand, which was grasping the board and Tando's hand, to pull the wrist back straight. This maneuver laid the board back down against Tando's proximal forearm.

Pell stared. Yes! The board lay flat against Tando's forearm! The arm was straight again! It even seemed like it was back to its original length!

Tears ran down Pell's cheeks.

He started to let go, expecting Tando's arm to stay straight. After all, the dislocated fingers had remained straight, after he'd reduced them. To his alarm, the arm started to bend again in a sickening fashion. Pell remembered that the rabbit's leg had done the same thing. He pushed the board back down against Tando's forearm—this held it straight.

He held it there with one hand and sat down on the bank to look at his work. Absently, Pell reached out, picked up another of the leather straps, beginning to wrap it around the proximal forearm to secure the board in place as a splint. While doing this Pell slowly came to realize that Tando was still pounding him weakly on the back, all the while gasping in great wracking sobs.

Pell turned, "Tando, it worked. Your arm looks straight!"

Tando looked at his arm, still gasping. His eyes rolled back and he collapsed onto his back. For several panic-stricken heartbeats, Pell feared Tando's spirit had left him. However, watching carefully, he could see Tando was still breathing. With a gasp, Pell started breathing again too.

Pell slowly began to wind even more leather straps into place. When he had Tando's arm firmly strapped to the wooden splint he propped it against the supine Tando's abdomen. To his amazement, a sense of complete exhaustion rolled over Pell. He considered the physical effort involved in what he'd just completed and it didn't seem like much.

However, Pell felt completely unraveled.

Trembling, he lay down next to Tando.

***

To hide her own tears and fears, Donte'd gone out collecting firewood while Pell whittled his little board.

Her nerves felt tattered by the battering alteration of despair and hope she'd been feeling for her only surviving child. She honestly didn't want to survive Pell's death, a death that she saw as inevitable unless Roley took him back into the Aldans. A squalid death in starvation, or a savage death in the jaws of some predator. In either case, it would be a desolate end for a mother's son.

However, her hopes had been buoyed high upon Gontra's admission that Pell—believe it or not, Donte's own son—had in fact been the one who'd straightened his dislocated finger.

The ability to perform such miracles was a Spirit-given gift that could make you welcome in any tribe, even if you *were* an abysmal hunter. Even if you were such an incompetent hunter that your own mother recognized your lack of skill. This was, after all, the boy Donte'd raised for thirteen summers—always watching for signs of the distinction a mother hopes to find in her child—without ever seeing a hunter's aptitude.

Pell had been a scrawny, clumsy child, and though initially friendly, after many beatings at the hands of his tormentor, Denit, he'd become fearful and shy. Only the similarly afflicted Boro had remained Pell's friend. However, Donte loved her son and had kept hoping against hope that he'd prove to have *some* distinctive skill. If not skill as a hunter, something else that would prove his worth.

When Tando asked her to take him to Pell, she'd begun praying to all the spirits she knew of. Praying for a miracle that Donte didn't believe could ever occur. On edge when Tando first asked Pell to reduce the wrist;

horrified when Tando became angry at Pell's initial poking; relieved when Pell calmly reassured Tando; then finally and desperately disappointed when Pell's first attempt failed. Donte's emotions had whipsawed back and forth so brutally that she'd finally stumbled back into the bushes to vomit.

Seeking solace in a familiar routine, she set out to gather wood. While dully collecting a leather strap full of dry sticks, Donte arrived at the conclusion that she must stay in Cold Springs Ravine with her son. Pell couldn't possibly survive without her, and she couldn't bear to rejoin the Aldans with a crippled Tando. Worse, word was *certain* to get out that, not only had Pell crippled the marvelous hunter that had been Tando, but that her son had tried and, of course, *failed* to amend the damage he'd wrought.

She arrived back at the little clearing below Pell's shelter in a leaden cloud of despair, ready to find Tando hostile and angry. She searched for words to brace Pell's spirits. Her load of wood clattered to the ground.

Pell and Tando lay inanimate by the edge of the stream, as if struck dead by the Spirits! Donte cried out, rushing to them. Her heart leaped with joy as Pell rose on one elbow to look at her. She stumbled to a halt, "What happened? Are you okay? What's wrong with Tando?"

Pell grimaced, "Yes, I'm fine. I think Tando'll be okay too; he's just had too much hemp. His wrist went back in place though."

Wildly, Donte turned to look at Tando's wrist. It was extensively bound to Pell's piece of driftwood and almost completely hidden from view by the leather straps. Just the same, it was obvious that the grotesque deformity she'd been seeing for the past two days was...

gone! Donte felt little prickles in her scalp. Lightheaded, but still staring at Tando's arm, she sat down with a "whump." Tears streamed freely down her face.

Pell got up and moved to her side, "Are you okay?"

"Yes," she sobbed, clinging to her son, "I'm fine. I'm fine..."

Chapter Three

When Tando regained consciousness, Pell and Donte helped him stumble back up to the little campsite under the overhang. Tando's arm had swollen further and Pell saw the leather straps were biting into his flesh. He carefully loosened them one at a time, worrying that the bones would slip back out of place. He wished he knew what herbs the medicine men used in the leafy compresses that they used for swelling.

While Pell sat fretting over Tando's arm, Donte went out gathering again. She returned with some small roots and even a few leaves she said were edible in a stew. Pell asked her if she'd take him gathering on her next trip and teach him how to recognize the useful plants. At first, she was surprised that he'd ask to learn "women's tasks," but after Pell explained his reasons, she agreed that he must learn to gather. They made and ate a stew containing some of the meat that Donte and Tando had brought with them while they discussed their plans for the next day.

During the night, Tando woke several times moaning about the pain. Not knowing what else to do, they had him chew more hemp. Each time he awakened, Pell looked at Tando's arm in the firelight. Twice during the night, he loosened the straps even further because of increased swelling. He worried that the swelling portended a dire outcome. He lay awake fretting about it. When he finally slept, he dreamed about Kana's horribly swollen finger.

The finger that'd eventually led to Kana's death.

The next morning Pell loosened Tando's bandages once again. Remembering how his swollen finger had felt better when he held it high in the air, Pell propped Tando's arm up on a few pieces of the firewood Donte'd gathered. Pell and Donte went out to do some gathering, leaving Tando lying at the back of the overhang.

He and Donte wandered from place to place through the forests in the little ravine and somewhat out onto the flatter areas below. Donte chattered animatedly about the different plants they were passing. They found some mint, early onions, small root vegetables and a few leafy plants that were edible. Donte pointed out bushes that would bear fruit later and grasses that would eventually have grain.

As they were inspecting some of the bushes they saw an animal thrashing about within the brambles. Excitedly Pell saw it was one of the bramble patches where he'd set a snare. Spirits! Pell thought, *It's a rabbit trapped in one of my nooses!* He speared it and dragged it out. For a moment he worried Donte'd recognize what'd happened, but she, knowing little of hunting, assumed that it'd simply become trapped in the brambles and that Pell had been lucky. While she wasn't looking Pell slipped the noose off its head and into his pouch.

Heading back up the ravine to the campsite, Donte got excited when she saw a whitish layer of sediment in the ravine wall. She rubbed her finger on it and licked it, then had Pell try it. It was salty! They gathered some in a pouch and took it back. Salt, even dirty salt such as they'd found, could be quite valuable for trading with other tribes. *Everyone* loved the flavor salt gave their food.

They returned at midday to find Tando awake, alert and grumpy. The hemp had worn off, leaving him quite sober. His arm remained swollen, but didn't seem any worse than when Pell and Donte had left that morning. Despite being irritable from the pain, Tando, when questioned, waxed ecstatic about the alignment of his wrist. To Pell's relief, neither Tando nor Donte associated the swelling of Tando's wrist with what'd happened with Kana and her finger.

Pell and Donte set about making a stew with the rabbit and the vegetables they had gathered. On several occasions Donte tried to brush Pell aside out of the old ingrained custom that a boy or man should not be involved in food preparation. Pell steadfastly remained involved, however, reminding her repeatedly how desperately he needed to understand all the steps of gathering and preparing food.

They made the stew in a large leather pouch, which they suspended on a tripod of sticks. Donte put some of the salty dirt in first, then several hot rocks from the fire. The dirty salt wasn't suitable for direct application to food, but it could easily flavor a stew. The salt dissolved into the water and the dirt and pebbles sank to the bottom. Some of the dirt, as well as ashes from the hot rocks floated to the surface. Donte skimmed that off. Next, she put the broken up rabbit, vegetables and some of Pell's young onions into the hot water. They settled back to wait, occasionally pulling out rocks that'd cooled and putting in fresh, hot ones.

~~~

Finally, Donte ladled stew into bowls for each of them and they sat about, slurping it up, scooping out chunks with their knives. Sitting back hugely satisfied, Pell decided it'd been the finest meal he'd ever eaten, better even than his earlier kill. The salt and onions made the stew savory in a fashion he'd not had before.

Tando made it even finer when he complimented Pell on killing the rabbit. Pell glanced at Donte, but she didn't contradict Tando.

Neither did Pell.

***

Over the next several days Donte gave Pell a considerable education in gathering various fruits, vegetables, and root vegetables. As they traveled about the nearby area, Pell slipped away and checked the snares he'd previously set.

He became more and more excited as he found two more rabbits, a hare, a squirrel, and a hedgehog in the snares, all of which he quickly reset. Out of this bounty, the hare and hedgehog had been mostly eaten and one rabbit partially consumed. Obviously, some kinds of carnivores had happened on his traps before he did.

These losses did little to dampen Pell's spirits. He felt sure that if he'd had a chance to check the snares daily, or better yet twice daily, the likelihood that they'd have been raided would be much less. The fact that other animals had chewed them allowed Pell to explain his sudden hunting success as mere fortune in finding small predators at their kills and driving them away.

With the undamaged rabbit and squirrel though, he couldn't resist claiming them as kills.

Struck by perfect throws, of course.

Over the next few days, Tando's swelling began to go down and Pell found it necessary to begin tightening rather than loosening the straps. As Tando began to feel better, he went hunting with Pell on several occasions. Tando thought that, though he couldn't really hunt himself or contribute otherwise, he might repay Pell's miraculous restoration of his arm by giving him some pointers on hunting.

Pell felt somewhat surprised at this since, after all, Tando's broken arm had been Pell's fault to begin with. Pell didn't feel that reducing the break even came close to repaying his debt. However, Tando apparently felt it did. A good part of Tando's generosity resulted from a simple reverence for anyone who could do what Pell had done with his wrist.

In any case, Pell certainly couldn't afford to refuse any charity. After watching some of Pell's wild throws, Tando shook his head and expressed amazement that Pell had managed to kill a rabbit and a squirrel in the past few days.

Pell feared Tando'd openly express doubt that Pell actually *had* killed the rabbit and squirrel, but Tando apparently accepted that Pell just made a few lucky throws. However, Tando strongly urged Pell to practice his throwing and actually sat with him while he did so, giving him pointers. He critiqued Pell's stealth as well.

After a few more days, Tando and Donte began talking about returning to the Aldans. Donte still felt that she should stay with Pell, but with his trapping success, he felt newly confident that he'd do okay for himself during the summer. He told her, "What I need is for you, and Tando if you can get him to help, to convince the tribe to take me back in. I'm pretty sure I'll live through the summer, but I need to be back with the tribe for the winter."

When they actually set out, Tando tried to give Pell a flint spear point. Pell stared at the offering with great desire, but realized that the chances he'd successfully hunt with a spear were small. "Tando," he said, looking the man in the eye, "rather than the spear point, what I really need is your friendship." Pell knelt and looked up at the older man, "I beg your forgiveness for breaking your arm. If you wish to repay me, which I admit I don't deserve, I'd be very grateful for your help asking the Aldans to take me back. I don't think I'll survive a winter alone."

Tando looked uneasy. "Uh, Pell, I don't think I can get Roley to take you back. At least not while Pont and Denit are both speaking against you."

Pell's spirits sank on hearing the truth in Tando's words. He almost took the spear point, but reconsidered. After all, he still wasn't going to be hunting with a spear. His char-point spears would do for defense. Finally, he said, "Just… if any opportunity comes, please speak in my favor."

***

The afternoon Donte and Tando left, the she-wolf turned up again. Pell had walked with Tando and Donte out of Cold Spring Ravine and seen them on their way, waving as they vanished around a bend.

As Pell walked sadly back to his lonely camp, the wolf appeared out of the bush and—as if she'd never been gone—once again trotted alongside him, tongue lolling. Her limp was gone and she gave the impression she was none the worse for the wear. She looked thin but healthy.

Pell checked some of his snares on the way back to his "cave" and found a fat porcupine in one of them. He carefully skinned it and gave a portion of the carcass to the wolf.

Pell wondered whether he was crazy to share his kill with a wild animal. He knew the Aldans would certainly think so, but his spirits had lifted a lot on the reemergence of his animal friend.

A wolf yes, but a friend nonetheless. A friend who'd come back in the midst of his desolate loneliness.

***

The next day Pell excitedly set about perfecting the art of trapping. The noose type snares were much easier to make and could be placed on almost any animal path. They didn't require a constricted tunnel like the ones with the barbed sticks—any narrow area on a path followed by little animals would work.

He set nooses up in many locations, from big ones on trails a little narrower than those he walked himself, to smaller snares where animals passed through brambles, to tiny ones on limbs where he saw squirrels run.

He suspended the bottom part of the noose at what he expected would be chest height for the size animal he thought would take that path and the rest of the noose he propped above. By sitting patiently and watching, he saw a couple snares in action as animals ran along a path, obviously expecting to simply push the chest high "twig" aside and thoroughly ensnaring themselves by fighting the noose once it came snug around their necks.

Sometimes larger creatures broke the noose. From stubs of cords left behind, he deduced that ensnared animals occasionally chewed through the cord themselves—or perhaps some carnivore bit through it when it carried off Pell's prize. Nonetheless, Pell found himself with more meat than he could eat and a large stack of furs.

Having decided he liked the flavor of the smoked meat, Pell began a system for smoking whatever he didn't immediately eat. Donte and Tando had never seemed to notice the strips of meat suspended in the back of the cave. Those had hung there during their entire stay.

Once they were gone, Pell tasted some of it. At first, he thought it'd been ruined because it was tough and difficult to chew. But, even many, many days after the kill, he could still eat the hard smoked meat! Because of his fear of starvation, he didn't discard the hard jerky even if it was difficult to chew.

One day, having mixed up some hard jerky with some of the more lightly smoked meat, he accidentally took a small bundle of the heavily smoked meat with him on the trail.

He'd traveled quite a distance that day and, being hungry with nothing else along, began gnawing on a piece. To his amazement, he found that after chewing at the leathery meat for a while, it moistened up to become quite tasty.

Thus with all the meat he was bringing in, now he smoked some of it lightly, but the rest for several days, making it hard and tough. He'd quickly learned that if he smoked it *too* lightly it didn't actually keep. It wasn't long before he became adept at telling by feel when it was smoked enough to store well.

Pell became especially ecstatic with a new discovery. He'd made another stew with meat, vegetables and a little too much salt. Of course, he ate it anyway, but unable to eat it all he smoked the remaining meat. To his delight, he really liked the salty taste of the tough leathery material this batch produced. He took to soaking all of his meat in salty water before he smoked it.

***

Needing less time to hunt, Pell began spending more effort on fixing up his shelter. Initially, his improvements focused on trying to stop the wind from blowing through. First, he dragged up some brush and piled it just outside his mud "drip lips." Though it slowed the wind some, it didn't help much. He needed a tighter fit so he started leaning poles up against the "drip lip."

Soon, he had poles braced across most of the opening, leaving only a small entrance. Some of the poles were unsteady, so he stuck them in place with more mud at the top and bottom. He hadn't been able to cut very many straight poles so there were significant gaps between them.

He wedged smaller sticks into those holes and used mud to stick the big poles together and hold the little sticks in place. That worked so well he began using mud to hold grass in even smaller holes. Eventually, he wound up with an entire wall slathered in mud and grass he carried up from the stream in a leather pouch. The heat of the morning sun baked it to a hard finish.

Looking at it one morning he realized he'd actually *created* a cave.

Unfortunately, the well-enclosed space trapped too much smoke. At first, he moved his fire near the entrance. The Aldans had kept their fire at the opening of their cave. But now the smoke didn't "pool" over the shelf in the back to smoke his meat. He considered this for a while.

Finally, he opened a spot at the top of the high end of his new wall to let the smoke escape. He moved his fire over under that opening. From there, some of the smoke still drifted back to pool in the upper back recess and smoke his meat. In addition, the smoke hole improved the air circulation and brought in some light. The extra light was nice because the wall he'd added had made it as dark inside as a real cave.

The smoke hole let water in until he put a drip-lip around it to divert the water running down the cliff side and under the roof of the cave.

Pell still kept his meat in the back of the cave, but after it was smoked, he wrapped it in skins and put it down lower to keep it from smoking even more. The leather didn't seal it as tight as he wanted and slowly even the lightly smoked meat dried out to become leathery or hard like the heavily smoked jerky.

He had an idea. To keep his meat from drying out and getting over-smoked, he began washing out intestines and stuffing chopped up bits of the mildly smoked meat into them. This worked even better when he also stuffed in bits of fat which kept the meat moist. He tied segments of the intestine off at the length of his fingers and smoked them a little more. He wrapped the "fingers," as he called his sausages, and his heavily smoked meat into some of the skins.

Using an old antler as a shovel, he covered entire skins full of meat with dirt in the back of the cave.

Tasting them occasionally over the next few hands of days convinced him that they were keeping well. Even better, burying them kept them from getting over-smoked.

The fatty sausages, which to Pell were among the finest delicacies he'd ever eaten, were truly delightful. He also felt fairly confident that his buried packages wouldn't be raided by animals in his absence. Burying his supplies minimized the meaty smell and he thought the small smoky fire he banked and left burning would keep scavengers out of the cave.

The animals he'd snared provided him with tendons and skins to make thongs for more snares and he soon had a regular production scheme going. In the morning he'd eat and set out to check his snares from the night before, picking up the snares and whatever bounty they'd provided. He soon realized that a snare didn't do well on the second day in the same location. He learned to move the snares to new locations each time.

As he walked his trap lines, he was constantly on the lookout for plants with edible roots and leaves. By midmorning, he'd be back in camp to skin his catch, cut the meat into strips and begin soaking it in a pouch of salty water.

The meat taken out of the pouch went to the back of the cave and into the smoke. Intestines were washed out and put in the salty water. Skins he scraped, rubbed with salty dirt and brains the way he'd seen the women do. He wished he'd watched more closely because his skins were coming out tough and stiff, not like good leather at all.

Then he'd eat, stuff some fingers, work on his shelter, repair or prepare snaring nooses and eventually set out in the late afternoon to recheck his trap line again.

The wolf made rounds of the trap lines with him. Pell was thrilled to have a friend along and took to having long conversations with her. After all, he didn't need to be silent like when he'd actually been hunting.

However, as opposed to when he'd been really trying to hunt and the wolf had been helpful, she was of little use while running his trap line. He took to calling her "Ginja" occasionally. This increased till he'd stopped calling her "Gimpy" at all.

Despite the name he'd given her, Pell didn't really think of her as useless. Thinking of the big cat that'd treed him always made him feel safer with Ginja around.

Pell kept Ginja away from the traps, fearing her scent would warn their quarry. He was pleasantly surprised to find that she quickly learned to stay back until he'd emptied a snare. She learned to stay even farther away when he was setting a new snare.

***

Hands of days passed. Pell slowly resigned himself to the fact that Tando and Donte weren't going to be able to talk Roley into letting him come back to the Aldans. His loneliness increased and he became depressed, especially when he thought about the oncoming winter and his impending death.

But, as time passed and Pell's store of smoked meat grew, he began to contemplate the possibility that he *might* survive a winter.

Without a tribe!

With some surprise, he comprehended that he already had more meat stored than would have been his share of what the Aldans usually stored in the big hunts they made right around the first freeze of winter. And, he had many moons to go before winter really set in! Of course, he couldn't be positive his smoked meat would last all the way through winter, but the tough meat that'd been heavily smoked didn't seem to have changed at all!

If he were to live through the winter, he knew he needed to find grains and roots to store. At least if he wanted to avoid the sickness that came from eating nothing but meat. He couldn't seem to find any grain growing in his area. Donte had shown him some grasses she said would have grain later, but he worried because he hadn't seen any kernels on them yet. The root vegetables he found continued to be small and it didn't seem like he'd ever find enough to last a winter.

With sadness, he decided that, despite his surprisingly large stores of meat, things still looked grim.

***

Pell was coming back into camp late one afternoon when a shout startled him. "Pell, look out!"

He looked up to see a figure casting a spear at him.

Pell dove into the bushes beside the path. The spear flew overhead to clatter onto the path behind him. Pell scrambled through the brush and, crouching, regained his feet. To his dismay, he dropped his own spear.

Thoughts rattled through Pell's mind. The shout sounded like Tando, but who just tried to kill me?

Would Tando have done that?

If not, how did Tando arrive at the same time as whoever attacked me?

How many are there?

Why are they after me?

Is it Pont?

What should I do?!

Pell dropped to his knees and was crawling further into the bush when he heard Tando calling again. "Pell, come on out, I scared it away."

Scared what away? Pell slowly raised his head and peered over the brush to see Tando standing there with a huge grin. He looked quite proud of himself. *Where's the guy who threw the spear?* "Tando, what happened to the other guy?"

"What guy?"

"The guy who threw the spear at me."

"*No one* threw a spear at *you*. *I* threw a spear at a wolf that was sneaking up behind you."

"Spirits! Did you hit her?!"

"Her? I didn't see any woman. Anyway, the spear didn't hit anyone. It did scare away that big wolf though."

Pell began to clamber back over the brush to the path. How was he going to explain Ginja to Tando? "Tando...."

"Yes?"

"Uh, the uhhh, wolf, you see, she's...the wolf's... my friend." He finished lamely.

Tando stared at Pell as if he'd grown a horn. "The wolf's a what?"

"She's my friend. Don't hurt her, okay?"

From Tando's expression, he now appeared to think Pell had grown several horns. Pell looked around for Ginja and saw her slinking about in the brush some distance away. "Ginja, come." He said this while unconsciously pulling a piece of the heavily smoked meat out of his pouch and waving it down low.

***

To Tando's utter amazement, the wolf slunk nearer, though warily. As it got closer, he could see the hair standing up on its back. It bared its teeth in Tando's direction. Eventually, it came right up to Pell and took something out of his hand. It lowered slowly down to its belly and began chewing on whatever Pell had given it. The whole time the wolf kept its ruff up and its attention focused on Tando.

Pell turned back to Tando. "How's your wrist?" he said eyeing Tando's arm cautiously. It looked swollen but, to his relief, it still appeared fairly straight. The wooden splint remained in place, though the straps looked loose.

"What? Oh, it's great!" Tando slid the splint out from under the loose leather straps and wiggled his wrist back and forth a little, flexing his fingers expansively. "It's kinda stiff, but it hardly hurts at all anymore. I didn't know if I could take your "healing stick" off yet. I feel safer with it on, but it feels good to take it off and move my hand around some too."

Pell stared at it for a moment, surprised that Tando thought of the stick as something that made his bone heal, rather than just something to hold the wrist straight while it healed itself. He hadn't explained to Tando why he'd strapped the stick to his wrist.

But it'd seemed so obvious.

"I guess it's okay to have it off. But why are you back? I'm happy to see you of course, but has something happened?" Pell didn't say it aloud, but he was hoping against all hope that Tando'd come to tell him that Roley'd agreed to take Pell back into the Aldans.

Without taking his eyes off the wolf lying at Pell's feet, Tando started a long ramble. "It's my mate Tellgif. She was sick when Donte and I found the Aldans at the summer hunting area. She started coughing; then she got hot. She alternated from hot and sweating to cold and clammy. She'd hack up terrible-looking stuff; coughing in great wracking heaves until she was exhausted. Slowly, she got weaker until eventually she couldn't even stand. She's been that way since.

"All Pont's medicines and rituals haven't made her any better. Sometimes he does things that seem to make her even worse. Like in some of his ceremonies, he makes her breathe smoke. When she does, it seems like she'll *never* stop coughing. He says she's coughing out the evil spirits, but it doesn't seem like it helps; instead, she just seems to get weaker."

Tando looked embarrassed, "When we first rejoined the Aldans, I pretended my arm had been straightened when I fell into a stream. Of course, Pont claimed that that was because he'd been praying to the water spirits for me.

I didn't object at first, but one night Pont had us all chewing hemp in one of his ceremonies for Tellgif. I, I... got kind of crazy like people do when they chew hemp. When Tellgif got even sicker during the ceremony I went berserk. I flew into a rage and started calling him a liar. I told them all I'd gone to *you*! I told them that *you* fixed my arm when Pont couldn't!"

Tando shook his head dispiritedly. "I was crazy enough to think they'd throw Pont out and take *you* as their medicine man instead. But they didn't. Pont went into a rage and cast a death spell on me. They threw *me* out. He said, if they didn't, the whole tribe would die just like Tellgif! And they took his word! Can you believe it?"

"Thinking back over the years I've been in the Aldans," Tando mused, "I'm not sure Pont's ever made anyone better. At least not someone I didn't think would have gotten better anyway! I think he just *claims* that the ones who did get better, got better because he did this or that ceremony or prayer."

Tando's gaze had dropped sorrowfully to his feet. After a moment he continued, "Anyway, Donte was the only one who stood by me and, since she came with me, now she's exiled too. Tellgif was so sick I was afraid to bring her with us, so she's still there." He looked down at his feet and mumbled, "I was afraid to leave her too, but Donte pointed out that it'd be better to get you quickly. Then you can heal her before she gets too much sicker."

"I can *what!?*" Pell said, aghast.

"You know, make her better."

Eyes wide, Pell said, "Tando, I don't know anything about healing! I only know one trick, and that one's *only* good for putting bones back in place."

"She's coughing stuff up."

"I don't know anything about coughing."

"She doesn't eat. She's hot; then she's cold. She says it hurts here." As he said this last, Tando pointed to his chest.

"Tando, I don't know *anything* to do for people who're hot and can't eat."

Tando tilted his head to one side, "Still, you're a better healer than Pont. All he ever does is give people hemp!"

"Sometimes he mixes in other herbs." Pell couldn't really believe he was defending Pont, but he desperately didn't want to become involved in Tellgif's illness. "I don't even know what they might be."

"Yeah, no one does." There was a long pause in which they both looked everywhere but at one another.

"Pell, surely you'll *try* to help Tellgif, won't you?" Tando finally said.

Pell was stunned. "How, Tando? I really don't know what to do!"

"Please, Pell? I'm begging you."

In frustration, Pell said, "I have to think. Let's get back to the campsite."

As they walked the rest of the way back to Pell's cave Tando practically started babbling.

"We already stopped by your campsite. Donte and I thought the way you made a cave out of that overhang was really amazing. Do you think something similar could be done in other places? Like the Aldans' drafty winter cave?"

Without waiting for a reply, he changed topics. "Also, Donte and I talked about your healing powers. I know you don't think you have any, but look what you did with my wrist! We're *sure* you could do something about Tellgif's illness if you just called on those same powers. Or spirits. Or whatever you call on.

"Donte and I also talked about how, once you've made Tellgif better, we could establish our own little tribe here at Cold Springs Ravine. It'd just be the four of us at first. I'd be the hunter, you'd be the healer and Donte and Tellgif would be our gatherers.

"I know the winters would be rough for such a small tribe, but others would join us as soon as word of your healing powers gets out."

Pell thought to himself that it was good the walk to the cave was short. He didn't know how long he could stand Tando's burbling enthusiasm. Especially, Tando's constant references to Pell as a "healer" and his unshakable confidence that, because Pell had fixed Tando's wrist, he'd be able to cure Tellgif's cough.

Evidently, Tando and Donte had talked themselves into an unbelievably optimistic frame of mind during the long walk to Cold Springs Ravine. Any difficulties that they might have contemplated had apparently been set aside for Pell to solve with his "healing powers."

Unfortunately, when they reached the cave Pell was assaulted by a similar chattering torrent from his own mother. Donte was also excited about Pell's cave, and worse, full of questions.

"Pell, what kind of mystical ceremony requires that strips of meat be hung over a bush back in the back of the cave?"

Pell opened his mouth to answer, but she continued, "Also, did you know there's a lot of smoke back in there? It's ruining the meat?" She held up a piece of his jerky and bent it, "See? It's stiff and dry." She turned to look back into the cave, "And, besides, what spirit do you pray to? One that gives you so much meat you can spare it for such a ceremony?"

Looking back at Pell wide-eyed, she asked, "Was it the Wolf Spirit? Because, there're wolf prints *everywhere* in your cave! Or, did a pack of wolves try to steal your cave for a den? Some of the wolf prints are on top of your prints so the wolves have been back to your cave since you left!"

"Oh." Donte almost whimpered when she saw Ginja. The young wolf had appeared at Pell's side in the doorway, hackles raised despite Pell's scratching behind her ears.

"Donte," Tando said in an awed tone, "he controls wild animals now!"

"No," Pell exclaimed, finally getting a word in. "Not wild animals, just this one wolf! She's my friend!" *My only friend,* he thought.

Donte sank to her haunches, staring ashen-faced at her son, much like she had after his successful bonesetting of Tando's wrist. "You *control* the Wolf Spirit!"

"No! No, she's just my friend. Just this one wolf, not the Wolf Spirit... I call her Ginja."

There followed a period of stunned silence during which both Tando and Donte alternately stared at the wolf, Pell, or each other. Tando cleared his throat and suggested that he and Pell go out hunting, so they'd have something to eat that night. "When they threw me out of the tribe they wouldn't let me take any food. Hah! I was the one who'd made the kill that day too. I should have taken *all* the food, but you know how it would've been trying to take it. I'd have had to fight Roley. Donte got some food when she left to join me, but we ate it all on the trip here."

Pell certainly understood why no one would want to take on Roley. "I have meat, but we should go gathering." Fumbling in his pouch he pulled out some of his jerky. He held out a piece for each of them.

They took it and smelled it. "It's meat isn't it?" Donte asked, "Is it some of the ceremonial meat from the back of the cave? It smells smoky enough!"

"Taste it!"

They nibbled tentatively, then with enthusiasm. "It's good! Is that why you hang meat in the smoky area in the back of the cave? To give it this flavor?"

"Well, yes, but mostly because once it's smoky, it doesn't spoil."

Tando and Donte gaped at him. After a moment Donte said, "It doesn't?"

"No, in fact, I got the rabbit you're eating *hands* of days ago, just a little while after you left to rejoin the Aldans."

Tando and Donte glanced at each other in astonishment. Tando whispered, "He's not just a healer Donte, he's a powerful mage as well! This smoked spirit meat's a sure sign of the Spirits' blessings."

Pell stared at them, "No, it's not magic! It's just the smoke. Look," he said grabbing his antler shovel and going to the back of the cave. He began digging in the soft dirt.

They were even more astonished when he pulled up one of his skins full of smoked meat and the stuffed sausages he'd made with intestine. He'd intended to demonstrate to them how well the meat had been keeping. But Tando stared at the trove of meat for a moment; then said with quiet envy, "So, you've become a mighty hunter as well! Do you use spirit magic to call animals to you, or do you have some secrets you could teach even me?"

In exasperation, Pell said, "It's not magic! Just smoke." He let it go at that by turning to bury the skin again, trying not to expose the other skins full of meat that lay beneath and beside the one he'd shown them.

From their reaction so far, he anticipated that the additional skins full of preserved meat wouldn't be comprehensible to Donte and Tando without further talk of magic. Pell had already begun to worry about how he was going to conceal the fact he didn't actually hunt at all.

***

They went out gathering. At first Tando hadn't wanted to go—gathering was women's work. Pell reminded him that, if they were going to have a tribe of only four, such a group would be far too small to honor the traditional division of labor.

They *must* have other food than meat, which at present they had plenty of. Eating plants would stave off sickness. Tando finally did agree to go gathering, but only because he wanted to start back to get Tellgif soon. He accepted that when they returned with her, they'd need to have other foods available to help restore her health. He could understand that more hands would make quicker gathering.

As they went out, Tando chattered about the future he envisioned. "After Pell cures Tellgif," began one sentence and shortly after that he'd moved on to, "I can't wait for Pont to see Pell make Tellgif better." Pell occasionally tried to protest again about how he didn't know anything about illnesses.

He tried to suggest to Tando that Tellgif would be better off with a "real" healer, if not Pont, perhaps one from another tribe. That brought an angry response from Tando. More of a tirade actually, concluding with

Tando's assessment that Pell had a "gift" for healing that *had to* extend beyond broken bones and joints.

As they gathered, Donte taught Pell to recognize several edible plants that hadn't been ready for harvest when she'd left hands of days earlier. After a while even Tando became interested in recognizing the different plants and, with his help, they'd gathered quite a bit by evening.

That night over their meal, they made plans to leave in the morning. Pell had finally stopped protesting his inability to help Tellgif. Instead, he'd begun sounding his concern that he shouldn't leave the cave for long for fear that a predator would break in and get to the stored meat.

However, Tando badly wanted Pell to go. He wanted to have two men to help carry Tellgif if she needed it. He also thought the sooner Tellgif came under Pell's care the better.

Pell continued to voice his concerns about leaving the cave, but Donte volunteered to stay and protect the meat. She proposed to continue gathering, looking especially for some of the medicinal herbs she'd gathered for Pont in the past. Pell would be able to use them to treat Tellgif when they came back.

Pell couldn't believe they thought he'd be able to decide which of the medicinal herbs were appropriate for Tellgif. He said, "I've never been trained in the use of herbs! Why would you even *think* I'd know which ones to use for a cough? I just don't know about this whole idea. We really should take her to another tribe's healer!"

To Pell's intense irritation, his own mother patted him on the shoulder and said, "Relax Pell, *you'll* know which ones are right. Just trust your instincts."

~~~

Pell and Tando set out the next morning. Tando was excited about traveling with the smoked spirit meat so that they didn't have to watch for game as they traveled. They also took a bit of early fruit and a few root vegetables to eat as they walked. They practiced their new gathering skills as they traveled, constantly keeping on the lookout for edibles. It pleased Pell no end when they proved so adept that they were finding more than they were able to eat or carry with them. They had to pass most of it up.

Passing it up pleased Tando, though in his case it was because he begrudged any moments spent picking instead of traveling.

They camped that night, but only after they had walked until it was too dark to see. Tando spurned Pell's suggestions that it was dangerous to travel at such a pace.

Leaving at dawn the next morning, they forged on, reaching the tribe's summer campsite on the plain by midmorning.

As Tando and Pell came within sight of their campsite, the Aldans, led by Pont in his finest ceremonial getup, were carrying someone out of camp on a bier. They carried her out... to the burial mound... Tellgif had died!

Tando flew into a frenzy, charging the burial mound. He sobbed on Tellgif's body. He raved at Pont for his incompetence. He ranted at Roley for turning him out at the healer's urging. He returned to Tellgif's body to lie, moaning, at her feet.

Pell stood woodenly by. Not knowing what to do, not knowing what could be done, wish mightily to be away from there, he nonetheless followed Tando, at some distance, from place to place. Gontra did stop and embrace his old friend Tando by the shoulders, but the rest of the tribe uncomfortably ignored the two of them.

They were, after all, exiles, by tradition to be ignored as if invisible, usually to be driven away. No one made to drive them away yet, they were too uncomfortable with Tando's grief. However, Pell felt sure it was just a matter of time before their annoyance would grow great enough to overcome their empathy. Pell saw Denit glaring at him and expected to be the butt of some derisive remark.

At least for now, Denit held his tongue.

***

Emotionally exhausted from being around Tando, Pell wandered off and sat on a small rise near the edge of the meadow containing the campsite. Pell watched the sun go down and chewed slowly on a particularly good piece of his smoked meat. He heard Tando calling his name.

"Tando, I'm over here."

"Pell, come back. *Do* something."

Pell walked slowly back down to where Tando stood by Tellgif's body. She lay in her finery awaiting burial. "What did you want Tando?"

"I want you to bring her back!"

"What!?"

"Bring her back. I *know* you can do it! I can't *take it* any longer! Bring her back, bring her back, bring her back…" Tando sobbed this last pitifully, casting himself back down to the ground at Tellgif's feet.

"How, Tando? *I* don't know spirit magic! I've told you, I don't even know healing magic. Only… only a simple trick for straightening bones!"

"You *do* know magic! You keep the spirit meat. You control the Wolf Spirit. Call on the Wolf Spirit to help her!"

Stunned, Pell contemplated the bizarre request. Pell felt sure there was nothing he could do, but was there? Could it be that I do have some kind of power? he wondered. Have I only been able to do the things I've done because I do have some kind of contact with the spirits? A contact I'm unaware of?

After being confronted with Donte and Tando's wonderment, even Pell felt somewhat astonished by the number of new things, never dreamed of before, that he'd accomplished in the past few moons. From reducing bones, to preserving meat, to trapping animals, they were all simple enough in isolation, but beyond belief in combination. Maybe they did suggest some… perhaps mystical power. *Maybe the spirits do listen to me?* After a bit, he murmured, "Okay Tando, I'll try, but, but… I really don't know what to do."

Tando rose to his knees and hugged Pell about the waist while sobbing in relief and thanking him effusively. Pell patted him uncomfortably on the shoulder and longed for him to let go. When Tando did release him, Pell found himself uncomfortably wishing he was back—he had absolutely no idea what to do or where to begin.

Pell sank to his own knees at Tellgif's side and reached out to take her hand. Her hand that was cold and stiff! Pell dropped her hand in revulsion, but, because of her stiffness, it didn't fall. He swallowed, then took her hand again.

He couldn't even grip it comfortably. Ill at ease, he let his eyes rove over Tellgif's body. She looked wasted away—for instance in her sunken cheeks—yet oddly swollen in other places. Death had drained the color from her and in the twilight her ghastly appearance raised the hairs on the back of Pell's neck.

Odors of death, sour smells of tired sweat, musty smells of Pont's herbs, they all clung to Tellgif in a repulsive miasma.

Pell felt frightened that the death specter still hung over her, and therefore over him. Nonetheless, he held to her hand and entreated the spirits, begging they return Tellgif to the living. He used a voice just loud enough for Tando to hear, but hopefully quiet enough that no one in the camp could hear.

Pell called out to the Wolf Spirit as Tando had asked; though only at the last moment did he remember not to address the wolf spirit as "Ginja." Pell petitioned the Spirits with his head bowed. After a time, he looked furtively up at Tellgif, hoping—though he had a hard time admitting his hopes even to himself—that he'd see some change in her dead face.

Nothing had happened.

Pell looked around the camp, continuing to chant to the Spirits. To his dismay, he saw Denit come out of his shelter and stand glaring at him. Denit turned and strode rapidly to the healer's shelter, a lean-to of poles bound with thongs and covered with sheaves of grass to keep the rain off. Denit leaned under the edge, saying something that Pell couldn't hear. Pell dropped Tellgif's hand, though again it didn't fall, and rose, stepping back from her body

A few seconds later the healer burst from under his shelter, roaring in a slurred fashion. He was obviously in another hemp-induced stupor, Pont had soon roused the whole tribe, claiming that some hyenas—as by convention he couldn't recognize exiles as human— were in camp disturbing Tellgif's body.

Under the healer's urging, the rest of the tribe's people gradually became threatening. Pell and Tando were eventually forced to back slowly away from Tellgif.

***

The next morning, after an endless night of Tando's sobbing, the two of them stood haggard on the little rise at the edge of the meadow. They watched as the tribe dug a pit at the edge of the burial mound. A mound that'd received many other friends and relatives over the years. With Pont officiating and the whole tribe chanting, Tellgif was lowered into the opening.

They placed a few of her things in the grave with her, Tando angrily observing that many of her most prized possessions were not to be seen. Presumably, they'd already been divided up amongst the other women. Pell sat in vigil with Tando for the remainder of the day. That night he went down with Tando and sat for hours while his friend lay prostrate and sobbing on Tellgif's grave.

As Pell sat uncomfortably waiting for Tando's grief to spend itself, his mind returned repeatedly to his loathing of Pont.

Pell mulled through his recollections of Pont's ceremonies and treatments. The more he considered Pont's treatments, the more he thought Pont didn't really know anything about healing.

Perhaps Pont only knew how to take credit that wasn't due, and the best way to lay any blame elsewhere. Pell resolved never to do that for any future bonesettings he might attempt.

***

When morning broke, Tando was dry-eyed and ready to leave. Before they could go, however, he dug a small pit near Tellgif's right hand and he placed some of the "spirit meat" there for her to enjoy in the afterlife.

As they traveled back to Cold Springs Ravine, Pell kept an eye out for gatherables, at first plucking only a few choice edibles such as berries. As they neared home, he began to stuff his pouches.

Tando stumbled along, oblivious to what might be collected. Pell, having filled his own pouches, began to fill Tando's. After a bit, Pell gave Tando a large leather to carry. He folded it to make a big pouch he stuffed with root vegetables. They arrived back at the cave heavily laden.

Donte greeted them joyfully, but then frowned, "Where's Tellgif?" Her eyes widened, "You didn't let Pont drive you away did you?!" A look of horror on her face, she accused them of lacking the courage to sneak back and steal Tellgif from the Aldan's.

In time, Tando's disconsolate expression penetrated and, without a word of explanation, Donte guessed the truth. With a wracking cry, she began her own grieving, leaving the cave and climbing up the hillside to sit above the cliff. From below, Pell could see her staring off into space and hear her chanting the melancholy laments the women of the tribe crooned in times of mourning.

Tando cast himself on one of the grass beds in the cave, lying there staring upward. Completely unresponsive to Pell's attempts to start a conversation, he did little more than blink. Pell unloaded his pouches, then Tando's, then emptied the big pouch of its root vegetables.

As Pell looked about the cave, he was pleased to find that while they were gone Donte had produced a moderate stack of bulbs of her own. She'd woven a couple of baskets and filled them with early grain and some sheaves of edible leaves.

To his surprise, when he looked back into the smoking recess, he found a number of objects back there in the smoke that hadn't been there when he left. He looked closer. There was rabbit meat and some sliced root vegetable. Also, a flat basket with a thin layer of grain and some spread out leaves. Why hadn't he thought of trying to smoke anything else after it'd worked on meat? Even more puzzling, who'd killed the rabbit?

When Donte came down from her vigil later that evening, he asked her excitedly about smoking roots and vegetables. "Did it work?"

"Well, not yet at least. I just started smoking those items today."

"That's a great idea! I'll bet it works—we'll see tomorrow. Where did the rabbit on the smoking shelf come from?"

To Pell's chagrin, she pulled one of his thongs out of her pouch. "You're not going to believe it. I found it strangled in this!" she exclaimed. "Was it your thong? I saw several thongs here and there in the bushes as I went out gathering. I couldn't figure out what they were for, so I left them alone, but then I found the rabbit stuck in this one. If more rabbits start getting tangled up in thongs you could give up hunting!"

Pell's eyes widened. He'd been ashamed of snaring instead of hunting, but it sounded like Donte wouldn't think that way. *Should I tell her?*

Tando saved Pell from making that decision by rising up from his bed to interrupt them. He'd decided that they should exhume Tellgif and bring her to Cold Springs. Then Pell could revive her at his leisure.

Pell spent the next several hours exhaustedly fending off Tando's more and more agonized pleas with repeated assertions that he knew nothing else to try.

***

The next morning Tando lay in a funk, refusing to get up or even eat. Donte stirred about moodily as well, responding dully to Pell's queries. Pell, feeling desperate to get away from the pall that hung over the cave, went out to check and set snares.

A brilliant morning walk, up along the burbling clear water of the creek and among the healthy green of the summer forest did much to improve his mood. Then he saw Ginja and his heart leaped! In the excitement of the trip, he'd only occasionally thought about the young wolf's absence, wistfully perhaps, but not often. Seeing her now made him aware of how much he'd truly missed his friend.

After a moment, presumably taken to be sure that Donte and Tando weren't around, the young wolf bounded up and rose on her hind legs, paws on his chest, tail wagging, tongue licking! Startled at first, Pell scratched behind her ears and wrestled her to the ground, much as he and Boro had often played when he was younger.

Ginja snarled and yapped in a playful way, gently biting his wrists. After they settled down he opened his pouch and gave her some smoked meat, which she enthusiastically bolted. Soon they were on their way again, Ginja leaping ahead at first, then settling down to her previous hunting routine of wary watchfulness.

Pell's snares were mostly empty, though several had obviously held prey that'd been eaten by other predators or scavengers in his absence. One held a few bits of a more recently trapped squirrel that he gave to Ginja. Pell repaired and reset his snares, placing them in new locations as they moved along.

Once they surprised a deer traveling on the same trail they were. It bolted back down the trail away from them. Watching it bound away startled Pell. He began thinking about a snare big enough to capture a deer or a boar. *That'd be really great! But I'd need a real rope. Maybe I could braid a rope out of a lot of smaller thongs?*

Pell and Ginja had almost reached the Cold Springs camp when Ginja bounded ahead. Pell, trailing behind, came upon the young wolf snarling at a sow. Ginja'd killed a piglet and was defending her kill from the piglet's mother.

The mother had other piglets to raise, so when Pell showed up at Ginja's side, she decided to cut her losses. The pigs quickly rustled off into the bushes. Expecting Ginja to stay with her kill, Pell started on his way back to the cave. He was surprised to find her following behind him dragging the piglet.

Piglet it might be, but it was still fairly good sized and dragging it seemed a lot of work for the young wolf. Pell felt surprised she wasn't just eating what she could. Puzzled he stopped to watch. She dragged it up and laid it at his feet. She looked up at him, tongue dangling from one side of her mouth.

As if she were saying, "Here, *you* take it."

He considered a moment. In the past, she'd growled at him if he came near her while she was eating. He reached down toward the piglet and she backed up a step, eyeing him curiously, tail wagging, not growling. He touched the pig—still no growling. Well! He picked the pig up, threw it over his shoulder and turned toward camp. Ginja bounded joyfully ahead, tongue still lolling.

Pell shook his head. This he didn't understand—a wolf's sharing its kill with him! *Almost as silly*, Pell chuckled, *as me giving a wolf some of* my *meat.*

Back at camp, Pell found Tando curled on his side. It didn't look like he'd moved since Pell left the cave. Upon finding Donte and Tando there, Ginja stopped just inside the cave entrance, rumbling low growls. In hopes of disposing Ginja more favorably toward them, Pell made a big show of friendship to them. He got no response from the catatonic Tando. Donte was no more than monosyllabic in her responses. Despite the one-way nature of the affection, Ginja settled down. She eventually took up residence just inside the entrance of the cave, head on her paws, alertly watching every move.

Pell gutted and skinned the small boar. After a bit, Donte sighed and set about trying to preserve the stomach for a water bag and the bristly skin for leather. "Pell! You let that damn wolf chew this little pig, didn't you! What were you thinking?!"

Pell sighed in return, "Momma, the wolf killed the pig for us. Of *course* the wolf chewed it."

There was a stunned silence in the cave. Pell gave the little boar's heart to the wolf with a piece of the liver. He cut up the rest of the liver for the three of them to share. Though he didn't personally like the taste of liver unless he was really hungry, he knew that eating liver made people better when they had the end of winter sickness. When Pell looked up again he saw both Tando and Donte staring at the wolf. For her part, Ginja lay contentedly tearing at her meal.

Glad to see him alert, Pell tried to talk to Tando, but, to Pell's dismay, Tando dropped back on the bedding, completely ignoring Pell's overtures. Donte sidled over to Pell and said quietly, "Tando takes Ginja's hunting for us as just one more bit of evidence demonstrating your astonishing powers. Powers that Tando thinks you're *refusing* to use to bring Tellgif back from the dead."

Pell pondered this revelation for a while; then went over to sit cross-legged beside Tando. After a moment he said, "Tando, you're a good hunter, right?"

"Yes."

"Would you hunt for me if I asked?"

Tando sat up and gave Pell an eager look, "Of course."

"Ah, but I don't want you to hunt for me, I want you to catch fish."

"Pell, I don't know how, but if you taught me how, I'd catch fish for you all day, every day, the rest of your life."

"No, Tando, I don't know how to catch fish either, I want *you* to do it."

Tando apparently didn't see where Pell was headed with this. His brow furrowed and he said, "But—I don't know how..."

"Tando! *I* don't know how to bring people back from the dead either! Now I've actually heard of people who can catch fish. I've even heard of people who can set bones. But, I've never heard of someone who can bring people back from the dead. Have you heard of someone who can do that?"

Tando cast himself back to lie flaccidly on the pile of leaves and grasses where he'd been sleeping. "No, but *you* could. If you'd only try." Tando stared disconsolately up at the roof of the cave, a tear trickling down his cheek.

"I did try—I can't do it Tando. I don't know how... I'm sorry," Pell trailed off into inaudibility. Pell turned and went out to climb up onto the cliffside rocks where Donte had spent the previous afternoon. He hunkered down, rocking on his heels and watching, unimpressed, the multicolored hues of a summer sunset. Donte climbed up to sit beside him. She chanted one of the women's mourning refrains for a while. Pell found the dirge comforting. They sat in companionable silence staring down the ravine and listening to the distant rush of the stream over the rocks.

After a while, without looking at Pell, Donte told him cheerlessly that Tando'd get over his funk eventually. Gloomily delivered, her promise raised little hope in Pell.

Despite his own statements regarding the impossibility of reviving the dead, Pell felt like a failure. A hunter in his prime, Tando, had begged him, a mere boy, for a favor.

And he hadn't been able to help.

That night Pell and Donte ate roast piglet with baked roots and handfuls of fresh berries that Donte'd gathered. Tando lay dully, staring at the ceiling and ignoring their attempts to entice him with food.

The next several days Pell ran his trap lines in the morning and went gathering with Donte in the afternoon. The trap lines continued to produce their bounty of several small animals per day. Donte delightedly exclaimed over the success of his "hunts", day after day after day. Pell struck the corpse of each of his "kills" with a rock to make it seem that he'd killed it with his new-found throwing talent. Kills chewed on by scavengers prior to retrieval were given to Ginja if their condition was too bad or were dismembered before being carried in if they were salvageable.

The majority of the meat they smoked for winter. Donte spent her mornings making the skins into leathers and furs, stitching skins into rough clothing, stuffing "fingers" of intestine with smoked meat and fat and weaving baskets for grain storage.

Tando continued to mourn listlessly, eating little and contributing nothing to their efforts.

As they picked berries one afternoon Donte said, "Tando's not doing his part."

Pell looked up, a puzzled look on his face. "He's been mourning."

Donte shrugged, "Bad things happen. We all have times when we're sad, but we *have* to keep working. The Aldans would have declared him ginja by now. Roley'd have said if you can't hunt, we're throwing you out."

Pell's eyebrows rose, "You think we should throw him out of our tribe of *three*?!"

"I don't know. Right now we can support him, but that might not always be true. You should be thinking about it."

Pell said, "He isn't eating much." Pell couldn't conceive of declaring someone ginja. Not after it'd happened to him. But he started looking at Tando differently. Pell wondered how he'd feel about it if they were hungry.

It didn't come to a head though. Tando woke two mornings later and declared he was hungry. To Pell's self-amusement, they willingly fed him a huge breakfast just a few days after debating the need to cast him out. It was just so good to see Tando up and moving around.

After the meal, Tando proclaimed himself ready to go along on Pell's morning hunt.

This shook Pell! He couldn't believe that he hadn't considered this problem before. How would he be considered a great hunter if Tando, or anyone for that matter, came along and watched him hunting?

It'd rained and they set out into a muggy summer morning miasma, steam seeming to rise from the lush summer vegetation. The day promised a scorching afternoon after the thin clouds burned away.

Ginja followed the duo cautiously at first. After a while she moved into the lead like she'd been doing recently when Pell was alone. Tando frowned at this and asked, "How are you able to sneak up on so much prey? You don't walk quietly, and, with the wolf out in front, surely it would have flushed any prey before you get to it?"

Pell dithered. As he wondered how to respond to Tando's questions, he abruptly realized he needed to follow a different route than he had the previous day. If he didn't, they'd come on the traps he'd laid out. With his hunter's eye, Tando'd surely notice them!

Pell decided to turn west, but before he could call the wolf in she bounded ahead with a little yip… directly to the site of the first trap he'd laid out the day before!

A frightened weasel scurried away from the site of the trap. When they arrived, Ginja stood guard over a slightly chewed squirrel. The squirrel hung by a thong noose from a branch Pell had propped against a tree.

Pell had observed squirrels running down sticks and branches that'd fallen against the trunks of trees. He'd taken to suspending his nooses over such squirrel paths. When that proved successful, he'd stooped to propping broken branches against trunks to make his own squirrel paths.

Pell tried to block Tando's view of the trapped squirrel in hopes of cutting it down and claiming Ginja'd merely driven away the weasel who was its rightful owner.

However, Tando quickly stepped in to examine the squirrel and the thong excitedly. "Pell! You made this little thong noose, didn't you? I've seen one of them dangling out of your pouch." His eyes narrowed, "But how did the squirrel get caught in it? Wait… Is that what the thongs are *for*?!" he asked excitedly. "Is *this* how you *hunt*?" Tando turned to look Pell in the eye, "You catch animals with these things, don't you?"

Pell stared shamefacedly down at his feet. He muttered, "Yes."

"That's incredible! How does it work?! Show me!! I've never seen anything like this! Can *I* do it? Or do you have to have the spirit power to set one?"

Pell slowly looked up. Tando *wasn't* making fun of him! In fact, Tando was so excited he was practically dancing. *Tando* didn't seem to think Pell was a hunting failure because he used snares. Though, Pell thought to himself, if Tando ever saw him throw, his inability to hit anything would still be a source of ridicule.

Nonetheless, at present, an awed Tando evidently thought the snares were just further evidence of Pell's amazing powers.

Pell, worried Tando would start demanding the revivification of Tellgif again, attempted to downplay the snares by explaining them as the simple tools they were.

"Of course you could do it Tando. There's nothing magical about it. You remember that rabbit I brought back to the Aldans' cave at the end of winter?"

"Yes?"

"I didn't actually kill it with a throw. I missed and saw it go into its burrow. So I sat by the burrow for a while hoping it'd come out so I could club it. It didn't come out, but while I was sitting there waiting, I thought of putting a noose around the burrow's exit. I hoped the noose would slow the rabbit down enough to give me a better chance to hit it. I'd given up and gone to check out a place some vultures were circling. So, I wasn't even there when the rabbit came out. But if the noose is placed right, most of the time when animals try to run through it, it pulls tight around their neck. The animals struggle as if they've been speared and the noose gets tighter and tighter until it chokes them. So I just go out every day and suspend nooses over the paths and trails where animals normally run."

Tando sank down on his buttocks as if he couldn't hold himself up. His eyes wide, still staring in amazement at the squirrel dangling in the noose, he said, "This is unbelievable! Why didn't I think of this?"

"I was just lucky. If that rabbit hadn't gone into a hole I could see, right when I had a thong with a noose tied in it, I'd never have thought of it either."

"No! Pell! You have a *gift* for seeing these kinds of things. You should thank the spirits for such an extraordinary talent."

Pell absentmindedly rubbed the thong with some manure to cover the smell of death and human, thinking it'd be difficult to explain such a strange practice to Tando. On the contrary, Tando immediately grasped the idea, again thinking that Pell was ingenious. "You do that so the animals won't smell your scent on the snare right?"

Pell shrugged, "Uh-huh."

They moved to a different location and Pell showed Tando how to set up a snare. They made the rounds of the rest of Pell's traps. As they did, Tando constantly questioned Pell about the snares, "Why put one here? How big should the loop be? Why do you drape grass or leaves over them?"

Tando's queries seemed endless, but Pell found they focused his own thoughts about the snares. Together he and Tando thought of several new ways to deploy them. The two hunters headed back to camp with a groundhog whose burrow entrance Pell had snared, a rabbit and two more squirrels. A fairly good haul, and one which had Tando agog. He steadily burbled over the possibilities opened up by the snares.

When they got back to the cave and encountered Donte, Tando launched excitedly into a description of the snares, their fabulous haul, and Pell's brilliance. Pell found the surfeit of praise embarrassing, yet he wished that the whole Aldans tribe could be there to hear praise heaped on their erstwhile ginja.

Donte, at first slow to understand, gradually became excited. Then she grasped that the rabbit, the one she'd found during Pell's absence with a thong about its neck, had been trapped purposely rather than accidentally. "Pell, why didn't you explain it to me before, when I showed you the thong my rabbit had been trapped in?"

Blushing, he said, "I thought that you might think it was a dishonorable way to hunt."

Donte and Tando both gaped at Pell, absolutely astounded to think he wouldn't be proud of his ingenuity.

Donte had questions of her own. "Why do the animals go into the snares?"

"Well, by accident, I think. I set the snares on paths where they travel. Like the branches that the squirrels like to run on and the small rabbit paths in the brambles and underbrush."

He explained how he positioned the loops to catch their necks. "I think the animals expect to push aside the bottom of the loop like a twig and don't expect it to drop around their neck and tighten. When they fight it, it tightens further. It works best with squirrels because they fall off the branch and their weight finishes tightening the noose. Even better, they hang high enough off the ground that some predators can't reach them."

"Why don't the animals see you've put something in their path? Surely they could just go around it?"

"I don't know, but I guess it's because it doesn't look dangerous and, often, they're running. Besides, I think many animals count on smell to recognize danger. I smear the thongs with the dung of plant eaters, so the snare doesn't smell dangerous to them."

~~~

They cut the rabbit and squirrels into narrow strips of meat and put them to soak in Pell's skin of salty water. That afternoon they all went gathering together, taking a new route that proved to be as bountiful of vegetables as the morning's trap run had of animals.

In the evening, while Pell and Tando suspended the strips of meat in the smoking nook, Donte began cooking up a feast from their profusion of fresh food. She spitted the groundhog on a couple of sticks and suspended it over the fire. The men took did stints rotating the spit while the groundhog roasted to a crusty brown on the outside.

Donte baked some root vegetables in the coals at the edge of the fire. They ate berries while they waited for everything to cook and talked excitedly of plans to make themselves self-sufficient for winter.

Pell was gratified that the other two had gotten over their funk and felt pleased to be planning for the winter he'd so long dreaded. Wiping his chin he said, "You know this little area of the overhang I walled off to make this cave is getting pretty tight for the three of us. Especially so, now that we're starting to accumulate a lot of food. I think we should spend some time making it bigger. The overhang has plenty of additional space we could wall in."

"Great idea Pell," Donte said, her eyebrows up. "I've been feeling crowded, and wondering where we could store more root vegetables and grains. I'd never thought of just making our cave bigger!"

Donte and Pell stiffened when Tando said, "Yeah Donte, why don't you get started on that tomorrow?" As one, they turned to stare at him but he had a big grin on his face. "Yeah, yeah, I know, no more 'women's work,' or 'men's work,' a tribe of three is 'too small for that'. I just wanted to see the expressions on your faces!" Pell and Donte laughed with Tando, Pell secretly feeling grateful that Tando could make a joke. They agreed each of them should start cutting and collecting poles for the enlargement whenever they had spare time.

Tando put some more wood on the fire and turned the roasting groundhog. While poking at the fire he told the other two, "I've been worrying that the smell of the smoked meat, even though we've buried it, might attract scavengers like hyenas or even some of the big cats that roam the area. Maybe one of us should stay nearby to stoke the fire all the time? I don't mean stay right in the cave. That'd be a waste when we could be out trying to gather or hunt, but maybe each day one of us should stay near. That person could come back and build up the fire a couple of times so that the fire would keep the animals away."

"But if we keep a big fire all day," Pell said, "we're going to be spending a lot of time just collecting wood!"

Donte said slowly, "I don't think we need a big fire, just a smoky one. Animals are afraid of smoke and if we're gone, the smoke won't bother us. In fact, it'll be good for the meat we're smoking. All a smoky fire requires is that someone drop by and put something green on the fire occasionally."

"Oh!" Pell said, "We could hang a skin over the smoke hole. Then the smoke would be trapped inside!"

Startled, Tando and Donte looked at each other, then turned to Pell, speaking in awed tones about what a good idea it was.

Discussing the smoky fire idea led Donte to talking about her attempts to smoke vegetables. "That idea turned out poorly," she said, pulling the root vegetables out of the fire and cutting them open to cool. "The leafy vegetables shriveled up and were almost inedible! The root vegetables and grain kept fairly well, but they keep well without being smoked. Berries and apple slices dried up on the smoking shelf. They don't rot, but the smoky taste ruins them." She turned to her son, "Pell, do you think *just* drying them might work?"

"Spirits, I don't know! I keep telling you two that this whole smoking thing was just an accident." Pell took the groundhog off the fire and began pulling it apart, handing pieces to Tando and Donte. He gave the head to Ginja. Cursing a burned finger, he said, "Maybe it's *just* the drying that makes the meat keep. It wouldn't hurt to try drying different foods, especially the things we have too much of. Even if they're ruined, we won't have lost much."

Donte said, "Tomorrow, I'll dry some fruit slices in the sun and see what happens."

Talk turned to equipment they needed, but didn't know how to make for themselves. They especially wanted better hand axes if they were going to be cutting more poles for the wall. However, they also wanted flint knives, scrapers and spear points, better leather, medicines, a sewing awl and other odds and ends.

"We need to go to a trading place," Tando said, wiping grease from the roast groundhog off of his lips. He reached for another piece.

Pell was startled. "What would we trade?"

Wide-eyed, "Are you kidding? Smoked meat, of course. Everyone'll love it!"

"But why would they trade for smoked meat? They could just make their own."

Tando snorted, "No they couldn't! Not if we don't tell them *how*. We'll tell them it takes powerful magic to preserve it… which just happens to give it a smoky flavor, not vice versa."

Pell frowned, "I think they'll figure it out pretty soon."

Tando grinned, "By then we'll have made a lot of good trades."

"Where would we go to trade?"

"About this time of summer, some tribes usually gather at the River Fork. You must remember going there, Pell. The Aldans went to River Fork some summers."

"I think they gather at River Fork a little later than this," said Donte. "We should work on the cave and some of our other projects a little longer… maybe go in one or two hands of days."

Stuffed from their feast, they talked on into the night about their projects and the trading mission. Over the next several days, they all pitched in to enlarge part of the cave with more mud and sticks, even while they continued trapping, gathering and smoking. Tando continued grumbling good-naturedly about having to do women's work.

Pell thought Tando was really good at building the wattle wall and that, despite his complaining, he secretly enjoyed the work.

***

Donte stopped Pell one morning to ask him about a white rind she'd noticed accumulating near the top of the skin Pell had been using to soak the meat in before smoking it. "Should I remove it or is it important? Why do you soak the meat anyway?"

"Oh, I soak it in that skin to make it salty. The skin has some of your rock salt in the bottom. I like the flavor of smoked meat that's soaked in the salty water before smoking better than plain smoked meat."

"Oh. What's the white stuff?" Donte scraped a little flake of it loose and tasted it. "Pell! It's salt! Clean salt!" She looked up, eyes flashing, "It tastes like the ocean salt the southern tribes bring up to trade sometimes."

Pell tasted it excitedly. "It's really good!" The accumulated rind of clean white salt that'd dried at the top of the soaking skin was much purer than the dirty salt they'd started with.

Donte said, "Let's try it on a bit of that roasted rabbit from last night." She picked up a few fragments of salt and crumbled them over a piece of the meat. Biting into it, she grinned at her son, "Oh! That's really good!" Donte held out the rest of the piece of roasted meat to Pell.

Pell tried it. Because salt was very precious, he'd never had any to just put onto meat like this before. He'd only tasted it in the broths they'd been making at the cave. Well, and in his jerky. His eyebrows rose, "Wow!"

Donte said, "Do you think I can set up several similar skins with water and rock salt to just leave out, even when there isn't any meat to salt? Maybe we'd get salt around the edges anyway?"

Pell shrugged, "I don't know. You could try it. Maybe it'd help to put in a lot more of the dirty salt than we put in with the meat."

Donte excitedly set up several skins filled with water and many handfuls of the dirty salt. Even though she didn't understand how it operated, evaporation still worked its miracle. Soon Donte was scraping up salt and leaving it out to dry. Because pure salt was rare and highly prized, it'd be a perfect product to take on their trading mission.

***

Pell began to get excited about the mission as well. Though he didn't admit it to the others, he'd started to dream of seeing girls again. When he'd last gone trading with the Aldans he'd viewed girls ambivalently, but still mostly as annoyances, to be ignored or on occasion to be teased. Recently, however, he'd begun thinking wistfully about them. They even entered his dreams sometimes. In one dream he'd found himself mating with one, the way he'd seen the men of the Aldans doing with their mates. He found the dreams wildly exciting.

After that he found himself thinking about mating when he was awake as well.

As they ate their meal one night, Tando turned to Pell, "Are you sure your magic will keep animals out of the cave while we're gone?"

Pell snorted, "No! There's no magic. I do hope the smell of the smoke will keep them away."

Tando said, "Maybe one of us should stay behind to protect our food?"

Pell thought it was a good idea as long as *he* wasn't the one who had to stay behind. Looking at Tando and Donte, he could tell they both really wanted to go as well. Looking at their eyes, Pell suspected that he might not be the only one thinking of meeting new mates. Pell finally said, "We can't leave a woman behind, Tando, it'd have to be you."

Tando gave Pell a disbelieving look, "You don't know how to dicker!"

"Maybe..." Donte said, "If we put heavy rocks on top of the dirt that covers the meat, it'd be hard for animals to dig up?"

Tando said, "We could find some fresh scat from one of the big cats and scatter it around the cave. It'd mask the smell of the meat and frighten away small predators."

Still worried that it wouldn't be enough, they completely covered the floor at the back of the cave with heavy rocks. Tando found some lion scat and spread it around. Pell and Tando lashed together some more poles into a panel big enough to cover the cave's doorway. The morning they planned to leave, they closed the smoke hole, built up their fire, and added green wood and leaves to it so that the smoldering fire would thoroughly smoke up the cave. They hoped the smell of the trapped smoke would drive animals away. Finally, they closed the doorway with the big panel and mudded it into place.

At mid-day they set out for River Fork. When rounding the bend, Tando looked back and said, "If you didn't know there was a cave there, you'd just think the rocks looked different."

Pell turned back and looked with fresh eyes, realizing Tando was right. However, still worried, Pell said, "I think animals depend a lot more on what they can smell than what they can see."

Tando shrugged, "I think the mud seals the smell in too."

They gathered as they went, so as not to use up the food they'd brought. Of course, they couldn't hunt with snares while traveling, but after all, they had a lot of smoked meat they were packing along to trade. As it was just after midsummer, the gathering was good. It turned out that they could actually have added to their stores as they traveled if they'd had room in their packs to carry more food.

It was a day and a half of tiring travel to the River Fork area, but their spirits were high. While walking, they talked gleefully about the successes they expected while trading. They all were excited about the potential value of the salt and spirit meat. If those traded high they could get a lot of new tools and other goods.

When the River Fork area came into view Pell lifted the "far-seer" that he'd started keeping on a thong around his neck. He used it to survey the area. It appeared they'd judged it about right. He saw by the smoke of campfires that there were several tribes already camped in the area.

"What're you looking through?" Tando asked Pell.

"It's a far-seer, like Roley uses on hunts."

"What?!" Tando reached out and Pell handed it to him. "Where'd you get it?"

"I made it. All you have to do is drill a small hole in a flat chip of wood."

Tando held Pell's far-seer up to his eye. When he took it away from his eye, he said with disappointment, "*I* don't see any better." He shrugged, "Of course, I couldn't see better with Roley's far-seer either. But a lot of the other hunters said they could."

Donte took the wood chip from Tando and held it up to her eye. "Hey! Everything is... *sharper* when you look through the little hole." She turned it to look at her hand, "Well, not things close to me." She looked to the distance again, "But, with the far-seer to my eye, I can tell the men from the women in that camp over there!" She looked at Pell, "This must take *powerful* spirit magic."

"No, mama. You just drill a little hole in something and look through it. In fact," he said, demonstrating with his own hands, "it even works if you just hold your fingers up so there's only a little hole between them. I think it's the same reason you squint when you 're trying to see things that're far away." He gave a puzzled look, "I don't know why it doesn't help Tando. Maybe his eyes are already really good?" Turning to Tando, he said, "Can you tell the men from the women in that camp without the far-seer?"

Tando glance that way and said, "Uh-huh, you can't?"

Pell shook his head.

To Donte's delight, Pell gave his mother the "far-seer." He had another in his pouch and, after all, it was easy to make more. She stood for a while, just looking about with it in amazement, exclaiming about the details of things she'd never seen before in the distance.

"Why do you have two of them, Pell?" Tando asked.

"I made two of them so I could try to see well with both eyes. But it's a lot of trouble to hold both of them up to my eyes." He shrugged, "So I never really use them that way. Besides, if you have them covering most of both eyes you can't see danger coming."

They moved closer to the trading area and to their relief, didn't see any Aldans. While evening fell, the three established their camp a short distance from the trading area. Ginja, uneasy at the proximity of the other tribes, began growling and whining. Pell felt relieved when the wolf faded back into the woods. As darkness fell, he saw her watching them from a hiding place a short distance back into the undergrowth.

They awoke excited the next morning. Because they didn't want to leave their goods unguarded, Donte stayed behind while Pell and Tando went in to the market area to look about.

As they approached, Pell found his heart pounding with excitement, even more so when he saw several young women striding along towards them. They were healthy looking, with the well-fed appearance of the members of a tribe that had good hunters and had fared well in an abundant summer. The shorter one on the left especially caught Pell's eye. Her muscular legs flashed from beneath the supple leather enclosing her hips, her long hair swung in thick braids and her breasts swayed enticingly as she strode along the path.

Pell's thoughts flashed to a mental picture in which he was mating with her. This image brought an immediate response from beneath his loincloth. To Pell's great dismay, the two young women noticed. One of them pointed to his groin and their heads went together as they giggled.

Tando also noticed when they pointed and, looking at Pell's groin himself, he let out an unrestrained guffaw. Pell flushed bright red. The murderous rage that followed quickly stifled his previous reaction.

Furious, Pell strode ahead of Tando into the market area and looked around. It was an ill-defined area at the juncture of two of the large rivers. Huge hardwood trees grew strong and tall and their dense canopy stifled much of the undergrowth. People walking around the annual trading marketplace beat down the rest.

Different groups staked out skins covered with trade goods beneath various trees.

Pell's eye immediately went to a flint worker plying his trade. The man sat at one corner of a large leather on which he'd laid out many flint implements. As Pell started toward the man, Tando caught him by the biceps. Tando whispered in his ear. "Don't go to the one whose goods are most desirable first. You'll seem too eager. They'll bargain harder with you. Wander about and look at *all* the goods, appearing disinterested. Return later to haggle. When you *do* bargain, act as if you've seen other items as good as or even better than the ones you're negotiating for."

Despite wanting to strangle Tando for laughing earlier, Pell thought the advice clever. So, he went first to a large leather laid out near that of the flint worker. Here an old hag had hundreds of medicinal bundles laid out. They were mostly herbs, crushed to powders so that they could be made into teas.

Also, Pell suspected, because in the form of powders it'd be difficult to guess the ingredients. Mixed into all the pulverized medicines were pungent, but useless herbs whose only purpose was to prevent the buyer from recognizing the smell of the active ingredients. "Do you have a particular sickness in your tribe?" the hag queried in a tremulous yet resonant voice. "I can advise you better on which medicines you want if you can describe the illness."

Pell thought the hag was probably the oldest human he'd ever seen. He wondered if this meant her medicines were successful since they'd kept her alive so long. *Perhaps they weren't any good or they would have kept her looking... healthier?* "Um, no, no one's sick at present."

"You should at least get some of this tea here. It keeps away the evil spirits, so it helps keep everyone healthy. You may also want some of this tea. It relieves pain. Injuries are bound to happen, and this tea will keep until someone needs it."

Intrigued with the concepts of the medicines, Pell thought her suggestions sounded practical. He felt pretty certain that the main ingredient of the pain reliever tea would be willow bark.

Unfortunately, he had no idea how to prepare willow bark himself, so the ready availability of willows didn't mean he could make his own pain medicine. He almost asked the hag what part of the willow bark was used in the teas, but then realized she'd just laugh at him. "Maybe later," he mumbled, suddenly worried that he hadn't appeared to be as uninterested as Tando'd suggested. He moved on to the next area, consciously moving away from the flint worker's place.

As he stepped away his eye was drawn back to the old hag's space. A beautiful girl had walked up, set herself down and begun talking with the hag. She was slender but not skinny. Instead, she was well muscled. She moved gracefully, like a tawny young cat in its prime. Her skin glowed as if she were at the very peak of health. Long, golden brown hair, sleekly combed and braided, fell nearly to her waist. Her eyes sparkled with amusement over the story she was relating to the old woman. As she laughed, Pell saw clean, healthy, white teeth. Pell didn't want to be caught staring, but he couldn't seem to tear his eyes away.

"Hey, watch your feet, fool!" a voice barked at him.

Pell looked around to see he'd nearly stepped on some of the carvings laid out at the next site. He stepped hastily back and gazed unseeingly at the carvings. He didn't think he could afford to trade for carvings, no matter their beauty or spiritual power, or whatever other properties they might have. But, whether he wanted carvings or not, he didn't want to move any farther away from the girl at the medicine woman's leather.

He kept watching her with furtive glances, finally deciding that she and the hag must be related. They appeared to be talking business now, using hushed voices as if speaking about trade secrets. After a few more moments, the beautiful young woman stood and walked away. Pell's eyes followed her until she disappeared from sight.

At last, released to continue his shopping, Pell practically staggered away from the carver's site. Mind spinning, he went on about the different sites trying to take in other wares on display.

He stopped at a site where a woman was quickly and deftly stitching a stack of soft leathers into various items of clothing. As Pell watched, one man was fitted for a pair of winter pantaloons. He stood, legs spread, while the woman laid various leathers against his legs and waist, deftly cutting them with a sharp flint.

He paid her with a stack of cured skins, agreeing to give her more skins when the pantaloons were complete. The woman eyed Pell's ragged leather loincloth with distaste. When Pell made no offer to trade, she went back to her stitching. Laid out on her leather were some examples of her work, including some short summer pantaloons, a vest and a winter hat made of fur.

There were also lots of leather items that didn't need to be fitted. Those were already made up.

Carrying bags, pouches, sheaths for flint knives and, most interestingly, a braided leather rope!

Pell dropped to his knees to examine the rope. Thick strips of pliable leather were twisted back and forth around each other in a manner he could not fathom. Every so often he could see a place where one strip was joined to another by cutting holes in both strips and sliding the tail of each strip through the other's hole to make a longer thong.

He'd done this himself, but it always made a weak link where the thong would break. Somehow, Pell had a feeling that braiding many thongs together made it much stronger than a group of thongs tied into a bundle like they'd done in the Aldans.

With a rope like this, he might be able to make a snare strong enough for a boar or a deer! He'd have to get Donte to look at it, maybe she could braid one without his having to trade for it. After all, the braiding looked similar to what many women did with their hair.

Pell moved on past a family selling bead jewelry, another woman with medicines, a group roasting a boar for people to eat later in the day, and a man with water bags made from the stomachs of various animals.

He came to another flint worker. There were serviceable scrapers and awls displayed. The knives and spear points were thick and somewhat clumsy looking, though better than the ones Pell tried to make for himself. While Pell was watching, the flint worker broke a blade he'd been working on and cursed in exasperation.

Pell thought back on some of the blades his father had made. Beautiful blades—blades that had been revered by the Aldans. Once again, Pell wished his father had lived long enough to teach him flint-knapping.

The flint worker, though obviously not a great talent like Pell's father, had many nice sharp flakes that would make perfectly serviceable general cutting tools. And, Pell thought, probably at a much lower cost than some of the finer products from better flint workers around the marketplace.

When Pell moved on he encountered Tando circulating the area and they conferred briefly. Tando said, "No one's offering sea salt, so Donte's should trade high." Tando'd seen two other flint workers and he thought the one near the medicine hag had the best blades.

Pell asked, "Should we get some general purpose medicines and some clothing?"

Tando snorted, "I *saw* you staring at that medicine girl! In fact, the whole marketplace probably saw you drooling." He laughed, "You looked like a man, weak with hunger, ravenously gawping at a freshly roasted piglet! You didn't think we needed medicines until you saw her did you?" He gave Pell a little nudge, "But you're our bonesetter, if you think we need to trade our hard-earned goods for medicines just so that you might have a chance to talk to a pretty girl, go ahead." He winked at Pell.

Embarrassed, Pell stared at his feet and mumbled, "I guess we shouldn't until we've obtained the more important items."

The roasting boar smelled good, but they decided they should probably do without until they knew how much their smoked meat and salt would be worth. They decided to try trading some smoked meat for a few small items to gauge its value and moved on in separate directions.

Pell tried trading some of his smoked meat for simple flint products at the next flint worker's sites. A dour looking woman sat behind a skin laid out with various flint implements. The flint worker himself sat leaning against the bole of a tree detaching flakes of flint from a thick spear point. Pell tried to appear disinterested as he looked over the products and finally picked out a simple scraper.

He could probably make something similar, *if* he had a large supply of flint so that he could afford to make mistakes. But, that fact meant that the scraper wouldn't have a high bargaining price. "I'd like to trade for this," he said to the woman watching the wares.

"What do you have to trade?"

Pell pulled out a bundle of the tougher, "traveling" smoked meat and, selecting a small piece, held it out.

"What do I want with a little stick?" she said suspiciously, eyeing the smoked meat.

"Oh. It's not a stick. It's 'spirit meat.' Here smell it."

Still not touching it, she leaned forward and sniffed. "It does *smell* a little like meat. But," she shook her head in disbelief, "why would I trade flint for meat that's been ruined?"

"It's not ruined," Pell said in exasperation. "It's been preserved with a powerful spirit magic." This was the ploy Tando and Donte had recommended. "This rabbit was killed four hands of days ago and the spirit meat's still good to eat." Pell took a bite to prove his claim and held the rest of the "spirit meat" out again.

Having seen him eat some of it, the woman took a little nibble herself. As she slowly chewed, her eyes widened a little at the salty, smoky taste flooding into her mouth. "It tastes funny," she remarked, frowning as if put off by the flavor. Pell noticed, however, that she kept chewing and didn't offer the rest of the piece back. "How do I know it's four hands of days old?"

Donte'd anticipated this question and suggested that they'd have to leave small pieces of spirit meat with various traders for a day or two to prove their claim. "Keep the rest till tomorrow, you'll see it doesn't spoil. I'll come back then and trade for the scraper." The woman nodded, sniffing the piece of meat she held again.

Pell moved on. Out of the corner of his eye, he saw the woman walk over to her mate, the flint worker and casually hand him a small fragment of the spirit meat. She whispered a few words to him. He put the fragment in his mouth and a delighted grin flashed across his face. She tucked the remainder in her pouch. Apparently, they'd test Pell's claim against spoilage on the morrow.

As Pell covertly watched them, the flint worker moved and Pell noticed the man's leg was deformed. It was bent just above the ankle and twisted outward as well. Pell didn't think it was a clubbed foot like his father's since it was bent in the opposite direction. He thought it must have been broken and subsequently healed in that awkward position.

The deformity would make it difficult to walk and hunt. The man was lucky he had the skill to work flint so he could trade for food. Unfortunately, he wasn't highly skilled. He'd have difficulty competing against some of the other flint workers in the trading area that day.

As Pell mused on this, he wondered whether his own trick for reducing bones would have worked for the man. Even if he couldn't have put an entire leg back into place like he had with the fingers and Tando's wrist, perhaps he could have held it straighter than it'd eventually healed if he'd just put on a splint like the one he'd applied to Tando's wrist?

The flint worker saw Pell staring at his leg and quickly drew the ankle back under the edge of the skin he had across his lap. The skin ostensibly protected him from flying flakes of flint, but the man wouldn't want anyone knowing he only worked the flint because his bad leg rendered him unable to hunt.

Pell's father'd probably started working flint *because* of his clubbed foot, but he'd had a tremendous skill for it nonetheless.

Pell moved on.

Pell didn't see anything else of great interest until he got to the third flint worker's site. He was amazed at the quality of workmanship of the blades available there. Though he tried to hide his interest, the sharp knives, excellent spear points, fine sewing awls and perfect hand axes practically had him drooling. Realizing he'd spent too long admiring the flint worker's wares, he moved on again to the medicine hag's display. There he expressed cautious interest in the general health tonic and the all-purpose pain reliever.

"What do you have to trade?" the old woman asked.

Once again, Pell pulled out a piece of his "spirit meat." Again, he had to explain its nature. The old hag expressed extreme doubt regarding any meat-preserving magic. She seemed to have the attitude that, if such magic actually existed, surely *she'd* already have been aware of it. "Well, at least taste it," Pell suggested.

With a doubtful expression, she gummed a small piece. "It's been ruined by cooking over a smoky fire!" she exclaimed. She apparently didn't find the flavor too dreadful though—she wadded up the rest of the piece of spirit meat and put it in her mouth. "How do I know it won't rot?" she asked with a sly grin. She kept slowly masticating the piece in her mouth with her few remaining teeth.

Pell shook his head at this obvious ploy, but gave her another piece to keep until the next day.

The old woman was still expressing her doubt about any preserving magic in the spirit meat—while continuing to inspect the second piece Pell had given her—when the beautiful young woman walked up. Pell had seen her coming and had already lost the train of the old hag's questions. The girl asked the old woman what she was looking at. As the young woman looked curiously at Pell, her penetrating gray eyes arrested him. She was slender and perfectly formed, having not a single deformity Pell could see. Scars of disease or injury, deformities of birth or accident, it seemed everyone had one or two, even if minor. Not this girl; her skin was flawless. Even her teeth were perfect.

"This young fool says this meat's preserved with magic so it won't spoil."

"Really?!" the young woman lifted a graceful eyebrow.

Pell desperately wanted to explain his spirit meat to this beautiful creature, but found himself completely tongue-tied. As he was struggling to get a word out, Tando spoke over his shoulder. "Oh yes, this is a very powerful magic, wrought by Pell, our Shaman and Medicine Man."

Pell stared at Tando in startlement. Shaman? Medicine Man? Where did Tando get these ideas?

"Shaman and Medicine man?" queried the old hag.

"Yes," said Tando. "Pell has immense powers. He has a magic for catching animals, and the one for preserving meat. In addition, he has powerful magic for bonesetting." He displayed his thick, but straight wrist. "Look at my arm, broken and horribly deformed at the beginning of this very summer!"

Pell's brows rose even farther. How could Tando call his little tricks powerful magic?

The old woman looked curiously around. "Where is this Shaman, 'Pell'?"

Tando put his hand on Pell's shoulder. "Right here. You didn't know who you were talking to?"

Pell felt the dubious gaze of the haggard old woman and curious eyes of the beautiful young woman bore into him. Surely they could see him quaking inside? To Pell, it seemed laughable that anyone would think of him as a powerful Shaman.

Certainly, he could comprehend the doubt in their eyes. Why would a "great Shaman" be wearing a loincloth made of poorly cured old leather? Surely any Medicine Man of power would wear something better? Feeling very self-conscious, Pell sensed heat rising in his face. Stomach flip-flopping, he almost turned and bolted.

The old woman grunted. "If this young upstart's such a powerful Medicine Man, why's he over here looking *at* my medicines?"

Pell was trying to get up the courage to disclaim himself as a Medicine Man when Tando responded, "So far his power has shown itself in bonesetting, but I'm sure he'll prove to be strong with medicines too. Look at my wrist! It was terribly deformed! My old tribe's medicine man tried seven times to straighten it without success. When I went to Pell he immediately made it perfect! He even applied a healing stick to it. The healing stick relieved the pain, held it straight and healed it in just hands of days!"

Tando turned an admiring gaze on Pell, "However, as yet, he hasn't gained his full powers with medicines so we *could* use some of your herbs. You keep that piece of spirit meat until tomorrow and, after you've seen it's still good, we'll discuss a fair trade for more of it."

Tando moved on without another word, as if he'd dismissed them. Pell followed, still tongue-tied and wishing fervently he'd been able to say something intelligent in front of the girl.

Eventually, after handing out a few more small pieces of spirit meat here and there, they walked back to their campsite and conferred with Donte. Donte and Tando went back to the market area so Donte could see what she might want to trade for. This time Pell stayed to guard the campsite.

Pell went over to where Ginja still hid in the bushes. He gave her some spirit meat and they played a while, wrestling around on the ground. Pell also explored the immediate area within sight of the camp in the hopes of finding some edible plants, roots or berries. He had no luck; presumably, the many people in the area to trade had already gathered everything edible. Back at the campsite, he lay down to take a nap. As he drifted off, he thought of the beautiful girl with the gray eyes.

He awoke from another of his erotic dreams—into a nightmare. Sneering, Pell's longtime nemesis, Denit, stood over him! The Aldans must have arrived at the River Fork trading area!

"Look at what I found." Denit's voice dripped vitriol. "That *girl* that used to live with our tribe—before she got thrown out for trying to hunt." Exen stood stiffly off to the side. He had an uncomfortable look on his face, but any remorse he might feel wasn't sufficient for him to interrupt Denit.

Pell started to sit up, but Denit dropped down to sit on his chest, boxing him on the side of the head.

Pell reached down, but Denit pulled Pell's knife out of its sheath and cast it aside.

Denit drew his own knife. Pell's eyes darted about desperately, but no one else was nearby. "What's the matter, little girl, no one here to save you this time?" Denit taunted, flicking his knife towards Pell's face.

Fear flashed through Pell, with no adults about to temper his judgment, Denit might seriously cut him! Or even kill him. Pell could easily believe Denit might murder someone—just for the fun of doing it.

Pell convulsed up, driving his knees into Denit's back with all the force he could muster. To Pell's own surprise this launched Denit off Pell's chest so that Denit smashed down onto his face.

Pell scrabbled to his feet, eyes darting about for his knife. To his dismay, Exen held Pell's knife. He didn't threaten Pell with it, but it didn't look like he was going to hand it back to Pell either. Pell looked about for a weapon—a club, a staff, a rock?

Nothing! Spirits!

Denit groaned and began to slowly push back to his feet! Denit held his back with both hands and heaved to get his breath. His color, at first pasty white, gradually took on an enraged red cast.

Pell dithered, what could he do? He thought of running for the market, but every time they'd raced, Denit had always been faster. Mentally, Pell berated himself for not attacking before Denit recovered from crashing on his face. Years of defeats in fights at Denit's hands had petrified him.

Uncertainly, Pell backed away. Denit finally stood all the way up. Startled, Pell realized that Denit wasn't as tall as Pell now! Huskier yes, but actually significantly shorter.

Pell knew he'd been growing rapidly all summer. He'd been eating more and better during his teen year's growth spurt than at any time in his life. He'd gotten to be *much* taller than Donte who was tall for a woman, but Pell had just assumed that Denit would be growing too. Denit was just *bigger* than Pell—had been for Pell's whole life. It had been a fact of Pell's existence.

Denit's eyes narrowed as he absorbed the change in their size differential, then he shook off any surprise and charged.

Pell, heart in his throat, dove to the left, out of Denit's path and into the dirt.

He scrambled back to his feet, expecting Denit to be almost on top of him.

To his surprise, Denit lay sprawled on the ground beyond him. With a snarl, Denit began to rise to his own feet. Blood dripped from Denit's knee! Unfortunately, if the injury was serious, Denit seemed unaware of it.

"What's the matter, Pell? Can't *fight* like a man? We all know you throw like a girl, but even I didn't think you'd scurry away from a fight like some kind of rabbit!"

Denit charged again, this time not so fast and with arms spread wide, wary of overshooting again.

Pell dodged to the right, away from Denit's knife hand.

Denit—expecting it this time—swerved to catch Pell about the waist, throwing them both to the ground.

Pell, once again amazed at Denit's strength, wrestled to escape, but Denit scrambled atop him. This time Denit didn't sit on his chest to be easily dislodged with a knee. After struggling, Pell found himself on his stomach, left arm agonizingly twisted up behind him. Denit, astride his back, took a lower, wider position to avoid being cast off. As if in the distance, a horrified Pell heard Denit ask Exen, "Where do you think her heart is? About here?"

Pell felt the prick of Denit's knife on the left side of his back. His heart hammered in his chest like a beast fighting for its own life. Mind wildly gyrating, he tried desperately to think of some way to beg for mercy. Something to say that wouldn't further inflame Denit's bestial nature. Such requests had always ended badly in the past. Pell surged again, trying to roll away, but Denit just forced Pell's hand higher, igniting agonizing pain in Pell's shoulder.

Pell rolled his head trying to see Exen. Might Exen help? It seemed unlikely Exen would think to thwart Denit now. But as far as Pell was aware, Denit hadn't ever actually killed any of the kids he'd tormented in the past. Maybe Exen'd draw the line and stop Denit before *that* happened? Agony lanced from Pell's back as the knife was driven in deeper. A grating torment pierced him as the blade struck a rib and stopped. Denit laughed and wiggled the flint point a little, seeking to slip it past the rib.

Pell realized with horror that he'd reached the end of his life...

A snarling explosion blasted Denit's weight from Pell's back!

Pell rolled away from the direction Denit had fallen and scrambled to his feet looking wildly about.

Denit lay struggling beneath Ginja, as the young wolf clawed and slashed for his throat. In his desperation to keep the wolf from his throat, Denit drove his wrist into the wolf's mouth.

Ginja shook her head from side to side, ripping at Denit's forearm.

Exen stood motionless, goggling at the events before him.

Denit's knife lay at Pell's feet and he picked it up. Pell took a step towards Exen.

Exen started back in fear, dropping Pell's own knife from paralyzed fingers.

Pell stepped over to where Denit and Ginja struggled, Denit beating at Ginja's side with his free arm. Pell stepped on the flailing arm on its down stroke and leaned down, laying his knife across Denit's throat. He tensed to sever the soft flesh at the front of Denit's neck, much as they did to finish off an animal during hunts. The knife creased the skin, but seeing the quailing, blanching dread in Denit's eyes, Pell couldn't go through with it. "Ginja," he said quietly.

Ginja let up on Denit's forearm a little. Though she continued to growl through her nose, she looked questioningly at Pell.

"Let him go, girl." After a moment spent with their eyes locked, Ginja slowly released Denit's bloody arm and backed away, growls still rumbling in her throat.

Pell looked down into Denit's panic-stricken eyes. "You would have killed me..." he said almost meditatively. "Really, I should finish you off, just so I don't have to worry about this happening again...."

"It, it—it won't," Denit rasped out pleadingly. "I *promise!*"

Pell eased up with the knife and slowly stood, both hands holding knives, Denit's in his left and his own in his right.

Both hands trembling in reaction and poised to strike.

Denit struggled back to his feet, holding his bloody right forearm in his left hand. His gaze alternated from Pell to the wolf and back—as if he saw demons. Denit and Exen slowly backed away from Pell's campsite. Reaching the path, they turned and scuttled away.

With a sudden rush of weakness, Pell precipitously sat on the boulder near the center of their campsite. He scratched absently behind Ginja's ear while the wolf continued to bristle and growl.

He wondered at the pounding sensation in his chest. Was that his heart? His back itched. He reached around to try to scratch it and his hand came away bloody.

He looked wonderingly at Denit's knife, resting in his palm. With some satisfaction, he noted its blade was of much better quality than his own.

Chapter Four

"Pell," Tando said as he strode excitedly into the clearing. "I just ran into Denit! The Aldans must have arrived here at the River Fork. You'll be glad to hear that Denit looked like he'd just wrestled a bear and barely survived, but I'm worried about..." Tando came up short, realizing something was wrong. "Spirits! What happened?"

Trembling and shifting the two flint knives from hand to hand, Pell described the course of his encounter with Denit. Tando's eyes, initially enraged, now took in the still bristling Ginja with a new look of awed respect. "And I complained that the wolf was eating a little of our meat!"

Shortly thereafter Donte arrived back in camp. Tando was surprised. "I was just going to go back to get you. I thought you'd be there the rest of the afternoon!"

"I probably would have been but Fellax and Teda came into the trading area. They started pointing at me and talking about 'cast outs.' The rest of the Aldans must be here somewhere. I think they're going to be trouble. We should make our trades as fast as we can so we can get out of here!"

Tando told Donte what had happened between Pell and Denit at the campsite while they'd been gone.

Donte also stared at Ginja for a moment. She said, "I'll never complain about that wolf again." Her eyes returned to the two men. "I ran into Tonday on one of the side paths and she brought me up to date on the gossip in the Aldans. She says Denit killed a boy from another tribe for some minor insult. She said the boy was much smaller than Denit and never had a chance. Oh, spirits, Denit's just… he's just *evil*! I'm sure he really *was* going to kill you. And for what? Just…" Donte shook her head in bewilderment, "I just don't know. Why would he *do* such things?" Donte sobbed despairingly.

~~~

The men waited quietly for Donte to get control of her emotions. After a while, she wiped her eyes and said, "We've got to get out of the River Fork area quickly." She glanced back at the trading area, "Let's go back, trade for what we can and leave tonight!"

Tando said, "The problem with that is, our spirit meat won't be worth much until morning because its preserving magic won't have been proven."

Glancing around Pell thought, *Denit won't honor his promise!* He thought to himself that Denit had to be out there somewhere, already planning his revenge. Finally, Pell said, "Let's trade as much as we can in the early morning and then leave."

He expected an argument, but to his surprise, the two adults just nodded agreement.

"In case something bad happens and we *have* to leave before morning," Donte said, "I'll take all the salt and head back to the trading area. I'll get as many of the things we want as I can before nightfall."

***

Donte returned just before dark and she reported trading high for her salt. However, she'd received threatening glances from several Aldans she'd encountered at the market. Even old friends hadn't really met her eyes when she'd spoken to them. From what'd been said, or in some cases left unsaid, Donte suspected Pont was blaming them for anything that went wrong in the Aldans. From bad luck to ill health, the three of them would either be scapegoats or root cause. They'd all seen the healer do it before, so, as soon as Donte suggested it, Tando and Pell both believed it.

Resolved to do whatever trading they could for their spirit meat early in the morning, even if it meant trading before the best of the traders appeared and settling for poor bargains, they tried to get to sleep.

    ***

The next morning Pell's back was sore from the wound Denit had inflicted. He and Tando headed for the trading area at first light. Donte, having finished trading her salt the day before, stayed behind to pack up and protect their little camp. They were disappointed, but not surprised to find that no one was ready to trade so early in the day. They sat down against the bole of one of the massive trees to wait, discussing their trade priorities in quiet voices.

The crippled flint worker was the first to begin setting up his wares. He looked up as they approached and said, "I'm not ready to begin trading yet."

"We just want to look at your tools as you set them out."

The cripple said nothing, getting out his wares and laying them out on the buffalo hide that served as his display area. The woman with the clothing arrived next, but Tando and Pell had discussed the fact that they couldn't wait for her to make anything for them. Nonetheless, in order to keep the flint worker from guessing the intensity of their interest in his tools, they went over to look at her display.

The old hag arrived next. Her legs evidently crippled by old age, she was practically carried in by a young man. Pell, hoping the girl would soon appear, went over to watch her set up while Tando went back to the flint worker's area. The hag looked sharply at Pell, "You're the one with the funny meat aren't you?"

"Yes," Pell said nervously, worrying that something had gone wrong. Had the meat spoiled or something?

"What magic do you use to make it keep like that?"

Her question had a calming effect on Pell. "Preparing the 'spirit meat' requires the help of the Spirit of the Spring," he intoned, internally somewhat surprised that his voice came out without a tremor. The three of them had agreed the night before that their smoked meat magic should be attributed to something in their own area so that others wouldn't be as likely to wonder if they could simply smoke meat for themselves.

Pell had briefly argued that they shouldn't try to keep their secret, because the knowledge might help others to live through harsh winters. He'd been persuaded finally by Tando's constant reminders of just how badly their little tribe of three needed some strong trades on this day, just to get themselves through the winter to come. Tando argued that others would probably figure out the secret for themselves soon enough, just from the meat's smoky taste.

In any case, Tando pointed out that even Pell didn't know if smoking worked if it wasn't done in the cave at

Cold Springs Ravine, or, for that matter, without Pell and his powers nearby.

The hag seemed to accept his claim without question. "Which Spring's Spirit is this?"

"We live at Cold Springs Ravine and call on the Spirit of the Spring there to bless our spirit meat."

"Humph, well, I'll trade you for some more. How much do you have and what medicines would you like in exchange?"

They settled down to haggling. The hag was getting the best of him, partly from her years of bargaining experience and partly because of Pell's mounting awkwardness when the girl arrived in the trading area. She began speaking to one of the other traders. Pell's speech stumbled every time he glanced over at the girl.

The old woman smiled slyly as she recognized his distraction and even more because she knew its source. She drove her bargains harder. The imbalance in the haggling got even worse when the girl saw Pell bargaining with the old woman and came over to ask occasional questions about Pell's bonesetting.

As she helped the old woman wrap up powdered herb packets in broad flat leaves and tie them with thongs she asked him how many bones he'd set and on what parts of the body. "Just three," he said, feeling as if three were far too few to justify calling him a bonesetter. "Really I just got lucky and discovered a trick that lets me put them back in place."

"Does your trick work every time?" the girl asked curiously.

"Well, it worked those three times. But I'm not sure it'll work every time." He blushed, "I hope it will."

She gave him an admiring glance, "Three out of three's pretty good!"

Her compliment made Pell's thoughts whirl even further out of control. He tried to explain his trick for setting bones and how he thought it worked from his examinations of the rabbit's broken leg, but he made a hash of the description. During his stammered attempts to clarify his method, the two women nearly cleaned him out of spirit meat; convincing him to trade for several herbs he'd had no thought of needing.

Though the hag appeared to be amused by the entire episode she looked quite pleased with her new trove of preserved meat.

Pell, for his part, left wishing that he needed more herbs and had plenty of spare spirit meat to trade for it. He wished he could think of another reason to stay near the girl.

When Pell finally wandered away from the medicine women's area he traded much of the rest of his spirit meat for a bundle of the braided leather ropes he'd admired the day before.

He found Tando haggling for hand axes with the last of his spirit meat. Pell added the last remnants of his own spirit meat to Tando's to take the bargain over the top and they packed up to leave.

When they turned to go they found Pont standing in the path back to their campsite!

As they approached, the healer drew himself up to his full height, which, Pell was surprised to realize, was now *much* less than his own. He began to mumble the incantations he'd always used to drive away evil. Pell and Tando skirted him and continued down the path, Pell's ears flushing red and a spot itching between his shoulder blades. Pont finished the chant with some shouted words about their "not being welcome" and "fleeing the area."

Angrily Tando said, "How dare he say we aren't welcome? This isn't *his* area! The trading area's supposed to be open to all tribes!" They hadn't gone far when Tando stopped in the middle of the path. "I'm going back to the trading area. I'll point out to everyone that Pont has no right to say stuff like that!"

Pell pulled him back. "We need to get out of here before we have an even worse encounter. What if we run into Roley?"

Sullenly, Tando allowed himself to be led away.

When they got back to their little camp, Donte sat with an arm around Ginja! She'd always feared the young wolf, so Pell was excited to see it. "Hey, when did you and Ginja get to be friends?" he asked jovially. Then he saw the tears drying on his mother's face.

It took a while, but eventually, she calmed down. Unable to meet their eyes she said wretchedly, "Denit and Exen came while you were gone."

At first tentative and sullenly angry about his injured arm, Denit had gradually worked himself up to an enraged state. He began stomping about the campsite, saying, "I'm going to *kill* Pell." Then he turned to sneer at Donte, "But before he dies he's going to watch me screw his mother!"

Denit gradually became more and more threatening. Exen, as before, merely stood by, not egging him on, but not trying to talk sense into him either. Becoming more and more agitated, Denit began to kick their gear around, spilling open some of their bundles. Donte fell to her knees, trying to salvage some herbs that spilled out of one pack. When she did, Denit had dropped down behind her, grasping her hips and rubbing obscenely against her buttocks. Donte struggled to get away and finally succeeded when his injured arm gave way.

But Denit stood, chased her a few steps and threw her to the ground. He growled in her ear, "When your coward of a son returns, he's going to find me *doing* you. When he whines about it, I'm going to kill him and make you watch."

Denit had just worked his body between Donte's thighs when Ginja had stalked out of the forest, bristling and snarling.

To Donte's amazement and relief, Denit had bolted to his feet in terror. He and Exen flew from the camp like rabbits. Ginja didn't chase them far, returning soon to sniff around the camp. After a bit the wolf came over to Donte, still emitting a low rumbling growl. Donte had stayed fearfully unmoving as the wolf came closer and closer.

As Donte lay trembling, grateful to Ginja, but terribly afraid of what might happen next, the wolf sat down next to her. Ginja'd studied Donte for a few minutes; then she leaned down to lick Donte's face.

Donte said, "I cried when I realized that Ginja'd just told me she was my friend."

~~~

Once Donte had regained control of her careening emotions she'd hastily repacked their gear. Since then, she'd sat with her arms around her new friend the wolf, anxiously waiting for Tando and Pell's return so they could get out of the area.

Tando flew into a rage and turned to leave, saying, "I'm going to kill Denit before he does anything else."

Pell's emotions surged from furious to fearful and back. *Denit, that pile of auroch's dung. I spared his life only yesterday. Then he tries to rape my mother today?!* But, he realized, the Aldans could easily destroy his entire little three-person tribe if they wanted. *Roley would probably kill all of us by himself if Tando hurt his son.*

Donte feared Roley's wrath as well. She pleaded with Tando's back as he stalked away. She turned her efforts to convincing Pell to stop Tando. She didn't want to go after Tando herself because she didn't want to leave Ginja.

Pell watched Tando's retreating back disappear out of sight and, finally spurred to action by Donte's pleading, set out after Tando. Rather than loping like he did when hunting, Tando stalked along in a towering rage. Pell readily caught up with him.

"Tando, come on back. Let's get out of here before something even worse happens."

"What?" Tando said, still fuming, "Are you still afraid of that worthless turd?"

"No, but I *am* afraid of what Roley and the whole tribe of Aldans will do to the three of us if you kill Denit!" Pell managed to make this statement without admitting, even to himself, that he actually did fear Denit.

"I'm not going to *kill* Denit," Tando said through clenched teeth, "I'm just going to teach him a lesson." He slowed his pace a little though.

"Denit's afraid of Ginja, Tando, he won't bother us anymore." Somehow, even as he spoke the words, Pell had a premonition they were untrue. Nonetheless, Tando slowed even further. After a little more cajoling,

Pell turned Tando about and got him headed back to their little campsite.

Already almost fully packed for travel, they quickly finished loading up and set out. Ginja trotted out of her usual hiding site in the bushes and was soon ranging cheerfully out in front of them like she usually did when Pell walked his snare lines.

Pell meditated on the bizarre conjunction between the day's peacefully brilliant blue sky and his own emotions which were raging in turmoil like a dark thunderstorm.

His thoughts churned from his own encounter with Denit, to Donte's.

They went from his confused, but elated thoughts about the medicine girl, to his daily trepidation that he, Donte, and Tando might not survive the winter.

His newfound height was exhilarating, but Denit's implacable strength was terrifying.

And his thoughts kept returning to his near death, and his friend Ginja—who'd saved him and his mother.

As the day passed peacefully, the tension slowly drained out of the Cold Springs tribe. Walking through mottled sunshine under the broken canopy of the forest, wispy swirls of breeze gradually cheered them. A few idle comments built up slowly into animated chatter about their dealings at the market. They excitedly discussed the items they'd traded for and their desire to get home to try them out.

Tando asked Pell about the herbs he'd traded for. He and Donte started laughing at Pell when he described haggling with the old medicine woman. Tando immediately guessed why Pell had bargained so poorly. Tando ventured that he found the beautiful young woman somewhat distracting himself, "Though not enough to completely lose my head like you did." They all chuckled some more.

Donte felt a little shiver at finding out that her son was excited about the girl. She'd been wondering whether he'd ever be able to find a mate.

Overall, the three were quite pleased with the value they'd gotten for their smoked meat and salt, especially in view of the rush they'd been in to make their trades and get away from River Fork.

Sure, they could've done better with more time to dicker, but Tando and Donte still felt they'd achieved a good rate of exchange. Certainly as high as they could've hoped under the circumstances. Unless other tribes rapidly discovered the secret of smoked meat, this trip suggested future trading trips could be even more fruitful.

They continued planning for their future. Further modifications of the cave were discussed as they walked, almost jauntily despite their burdens. Furs needed to be sewn together to make winter leggings like they'd seen, as well as hats and cloaks. "Now that we traded away some of our smoked meat at River Fork, we need to build our stocks of smoked meat back up for this winter," Tando said.

Donte said, "We're coming up on the best part of summer for finding more grains and roots for winter. We need to harvest those first. We can get more meat right before winter." The two men turned to stare at her, Pell curiously and Tando as if she were crazy.

She said, "Really! There's a time at the end of summer when the harvesting is at its best. *That's* when we need to be out there getting roots and grains!"

Men usually thought of hunting as far more important than gathering, but Pell realized that in their situation the gathering might be much more important. Before Tando could dismiss Donte's suggestion, Pell said, "You're probably right Mother. I hope your idea of drying fruit is successful in preserving it all winter; I'd really like to have something besides meat in late winter." Lifting an eyebrow, "I hope you get ideas for preserving other kinds of foods."

A moment of silence came as they contemplated the possibility of eating some version of summer's sweet bounty during winter's dearth.

***

As they approached the Cold Springs campsite, they looked about for new gatherables that might have ripened since they left. Not necessarily to gather now, as they were heavily loaded from their trading, but to get on a return trip. They found a small meadow with several patches of ripening grain. They did stop to eat some blueberries that'd just begun to ripen. They took careful note of the locations of the lowbush berries and grain so that they could make return visits.

Arriving back at the cave with bellies pleasantly full of sweet, tart, berries, they were happy to see the walls they'd used to close off the cave were undisturbed. The entire structure fairly reeked of smoke, which probably counted as much as the strength of the barrier for the lack of animal intrusion.

They opened the smoke hole, then the door. Finally, they cleaned out the carnivore dung they'd scattered about. Despite their cleaning, the cave stank badly enough that they slept outside the first night.

Fortunately, nature provided them with a beautiful, cloudless summer night beneath the stars.

***

The next day they continued cleaning up their campsite. They gathered fresh grasses for bedding. When Donte started weaving storage baskets for the new supplies, Pell sat down next to her, "Show me how to make baskets."

She gave him a quick look of surprise, then remembered his desire to learn women's tasks. Tando watched them for a few minutes. Eventually, he sat down with a disconsolate sigh, "I guess if Pell's going to do it, I need to learn to be a woman as well."

They all had a little chuckle.

The next day, Tando and Pell made an early morning run to set out a fresh trap line and came back with some blackberries. Donte excitedly showed them some of the fruit she'd set out to dry before they left. She'd placed it on the cliffside rocks above the cave, in the sun, but under a loosely woven inverted basket to keep the birds from getting to it. "Look! The berries dried into small, tough, chewy things, but we can still eat them. And they have a *lot* of flavor!"

Tando and Pell each ate a few. Tando said, "I like them better fresh."

Pell raised an eyebrow, "But you'll be glad to have them in the winter when there's *no* fruit to be seen, won't you?"

Tando snorted, "Yeah, there's that."

Bigger fruits like apples had rotted rather than drying—except where Donte'd sliced them thinly like the spirit meat. The slices dried into leathery, edible pieces. Though tough to chew, they were tangy and flavorful! Excitement over the dried fruit was intense.

Examining an apple slice, Tando said, "If this dried fruit keeps through winter, that'll be *so* wonderful!"

Pell grinned at him, "So, are you ready to gather as much as we can while the gathering's good, and help dry all of it that we can't eat?"

Tando rolled his eyes, "We need more *real* women in this tribe!"

***

The next hands of days passed in a blur. It was reaching the height of the best gathering time. They almost completely stopped trapping, only putting out a few snares to keep them in fresh meat, but not smoking any except when the snares were unusually productive. They figured they'd be able to trap for quite a while after the summer harvest.

They spent the biggest parts of their days searching out ripening fruits and grains and trying to harvest them before the birds did. In the evenings, they wove big, loose baskets and in the mornings they set the fruit out to dry under the large mesh baskets held in place with rocks.

After talking about "dried fruit" for days, Pell thought about how deep baskets full of grain had rotted over the winter in the Aldan's cave. As he remembered it, the rot occurred in the middle and bottom of the baskets.

When asked, Donte confirmed this recollection. Pell thought the rotten grain had seemed wet and, with their new discovery that drying preserved food, asked if wetness might be the culprit that caused the rot.

After discussing the idea with growing excitement, they began making shallow, slightly loose baskets to store their dried fruit and grain in, hoping that the foodstuffs would stay drier and therefore last longer. They also talked about how they could turn the grain every hand of days during the winter to help it keep dry.

They didn't fill the baskets completely and tried to stack them in such a fashion that there'd be some space for air circulation between the shallow baskets. They couldn't stack the baskets very high and so they were having difficulty storing the quantities of grain they wanted.

They spoke of further enlarging their cave but Tando dragged a broken treetop back to the cave. At first, Pell and Donte couldn't understand his idea. Tando demonstrated, using branches of the treetop that he'd laid on its side, how it could hold a large basket. This large basket formed a sort of shelf on which more baskets could be stacked.

They broke their doorway open a little wider and dragged the treetop inside. They chivvied and prodded it into place against the back wall, far from the smoke, and trimmed off smaller branches to leave larger ones in good locations. They stacked "basket shelves" on its limbs to substantial heights. They started making those baskets oblong so that, by alternating directions they could stack them without squishing their contents. They also found that if they left roots on their root vegetables and tied the roots of a group of them together with a thong, they could hang them in bunches from smaller branches on the tree.

Despite their improved storage, they were soon sleeping outside for lack of room, now that they were trying to get all they could gather instead of just what they could eat that day.

They didn't understand it, but in addition to their industriousness in gathering, their traps' harvest of smaller animals had decreased the competition for edible fruits, grains, roots, and vegetables in their area.

As the harvest season dropped off, they eventually did move the wall of their cave further outward. They started searching harder for edible roots. Again associating moisture with the rotten roots at the bottom of the stack in previous winters, they looked for more ways to stack and suspend the roots so air could circulate through.

More dead treetops were dragged in and fitted with large shallow baskets.

***

As they wove baskets in the evenings, they talked about their old friends in the Aldans, whom they missed, and their old enemies in the tribe, whom they were glad to be away from.

Donte said bleakly, "I wonder what'll happen to the tribe when Roley gets old and Denit tries to take over as leader?"

Pell frowned, "Will he become the leader just because his father was?"

Tando said, "Sons usually follow in their father's footsteps, but it isn't a sure thing."

Donte said, "But *Denit* will *assume* he should be the Aldans' leader."

Pell grimaced, "I'll bet Roley'll try to hand over the leadership to Denit. I wonder if everyone else thinks he'll be a terrible leader?"

Tando shrugged, "There could be a fight. Or the tribe might split, with some going off to follow another leader or to join another tribe. A tribe half the size of the Aldans could have a rough time though."

Pell laughed, "Here we are, thinking that a splinter off the Aldans would be too small to make a go of it—we, the 'Cold Springs tribe of three!'"

The other two laughed as well. Tando shook his head wonderingly. "You're right Pell, but I'm not as worried about the three of us surviving this coming winter as I am the Aldans. They'll have a tough time making it through, even bigger than we are. These new, snaring and smoking ideas of yours, Pell; they've changed our lives. If an illness strikes, we wouldn't even have to declare the sickly one ginja for quite a while because we have so much food stored up!"

***

The next afternoon, Pell was weaving baskets when he looked up to see Tando striding back into camp from checking their trap line.

Tando had a following! There was a young man who carried a child "pig-a-back" and a young woman following them. Pell sat transfixed when he recognized the young woman as the "medicine girl" who, with the old hag, had bested him while trading medicines back at the River Fork market area. Pell stared at her from his seat. She looked distraught and had none of the amused by the world look she'd had at River Fork.

As she approached, her expression became appraising. As before, Pell felt that she somehow saw into his very core. He wondered what they were doing in the area. It didn't seem that Cold Springs Ravine was likely to be on their way from one place to another. If it was, Pell thought he'd have met them before in some other chance meetings between passing tribes. Pell started to ask why they were there, but the words seemed to stick in his throat. Who was the young man? Was he her mate?! Was that their child?

"Pell! Get a grip on Ginja!" Tando's words broke through Pell's reverie. Ginja had risen from the bushes where she'd been lying and stalked into the small clearing between the creek and the front of their cave. She bristled, snarled, and curled her lips back.

The wolf had come to accept Tando and Donte's comings and goings without challenge over the past hands of days, but apparently her tolerance didn't extend to strangers.

Pell scrambled to his feet saying "Ginja! No!" He strode over, grasped her by the ruff of her neck and pulled her back. The newcomers stared with undisguised amazement as Pell manhandled the wolf. As the wolf settled down to a low-pitched rumbling growl, Pell became embarrassed that he'd as yet made no greeting to the visitors.

Before Pell could say anything, the medicine girl held her hand up, palm forward. Speaking in a formal fashion, she said, "Hello Bonesetter, I am Gia and I greet you in the name of my grandmother Agan. These are my brothers, Manute and Falin. Falin, as you can see, has broken his ankle. It's deformed. Having seen the evidence of your skill in the wrist of Tando, we've come to ask that you perform a bonesetting for Falin."

~~~

Through the entirety of her little speech Gia's eyes never left the wolf, still bristling at Pell's side. She felt amazed, seeing the wolf not only letting Pell touch her, but even allowing him to grasp the skin of her neck so hard it looked as if it'd hurt!

She'd wondered about their claims that he was a bonesetter and worried that this would be a wasted trip.

Now she stared at the handsome young man with sudden respect.

Though Pell hadn't really noticed, the young wolf, well fed by Pell's traps during her growth period, had become larger than almost any wolf in the wild. To the young medicine girl, his control of the huge wolf stood as formidable evidence of his awesome power.

~~~

Not noticing her fixation on the wolf, Pell's eyes had dropped to Falin's ankle. Twisted and swollen, it was a dark purple. Embarrassment flushed over him. His inner voice questioned the skill of a supposed bonesetter who could've overlooked such a grotesque deformity in a boy being carried on his brother's back. A boy who had such a pale, taut face! Embarrassment gave way to dismay as he recognized the enormity of the task that'd just been thrust upon him.

And the high probability of his failure.

Without noticing Pell's consternation, Tando forged excitedly ahead. "Pell, I've been telling them all about your finger and Gontra's, as well as what you did for my wrist. As you can see, this boy's never going to walk again without the benefit of your gift. Thank the Spirits that we saw his sister and grandmother at the trading area so they'd know to bring him to you!" Tando glanced around, "Should Falin start chewing hemp right away?"

"Uh, I don't know," Pell ventured lamely, his eyes darting from Tando to the medicine girl and back to Falin's ankle. He looked back at the medicine girl, whose eyes, he realized, had opened wider at Tando's suggestion of hemp. "She knows much more about medicinal herbs than we do Tando, we should let her decide what to use to relieve the pain."

"Oh, yes, yes of course. Gia, what should we use?" Tando asked brightly.

Tando's blithe expectation of a triumphant conclusion to the "simple" problem of Falin's ankle didn't help the gnawing ache in Pell's stomach over the prospect of a botched attempt to straighten the boy's leg.

For her part, Gia pursed her lips in consideration. She seemed to have forgotten the wolf while thinking about a problem posed in her own field. "It depends on how long until Pell's ready to set Falin's bone."

Upon these words, Falin started sobbing. Though he did so quietly, his agonized fear was evident in his expression and in the tears that began to roll down his cheeks.

Tando spoke up brightly, "Falin's scared because someone in his home tribe already tried to straighten his ankle four times. Even after all that terrible pain, his leg isn't a bit straighter. I told him not to worry. After all, the same thing happened to me and you fixed my wrist just fine."

Tando brandished his wrist to emphasize his point.

Falin didn't look reassured.

Pell's gaze was again drawn to Falin's grossly deformed ankle and he moved closer to see it better. Manute carefully lowered Falin to the ground while

Falin grasped the shin of his injured extremity with both hands to keep it from striking the ground.

Pell saw Falin's left foot was twisted outward as well as bent almost perpendicularly to the side. He'd never be able to walk on it in its current position, not even with a limp. Purplish bruising extended all around the ankle, in the foot all the way down to the toes, and in the back of the leg all the way up to the upper calf area. The leg was swollen from the knee to the toes and the boy's toes looked like little sausages.

Glumly, Pell thought to himself that this ankle looked worse than the fingers he'd reduced. Worse even than Tando's wrist. He reached out a tentative finger to touch, but Falin drew the deformed limb back with a cry, "No! Medicine first!"

Gia rushed to his side. "Falin, don't worry, of *course* you can have some medicine first!" she said, shooting a glare at Pell.

Pell had jerked the offending finger back as if burned. "Oh, yes, sorry," he mumbled. Thinking back to the splint he'd used to put Tando's arm back in place and hold it straight, he said, "I'll need to make wooden splints for your ankle in case I'm able to reduce it. Your sister Gia can give you some medicine while I'm doing that." Pell turned to beat a retreat.

Tando said, "Pell, you'd better take Ginja with you. I don't think they're very comfortable around her."

Pell turned back to see Ginja still bristling, a ridge of hair standing up on her back. "Ginja, come." The three visitors appeared even more astonished when he walked away and the wolf turned slowly and stalked away behind him. As he departed, Pell heard Tando begin to regale them with tales of Pell's "powers over animals." This embarrassed Pell.

However, it simultaneously filled him with pride.

Once out of their sight, Pell's mind started to whirl with distressing images of Falin screaming during the bonesetting. But then he imagined Falin's ankle back in place and Gia grateful to him. Perhaps she'd even throw her arms about him?

His vision metamorphosed again—Falin's bone bursting through the skin during Pell's attempt to force it back in place—the boy dying slowly in the same tortured throes that Kana'd suffered after her crushed finger got infected. He had visions of Gia's growing resentment and loathing.

Pell took a deep breath and tried to calm his own thoughts. Eventually, he found some pieces of deadfall wood that he thought were about the right size to make splints and headed back to the camp.

Ginja appeared to be more accepting of the visitors by the time she and Pell arrived back in camp. In addition, the newcomers appeared to have been calmed by Tando's stories of Pell's powers over the wolf.

After measuring the branches he'd chosen against Falin's good limb, Pell chose one that was almost the right length and began to trim it with a hand axe. As he worked, Pell worried about the engorgement in Falin's ankle. Remembering how the puffiness in his finger had diminished after he'd begun propping it high in the air to decrease the pain, Pell suggested that they prop Falin's leg up as well. Manute carried Falin over near the creek and they put his leg up on an inverted basket covered with furs.

To Pell's relief, the boy said it felt better up on the basket. "It doesn't throb as much," he reported with a sob of relief.

Pell continued work on his splints. The boy's ankle was so deformed that Pell had to guess at its normal shape by looking at the shape of his other leg while imagining it swollen. The inner surfaces of the two pieces he'd chosen were rough, so Pell began scraping them smooth with one of the new scrapers they'd obtained at the trading area.

When they were smooth, he returned to hold them up against Falin's good leg, one against the inner or medial side of the leg and the other against the outer or lateral side. Though they were about the right length, they didn't fit very well against Falin's leg. They lay nicely up against the calf but gapped away over the lower shin and rested hard on the point of the knobby malleolar bones that stuck out on either side of the ankle itself. Pell went back to work with his scraper to make hollows in the splints for Falin's malleolar bones to fit into.

Donte arrived back in the area and, once apprised of the situation, asked what she could do. Pell set her to cutting soft leather strips with which to bind the splints to Falin's leg.

Meanwhile, Gia brewed a concoction that produced some sharp odors. Pell could identify hemp leaves and willow bark, both of which he knew Pont used, even though it always seemed that Pont's major ingredient was hemp. Hemp—marijuana—mostly produced a feeling of euphoria and well-being. It wasn't a powerful pain reliever. Pell had heard that many healers used willow bark tea to relieve minor pains. Aspirin would one day be derived from that kind of bark.

Pell's respect for the medicine girl went up a notch when he saw her working with a fine, black sand that he thought had to be poppy seeds. Poppy seeds contained a very powerful pain reliever and euphoric. They had to be harvested at just the right time and prepared with great care or they could be very dangerous. Garlic and the leaves, stems, seeds, and roots of several other plants also went into Gia's concoction, but Pell couldn't identify most of them.

***

Towards evening Pell had splints shaped that he thought would fit Falin's leg.

If Pell could straighten it.

Gia pronounced her medication ready.

Donte not only prepared straps to tie the splints in place, but had also prepared some soft rabbit skins for padding.

After anguishing about whether any other preparations should be made first, Pell told Gia to go ahead and give the boy her medicine. She carefully measured out a quantity into a bowl and had Falin scoop it up and swallow it. They waited, Pell growing more and more nervous. All too soon, Falin visibly drooped. Pell had Manute move him to the edge of the stream.

Pell tested the water and found it icy cold as usual. Remembering some of the difficulties he'd had gripping Tando's wrist during that reduction, Pell laid the inside or medial splint in place against the surface of his broken ankle and foot. Because the foot was twisted externally and bent outward, away from the other leg, the long part of the splint stood away from the medial side of the calf when the distal part was pressed against the medial foot and ankle.

Pell began securing the medial splint to the foot and ankle with the straps. He tightened them, especially at the ankle where they'd have to pull hard to bend the bone back. This would be necessary in order to bend the ankle even farther and increase the deformity, like he'd had to do during his other bonesettings.

Pell was pleased these manipulations didn't seem to affect the boy much in his drugged state, though Falin did moan some while Pell was tightening the straps. Pell placed the boy's leg in the icy water up to the knee. With a small cry, Falin woke from the shock of it. After a brief struggle to pull the leg back out of the water, Falin dozed off again.

Pell began to worry about how best to apply the tremendous amount of force that he was sure would be required to put an ankle back into place. Reducing Tando's wrist had required most of Pell's strength, so he felt certain that an ankle, even a boy's ankle, would be even more difficult. He looked up to see Tando, Donte, Gia, and Manute looking expectantly at him.

Gia and Manute looked like they were hoping against hope, but still expecting an almost certain failure. Unfortunately, this was pretty close to Pell's own expectations.

Donte's expression held a mother's pride, tinged with the fear her son might fail this time.

Tando's blasé countenance evinced someone awaiting a routine miracle.

Pell found Tando's nonchalant expectation irritating. In a pique, he asked Tando to step down into the stream to hold Falin's leg under water while Pell considered the best method for putting the bone back in place.

Tando grumbled briefly, but he did get down into the icy water to do so.

Trying to imagine how best to place his hands to pull on the boy's ankle, Pell found himself wishing for a model. He looked around at the others and saw that Gia's leg was closest in size to Falin's. Nervously turning to her, he asked, "Can I have your help? I've never done this on an ankle before. I need to figure out how to position Falin and how to place my hands so I have the best chance of doing it in one try. Since your leg is closest in size to Falin's, I'd like to try some different ways to position it."

He felt like he was babbling.

Gia said, "Of course," but was obviously puzzled as to his intent. She became even more puzzled when he asked her to lie down, nonetheless she did so. He knelt down at her feet and grasped her ankle, but even a mildly strong pull on her ankle simply scooted her butt along the ground. With both hands on her ankle in order to provide a grip capable of great force, he had no other hand to apply counterforce at her knee.

Pell turned to Manute, "I need something to pull against. Can you grip her knee and pull the other way?"

Frowning, Manute knelt and grabbed Gia's knee. Unfortunately, Manute couldn't get much of a grip, so his hands slid, giving her a friction burn.

Pell tilted his head as he studied the problem. "Try bending her knee up and pulling against the back of her thigh."

Manute didn't understand Pell's directions so Pell had to put her leg in position. Pell pulled on Gia's ankle while Manute pulled her thigh the opposite direction. Pell thought this had some potential, but he and Manute had difficulty coordinating efforts. They wound up tugging her leg back and forth between themselves, rather than applying the powerful traction Pell knew would be necessary.

Thinking that he had to find a way to apply both force and counterforce himself, Pell sat on his buttocks at her feet. Grasping her ankle, he began to reach out with his own feet, looking for a place to put them in order to achieve purchase for application of such a counterforce.

Her crotch provided an obvious stirrup in which to place his foot. Thinking hard about the problem and its solution, he began to slide his foot in that direction. Suddenly he realized she was watching his foot with wide eyes. Pell realized what he'd been about to do and his hormones burst onto the scene.

Both embarrassed and sexually stimulated, he jerked his foot back and scrambled to his feet. Not knowing that in the twilight they couldn't see either his red face or his erection, he abruptly turned away.

"Have you figured it out yet?" Gia asked curiously.

Hardly trusting himself to speak, Pell choked out, "Not yet." After a moment, when he judged he had control of his voice, he asked her to turn on her stomach.

Pell backed up a little to stand over her knee and, bending her knee, brought her foot up behind her so that her calf stood straight up in the air. Placing his foot on the less arousing back of her thigh, he decided he could obtain a powerful grip on her foot and ankle. "Okay, this should work," he said staring off into the distance. "Manute, help Tando roll Falin onto his stomach."

They rolled the boy quickly and stared at Pell, awaiting his next move. Pell looked at the boy, face down in the dirt and said, "For the Spirit's sake, turn his head so he can breathe."

Manute quickly did this while Gia knelt by his face, brushing dirt from Falin's listless mouth.

Pell picked up the boy's ankle by the board splint attached to it just as Gia cried out. "He's not breathing!" Gia exclaimed.

Pell had begun to pull on his ankle just as she said the words. The pain roused the boy so that he gasped in a torpid fashion. "Oh! Do that again! The pain makes him breathe! Keep going!"

Pell had let go at Gia's exclamation. Now, thinking he'd never been told to hurt someone before, Pell grasped the splint and used it as a lever to bend the leg into an even more deformed position than before, just as he'd done with each of his successful bonesettings in the past.

The boy gasped and struggled, flailing weakly about, but Tando and Manute easily controlled him.

Pell placed his instep on the back of the boy's distal thigh and began pulling hard on the splint with one hand and the foot with the other. He felt the bones grating sickeningly together and wanted to stop.

Instead, remembering his false try with Tando, he continued to pull harder and harder. He straightened his back, heaving as hard as he could as the boy continued flailing weakly beneath him.

Gia cried out, "The leather straps are cutting into his skin! Stop! You're pulling too hard! Stop!"

Pell, fearing that he hadn't pulled long enough or hard enough, nonetheless began pulling less on the splint and more on the foot in order to rock it back out straight. There was some crunching of the bones beneath his hands and the ankle rocked back into a better alignment.

Letting out a gasp, Pell bent down to look at the ankle, but before Pell could even see, Manute shouted, "You did it!"

Hoping it had indeed been enough, Pell tried to press the splint against the calf where he'd shaped it to fit but it wouldn't go. Holding the splint near the leg, he crouched down to see why, surprised to find himself shaking from the effort he'd just completed. He saw immediately that the ankle was much better, no longer flopping off to the side as it had. However, it wasn't quite straight, still having a small bend out laterally so the splint wouldn't fit against the medial side of the calf. It also looked as if the foot still wouldn't go quite flat on the ground when Falin stood on it.

Manute and Tando also gathered close to inspect the outcome. They both jumped back when Gia cried out yet again.

"He's stopped breathing again! Pell, work on his ankle some more, it keeps him going!"

Pell'd been wondering whether he should try again, fearing his next try might not even be as good as the one he'd just finished. Gia's pleas decided the matter. He stood and once again grasped the splint in one hand and the foot in the other, placing his foot on the back of the boy's thigh. He increased the deformity anew, pulling as hard as he could while the boy once more began to gasp and cry out. Pell tried to pull the foot over medially to correct the deformity that had remained after his last try, but the leg just came with him when he moved the foot in that direction.

"Tando, come pull on the leg!" he gritted out. "Yes, yes, grasp it there, just above the ankle. Move it outwards! No dammit, outwards, toward you! No! The other way! Yes, yes!"

Now that Tando had given him something to work against, Pell pushed the foot over onto the end of the leg, shoving mightily until it wouldn't go any farther. His own muscles protested until he didn't think he could pull any more. He tilted the foot back straight again. Holding the splint against the calf he stooped down to look; then he sank to the ground beside it, exhausted. The leg was much straighter now. *Still not quite perfect*, he thought, but pretty good. It was hard to tell for sure because he was trembling so much from the exertion.

Tando and Manute were exulting over what looked to them like a flawless job.

Gia was sobbing into Falin's ear, begging forgiveness for giving him too much medicine.

Donte tried to tell Gia it wasn't her fault; she just hadn't wanted him to suffer. "Better to suffer than die!" Gia wailed, fluttering about the boy's face, begging him to breathe deeper.

Pell strapped the splint to Falin's calf with two of the leather straps that Donte'd cut earlier. He asked Gia if she wanted him on his back now. When she nodded, they rolled the boy over and Pell began to worry about fitting the other splint into position. He padded it with the soft fur Donte'd cut for that purpose and placed it against the lateral side of the ankle. To his relief, it fit fairly well. While peering at the fit he noticed in dismay that, as Gia had said, the wet straps from the first splint had cut into the swollen flesh. Blood was oozing from beneath one of the straps and the other was deeply creasing the skin.

Using one hand to squeeze the two splints towards one another, and thus against the sides of the ankle, he tried to use the other hand to worry the knots in the straps loose. "Tando, I need help. Can you get these knots loose? No? Well, cut the straps." Pell held the splints firmly situated while Tando did so.

It was difficult to see in the twilight and under the edges of the splint, but the skin appeared to be broken where the straps had cut in. However, Pell thought the tear in the skin wasn't deep. Carefully holding the ankle against the lateral splint, he pulled away the medial splint and had Tando pad it with fur like the lateral one. With both splints back in position, Pell held them in place and had Tando bind the two splints to the leg with fresh straps from the pile Donte'd made.

Through all this, the constant small manipulations of Falin's painful ankle kept the boy gasping in pain. Shortly after they finished the splinting, however, Falin began to breathe shallowly again. This caused Gia a great deal of distress and she begged Pell to undo the splints and wiggle his ankle again.

To his surprise Pell found himself disagreeing, "No!" Before that moment, he'd have thought that he'd do *anything* the girl asked. "If we move his ankle too many times I'm afraid the swelling will get a lot worse. Better he dies now, rather than later of a limb with the swelling sickness!"

Though they didn't understand the infection that caused such deaths, everyone knew that the deaths that came from a limb which swelled too much could be horrifying.

"The pain of your working on his ankle is the only thing that's kept him breathing so far!" Gia sobbed, "Would you really rather he just died right now? At least there's a *chance* that he might survive the swelling."

"There must be other ways to cause pain than to damage his ankle more." Saying this Pell grasped the boy's fingers and bent them back the way Denit had done to him many times when they were younger. This brought a small moan from Falin, but only after he'd bent the fingers back so far Pell feared they might break.

Tando leaned forward and grasped the boy's other arm, pushing the bones together just below the wrist. "My big brother used to do this to me when I was little—it hurts a lot." Falin moaned and took a deep breath, thrashing about a little.

The group took turns sitting with the boy, stimulating him in various painful ways in order to keep him breathing until Gia's concoction wore off. Continuing to worry about the swelling, Pell propped the boy's leg back up on the inverted basket. With time, Falin gradually resumed breathing steadily. Working beside Pell to care for the boy, Gia's thigh briefly pressed against Pell's.

His breath caught at the touch. The warmth of her touch seared into him, then raised goosebumps on that whole side of his body. She asked an innocent question and he stammered a reply, but a moment later couldn't remember what the question had been. Shortly after that, Pell staggered away, feeling like Pont on too much hemp, cursing himself for being unable to talk to the girl of his dreams.

Donte and Tando were laughing off to one side. Happy to see them in a good mood, Pell forgot his own distress. He went over and asked them what was so funny. "Oh Pell," Donte giggled, "You are *so* moony-eyed over that girl. It's *obvious* you adore her, why don't you at least say a few words to her? You're nothing but business!"

Pell felt his face flush again. "I, I... I don't know what to say," he mumbled, scuffing his foot in the dirt.

To Pell's chagrin, Tando guffawed, "Boy, if you can't talk to the pretty ones you're going to end up mated to some bristly old sow." He chuckled at his own joke and Pell's own mother giggled with him.

Seeing how embarrassed and miserable her son was, Donte asked him to help her put together some food for a feast, saying, "We need to celebrate the success of your bonesetting." As they walked up to the cave, she quietly suggested he pretend Gia was one of the girls from the Aldans that he hadn't seen for a while. "Talk to her, but imagine that she's an old friend. Ask her questions. Then she'll do most of the talking and you can just listen."

At the feast that night, Gia and Manute shared some "traveling food" which they'd brought for their trip. It consisted of cooked grains and root fragments that were packed into little cakes using the fat drippings from a roasted animal. They tasted as if they'd been savory initially, but now, several days after they'd set out, the cakes had started to sour.

The three hosts ate some of the cakes out of politeness, but they'd been spoiled by the consistently better fare provided by their trap lines and diligent gathering.

They furnished a roasted rabbit from Tando's harvest of the trap line that morning. They also contributed some freshly baked roots and handfuls of fresh berries Donte'd picked earlier in the day. Gia brewed up a special tea that tasted of mint and hemp.

The sumptuous meal, along with the mild euphoria from the tea, induced a happy feast.

They ate out in the small clearing where Falin was lying by the stream. Afterward, they sat around a fire built there, telling stories and monitoring the boy's progress.

Though Gia continued casting worried looks at her little brother, she and Manute repeatedly expressed amazement at what Pell had been able to do with Falin's ankle. Such a deformity would likely have cost him his life eventually, as unable to walk, much less run, he wouldn't have been able to do his part in a tribe.

No one said anything about it, as if for fear of bad luck. As well, their enthusiasm was tempered by the knowledge he might still come to a bad end from the swelling.

Pell looked up with some surprise to see Tando carrying sleeping furs down from the cave to the clearing. "What are you doing with the bedding, Tando?

"I didn't think we should move the boy, so I thought it would be better if we all slept down here in the clearing with him."

"Oh, that's ridiculous; surely we could carry him up to the cave if we're careful."

Tando shot Pell a meaningful look and, while jerking his head off to the side to ask for a private conference, said, "No, no, he'll rest easier if we don't move him. Besides, there's hardly room for six in the cave."

Thinking that there was *easily* room for more than six in their newly expanded cave, Pell nonetheless said nothing. He got up and walked back up to the cave with Tando for the conference Tando so obviously wanted.

As soon as they were out of earshot, Pell turned. "Why do you want to be such poor hosts? There's plenty of room for them to sleep in the cave and I'm sure we could move Falin safely."

"Pell, if they sleep in the cave, they might learn the secret of our smoked meat! Soon everyone'll be making it. We'll never have a chance to really do well at a trading place like River Fork!" He shook his head, "We shouldn't let anyone outside our own little tribe into our cave. Not until we find some way to hide our secrets."

Pell shook his head. "I've said it before, I don't think we should keep meat smoking a secret. It could help a lot of people—people who might otherwise die—live through the winter."

"Believe me; it won't stay secret for long. From the taste alone, someone's going to figure it out pretty soon. But, I'll give you another reason why no one else should be in our cave. We've got a lot of smoked meat, grains, roots, and dried fruit hidden in there. If word gets out about what we've got stored up, someone may come back to take some of it later this winter.

Remember, large tribes raid small ones when winters are tough. The three of us wouldn't be able to protect ourselves. Raiding's one of the reasons it's so bad to be part of a really small tribe. Not only is it harder to hunt, but when big tribes get hungry in the winter, they just kill you and take what you've got."

Pell thought with dismay of the Aldans. If they were hungry, it'd be easy for Denit to bring the Aldans' hunters down to massacre Pell, Tando, and Donte. Denit would do it for a *little* smoked meat, much less the quantity they had hidden away. Denit would do it for fun! "I hadn't thought of that." He reflected a moment, "I don't think Gia or Manute would do that though."

"No…" Tando shrugged, then continued darkly, "but maybe her tribe would. We don't know anything about them you know. Even if she just brought them here to *trade* for meat this winter—once some of them figure out how small our tribe is, we could be in trouble. And, she might just *talk* about it. She may not understand how dangerous it could be for us if other tribes knew we have stores of food. Think if she just mentioned to someone in passing how amazed she was at how much meat we had saved up. If she did, we could die this winter despite our stores."

"Well…" Pell said unhappily, "maybe you're right. There aren't any clouds, so probably no rain. It looks okay for us to sleep outside, at least tonight." Pell returned to the fire with more sleeping furs for the group. His mind stirred over these new problems until long after the rest of the little party was sound asleep.

***

The quiet of the night was broken by Falin's painful cries. Pell woke frequently to check on his leg. It was even more swollen. Pell loosened the straps and Gia sparingly gave the boy some more of her potion, fretting aloud about the earlier overdose. After a while, Falin got more comfortable. Nonetheless, he continued occasionally crying out during the night.

***

By morning, blisters had popped up on Falin's grotesquely swollen ankle. Pell felt his heart thumping in his chest as he recognized that new bruises had appeared as well. The blisters had formed in the areas where Pell's straps had cut into the skin during the bonesetting. The ankle felt hot so he doused it briefly in water from the cold stream to cool it off. The cooling effect didn't last long, so Pell scooped up some chilly mud from the creek bottom and packed it around the leg and ankle. Falin moaned and sat up. "Bonesetter, what's the mud for? It's really cold."

Pell shook his head, "I thought it might take some of the heat out of your ankle. Heat can be bad." Pell didn't say anything about the fevers he'd seen kill people. He began changing the mud whenever it warmed up. An unexpected benefit, though it made him feel dishonest, was that the mud covered the ugly bruising and blistering to some extent. No one else seemed to have noticed the injured skin and the concealing mud made them less likely to blame Pell for additional injuries.

At least for now.

Pell's thoughts scampered about, feeling somehow that it was wrong to hide the additional injuries since they were his fault. But, he thought to himself that there'd been no other way to straighten the leg. If he'd left it as it was, the leg, and therefore Falin, would be useless. Regardless, he knew that many members of his old tribe would blame him if Falin died, whether it was Falin's only hope or not.

To Pell's relief, Falin said that the chilled mud made his ankle hurt less and he began requesting that the mud be changed as soon as it started to warm up. Falin also liked having his ankle propped up because it didn't throb as much, so Pell kept it up on the inverted basket. By evening, it seemed the swelling was beginning to go back down. Pell was able to retighten the straps a little.

The next few days passed uneventfully. It stayed clear and cloudless so there was no problem sleeping outside. Little by little the swelling in Falin's ankle went down. The boy gradually felt better and asked for Gia's medicine less often. Pell tightened the straps on the splints twice a day and the little boards began to fit the way he'd intended when he first carved them.

Manute hunted a few times with Pell and Tando, excitedly at first, expecting unusually easy hunting after seeing Pell or Tando return the first few days of his stay with three to six small animals each time. Of course, when Manute went along, they stayed away from the trap lines. When he and they returned with only an occasional kill he became dismayed. "What am I doing wrong?" he asked. "I don't think I'm making more noise than you are, am I? Is it something else?"

Tando laughed it off, "Some days the hunting's good, some days it's not."

***

Manute gasped in awe at the haul Pell made the next time he went out and Manute stayed in camp. So big a haul that Pell said, "I had to stop to clean, skin and cut them up because they were so heavy." He'd carried them back in a big leather pouch he'd taken with him.

Actually, after two days untended, the trap line had been full of partially eaten prey and Pell had cut them up to disguise the fact.

***

As the days passed, Manute found he could carry his little brother around for short periods without causing him too much pain. They began to talk of returning to their own tribe.

As they contemplated leaving, Gia steeled her nerves and came to sit next to Pell. In awe of the handsome young man, no matter how much she wanted to get to know him, she found it hard to talk to him about anything except the care of her younger brother. "Bonesetter, can I ask you how to take care of Falin's ankle after we leave?"

Pell didn't say anything for a moment, though Gia didn't understand he was tongue-tied, as always. He found it especially unnerving to be addressed as "Bonesetter," an honorific that seemed so undeserved.

"Um, one thing you'll need to do is retighten the straps almost every day so the splints stay snug."

Gia gave him a curious look, "Why is that?"

"As the swelling goes down they'll get loose."

"How long does he need to keep the splints in place?"

Pell swallowed. "I'm not sure."

"What?" she said, disbelievingly.

"I told you I've never taken care of an ankle before. I think Falin will know when his leg is healed enough to go without the splints."

"You're saying he can walk on it now if he wants?!"

"Well not now!"

"When?"

"I'm not sure. When *he* thinks he can. When it feels okay." She still looked unbelievingly at him, so he elaborated, "When it doesn't hurt."

"You don't seem to be sure of anything!" she said doubtfully. "I thought you were a bonesetter?"

Pell felt a flush rising on his neck, "Well, no, I'm *not* sure. And I've told you I don't really consider myself a bonesetter. Just someone who's got a trick for putting bones back in place when they're broken." At the dubious look she gave him, he wondered if he should just invent answers to her questions. However, memories of the disgust he'd felt when he'd realized how often Pont lied rose to silence him.

Gia got up, pondering the humility of the young man she admired so. As she walked away, she said to herself, "'Just a trick for putting bones back in place.' Huh! What is a bonesetter then?"

***

Despite Gia's dissatisfaction with Pell's answers, she stopped Pell the next day. She laid out a bundle of assorted medicines before him. "Bonesetter, I have medicines for a cough, medicines for pain, medicines for a fever, poultices for redness and heat—what will you take in payment for Falin's treatment?"

Pell's ears grew warm. As before, the "Bonesetter" appellation felt splendid… but undeserved. He considered the different medicines she'd arrayed before him. "I'd rather that you taught me how to make the powerful pain medicine that allowed me to set Falin's leg without suffering."

"No! It's much too dangerous! *Even I* nearly killed Falin by giving him too much. Besides, when you use the correct amount they do feel some of the pain."

"Well, I know that was too much. Teach me the mixture and I'll just use less."

"How can you say that? You have to give more to big people and less to little children. I misjudged Falin's size, not the dose of the medicine." Her voice took on a musing tone. "Even if you judge the size correctly, sometimes the medicine seems to be more powerful than other times. Even when prepared in the same way and given to the same person." She looked up sharply. "It has poppy seeds in it—when they're harvested on different days, they have different potency." She shook her head exasperatedly, "In any case, it's really easy to misjudge, as I did, and much too dangerous for someone inexperienced with such medicines."

"But, it made the bonesetting so... much less painful. If, in the future, I'm called upon to set more bones, it'd be a real kindness to give them some of your medicine, even if I use much too small a dose."

Gia looked at Pell curiously. "Well, maybe you're right, but the magic in this pain reliever is too strong for you to make by yourself." She'd said this much with a sly tone. She shook herself and with a more open look said, "Besides, my grandmother would kill me if I gave away her secret! However, I'll make quite a bit for you, perhaps enough for five or six more 'bonesettings', and leave it. If you need more, you can come trade with me for it in the future."

Pell agreed, happily looking forward to meeting her again someday.

She started making up the mixture. He was chagrined when she appeared later with several ingredients for him and set about giving him careful directions for them. Some parts had to be ground, then steeped. Others steeped without grinding. The liquid from one mixture was combined with the dregs of another and words must be said at each step! Finally, there were careful instructions for dosing children and varying sizes of adults.

At first, Pell thought that he could never remember it all. Astonishment came over him when he considered that this was just *part* of *one* of many recipes she must carry around in her head. Despite his feeling of hopelessness, she—having had to learn recipes herself—knew the trick of it. She drilled him over and over with questions and repetitions until she was sure he'd learned the recipe and wouldn't forget it.

***

Gia and her brothers packed to leave. She didn't notice Pell walking up behind her and Manute as they were wrapping a bundle. He'd slowed, admiring Gia's legs as she bent over the bundle. The pause let him overhear as Manute said, "I just don't understand the way they hunt! Almost every time they go hunting, they return with game. Usually, a lot of it! The few times they've let me go with them we've been no luckier than any other time I've been hunting. Tando strikes me as a very skilled hunter, but Pell; Pell just isn't a very good throw. Yet even when Pell goes hunting alone he comes home laden..." Manute snorted, "Unless *I* go with him, that is."

A little irritated to have Manute disparaging the young man she'd come to admire, Gia said, "Well they must be good if they always get game! Maybe you just scare it away."

"No, I thought of that. In our tribe, I'm considered stealthy, but I thought that perhaps they were even better. So, I've listened carefully. They're just as noisy on the trails as I am; in fact, Pell makes a lot of noise. They always lead the way though, and there are some areas they don't hunt. When I tried to get Tando to go down one of the trails, he said it was inhabited by spirits."

"Well, maybe they've just been keeping you away from their best hunting areas?"

"Maybe..." Manute sounded doubtful though.

Pell cleared his throat. They quickly glanced around. "I brought you some of our special 'spirit blessed' meat for your trip back."

They looked embarrassed, as if wondering what he'd heard, but thanked him and packed it away.

The next morning, they headed out with Falin perched on Manute's shoulders. Taking their leave, they were effusive in their thanks. Over and over, they expressed their amazement over Pell's correction of Falin's deformity and their gratitude that their brother might walk again. Falin touched all of their hearts when he tried to thank Pell as well, bursting into tears instead. They declared their readiness to help Cold Springs' little tribe of three at any time they might need it.

Pell thanked Gia for the doses of her powerful pain reliever. He'd thought he was getting comfortable around her, especially while she was teaching him about the medicine. However, he stammered again while thanking her.

After they departed, Pell spent days in a depressed funk, rebuffing any attempts at conversation by Tando or Donte. He couldn't admit to himself that his dejection had to do with Gia's absence, nonetheless, all his thoughts revolved around her.

He should have told them Falin needed to stay longer.

Pell thought of all the witty conversations he should have had with Gia.

He even considered pretending to be sick so he could travel to seek her care.

Chapter Five

Several evenings later Tando again brought up his fear that another tribe might attack to steal their stores of food. "The Aldans would do it for sure if they knew we had so much food. I've been worrying they might have talked to other people at the trading place after we left. They may know about our spirit meat and, worse yet, might think that we must have a lot if we're using it for trade." He shook his head sadly, "This winter, when times get hungry, even if they just think we have a *little* bit of spirit meat, Denit'll try to talk Roley into killing us! We've *got* to protect ourselves somehow."

"Maybe we should move farther away," suggested Donte.

"No!" Pell surprised even himself with his emphatic veto of this idea. Dismay had flashed over him at the prospect of moving to a new location. *If we move, Gia might not be able to find us!* Though Manute and Gia had given directions to their home cave when they departed, Pell was none too sure he could follow them. Anyway, he wasn't sure he'd get up the courage to go to the area where she lived without a good excuse, such as an illness.

But, daily, Pell dreamed about her returning with another injured tribesman for Pell to treat.

Aloud, Pell said, "We've worked too hard to fix up the cave here! Besides, imagine how hard it would be for the three of us to move all the stuff we have in this cave to a location far enough away that Roley and Denit couldn't find us. *And,* if anyone else comes with an injury for me to reduce, we wouldn't have the stream's cold water to deaden the pain."

Donte grinned at him, then turned to Tando. "I think he's just worried that he wouldn't see Gia again," she said—as if she'd been peering directly into Pell's spirit.

Pell flushed brightly. "I am not!"

Tando was also smiling broadly. He teased in a singsong voice, "Pell's in love. Pell's in love with Gia."

"No!" Pell hung his head and scuffed a toe in the dirt. "Anyway, she doesn't want me!"

"I'm sure she does," Tando said, grinning. "An amazing bonesetter like you?" He lifted an eyebrow, "Women are crazy about men with *powers.*"

Pell retreated with his head spinning. He went to sit outside with Ginja in the moonlight, saying that he wanted to think about Tando's concerns. Instead, his thoughts kept returning to Gia. *Why didn't I ask if the three of us could join Gia's tribe? Will I ever see her again? Do I love her? Is that what these feelings are? Could she love me? Would she... possibly even... mate with me?*

When he returned to the cave, Tando and Donte were still arguing about the possibility of being raided. Donte still advocated a move while Tando wanted to strengthen their ability to fight.

"I don't see how we could get strong enough to protect ourselves from the Aldans." Pell put in. "They have too many hunters. They'd surely kill all three of us if they came after us, no matter how many spears we'd prepared."

"We might be able to defend this place if we had a few more hunters and narrowed the mouth of the cave. Two men with spears can defend a cave with a narrow mouth. I heard once that the Brekko tribe defended a small-mouthed cave for four days with just five hunters."

"But one wall of our 'cave' is made of wood! All Roley would have to do is set in on fire and it'd be destroyed in no time."

"*We* know it's made of wood, but Roley doesn't. We could put more mud on so it'd really blend into the mountainside. It already blends pretty well. Besides, with enough mud, it'll be almost impossible to burn."

"Well, that might help, but we'd still have the problem of needing more men to defend the opening," Donte said with a shrug.

"One thing at a time Donte," Tando said. "I'm just pointing out that this cave could be defended. Anywhere we go we could have the same problem of others wanting to raid us. It doesn't have to be the Aldans. Some other tribe might try to take our food. But, you're right, we do need more hunters. We should've tried to recruit Manute."

Pell was aghast, "Manute wouldn't leave his sister!"

Donte and Tando laughed. Donte said, "He probably wouldn't come without his Granny or his little brother either. Aren't you worried about them?"

"Well… yeah." Pell looked sheepishly down at his feet, but his heart was lifted by the simple contemplation of Gia's presence in his own tribe. "But, I think she's from a really strong tribe. The four of them would have to be crazy to leave their tribe and join ours."

Donte smiled at her son's obsession with the girl, but decided not to tease him any further about it. "Maybe we'll run into someone else who'll join us. In the meantime, since you two are too lazy to move, what else could we do to protect ourselves here?"

Tando said, "Well, as I said before, first we should make more weapons. I could put more of those spear points we got at the trading place onto good shafts. In fact, I probably should put them *all* on shafts. If we're using them for defense we may need them all at once, not one at a time, like when we're hunting."

Pell considered this with some dismay. He didn't think he'd do very well in a fight with spears. On the other hand, if he did get in a fight with someone wielding a spear, he'd certainly do better if he had one himself. He thought back to his father's advice, "We're not good hunters, but we *are* good tool makers." *Should I be trying to devise a "tool" for protection? But, how could we protect ourselves with tools?* A thought struck. "Maybe we could rig up some kind of snares that would trap people who were attacking us."

Tando looked at him with some surprise. "If it worked, that'd be great. But a *man* wouldn't stick his head in a noose. Even if he did, the snare'd only trap one hunter. He'd probably get himself free from the noose. If he couldn't, his fellow hunters'd cut him loose."

"Maybe you're right," Pell said, frustrated.

Donte said, "Even if you guys won't move, we should at least take some of our stores to another location to keep them safe. Then, even if they chase us out of our cave, all we'd have to do is get away from them. After we escaped, we'd have a place we could go where we'd have food and equipment."

Tando and Pell looked at each other, then at Donte. "That's a great idea!" Pell said. "It'd give us more room here in the cave too." He looked out across the ravine,

"Maybe we could put stuff in a couple of different locations?"

They fell to talking about possible locations and what to store in them. Their discussions ran late into the evening, laying out plans for the next few days.

The next morning erupted with activity. It reminded Pell of the days when they'd worked hard all day, every day, trying to improve the cave and build up their winter stores. Tando began cutting poles and assembling spears. Donte and Pell loaded up big packs with smoked meat, roots and other stored foods as well as two of the three spears that were already available. Pell and his mother started hiking out to a site they knew of from their trapping runs.

When they reached the site they'd discussed the night before, it was much as Pell had remembered it. A large slab of rock had fallen from the side of a cliff and landed on a shelf leaned up against the cliff wall. There was a substantial cavity beneath it. With some difficulty, Pell scrambled up to the shelf where it stood, then climbed underneath the slab. He explored the crevice between the slab and the cliff wall. It bore little spoor to indicate animal visits, but that wasn't surprising since it was relatively inaccessible and absolutely nothing was growing up there. It wasn't big enough to make a satisfactory long-term living site, but it did provide a good, if cramped, sheltered area.

Pell dropped the end of one of their new ropes to Donte. While she was wrapping their supplies and tying them to the rope, he dragged loose shale out of the crevice and put it to one side. He pulled up the bundles of leather wrapped supplies and pushed them deep into the crack.

Covering them with some strong-smelling, bitter leaves he stacked the loose shale up in front of it. Finally, he added some lion dung they'd gathered on their trip. They hoped the scat would both disguise the smell of the smoked meat and discourage smaller predators.

While he was doing this, Donte gathered wood. Once he had the supplies stashed away, Pell piled up the wood and used the coal they'd brought to start a campfire in the mouth of the crevice. The ashes would discourage animals for a while.

While the fire burned down, he pulled up rocks Donte tied to the rope and spent a couple of hours wedging them into the other end of the little tunnel, thus closing it off to become a one-ended cave. Before they left, Pell helped Donte up onto the shelf and she sniffed around their stores. Her sensitive nose declared the medley of herbs, scat, and charcoal, quite horrid.

She thought the cache would be relatively safe from predators. However, she suggested cutting a thorny bramble bush and stuffing it into the open end of the crevice as well.

On the way back to the cave, they gathered some grain in a small meadow and Donte found some apples they hadn't noticed before. They talked about ideas for creating other cache sites.

Pell was excited because he envisioned using sites like the one they'd just set up to extend their trapping range in the winter. They could make two-day trips staying at the cache shelters during the nights between. The bounty of the land in the summer was so plentiful such trips weren't necessary. But he knew the winter landscape would be a different thing altogether.

Over the next hand of days, they took more food and equipment to two more sites, investing enough effort at each to make them into minimally livable campsites or, as they'd begun calling them, "getaway sites." The other two sites were both little cavities in the rock walls of ravines. The cavities were too small to live in, but they filled them with food and walled off the openings with piled rocks.

Donte found some soft limestone they pounded to a powder. They dusted the powder all about the rock closures and over the supplies inside to help keep ants and other insects out. They even took some home and put it over their stores in the main cave.

Pell and Tando revisited the first site to make sure that animals hadn't disturbed it. They also took more supplies to it for storage. Animals hadn't gotten into it, but the grain wasn't staying as dry as they would have liked. They wove more basket trays and spread the grain amongst them in thinner layers so air could move through it more easily. They covered the stored meat with dirt in hopes of obscuring its scent more thoroughly. Finally, they spread limestone powder everywhere and blocked shut the open end of the crevice.

When they were piling the rocks for the closure, Pell was surprised to find that he could reach higher than Tando. To his astonishment, he realized he'd even gotten taller than Tando!

He remembered his fight with Denit, when he'd suddenly recognized he'd outgrown his erstwhile tormentor. He'd known then that this was apparently his year to grow, but he'd not really grasped how much the unrestricted diet provided by his trapping had been doing to his teenage growth spurt. Whereas most members of the Aldans and other tribes had all been at least somewhat stunted by chronic hunger during their youth, Pell was reaching the full potential of the height prescribed by his genes.

***

As they dug up supplies from their primary cave to move them out, Pell was astonished at the sheer volume of smoked meat they'd already preserved. They also had a great deal more grain and root vegetables than he'd realized.

The Aldans, like other hunter-gatherers, had spent only a few hours per day procuring food during the summer plenty. With little ability to store it except in their own fat, what was the point? Then they'd spent long hours searching for food during winter's dearth, to little benefit.

For the Cold Springs three, their new ability to store food and their fear of starvation in winter had led to their working long hours in the summer for the first time in their lives.

The hours they'd put in during abundant times, in combination with the rate that they were able to snare small wildlife, had led to a cornucopia such as they'd never before experienced or expected. Because small game was difficult to hit with spears or stones, the Aldans had mostly hunted large game in big groups. Pell became aware that the men of the Aldans probably had no idea just how many little animals were actually available in this bountiful land.

They kept moving stores out. After several more trips to stock the three escape sites, they'd mostly cleaned out their stores in the Cold Springs cave.

However, Pell now judged that any one of the three sites could get them through the oncoming winter, even with minimal success at winter hunting or trapping.

They'd be quite hungry, but they'd survive without as much difficulty as they'd had during most of the winters he'd spent with the Aldans. Even more amazingly, they all believed that, if they kept working at the pace that they'd been going, they could restock their primary cave before winter came.

As they set about replenishing those stores, they directed most of their effort to restocking grains and fruit since they'd become scarce before the hunting ran out.

Tando had an idea about their storage. At first, they'd covered their meat with the soft dirt they dug up at the back of the cave. They'd started putting their stores down in the hole they'd dug getting the covering dirt. Now, as they dug their stores back up, they were left with a huge hole *and* quite a bit more living room. As they stood looking with some surprise at the size of it, Tando said, "Let's dig an even *bigger* hole. We'll roof it over with poles we can lash together in a criss-cross pattern like the rafts some tribes use."

It took a bit of explanation before the other two understood what he wanted to do, but then they all worked enthusiastically. They dug a hole so big they joked that it was "another cave" and spread lime in it. As time passed they put the bulk of their new jerky, sausage, roots, grain and dried fruit into the cellar they'd created. They stacked supplies with room to spare for air circulation so things would stay dry.

Tando built the cover for the cellar much like the wall of the cave and applied mud to it. He left it out to bake in the sun for a few days. The cover had some holes for ventilation. When they had their cellar fairly full and put the lid on, they covered the lid with dirt and moved their bedding over on top of that. They hid the ventilation holes under loosely woven baskets.

Pell stood looking at it after they finished closing it up. "It's going to be hard having to open this each time we get a little more food we want to hide."

"Oh, we want to build up quite a bit of food here in the cave itself," Tando said. If someone robs us, that's what we want them to take. If we don't have anything here in the main part of the cave, they'll start searching." He looked around and shrugged, "We want to have enough visible that they don't think we're hiding it, but not so much that we look like a really good target for a raid."

***

As the cool crisp days of autumn rolled past, they felt well prepared for winter. They felt relieved to think they could survive even if they got robbed or driven away from their primary cave, though they certainly didn't want to be driven away from the fruits of all the hard work they'd put in.

They did worry about the very real dangers of the fight that would force them out. Despite Tando's original doubts, Pell thought more about his "man-sized snare." He tried building large snares for animals as a way to test his ideas. A loop of the braided leather he'd bought, suspended across a deer trail with a little ivy wrapped around it for disguise successfully snared a deer.

Pell stayed to watch the snare in hopes of learning something about how a big snare would work. The deer walked into the loop, no doubt expecting the ivy to be easily pushed out of its way. When the remainder of the loop had dropped onto its back, the deer startled violently, then bolted, drawing the noose tight around its neck and throwing itself to the ground. It thrashed so violently that he thought it broke its own neck before the noose choked it.

In any case, it died before Pell could get a spear into it.

Snaring a deer was pretty exciting, but as he thought about it, Pell realized Tando had been right. He couldn't count on its working on a person. People would see and understand what the rope was. Even if their enemy didn't avoid the rope, a man bolting to draw a noose tight on his own neck didn't seem likely.

Besides, how could Pell set it up to trap *only* his enemies? When he arrived back in camp with the deer about his neck the excitement was huge. At first Tando and Donte assumed that he must have speared it as they hadn't made a snare that large before.

Learning that he'd successfully made a deer snare created so much excitement that the implication of trapping a human never came up. They all set to work harvesting and curing the large skin provided by the deer as well as its stomach which would make an excellent water bag. Then there was the meat to slice and smoke.

They had so much meat now they decided from now on they should only put out enough snares to catch what they ate each day.

***

Pell couldn't stop thinking about his "man snare" though. He worked for a while trying to set up a noose that drew *itself* tight. He could make this work with a small noose by tying it to a springy branch he'd bent. When he released the branch with his finger inside the loop, the noose snapped painfully tight. However, he couldn't envision any branch he'd be able to bend that'd be strong enough to seriously injure another person with its noose. Besides, he couldn't very well stand around waiting to release the branch!

Nonetheless, Pell invested one of the days when it was his turn to stay in the camp. He laid out nooses in front of the cave where he could imagine confronting a group that came to rob them. It wasn't difficult to bury the noose in the dirt so it wasn't visible.

When Tando returned from checking their traps, Pell had him stand in the noose while he stood up on the cliff above and jerked up on the rope. He did trap Tando in it, but couldn't figure out how he could pull on the noose with sufficient force to stop a group of attackers. He left the tail end of the rope hanging over the base of a small tree up on the cliff so he could think about it more.

The next morning, he looked up at it and saw that if he pulled down on the tail of the rope, the noose would be pulled up over the tree. He tied two fairly big rocks to the end of the rope, propping them in place with a stick that could be jerked out from under them. This worked, jerking the noose up into the air, though the two rocks weren't heavy enough to accomplish much.

After thinking a while, he fashioned a net of cords into a pouch at the end of the rope. Then he carried rock after rock up to place them in the pouch, bracing the big bundle of stones with a limb wedged in place with a stick. He set up a smaller rope to pull out the wedging stick and tied it off inside the cave. Thus, the cave's defenders could work the trap by jerking the end of the small rope. Pell wanted to try it out and see what it did to someone trapped in the noose, but he couldn't bear the thought of climbing back up the cliff with all those rocks.

***

The leaves turned colors and the mornings started getting cold. The snares still brought in a fair bounty of summer-fattened animals. However, using shorter trap lines, the three caught barely more than they ate, only building their stores a little. They worked hard on rooting now as the roots they found were large and juicy with a summer's worth of storage. These roots they stacked up in the "visible" area of the cave. However, Donte brought in so many that they had to dig another "hidden cellar," putting more roots and some of their freshly smoked meat down there.

As they closed off the new cellar, Pell said, "We should check how things are keeping in the other cellar. If stuff's rotting in there, we need to know."

Tando's eyes widened, "You want to dig it up just to *look*?"

Donte looked back and forth at the two men, "We just have to move the stuff off it and lift the cover. It isn't as if we really have to dig. And Pell's right, we need to know before we keep putting more stuff in cellars."

When they got it open, they were pleased to see the vents were keeping things in their cellar pretty dry. So far, there seemed to be little or no spoilage. They turned the grain while they had it open.

Then they checked the food in their getaway sites and found it was okay as well.

***

One morning, returning from checking the snares, Pell found a small group of people ahead of him on the path back to the cave. He slowed furtively to follow them. They were a pretty bedraggled looking group, six in all, with two of the group riding pig-a-back on the others. Of the two walking, one was a boy with a limp and the other a young man.

He was startled to see that one of the carriers was a young woman. He couldn't understand why she had someone on her back when the young man didn't. But then they stopped for a rest and the young man helped relieve her of her burden. When she straightened, Pell's heart leaped! It was Gia! With that, he recognized the young man as Manute and the limping boy as Falin. Pell quickened his stride, calling out, "Gia, Manute, What's happened?"

As he came up, they stood wearily from lowering their burdens to the ground. He stopped a few paces away, holding Ginja by the ruff while she growled and bristled as if she'd never seen them before. He noticed then that some of them were indeed new to Ginja.

A quick glance showed Pell that Gia's burden had been her hag of a grandmother, Agan. The other man of the party carried a woman with a deformed leg who looked sick. Pell embraced Manute, nodded respect to Agan, and ruffled Falin's hair. To his dismay, he couldn't muster the courage to greet Gia with anything more than a shy smile and a "Hello." Again, he asked, "What's happened?"

Gia formally drew herself up to her full height and waved at the old woman. "Pell, this, as I believe you remember, is my grandmother Agan. Of course, you remember Falin and Manute. These other two are my cousin Deltin and his mate Panute." She turned to Deltin and Panute. "This is Pell, the bonesetter Manute and I have spoken of. He controls the Wolf Spirit so you need not fear the wolf, who is called 'Ginja'." She turned to her cousin's mate, "Panute, if anyone can help you, it is he."

Surprised as always to hear someone speak reverently of his skills, Pell's eyes swept over to Panute and fastened on her leg. It was angled and twisted so that it turned inwardly between the knee and ankle. The leg was swollen, but Panute looked much sicker than he'd have expected from a broken leg. She appeared fevered, leaning listlessly against the tree Deltin had set her against.

Pell was puzzled for a moment; then his eyes caught on her hand. Her pointer and long fingers were swollen and dark. There was a fetid ooze emanating from the mid portion of the long finger. The hand itself was bright red, with streaks of red running up the arm. With dismay, he saw her fingers looked much the way Kana's had a few days before Kana died.

Pell remembered his panic when he'd thought his own finger might kill him like Kana's had. *Panute's going to die...* he thought to himself, *soon.* He tried to keep the grim thought from showing on his face. Looking around the group, he saw despair on Panute's countenance. Doubt showed in the faces of Deltin and Agan. Unbelievably, he thought Gia, Manute, and Falin looked as if they expected Pell to be able to solve this problem. Infuriatingly, it reminded Pell of Tando's constant and blasé assumption that Pell could right any kind of physical problem.

Aloud, Pell said, "Well, let's get you to our camp and see what we can do. You can tell me what happened on the way. I'll carry Panute if you'll carry this rabbit and squirrel."

They helped get Panute up on Pell's back and Agan up on Manute's. Ginja, distressed by the large group of strangers, plunged off into the forest. As they walked, they told Pell a tale of disaster.

Their tribe lived in a cave cut deep into a cliffside by a creek like the one at Cold Springs. As they described it, it sounded to Pell like a wonderful location. The water had been cutting back underneath their cave so the lip of the cave's floor hung above the stream.

This meant that there was water five to ten feet below the cave that they could haul up in skins with a rope, not even having to walk to fetch it. A ledge from the cave went upstream a way and curved out onto a flat, rich meadow. Every few years though, when storms were heavy, the stream rose high enough to flood the cave. Although inconvenient, when that happened, they simply moved out for a day or so and came back to a clean cave when the flooding went back down. There was a smaller, much less convenient cave higher on the same hillside where they stayed on those rare occasions.

Five nights ago, the water had risen rapidly during the night. The rains had been heavy and the water had been rising, so they'd thought they might have to move out. Unfortunately, when water first trickled into the cave, it was the middle of the night and caught them by surprise. Nonetheless, they'd thought that, as in previous floods, they'd have time to save their possessions. When the water first entered, Manute immediately carried Agan up to the small cave and Falin had limped up to sit with her. The other members of their tribe were still gathering possessions when the first trickle was followed by a huge surge of water that filled the entire cave in minutes.

Gia had been away at a neighboring tribe, ministering to a sick child. After depositing Agan in the little cave, Manute went back to get their important possessions but hadn't been able to reach the big cave because it was completely beneath the raging water. For a time he'd hoped that the others had gotten to safety and that he just missed them in the darkness and downpour.

Unfortunately, when Manute returned to the small cave he found none of the others had arrived. Agan, Manute, and Falin waited in growing dread as the night passed, reassuring each other that the missing members of their tribe simply couldn't find their way in the dark. When the next morning dawned they went out to search with growing anxiety.

By evening they recognized the appalling truth.

Deltin and Panute were the only other survivors from a cave of twenty-three people. They only lived because the two of them had started shortly behind Manute, Agan, and Falin, carrying a large basket of grain.

They were swept off the path by the waters just after leaving the cave, but they'd already spilled most of the grain, struggling in the knee-high water. The nearly empty basket floated and they clung to it in the surging waters. The rushing torrent flung them to a landing on a rocky bight in the stream. Immediately after they landed, a log came aground on top of Panute, breaking her leg and crushing her fingers.

Amazingly enough, Deltin had been almost uninjured. He was already carrying her back towards the cave when Manute, searching downstream for survivors, found them. Though they'd hoped a few more people may have floated even farther and come to shore way downstream, it seemed more and more likely that no one else had survived.

Gia and Agan, striving to stop the swelling and fever in Panute's hand, had tried every poultice or tea they knew to no avail. Despairing, with nowhere else to turn, the group of six had set out for Cold Springs in hopes that Pell could work a miracle.

Pell's mind was racing. Why would they think that *he* could do something for Panute's finger they couldn't!? A broken leg, yes, Pell could accept that perhaps he was the right person to treat that—but a finger with the wound fever? *He* wasn't the right one to treat wound fever. That was for a medicine woman like Agan or Gia, or even, though he hated to admit it, perhaps for Pont.

Not for me!

Pell didn't have any idea which medicines might be of use for wound fever.

Next Pell began to worry about where they'd all sleep if it rained, which the dark clouds overhead were threatening. Should he try to convince Tando it was okay for their guests to sleep inside, now that most of their stores were hidden? How were Gia and her tiny tribe going to survive the winter with only two hunters and all their summer stores washed away?

Through it all, the fetid odor of Panute's finger dangling limply about his neck kept reminding Pell of how horribly Kana'd died.

They walked into the clearing below the Cold Springs cave and Pell saw Tando standing in the entrance. When he called out to Tando, Tando raised his hand and waved. Pell found himself staring at the missing small finger on Tando's hand and goosebumps rose on his neck. Tando'd crushed his finger under the same rock as Kana! But his finger had been cut away completely and he'd never even *started* to get the wound fever!

All of a sudden Pell remembered that, when he'd seen his own finger turning dark, he'd thought of cutting it off like Tando's. He'd hoped that would keep the wound fever away. Might the same treatment work even after wound fever had started?

Shortly they were all gathered in the clearing while the tale of flooding and woe was repeated to Tando and Donte. When telling Pell their tale earlier, the little group of six had held up bravely. Now, perhaps because of their sheer exhaustion, tears ran freely. Especially, as they spoke of Gia's father, aunt and many cousins who'd died in the disaster.

Pell recognized the dismay on Donte's face as she looked at Panute's hand. However, as Tando studied the infected hand, his face filled with excitement and anticipation. Tando looked brightly at Pell and said, "Well, Pell, what do we do first? Shall I gather wood for splints? Shall we move her down by the stream?"

Once again, Pell was taken aback over Tando's matter of fact expectation that Pell *could* treat Panute's hand. And his expectation that Pell could treat it successfully! Pell almost responded angrily. He stopped himself, because the dying Panute would hear whatever he said. "I'm not sure, Tando." He turned to the others, "I only have a trick for setting bones. I'm not at all sure what might be done for Panute."

Pell felt their almost palpable dismay like a visceral blow and so, against his better judgment, he weakly offered, "I have an… an idea, but I don't know if it'll work. I've never attempted it before. I've never even *tried* to cure anyone with a wound fever before."

"Well, for spirit's sake, Pell, do it!" Tando exploded. "No one else knows how to treat wound fever! You can *hardly* make it worse."

"Tando! You don't even know what the idea is! It certainly *could* make the wound fever worse. Besides, Gia and Agan know treatments for fever—they've been using them."

"They've *been* using them and they *haven't* been working! Haven't you been listening? It *can't* be worse, Pell. She's going to *die* if nothing's done and you know it! Use your gift!"

Despite having lived around the man for years, Pell was shocked by Tando's bluntness. How could anyone speak of Panute's impending death in front of her? Pell's gaze darted to Panute and saw her eyes wide with shock. "Panute," Pell hesitated, "Tando doesn't know what he's talking about. You aren't going to die…"

Panute shook her head and interrupted. "Yes, I am. I knew it myself. I was just surprised to hear *him* say it. Everyone else's been pretending that my hand isn't so bad." She snorted, "I can smell it too, you know. I'd like you to try your idea… whatever it is. Otherwise…" she looked out at the horizon, "I'm finished."

Gia looked at Pell as if she expected him to begin spouting the spirits' own truths. "What should we do, Pell? What's your idea?"

"Well, in our old cave… Once… Uh, once Tando and Kana's fingers were both crushed under a large rock. Tando's finger was cut completely off, but it healed cleanly with a little stump as you see."

Tando held up his hand and proudly waggled the stubby finger at everyone.

Pell would've giggled if the situation weren't so serious. "Kana's finger was crushed, but stayed on her hand. At first, we thought Kana had the less serious injury because her finger was still attached to her hand, but it soon swelled with the wound fever. Redness and swelling raced up her arm. Um…" Pell ran down as he realized what he'd been about to say in front of Panute.

"Um, what, Pell? What happened?"

"Um…" Pell paused. Unable to think of a way to soften the blow he practically whispered, "She died about two hands of days after her injury." Pell did refrain from describing the horrible nature of that death. He looked around at his audience.

Tando wore a puzzled look. "So what *should* we have done to save Kana?"

Pell was taken aback. He'd thought that his story would make his suggestion obvious to everyone without his having to state it baldly. "Well… I don't know… I'm just pointing out that people whose fingers get cut off do better than people whose fingers are crushed but still attached…"

The others looked puzzled and Tando was exasperated. "Okay, but what should we do for Panute? Her fingers are crushed, not cut off!"

Pell looked down. "I thought… I thought perhaps…" he finished weakly in a rush, "I thought maybe we should cut the bad fingers off."

They all stared at him.

Tando blinked a couple of times and said, "Do what!?"

"Cut them off. When I thought my own finger was going bad, I tried to cut it off," he said. "I couldn't bring myself to cut my own finger though, so I tried to break it off—that's when it went back into place—and, how I learned the trick of bonesetting..."

A moment of astonished silence passed. Agan rolled her eyes back and baldly stated that she'd never heard anything quite so absurd. A rush of argument followed. Gia argued that Pell had a gift and, if the spirits had told him to do this, it must be the right thing to do. Manute, having seen Pell work an apparent miracle with Falin's leg, also thought if Pell recommended it, that of course they should do it.

Pell, now crushed with doubt, began to think it was a *terrible* idea.

While the others were arguing, Donte raised Pell's anxiety by whispering in his ear that a gift for reducing fingers might not be the same as a gift for cutting them off.

Tando, though initially appalled, shortly segued to his usual opinion that the spirits would bless *anything* Pell suggested in the way of healing. In fact, Tando took an aggrieved tone with those who were arguing against Pell's proposed amputation.

The dispute had been surging back and forth for some time and it began to seem that, despite their great respect for Agan, the tide was in favor of the amputations. At that point, Deltin, who'd been quiet 'til then, burst out, "But, how will Panute take care of herself if she's got two fingers missing?"

A pause followed that was broken when an exhausted Panute said, "How am I going to take care of myself if I'm dead, Deltin?"

Pell realized this was the first time she'd spoken during the entire argument.

Everyone turned to look at Panute with surprise. Pell thought guiltily that they'd been talking about her almost as if she wasn't there. She said, "I've been looking at these fingers and thinking they were going to kill me for days. I've been *hating* these two fingers and wishing they were gone. Even if I live, they'll surely do me no good. Look at them. They don't even move. If Pell thinks cutting them off might save me, I want him to do it."

Everyone turned to look at Pell and he felt panic rising. When he'd said, "We should try to cut them off" the picture in his mind had been of Tando cutting them off. He'd once watched Tando deftly removing fingers from a corpse after Pell had been assigned the task and failed.

Pell felt queasy at the mere thought of trying to cut Panute's fingers off while she was alive. He looked at Tando, "No, Tando should do it. He's had practice cutting off fingers..."

"Oh, No. Spirits, no!" Tando exploded in dismay, "No, I couldn't *possibly* do it. I'm not a healer or a bonesetter. I couldn't do it. I shouldn't do it...! It... it was your idea anyway." He drew back for a moment. "Besides, *I* don't have the healing powers, you do."

Perplexed, Pell thought the group had accepted the idea of cutting the fingers off more readily than he could accept the possibility of doing it himself. He dithered some more, trying to convince them someone else should do it. Having accepted Panute's plea that it should be done, the group now became resolute that Pell should do it and do it as soon as possible.

Except for Agan, that is. She merely stared unseeingly into the distance.

Eventually, Pell succumbed to the inevitable. "Gia," he turned to her, "could you and Agan make Panute some of your powerful pain medicine while we're figuring out how to do it? Donte could probably help you find new herbs to replace ones you lost in the flood."

Agan snorted and looked away, obviously not intending to help with a procedure she considered unsound. To Pell's surprise Gia brightened, "Oh, I have my herbs with me. I'd taken them to the other village on the night of the flood. I'll get started preparing the potion."

Tando turned to Pell and said, "Shall I get wood for splints?" At this Pell exploded, "For spirit's sake, Tando, why would we need splints if we're cutting her fingers off!?"

"I don't know! I've never even *heard* of cutting parts off of people! You've always used splints before when you do your magic. How am I supposed to know what you need each different time?"

"Sorry Tando," Pell said dispiritedly. "It's not magic, we're just going to cut her fingers off and then pray to the spirits that it helps." Pell lowered his voice and said tiredly. "I'm not even sure how to cut them off, or even if I can bring myself to do it. What if she starts screaming?"

"Just do it so fast it'll be done before she starts screaming."

"How am I going to do that!?"

"I don't know. Maybe with a big hand axe?"

"Yeah, sure!" Pell snorted. "You've seen me using a hand axe before! I'd probably cut off the wrong two fingers!"

"Fold the other fingers back out of the way?"

"The way I swing an axe, I'd probably cut her hand off at the wrist. We've *got* to do better than that."

Pell and Tando moved off to the other side of the clearing and sat for a while, experimenting with ways to place fingers on a stump so that only two of them were exposed. They laid another flat piece of wood over the rest of the hand so that it would protect the other fingers from a wild blow. Next, Pell worried about striking too distally and having to strike again to cut them off up closer. "This has to be right the first time, Tando," he said in exasperation. "Why won't *you* do it? You're *good* with a hand axe!"

"I couldn't Pell. I just couldn't. I'd probably pull the blow and only cut them halfway off. Besides, *you're* the bonesetter. You have the healing hands. It *has* to be you who does it."

When, an hour or so later, Gia announced that Panute was ready and asked, "Where are you going to do it?" Tando and Pell were still trying to figure a way to protect the good fingers from the blow of the hand axe.

Hoping to stem the tide of his rising panic, Pell carried over the large chunk of deadfall wood that they'd picked out for a cutting block. It had a knothole that the good fingers could be placed in to protect them from misaimed blows. He had Tando hold the hand axe in approximately the correct place while he tried to position a slab of wood to protect the rest of her hand and wrist. He slipped and almost dropped the slab on the axe. With great suddenness and clarity, he saw how to do it safely.

With a trembling hand, Pell took the hand axe from Tando. He carefully placed it a finger's breadth proximal to the edge of the dark, sick-looking skin, so that the axe lay over the bright red skin on the back of Panute's hand.

Pell felt to check the location of his good flint knife at his belt, looked down at Panute's snoring face and then up at the sky.

With the thunderclouds that were storming in his own mind, he was bemused to see the clouds in the sky thinning and beginning to pink up toward what promised to be a gorgeous sunset.

Pell rechecked the position of Panute's fingers and found the area under the hand axe was hanging over the void of the big knothole. He repositioned the hand flat and simply placed the axe so its blade was over the base of the pointer and long fingers and did not extend over the small or ring finger. Once again, he checked the location of his knife and the beatific face of Panute.

Then, with grim determination, he picked up a large stone and struck the back of the hand axe a powerful blow.

The hand axe shattered and the sleeping Panute convulsed upward, screaming like she'd risen from the dead.

Pell grabbed her wrist and saw with dismay that all four fingers remained on her hand. Then he saw that the pointer and long fingers were only hanging on by a small strip of skin. Without volition, his hand pulled the flint knife from his holster and cut that strip. He cast the two fingers away into the bushes.

Blood was pouring out of Panute's hand! Panute herself had fallen back in a faint, eyes rolled back in her head and mouth gaping open. Pell looked up from the gushing blood to see the others standing stricken, also staring at Panute's lifeblood as it poured out onto the ground. "Gia, your poultice for the wound?" Pell felt he'd shouted, but later the others would remark on his calm demeanor. Gia started, then wordlessly raised the hand in which she held the poultice, holding the wad of leaves and herbs out to Pell.

This surprised Pell again. Somehow, he'd expected Gia would take over from this point. She had, after all, treated many wounds in her role as a medicine woman. Other than a few small cuts of his own, Pell had never cared for a wound at all. But Gia looked stunned by the violence of the amputation and seemed reluctant to intervene in what she considered to be Pell's domain.

He took the poultice in one hand and seized Panute's hand with the other. When he grasped her hand, it felt like a rotten fruit bursting. In revulsion and astonishment, he saw a river of pus cascade from the amputation wound. Knowing that when the evil humours in pus left a person, the person often got better, he squeezed the squishy feeling area until no more pus came out, then placed the poultice over the wound.

The poultice rapidly became soaked in blood and, squeezing hard, Pell turned again to Gia. "Will this poultice stop the bleeding?"

Gia gasped, "No! Oh! I *should've* known we'd need an astringent poultice! I'll make one now!"

Gia turned to go and Pell found himself sitting alone by Panute, compressing the poultice and trying to stanch the bleeding. Deltin was at the edge of the clearing throwing up. From the looks of his heaving, he'd found the bottom of his stomach and would soon throw that up as well.

Manute was comforting him while Donte poked around in the bushes, looking for Pell knew not what.

Tando said he needed to check the fire up in the cave. From his white face Pell knew he'd been badly shaken by the entire episode and probably just wanted to be away from it.

Agan was still sitting on the rock where Pell had placed her when their group arrived in camp. However, she'd managed to turn away from the whole thing. She sat staring off down the valley with her rheumy eyes, chanting under her breath.

The wide-eyed Falin *was* still there with Pell and Panute. Unfortunately, the presence of the young boy didn't keep Pell from feeling dreadfully alone.

He sat, pressed the poultice into the unconscious woman's wound and wished the flow of blood would stop.

Falin asked if there was anything he could do, so Pell sent him to the creek for some water. When he returned, Panute was rousing and Pell wound up giving the water to her rather than drinking it himself. He sent Falin back for more. Panute promptly threw up the water, broke into a sweat and proclaimed herself chilled.

Stricken with fear that the chills portended Panute's impending death, Pell felt his own stomach go queasy. He fervently wished Gia would return with the astringent poultice. Perhaps he could get her to apply and hold it. At least he could ask her what she thought about Panute's chills.

Deltin returned from where he'd been dowsing his head in the creek after spewing his guts. Pell sent him up to the cave to ask Tando for furs to cover Panute. He asked Deltin to bring Tando back with him when he brought the furs.

When they returned and Panute had been covered to Pell's satisfaction, Pell turned to Tando and asked, "Do you think there's room for them in the cave now that we moved all that stuff? I think it's going to rain and I don't think Panute should be out in it."

Tando appeared to be surprised by the question. Though whether he hadn't considered letting them stay in the cave or whether he hadn't considered *not* letting them stay in the cave Pell couldn't tell. "Sure, there's plenty of room now," he said with a wink. "When are you going to fix her leg?"

"Spirits! I forgot about her leg!" Pell gave Tando a wide-eyed look, "Sorry, that's probably why you thought I would want to make splints earlier, isn't it?" He looked down at Panute, "I don't think we should put her through a bonesetting though, at least until we see if she recovers from losing her fingers. We probably *should* make the splints for her leg though. We might even put them on, just to hold it a little straighter and keep it from getting bumped."

Pell turned to see if Panute looked like she was up to the splinting, but she'd passed out again. He looked at her chest a moment to be sure that she was breathing then turned back to Tando. "We really could use some wood for splints. Do you want to go, or would you rather sit with Panute while I look for wood?"

"No! No, I'll go get the wood!" Tando said anxiously, obviously ill at ease at the thought of being left with the unconscious Panute. Once again, Pell had nothing to do but sit, squeeze Panute's hand, and worry.

Panute intermittently broke into an uncontrolled shivering, but when Pell looked over at Agan in hopes of her help, the look she gave him was filled with scorn. In his gut, he felt sure that when Panute died, Agan would declare her death a consequence of Pell and his treatment rather than the result of an untreatable wound fever.

That's what Pont would have done.

Unfortunately, Pell thought Agan might be right. Panute had looked bad before, but she looked worse now.

Donte came back from scrabbling around in the bushes to talk to Agan. She had Panute's fingers! Pell vaguely recollected throwing them into the bushes when he'd finished cutting them off. Apparently, they were what Donte had been looking for all of this time.

Shortly Donte and Agan engaged themselves in some kind of ceremony involving the fingers. It looked to be some kind of burial rite. Shame spread over Pell as he realized that he hadn't even considered that a ritual for the amputated parts might be needed. Considering it, he thought to himself that Pont would've made a huge event out of it. He probably wouldn't have had much time for Panute after all the time he'd spent consigning her fingers to the afterlife.

Pell snorted softly.

Falin came up to ask if there was anything else he could do and Pell sent him for more furs to cover the shivering Panute. When the boy returned and Pell went to add the extra layers, he was astonished to find her flesh hot to the touch. Pell was pondering whether to add the extra furs anyway when Gia returned with her new poultice.

As he applied the poultice Pell told Gia about Panute's shivering despite her fever. Gia advised against adding more furs and, after more discussion, they decided to remove some instead. Relief flowed over Pell when he removed the first poultice and saw that most of the bleeding had already stopped. He wrapped the astringent poultice on with a couple of the soft leather straps that Donte'd prepared for the splints to go on Panute's leg. Gia went to Agan to consult with her regarding a tea to break Panute's fever.

Gia called out to Pell, "Can you help me move Agan so she can look at Panute?"

Pell was grateful to be asked. From Agan's withering looks earlier, Pell had feared that she'd refuse to have anything to do with his treatment of Panute. "Sure," he said. As he and Gia helped Agan stand and shuffle over to Panute, he asked, "How will we get Panute to drink the tea?"

Agan snorted, "She'll wake soon enough. As soon as the pain herbs wear off... unless she dies first." This last was muttered darkly and in a tone that left little doubt as to whom Agan would hold accountable.

Pell's heart fluttered when Gia came to his defense, "Agan, Panute was *going* to die, even if Pell didn't cut off her fingers. You know that."

"Maybe," Agan begrudged, "but I don't think it would've been so soon."

Agan and Gia inspected Panute and consulted with one another regarding the proper herbs for their tea.

Pell sat down with Deltin and Tando to begin shaping splints for Panute's leg. It was soon obvious that Deltin had a phenomenal skill for shaping wood. Watching him, Pell asked about it.

Deltin said, "I've made the spear shafts for our tribe for several summers now." He wiped at a tear. "Ever since my father died. He taught me." He glanced over at

Panute and sighed. "I learned everything I know about working wood from him. And now he's gone…"

Pell watched Deltin work in awe, carefully trying to duplicate his techniques as he used hand axe, scraper and flint knife.

Deltin worked in silence briefly. He held up the piece of wood he'd been working on and said, "I make other wooden things for the tribe. A two-pronged eating utensil for spearing meat when eating. Bowls scraped out of wood, totems to ward off evil spirits, and spits for roasting meat over a fire. But I've never made 'splints.'" He flipped the splint over and said, "A chisel would be very helpful for this."

"What's a chisel?"

Deltin described a specially shaped flint knife, made to cut on the end instead of the side. "All of ours probably washed away in the flood," he said morosely.

Pell occasionally gave Deltin directions regarding how the splint should be shaped, but the woodworker readily enough grasped the idea that it should fit Panute's good leg and made rapid progress towards shaping it to do just that.

As Deltin tested his splint against Panute's leg, he said mournfully, "I hope she lives to use these splints." He looked up, "Who taught you the art of carving them?"

Pell dumbfounded him when he said, "No one. I don't even have training in how to work wood. I've had to figure it out all by myself."

"How did you learn to make magical splints like the ones that healed Falin?"

Pell drew back, "They're not magical."

Deltin gave Pell a skeptical look.

"Really. There aren't any spells or spirits or anything in a splint! It's just a tool that holds the limb straight while it's healing, like... like a stretcher holds a skin while it's curing."

"Well, how did you learn to make 'non-magical' splints?"

Pell paused to consider, "I just thought about what it would take to hold Tando's wrist straight. I thought a straight stick would work if the limb was strapped to it. But since arms and legs are bumpy, a completely straight stick wouldn't fit very well—so I just pictured how it would have to be shaped to fit his arm when the wrist was straight. I tried to shape it that way by scraping and chopping. The others I've made took a lot longer to make than this one. I've learned *so much* from watching you."

"You *must* have an amazing gift to make healing sticks like Falin wore without anyone to teach you." Deltin glanced again at Panute who still lay unconscious. After a moment he said, "I've seen Falin walk when I was sure he wouldn't—that's a miraculous gift. I don't know whether what you've done will help Panute, but I think she was right. It couldn't make her any worse than... than dead." He took a shuddering breath, "I won't hold it against you if she dies." Tears rolled down Deltin's cheeks as he whispered this last.

Enormously relieved by Deltin's halting statement, but unsure of what to say in response, Pell continued scraping for a while. Eventually, he said, "I hope... I, uh, hope... all turns out well for her."

~~~

It was dark when they had scraped and shaped the splints to Pell's satisfaction. He looked at her leg for a while, pondering. He'd always made the deformity worse then pulled or pushed the limb back into place when doing his "bonesettings." But with the other cases, the deformity had always consisted of a limb *stuck* in a bent position.

Panute's leg seemed "floppy," lying angled in whichever position it'd been laid down. Generally, it lay with an outward twist so that when she was on her back, the foot turned out to the side. However, sometimes it was bent one way, sometimes another.

Perhaps it doesn't need a "bonesetting," he thought. *Maybe it only needs something like the splints to hold it straight?* He grasped her foot and turned it up slowly, then gently pulled the leg straight. She moaned a little, but didn't waken. With his other hand, he placed one splint on the medial side where it seemed to fit well. Deltin tentatively held the other in place on the lateral side of her leg.

Because of the swelling in the middle of the leg, both splints touched the leg in the middle but not at the ends. Pell considered scraping more wood away, but feared that more thinning would weaken the splints too much. They'd already been scraped until they were very slender in their central sections. Also, he thought that, as the swelling went down, they'd get loose in those areas.

After more thought, Pell went up to the cave to get some small furs. He used them to make pads that he placed between the splints and the ankle and between the splints and the knee to tighten the contact in those areas. With Tando and Deltin's help, he bound the splints to her leg with Donte's soft leather straps. The splints held her leg fairly straight, though Pell feared they'd be knocked loose when they picked her up to carry her to the cave.

When he discussed this problem with Tando and Deltin, Deltin described a carrying device he'd seen once made of two spear shafts with skins stretched between them. It took a while longer, but they constructed a stretcher like that and carried Panute up to the cave. They put her on a bed of straw and furs that Donte and Gia had prepared.

Donte had inverted a basket at the end of the bedding where Panute's leg could be propped up. She'd even put one beside the bed for the arm to be placed on. When Deltin asked about them, she said, "That's how Pell took care of Falin's leg," as if that concluded the matter.

As they got Panute settled in on the bed, Deltin stared around the cave in astonishment. He exclaimed over the way the cave had been walled in with the poles and mud daub wattle. "You could make it even bigger by walling in more of the overhanging area! What a great idea!"

Manute showed up in the cave carrying Agan. They had the same astonished reaction that Deltin evinced.

Pell noticed Gia smiling at her tribespeople's reaction as if she took pride in it herself. She said, "Our cave'd be warmer in winter if we narrowed the opening like this."

"Oh, and look," Manute said, "they just made a hole in the wall for the smoke to get out through. With a smoke hole like that, they can put their fire far from the opening of the cave."

Pell watched Agan and saw her dart a few glances around the cave to look at the things her people were pointing out. He got the feeling she was trying not to appear awed.

Deltin turned to Tando who was setting up more bedding. "Where'd you learn to close in an overhang to make it into a cave?"

Tando inclined his head to where Pell was sitting with Panute, "Better ask Pell, he's the cave builder."

The group was astonished to learn someone as young as Pell had thought of walling in the overhang by himself. "No one showed you how?"

"Well no. There wasn't a good cave in Cold Springs Ravine, just this overhang. And the overhang dripped. I made a "drip-lip" but the wind and rain still blew through. Then I started leaning poles against the mud of the drip lip, trying to stop the wind. After that, mudding the gaps to block even more wind just seemed natural."

Manute said, "You just *thought this up*?!" He turned his head to look around and then stared wide-eyed at Pell. "How many summers do you have?!"

Sheepishly, Pell said, "Fourteen."

Deltin drew back in surprise, then narrowed his eyes to ask, "Did you ask the spirits for help and they told you what to do?"

Pell tried to explain, "No, no. I was just trying to fix one little problem after another..."

Still looking around, Gia finally swallowed her awe. She said, "We can teach you to weave deeper baskets. Those shallow grain storage baskets you have propped in that dead tree waste a lot of the space in your cave."

Donte shook her head, "We used to keep ours in deep baskets too. But Pell pointed out that the grain in the bottom of the basket went bad. And the roots in the bottoms of deep baskets get crushed and they go bad too. Even if it doesn't rot, the rest of the grains and roots sprout into the wet mess of the ones that went bad and they're ruined too. Pell thinks propping them up lets little winds blow through and keep the food dry. The grain and roots at the bottoms of these shallow baskets still sometimes go bad, but they do it a lot less than they did in our old deep baskets. He's also got us turning the grain every so often to keep it dry."

Pell blinked. He remembered the three of them talking about bad grain and roots and thought they'd come up with the shallow basket idea together. He was about to say something when Gia peered into a basket and said, "What are these?"

Donte leaned over, "Let me see. Oh, those are dried apple slices."

Gia frowned, "Apples? They're ruined!"

Undaunted, Donte shrugged, "You can still eat them. Here, taste one. They aren't as good as fresh apples, but they don't spoil either. We slice them thin and dry them in the sun. We're hoping they'll last most of the winter."

Gia chewed thoughtfully on a slice, blinked and smiled, "It's like your spirit meat, tough and chewy, but still full of flavor. Can I give a piece to Agan?"

When Donte handed her a piece Gia carefully took it to her grandmother. Pell thought Agan took it reluctantly and tried not to express any surprise at the taste while she gummed it.

They made a stew of the rabbit and squirrel Pell'd been carrying when he met them that morning. The group continued talking about the innovations in the cave while the stew cooked.

So much had happened that Pell could hardly believe it was the same day. The stew contained some of Donte's older stored roots. The fresh, fat roots Donte'd dug up earlier that day were placed in storage in an effort to keep their root stores as fresh as possible.

The visitors enthused over the flavor of the stew. Not having a source of salt like the Cold Springs tribe, they'd never been able to put much salt in their food. That alone made it wonderful to people who spent much of the summer sweating away more salt than they got in their diet. In addition, Donte had added some onions and "bitter berries" to the stew. These were berries she'd discovered were too bitter to eat by themselves, but still added an interesting flavor to stews. When she described them to Agan, the old hag nodded knowingly and proclaimed that they were also good for wounds that weren't healing.

Agan asked for Gia's bag of herbs and medicines. Taking out one of the packets she had Gia crush some dried leaves and add them to the remaining stew. After stirring it in for a while, everyone had some more stew and they remarked on the further enhancement of the flavor. Then Agan had them taste the herb itself. It had a sharp and unpleasant taste. She said there were several other herbs that added interesting flavors to stews, even though they tasted bad by themselves.

Pell hung on every word, awed by the breadth of Agan's knowledge of herbs, medicines, and cooking.

~~~

As they sat in the dim firelight, the conversation drifted back to the flood that'd killed the other members of Gia's tribe. Tears were rolling down cheeks as they reminisced, but then Panute wakened, moaning and somewhat out of her head. This brought their attention back to the present and at Gia's suggestion, they managed to get some stew into Panute. After taking a few sips she broke into a sweat, cast off all her covers, thrashed about a while, and fell back into a disturbed sleep. During her thrashing about, she disturbed the poultice that Pell had wrapped onto her hand and her hand started bleeding again. Gia prepared another poultice while Pell gently removed the old one.

They wrapped the fresh poultice on together. Working with Gia left Pell stuttering again.

Soon after that Panute was shivering again and Deltin covered her back up with furs. It wasn't long before her tossing and turning had again cast them off and she began shivering anew.

Pell suggested they take turns staying awake during the night to tend Panute. They worked out a rotation, changing each time a piece of firewood as thick as a forearm burned through.

Pell sat with Panute the last watch before dawn, by which time she'd become fairly calm again. With nothing to do, Pell looked about for Ginja. He felt sad when he realized his wolf friend hadn't come back. He sat, worrying about her and feeling surprised by the depths of his friendship with the animal.

When the sun rose, Panute awakened as well, this time clear in the head, though she still looked drawn and weak. When Gia awoke, they changed the poultice again. Pell was dismayed that Panute's hand remained swollen. To himself, he thought with chagrin that amputating her fingers had been for naught. He was wondering whether to try to hide the bad news from Panute, when Gia exclaimed, "Pell, look!" She was pointing to Panute's forearm up near the elbow. Pell couldn't imagine why. Gia said, "The redness in her arm is less!"

Pell couldn't remember how far the redness had extended the day before, but Gia said it had gone above the elbow. Believing Gia, he felt elated that it no longer did. "Great!" he said, then looked back at her hand and felt dismayed when he saw more pus leaking out.

Gia saw him staring at the pus. "Oh, and look, more of the evil humours are draining out! I saw them coming out yesterday after you cut off her fingers. Krill, in our tribe, he got really sick when a wound went foul. It swelled and he seemed on the verge of dying, but it burst open, letting out putrid humours like those. He got better shortly after that. When I've talked with other healers, many speak of people getting better when the evil humours escape from their bodies." She looked at Pell musingly, "But I've never heard of someone bold enough to think of cutting people open to let the bad humours out!"

Panute had been staring at the pus with revulsion, but she took heart at Gia's words and smiled for the first time since Pell had met her the day before. A weak and tremulous smile, but a smile nonetheless. Pell took heart from it.

Soon the rest of the group was up. They ate leftover stew and grain. Gia ground some grain between two rocks and made a paste with fat and water. She spread the paste on hot rocks pulled out of the fire. The little cakes she produced were something new to Pell and he thought they were wonderful. The group sat about, talking pleasantly for a time. Then, to Pell's dismay, Manute proposed the four men go hunting in hopes of getting bigger game than rabbits.

Pell wanted to tell them they had enough smoked meat to feed everyone without a hunt, but knew Tando wouldn't want to reveal their hidden stores. Pell had no good reason not to hunt, except for his fear that the newcomers would find out how clumsy he was with a spear.

To Pell's consternation, Tando thought a hunt sounded like a great idea. Listening to him talk about past hunts, Pell realized that Tando really enjoyed the entire process of going out hunting with other men. Tando fetched a couple of the spears he'd stored near the opening of the cave for fighting off attacks. He gave them to Manute and Deltin as gifts. Then Tando got a pair for Pell and himself.

Pell protested weakly that he should stay with Panute, but Agan grumpily said that watching Panute was one of the few tasks an old woman with bad knees could take on. A task she could do while the men hunted and Donte and Gia went out gathering. Soon the four men and Falin set out on their hunt. Falin carried a sharpened wooden spear that Deltin quickly cut to his size from one of the shafts Tando had stored away.

~~~

To Pell's immense relief, the hunt wasn't the disaster he'd envisioned. As Pell expected, Tando led them away from the area where they'd set snares the day before. Instead, they went out into the mature forest that lay down river from the ravine.

Scouting carefully beneath the canopy, they saw little in the way of game. Because the crunchy autumn leaves on the ground made it difficult to walk quietly, they had a hard time closing on the little game they did see.

Eventually, they saw some deer in a small meadow. The clear meadow was closed in pretty solidly around the edges because sunshine had promoted growth of the underbrush. However, it had a narrow area on the upwind end where a big gap in the underbrush opened into the open lower layers of the forest.

Tando spared Pell the embarrassment he'd feared by asking if he'd work his way around through the forest to the downwind end, then drive the deer toward the upwind opening. The other three men and the boy would hide near the meadow's easy exit point.

Pell's tensions eased. Most hunters would be hurt to be asked to drive rather than participating in the actual kill. Therefore, the youngest hunters were usually the drivers. However, Falin was a little too young and still limping on his healing ankle.

In any case, Pell felt grateful he wouldn't have to cast a spear in front of the others.

While the other four slowly made their way into position at the upwind opening, Pell took his time, working far around the clearing. He knew he wasn't as quiet as other hunters, but he stayed wide of the clearing and managed not to spook the deer. Pell's scent did start exciting the deer right before he stepped into the upwind opening of the clearing.

He began striding noisily towards them. Looking frequently back at Pell, the deer moved up the clearing to the relatively narrow exit. The deer stayed focused on Pell and didn't notice the other hunters. Tando leaped out from behind a tree to plunge a spear into the closest deer. Unhurt by the cast spears of Deltin, Manute, and Falin, the other deer bounded away, but the one Tando had struck only made it a few hundred yards. It probably would have led them on quite a chase, but a large wolf abruptly appeared and brought it down. Pell's heart leaped.

Ginja was back!

Laughing, Tando restrained Deltin from charging the wolf with his spear to reclaim their kill. "Stop! Deltin stop, that's *Pell's* wolf," he chuckled, grasping Deltin's spear arm. Deltin looked on with amazement when the wolf lifted its head up from the neck of the deer it had just brought down.

Not to snarl, but to nuzzle Pell's hand when he trotted up.

Carrying the gutted deer on a pole back to camp, their spirits rose as they bantered back and forth. The successful hunt seemed an extraordinary omen to the two men from the shattered tribe. Pell was happy to see Tando so obviously enjoying the hunt. When Manute and Deltin took their turn carrying the deer Tando slowed his walk so they pulled ahead of himself and Pell. "That was great fun, eh?"

Pell, though he'd only been the hunt's driver, nonetheless exulted in relief at having been spared the embarrassment he'd so feared. "Yes! And a great omen for them too, I agree."

"I think you should invite them to join your tribe."

Pell was startled. "My tribe? It doesn't seem to me that we're really a tribe, but if the three of us make a tribe, it must be *your* tribe. You're the biggest, the strongest, and the best hunter. Anyhow, I'm not sure they want to join us?"

"Why wouldn't they join us?! Think Pell! They're homeless, hurt and they've lost all the winter stores their tribe had set aside. The question should be, 'Why would you let them join us?' *You're* the one who has all the food stored for the winter. You're the one who has no fear of starving during the cold months. The only dangers you face are attacks by other tribes." Tando looked musingly ahead at Manute and Deltin, "Anyway, I think that you've got more than enough smoked meat to feed the three of us, *and* the six of them, through the winter. It'd be worth sharing our stores so we'd have the extra hands for defense." He shrugged, "Besides, with a few more deer smoked away, even nine of us wouldn't go hungry."

They walked in silence a little way. Pell spoke, "I guess you're right. We should invite them to join us, but I just can't think of myself as the leader of our tribe. If one of them disagreed with me, I could never enforce a decision. Roley could tell anyone to do anything without getting an argument because he's so strong. I don't even think of the things a leader should, like whether their tribe would join us. I know that you're grateful for the fact that I set your wrist, but, 'my tribe?' No, it's not mine."

"You were here first. You saved my arm and… therefore my life," Tando said, emotion thick in his voice. "So I owe you my allegiance. The spirits taught you about the snares that have provided us with such a profusion of game, and the smoking that preserves it for us. But," he shrugged, "if you want, I could be the leader." He lowered his voice, "I'd still do what you say."

"Well, I suppose… that'd be okay. When will you ask them to join us?"

"Soon."

They caught up with Deltin and Manute and took a turn carrying the deer. Tando asked the other two what they planned to do when Panute was better. The matter of fact way Tando assumed Panute would recover astonished Pell, and he suspected it surprised Deltin and Manute as well. However much Deltin and Manute might think Tando's assumption was unwarranted, they made no comment on it.

As Tando talked to them, it soon became apparent they had no real plans as yet. They'd been assuming they'd return to the area of their previous cave, or to the area where they'd traditionally wintered. Their winter location was a smaller, more closed off cave in a small valley branching from the big river. They said, even in winter, some small game could usually be found in the little valley. Although they didn't say as much, Pell could tell the two were worried about how they'd survive the coming winter without the grain and roots the tribe had stored in their river cave.

In his mind's eye, Pell pictured Panute surviving her illness, only to starve in the winter due to her weakened state. He realized that in a similar situation, Roley would already have declared Agan and Panute ginja. Knowing the tribe couldn't possibly survive the winter while trying to support them, he'd have cast them out immediately so they wouldn't diminish what few stores the tribe could still put by for the winter.

Roley certainly wouldn't have spent time and energy traveling somewhere in an attempt to heal someone in Panute's condition. With dismay Pell recognized that he considered such a decision, the very same abhorrent decision he'd have despised Roley for making, to be wiser than risking the lives of the entire tribe during what was sure to be a difficult winter even for its healthy members.

Pell wondered if Gia's tribe didn't cast people out, or whether they *would* declare the two sickly ones ginja, but only when it was too late because the death spirit already hung over the entire tribe.

Tando looked over at the two of them as they walked alongside. "Who leads your tribe now?"

"Agan still leads us," Manute said, seeming surprised it wasn't obvious. "She's led our tribe for over twenty summers. It's why we're known as 'Aganstribe.'"

"Agan?!" Nonplused, Pell said, "How can she be your leader? Anyone who disagreed with her could simply… c-cast her aside. Then they could proclaim themselves the leader."

Deltin stared at Pell. "The tribe chooses her as leader because she's so wise. She always consults with the people of the tribe before making up her mind. We have our say before she makes any decisions. I guess if she starts making bad ones, we'll choose someone else, but it hasn't happened yet. We choose anew at the midwinter feast each year."

Tando blinked, "How do you 'choose' a leader?"

"Well, you'd be surprised at how complex we've made it! Five adults are chosen from volunteers by voice acclamation of the tribe at a feast the night before.

"Those five pick from a pile of river pebbles, taking turns and each trying to get the largest but, of course, eventually getting some pebbles that are pretty small. When each of the five has one pebble for each member of the tribe, they dole them out to tribe members after the people lie down to sleep that night, putting them in small baskets at the head of each person's sleeping place.

"They give pebbles out to people according to the value they feel that person has to the tribe; good hunters, powerful medicine makers and excellent mothers get large pebbles while children and those who've been lazy are given small pebbles.

"Before anyone moves, Agan designates someone to check each basket and be sure that each person has five pebbles, one for each of the five 'valuators'. Agan thinks that the next part is the most important event of the year, when each person finds out how they're viewed by the members of the tribe.

"Believe me your heart's pounding with fear that you might find five tiny pebbles in your basket! Some, when they've been particularly slothful, have found grains of sand. You hold your pebbles in your possession until the next night, when you place your pebbles in the basket of the person you feel would make the best leader.

"The person with the heaviest basket at the end of the night becomes the next year's leader. Sometimes, in the past twenty winters, others besides Agan have had quite a few pebbles in their baskets, but never enough to make it close. Those people always give any pebbles they accumulate to Agan when they realize they can't win. She finishes the night with all the pebbles every year."

Reminiscing about it brought tears to the eyes of Manute and Deltin, especially when they spoke of the people of their decimated tribe. Neither Tando nor Pell knew what to say, so the group walked on in silence for a while.

Pell pondered the concept of the leader "consulting" with the tribe before making important decisions. It seemed to be a good thing to do, but it was hard to imagine Roley ever doing such a thing.

Pell felt bad that he and Tando had, just a few minutes ago, decided to ask the others to join their tribe without thinking about whether Donte might welcome them.

Tando didn't say anything about joining the tribes for the rest of the walk back to the cave. Instead, once Manute and Deltin regained their composure, he carried on a cheery conversation about hunting techniques and enthusiastically described some of the big kills he'd been in on.

~~~

They and their deer were welcomed back at the cave with a great deal of excitement. Agan and Gia immediately began preparing the heart and liver of the deer for Panute, saying that some of the spirit of the deer resided there and would help her heal.

When Pell heard the words, "help her heal," he felt the hair prickle on the back of his neck and looked at Panute more closely. He'd avoided looking at her when they first got back, fearing the worst. Elated, he saw she *did* look better. Still wan, but now even he could tell some of the redness had faded from her arm.

Pell's insides did little gyrations and he wanted to jump up and down. He looked over to see if Tando and Donte had noticed Panute's condition as well and saw them in deep conversation off to one side. So instead, he went over to speak to Panute. As he approached, she smiled, waving with her good hand at her bad arm. "It's much better, Pell! It doesn't hurt as much and I'm not so feverish. I thank you, and beg you to thank the spirits for me."

She tilted her head indicating mild puzzlement, "Whichever spirits you called on?"

Pell was embarrassed. How could he tell Panute that he really didn't know much about the spirits? He momentarily considered pretending he did, but remembered his promise not to act like Pont had. Without speaking much, he adjusted the splints on her leg, changed the poultice on her hand and retreated to the cooking fire where he carefully watched the special preparations of the deer's organs.

Preparing them involved cooking the strips briefly and rolling them in crushed herbs. Before presenting them to Panute, Gia and Agan chanted mystically over them awhile, their voices weaving a strange harmony.

When they brought the strips to Panute, she frowned and said, "It doesn't matter how many herbs you put on it, I'm still not going to like the taste of the liver." Nonetheless, she dutifully ate several strips of it. On the other hand, she consumed her portion of the heart with relish.

Gia set much of the rest aside for Panute to eat over the next two days, but everyone else got a small strip of heart and liver at dinner. Pell found the heart edible but, as usual, almost couldn't choke the liver down. Gia talked about how eating them strengthened your own heart and liver. Listening to her, Pell managed to swallow it. In fact, by focusing on how Gia's gray eyes flashed as she spoke, he got it down without noticing the flavor all that much.

A pause came in the conversation and Tando cleared his throat. "I've spoken with Pell and Donte and our group of three here at Cold Springs, has a proposition for you members of Aganstribe." Pell stared at Tando. *So, that's what Tando had been talking to Donte about earlier?*

Pell didn't think Tando would've considered talking to Donte about uniting the groups before hearing Deltin's description of how things were done in Aganstribe. Pell realized that the descriptions of Agan's consultations must have made as big an impression on Tando as they had on him.

Everyone turned to listen so Tando went on, "Your poor tribe's been so badly damaged that it's too small to be safe. You'll have a hard time hunting for enough food... especially with winter coming. We'd like to invite you to join us here in Cold Springs. We believe the successful hunt today was a good omen."

Startled looks passed among Agan's group. Surprise and disbelief held the greatest sway. They all eventually looked to Agan. The old woman slowly looked from Tando, to Donte, to Pell, and then back into the fire. After gazing there for a while she began, "This is a generous offer to make, late in the fall, to a group with one old woman, one sick woman, one child and no stores laid by. We must think on it well. I myself do not know you well enough to say yes, having only met you one time before yesterday. I must admit that yesterday... yesterday, I thought it had been a great mistake to come here." This last came out in a rush.

Everyone waited while Agan continued staring into the fire for a while. Finally, she looked up at Pell, "I... I had... had never heard of such a thing as to cut away a part of someone. *Certainly*, I'd never considered the possibility that inflicting an additional injury might help to heal a person and so... I thought it, at best—a terrible mistake, at worst—a grievous depravity."

She reached up to wipe a tear from her eye and continued emotionally, "And now I see... see clearly that I'm just too simple to understand what Pell was doing. Now, I understand that all that I've truly learned of the three of you," she swept her gaze over them, "has been good. Both from what Gia told me of the time you helped with Falin's ankle, and from this time when you've helped Panute. Now…" her voice broke to a whisper, "now you offer to help us through a winter that will almost certainly claim my life, and possibly the lives of the rest of my tribe."

Agan turned to gaze into the fire again.

Still, no one else tried to say anything.

Eventually, she looked back up. "Grateful as I am, as all of us in our broken little tribe should be, we must talk on this joining. Both of our groups look to be in for a *very* hard winter. You have a *little* food stored up, while we have *none*. We know how to hunt in our regular wintering area, but we don't know how to hunt here. For that matter, I understand this is your first winter at Cold Springs as well. Perhaps you won't know how to hunt winter game in this area either? If our two tribes did join, perhaps it should be in our area? Before we decide whether to join, let's talk about how things would be decided, and, who would be our leader."

Pell hadn't heard the old matron say so much at one time before—later he'd appreciate that she seldom said much, preferring to listen and steer the conversations of others with a word or two now and then.

However, he felt astonished not only at the length of her speech, but the wisdom it contained.

~~~

Discussion of the union of the two groups ranged on late into the evening and spanned many topics. They spoke of the dangers of being raided by another tribe— here it seemed that the members of Aganstribe had little fear, having gotten on well with their neighbors for many years. First because of Agan's and now because of

Gia's reputation as a healer, the tribes near them truly wanted to remain their friends.

Another factor mitigating any rush to join the Cold Springs band on their part was the expectation that they had a good chance of being taken in by one of those neighboring tribes. However, they worried they might have to split up and go to two separate tribes if no one tribe felt it could take all six of them.

As they talked, Pell gathered that Aganstribe's plight wasn't as wretched as he and Tando'd imagined. In fact, as the conversation continued, he realized that most other tribes were less tyrannical and aggressive than the Aldans had been. Few, perhaps, were as democratic as Aganstribe, but it appeared the risk that Agan's little band might be massacred by their neighbors was much lower than the risk for those at Cold Springs.

They spoke of winter stores, where it appeared that Agan's group had nothing. Agan acknowledged that Pell's group had stores, but she didn't think their stores were enough by any means. Pell said, "We have some spirit meat hidden away..." but he caught Tando's warning glance. It looked as though Tando had wanted to keep that secret a little longer. When Pell asked him about it later, Tando said that he hadn't wanted Agan's group joining just to get access to their stored food, but rather because they were willing to work together to survive the winter.

Revealing they had some hidden meat had some benefit though, for when Agan heard that they had hidden food stores, she shrugged, "Actually, our little tribe had already stored some grain at their winter cave before the flood. If you have some extra meat, our stored grain makes a good match."

They moved on to talking about governance. After hearing more of how Agan's tribe had worked out their differences, the Cold Springs band agreed it seemed much fairer than what they were used to. However, that form of democracy depended on everyone in the tribe knowing each other well, a situation that didn't exist as yet for any joined group they might form.

They decided to talk about what each person's particular skills were. Agan described Manute as a hunter with a second skill in leatherwork, Deltin as a woodworker with a second skill in hunting and Panute as a gatherer with secondary skills for cooking and basket weaving. She and Gia were medicine women who also gathered; though, due to her arthritic joints, Agan could no longer gather. Falin was too young to have shown a skill yet.

Tando described himself as a hunter with a second skill for flint-working, Donte as a gatherer, basket weaver and cook, and Pell as a bonesetter and a toolmaker. Tando grinned a moment, then said, "And, if you do join us, I promise you'll be surprised by some of the tools he makes!"

Pell wondered a moment what "tools" Tando spoke of, but realized that he was probably referring to the snares.

Agan thought for a moment, then said, "We'll need other skills, a maker of clay pots, a fire starter and keeper, and a real flint worker. I'm sorry Tando, but I've seen some of the flints you've worked yourself, they're serviceable tools, but we'll want better. We need more good hunters and gatherers, even though I can tell from the quantities of grain and root vegetables you have here that Donte gathers more than most women can." Pell thought for a moment of interrupting to tell her that he and Tando also knew how to gather, and that their efforts had contributed to the volume of the Cold Springs' stores. He thought better of it, *Tando may not want them to know that yet either.*

Agan frowned and went on, "And, we have far too many healers. We may be able to trade our healing services to other tribes someday, but that won't happen until other tribes learn of our skills." She shook her head despairingly, "Even joined, our tribe will still be too small, though better than if we remain separate."

They talked on and on until much later than their usual sleeping time. Agan ultimately said, "Well, we've learned a lot about one another. Nonetheless, we have much more to learn during the following days while we wait until Panute might be well enough to travel. We need not decide whether we should join our tribes until she's healthy. Let's *all* think on the wisdom of this joining over the next days."

***

The next day dawned crisp and clear with leaves raining down out of the trees, blowing and swirling, sure signs of winter's approach. They talked more during breakfast. Manute asked about their hunting techniques. At first, Tando described typical hunting techniques such as they'd used when they lived with Roley. Manute continued to probe, asking about the smaller animals they brought in so frequently. Animals that didn't look like they'd been speared...

The conversation stopped briefly while Tando gazed at him, brow furrowed. After a moment he said, "You suspect that we have *another* means of hunting. We do. But it's a very important secret for us." He shrugged,

"One so effective that we believe it can get us *and* you through the winter with enough meat. We'll share this secret with you *if* our tribes join. Perhaps you feel that we should share our secret freely, even if we don't join, for it's true that our ability to hunt wouldn't be diminished by sharing our secret. But... just as much as you *need* to learn our new hunting methods and our technique for preserving meat, so we *need* more strong hunters to protect ourselves from raiding by larger tribes."

Pell felt guilty. He felt they should share their secrets with their friends. However, he definitely felt the same need that Tando felt. Pell really wanted to have more strong men at his side during any confrontations with the Aldans. Any inner shame he had didn't overrule such self-interest.

After eating, Manute began preparing the skin of the deer from the previous day's kill. While Pell and Tando cut the meat into strips for smoking, Pell watched Manute's preparations with great interest. As he scraped away at the skin, Manute cheerfully described each of the many steps required to make the skin into supple leather.

Pell pulled Tando aside and suggested they teach Agan's group how to smoke meat. He felt it'd be a gesture of good faith toward the joining of the tribes. As before, Tando opposed sharing their most powerful secrets. Pell, however, pointed out that it was going to be hard to hide the technique, unless they wanted to try to set up a completely new smoking site. Otherwise, they'd be smoking meat in the cave right there in front of their guests. Surely Aganstribe would divine the important principles without explanation.

Tando finally agreed. But then he made a big show of how, in their gratitude for Manute's lessons on working leather, they were going to teach their guests from Aganstribe the secret of preserving meat. They brought in some lumps of the dirty rock salt and put them in a skin full of water. After enough had dissolved to make the water taste quite salty, they soaked thinly sliced strips of deer meat in it. Next, they stretched the meat over the branches of the dead bush in the high recess where their smoking occurred.

During a pause in the meat-smoking lesson, Manute cracked open the deer's skull and scooped out the brains. He rubbed the brains into the deerskin, continuing to demonstrate more of the steps in the leather working process. As they came to trust one another more, they went into more and more detail on the techniques, eventually holding back none of their little secrets.

Deltin finished making a new spear shaft to replace one damaged while killing the deer the day before. Then, while the others kept working on their projects, he lashed together a frame of small straight, wooden shafts. Pell studied the frame in puzzlement, finally asking what it was for. To his surprise, Deltin told him it was for smoking their meat strips. Pell immediately saw how this regular frame would be more effective and efficient than the random arrangement of branches in the dead bush they'd been using.

***

Pell and Gia worked together to change poultices on Panute's hand. At first, he'd been surprised when she didn't just do it herself. On the third day after the amputation, Pell had been about to leave to check their snares. Gia'd said, "Before you go, shouldn't we change Panute' bandage?"

Pell had turned slowly in surprise. Gia looked concerned. He said, "Uh, I thought you were the expert with bandages and poultices?"

Gia looked at him for a moment. Then, eyes twinkling, she said, "But I don't know anything about finger removal. You *have* to help me."

Rather than remind Gia that he didn't know anything about amputation wounds himself, Pell untied the soft leather of the bandage and tugged off the old poultice. He saw a puffy area on the back of the hand and touched it with a finger. When he did, pus immediately gushed out of the wound.

Gia's eyes had widened, "See! I wouldn't have known to do that. The evil humours would have remained in her hand!"

Too embarrassed to say he'd had no idea that touching it would squeeze pus out, Pell shrugged and massaged it to squeeze out a little more. When Gia put the new poultice in place, she held it with one hand, then put Pell's hand on top of hers and her other hand on top of his. She intoned a brief chant while Pell stared at their intertwined hands. Her hands felt so warm!

Pell had goosebumps all up his arm.

This became their routine, Pell taking off the dressing and gently massaging Panute's hand, Gia putting on the new poultice and then they'd sit with their hands intertwined for a few moments while Gia chanted.

The intertwining of their hands quickly became the highlight of each of Pell's days.

***

Days passed and stretched into hands of days. Panute's sickness faded and her leg began to hurt less. The wound where her fingers had been cut off turned bright red and became fragile, bleeding easily when it was disturbed during the dressing changes. This worried Pell, but with time the wound slowly contracted and got smaller.

Panute began using her remaining two fingers and thumb, soon becoming remarkably facile with them, weaving light baskets and sewing furs into winter clothing. Saying she preferred to stay busy, as long as someone brought her materials to work with, she made what she could. The swelling in her leg slowly went down and Pell took out the fur padding a little at a time, gradually snugging up the straps around the splints.

Her leg looked straight, though it was a little shorter than the other leg. It also continued to turn somewhat outward at the foot. This twisted, shortened condition worried Pell a great deal, but, because her leg hurt so much less as time passed, Panute seemed ecstatic about it.

Rather than being concerned about the remaining deformity, Panute enthused regularly about how much straighter it was than Rasad's. Rasad, a man from her old tribe, had broken his leg and had simply lain unsplinted in his bedding until it'd eventually healed. Healed, yes, but twisted and bowed, it rendered him a cripple for the rest of his life.

He'd apparently been reduced to performing menial tasks about the cave and staying home to defend their stores from animals while the tribe foraged. Pell thought such a life sounded sad, but much better than how such a person would have fared in the Aldans. Lucky if he wasn't cast out while the leg was healing. Certainly, he'd have been cast out when his twisted leg rendered him a cripple.

***

Panute sat up more and more, resting her back against a large bole of wood the men rolled in for her. One day Pell came in and, to his surprise, found her perched on top of the bole, feet resting on the ground. Pell'd rarely seen anyone sit anywhere other than on the ground, but she began to sit up there most of the day, saying her leg was more comfortable upright than laid out on the ground.

Not long after that Panute began to hop from place to place about the cave—and hop outside to urinate and move her bowels. She'd hated going in the rough clay pot they'd made for her and having to ask someone else to carry it away.

Tando and Pell continued to check the trap lines by themselves so that the others wouldn't learn the snaring secret unless they joined the tribe. They also went on group hunts with Manute and Deltin. Sometimes they made another kill. But the occasional large bounty from those hunts couldn't match the steady stream of small game provided by the snares. The profusion of small game was dropping off as the weather steadily grew cooler, but remained high enough that they were still smoking extra meat more often than they took any out of storage.

***

One day, when she awoke Panute said, "Pell when can I begin walking on my leg?" She'd already been resting its own weight on the ground without pain.

Knowing better than to protest that he didn't know, Pell said, "Let me look." He took her splints off and tested the bones. The leg was nothing like the floppy bag of bones he'd felt initially. Though her leg was swollen, the bones seemed solid to him. Hoping it was the right thing to do, he tied the splints back on and said, "I think you should put as much weight on your leg as you can, as long as it doesn't cause pain."

Panute immediately began carrying some weight on each step, even though her gait mostly remained a hop.

***

In the evenings, they sat around the fire and told stories. Agan had a talent for storytelling. Many of her stories were of true experiences from her long life, but some were stories she'd heard from travelers.

Gia told stories as well and Pell hung on her every word. Her stories, she said, were "pretend." They featured young lovers, meeting for the first time and being swept away. These young strangers often met at places where tribes met to trade. Remembering that he'd met Gia at the River Fork trading area, his heart leaped when she started one that way.

At Tando's urging, Agan at last agreed to another discussion of the subject of the joining of the tribes. In a good mood after a successful group hunt that had brought in a small pig, they discussed it in the evening over roast boar and grain stew. The group talked about it cheerfully, bantering back and forth. It soon appeared that everyone was comfortable making up a combined tribe and contented with the rules of governance that Aganstribe had used. However, there was disagreement about where they should live. The Cold Springs site provided the best cave, excellent water, and good hunting.

Privately, Pell and Tando thought their snares would probably work as well anywhere—perhaps better in a new location. After all, a snare always worked better when it was moved to a new site in the Cold Springs area. But they didn't know for sure whether snares would work at all in the Aganstribe area. Tando worried that it might be the spirits near Cold Springs that made snares work and that they'd only function in that one region.

Another point in favor of Cold Springs was that the cave was ready to be lived in, whereas a lot of work would be necessary at the Aganstribe winter cave. However, at the Aganstribe winter site, the neighbors were well known and friendly, while at Cold Springs, the Aldans and possibly other raiders could be a major concern.

They went through the baskets and pebbles routine to decide who would be their leader. Gia, Tando, Donte, and Deltin assigned the initial pebbles to decide worth. Pell felt greatly relieved that his basket didn't contain any tiny pebbles. In fact, he realized with surprise, his basket contained four of the largest pebbles from the initial pile! The next night when they redistributed the pebbles to decide leadership Pell was again surprised to find some pebbles in his basket, but he quickly passed them on, giving half to Tando and half to Agan, just as he had his original pebbles. Soon, Tando and Agan had most of the pebbles.

Pell was pretty sure that Agan had more than Tando, but before he could really see who had the most, Tando stood and carried his basket over, pouring its contents into Agan's. He looked around the group and said, "I thank those of you who gave me pebbles, but in the short time we've been together I've come to recognize Agan's wisdom. That first night when she admitted that she was wrong about Pell and the treatment of Panute, I was startled. I'd never been around a leader who admitted being wrong. I thought it was a sign of weakness. I've come to recognize it's not a sign of weakness, but of wisdom. She'll make a much better leader than I."

Though Pell had, out of loyalty, felt compelled to give half of his pebbles to Tando, secretly he agreed Agan would make a better leader.

Chapter Six

The next day Agan began talking to everyone, even Falin, about whether or not to move. Gradually it became evident that the vote would be for a move to the Aganstribe's winter cave for safety's sake. Tando pulled Pell and Donte aside and said, "I think it's time to tell them about the rest of our stores, don't you?"

They both nodded, they'd both been willing before, but neither pointed out that Tando had been the reticent one.

As they sat to eat their evening meal, Tando said, "There's another problem with moving that you don't know about yet."

Manute smiled broadly, "Let me guess. There's a place near here you haven't shown us. A place where rabbits, hares, groundhogs, squirrels and other small animals just walk up to you and wait to be clubbed?"

"No," Tando said with a grin, "though we're also worried that we might not be able to hunt those small animals as well near the Aganstribe cave as we can here." He shrugged, "Actually we hunt small animals pretty much wherever we want by using another of Pell's inventions."

"Inventions?" Manute said, frowning.

Tando looked at Pell, so Pell said, "It's a word I made up for a new way to do something."

Deltin looked back and forth from Tando to Pell. "How can there be a *new* way to hunt? You have to either spear or club animals. You can throw the spear or throw a rock, but those are just variations on spearing or clubbing. How else can you possibly kill them?"

Tando snorted, "I'd have asked *exactly* the same question. But Pell looks at things *sideways*. Tomorrow, we'll take you to see some 'traps.'"

"Traps? What's a trap?"

"It'll be easier to show you tomorrow."

"I won't be able to sleep tonight!" Manute protested.

"Hah! Well, let me give you something else to wonder about as you try to sleep," Tando said, rising and walking over to the side of the cave. He pushed a pile of bedding leaves to one side as Manute, Deltin, Gia, and Falin got up to come over and look as well. Eager to participate in the excitement, Panute heaved herself up off her log and hobbled over to watch Tando scrape dirt away from the floor of the cave. A moment later Pell and Donte started helping him.

They'd soon exposed a row of poles bound and woven to one another.

Gia said, "It's like the wall of the cave! Was there another opening here, in the floor instead of the wall?"

Tando grinned up at her, "No, we had to *dig* this opening in the cave." He started to heave up on the raft, tugging it loose until it came free and could be lifted into the air. Tando said, "We call it a cellar."

The old members of Aganstribe stood staring down into the exposed pit in the floor. A pit filled with bundles of smoked meat, piles of edible roots, and stacks of shallow baskets filled with grain or dried fruit!

"Spirits!" exclaimed Manute.

"What is it?" Agan asked, picking up her sticks and trying to push herself to her feet. A moment later Manute came over to help Agan get up and over to the edge of the hole. She blinked several times, then she also exclaimed, "Spirits," in a hushed and reverential tone. The previous members of Aganstribe glanced at one another. With cracked emotion, Agan said, "And I thought we'd be doing the Cold Springs people a favor by letting them into our tribe..." she shook her head. "How *did* you put so much aside?"

Tando and Donte both looked at Pell.

Pell only shrugged shyly.

Tando grinned around at the group. "It's these crazy ideas of Pell's. Trapping brings in so much meat. Smoking lets us preserve it, hopefully, so it'll last all winter. And," he dropped his voice to a near whisper, "the craziest idea of them all... that men can do women's work and women can do men's work!"

Gia frowned, then smiled. If this was true, it made Pell even more attractive in her eyes, "You mean Donte didn't gather all these roots, grains and fruit herself?! You men helped?!"

Donte grinned and nodded.

Agan said musingly, "This'll make it quite a bit harder to move to our old home. It'd require more than one trip."

Tando snorted, "And this is our *small* cellar."

Eyes widened, the Aganstribers stared. Finally, Agan said unbelievingly, "There's *more*?"

Tando nodded. "There's a bigger cellar on the other side of the cave. And..." he paused, grinning.

"And *what?!*" Gia exploded.

"We've stored supplies elsewhere in case we're attacked here and someone takes over our cave and everything in it."

Gia drew her head back, "How much do you have there?"

Tando looked at Pell, "He figured it."

Pell, finding everyone looking at him, scuffed a foot in the dirt. He said, "I did some counting and I thought the 'broken slab' site would have enough to keep the three of us through the winter if we could be just a little bit successful hunting. We'd be hungry though."

"So, with nine of us we'd be *really* hungry," Agan said.

Gia said, "You know how to count?! Who taught you?"

To Gia, Pell said, "Our medicine man, Pont. He spoke the counting words a lot in his ceremonies. Even though he didn't use them for anything, I think they're helpful for figuring out if you have enough of something." Pell turned to answer Agan with a shrug, "We'd be *very* hungry if we could only get access to the broken slab site."

Agan's eyebrows rose, "There's more than one site?!"

Pell ducked his head, "We have two other sites besides the one at the broken slab."

"It'd take a *lot* of trips to move all of it," Tando said.

"Wow," Manute said shaking his head. "I don't want to even think about how hard it would be moving that much stuff."

Deltin said, "Maybe we could just move some now, then come back later when we needed more."

Shaking his head, Tando said, "I wouldn't want to have to carry big loads in the middle of winter. Besides, living here, we check on the three other sites when we go out trapping to be sure nothing's disturbing them."

"You've got to teach us this 'trapping' soon," Manute said.

They turned the grain in the cellar. Then while they were covering the cellar back up and the former Aganstribe members were trying to come to grips with the astonishing quantity of stores at Cold Springs, Ginja began growling.

She rose up from her place beside the fire. Bristling, she stalked toward the opening of the cave and stuck her head through the heavy patchwork curtain of skins Manute had hung there to keep the cold autumn breezes out. Looking at each other, the men quickly rose and got their spears.

Tando unlashed the stack of spears near the door and took a second spear in his left hand. He offered a second spear to the other men, but only Manute took one. Tando whispered to Donte and she and Gia lifted a quilt of small animal furs off one of the beds and held it between the fire and the door to cast the cave opening in darkness.

After all their talk, Pell felt in his bones that raiders must be coming to attack. With embarrassment, he felt himself trembling.

After his eyes had adjusted to the dark, Tando moved to the edge of the door and carefully peered out through one of the gaps between the opening and the hanging leather. After a moment, he said, "Boro?"

"Tando?"

Pell peered out too. Sure enough, it was Pell's former friend Boro. Pell was shocked at his appearance. The boy shuffled up, emaciated, shivering and foul smelling.

As well, Boro seemed short. Really short. Pell quickly realized this was only in comparison to his own unrestricted adolescent growth spurt. They had difficulty getting Ginja to let Boro into the cave and more difficulty convincing the boy that it was okay to come into a dwelling where there was a growling wolf.

Eventually they got him settled in front of the fire. They fed him the remnants of their dinner. Boro's eyes gleamed at the food laid out before him, roast boar, boiled roots, Gia's bread cakes and a little stewed grain. Though Agan told him to eat slowly, he wolfed the food down—then bolted for the cave mouth to vomit. When he returned, he ate a smaller quantity at a slower pace under Agan's watchful eye.

Once Boro had some food in him, they began to ply him with questions. His story was grim, but as it unfolded it made them all, even Pell, wonder if they shouldn't move away from the area.

~~~

"Things first started to get bad when my father, Bonat, was killed in a hunt," Boro told them. "The hunters had chased a boar into a small ravine and cornered it. Bonat and that coward Denit had blocked the boar in." Boro's tone dripped loathing as he spoke of Denit, then he choked up about his father. After a moment Boro continued, "The boar turned the tables on them, breaking Bonat's spear point, then catching Bonat in a twist of the ravine.

Denit had a good angle of attack on the boar's left side because the boar had focused on my father, but, because the boar was raging, Denit held back—like the coward he is. He only surged in to spear the boar when Gontra arrived to spear it as well. But, while Denit was trying to chivvy up some courage, the boar tusked Bonat's arm..."

Boro's voice broke again and he paused for a bit. When he returned to the story he spoke hoarsely, "Bonat didn't die right away. He lingered for days while the tusk wounds developed the fever. He got delirious at the end, openly and repeatedly accusing Denit of cowardice."

"I'll bet that pissed Roley off," Tando said.

Boro shook his head, "Roley just got sad when he first heard someone else's honest opinion of his son. So sad that for a while he stopped getting out of his bed. He didn't take the band out on hunts. We ate fairly well on what the women gathered, because it was the best part of summer. However, everyone was upset because it was the "fat" part of the summer when we normally gorge ourselves to build our fat for the winter.

When we did start hunting again, Roley seemed detached. The hunts were disorganized and they rarely succeeded. Roley lost command of the group. Hunt after hunt failed. Finally, someone suggested that, to change their luck, someone else should lead a hunt. Roley shrugged and said, 'Okay' but before anyone else stepped up, *Denit* volunteered!"

Boro looked at Tando and lifted an eyebrow. "Believe it or not, Roley said, that was a good idea!"

Boro said astonishment engulfed the Aldans' hunters as they found themselves led out on an extremely important hunt by such a young and inexperienced hunter. However, since they'd all feared Roley would refuse to let *anyone* else lead a hunt, they initially viewed it as somewhat of a success.

However, Denit's hunt strategies were crazy. Every animal bolted before anyone even came close to getting a spear into it. Frustration mounted as, unexpectedly, their bellies growled even in the summer.

Boro sighed, "Rather than admit there was a problem, Denit got even more arrogant."

Interrupting with a snort, Tando said, "I didn't think *that* was possible."

"Yeah, well, he did." Boro said, "And he never even *considered* letting someone else lead a hunt. Roley backed Denit's decisions and, strong as he is, no one argued with him."

"Pell, after you were cast out, Denit turned on me," Boro said. "I started getting the brunt of Denit's bullying."

Boro told how Denit's mood darkened through failed hunt after failed hunt. He began to deride Boro, blaming him for everything that went wrong. One day Denit accused Boro of somehow alerting a small herd of antelope.

In an angry response, Boro made the ultimate mistake of repeating his father's accusations about Denit's cowardice.

By that time Denit was only bullying, not leading the hunters. He only got away with it under the threat of his increasingly irrational father's violence.

Upon Boro's explosion, Denit cast Boro out. Roley stood sullenly and wordlessly beside Denit as he did it, so no one had had the courage to take Boro's side.

Pell realized that being cast out at the beginning of winter—rather than the beginning of spring like Pell had been—would have been much more difficult. Boro hadn't had a boar's carcass to start his isolation with either. He'd unearthed a few root vegetables occasionally, but that'd been mostly by accident, since he didn't really have a clue how to find them. He just pulled up random plants, hoping they might have edible roots, but finding few. The root vegetables made a poor diet by themselves. Boro mixed them with the relatively abundant wild onions hoping that some variety might make his diet a little healthier.

Boro'd hung around the periphery of the Aldan's camp, hoping they might take pity and let him back in. Instead, Denit organized stone throwing parties to chase him away, accusing him of continuing to bring them bad luck.

Boro's mother had covertly taken grain out to him once or twice, but that was a dangerous undertaking when Roley was in such an unstable state of mind. Especially with the vindictive Denit steering Roley's actions. The last time Boro's mother came out to him, she told him, "You should go to Cold Springs Ravine. That's where Tando and Donte went when they wanted to find Pell. If they're still alive, maybe you could join them."

Pell, whose emotions had been mixed on first seeing Boro, virtually exploded. "You! You come to *my* camp asking for *help*! Did you help me when Roley was casting me out? No! You chanted 'ginja' alongside the others! *I* 'set' Gontra's finger— you and Gontra and Exen should have stood by me! But *you,* you especially should have stood with me! We swore an oath! You were supposed to leave… with me."

Boro blanched in terror. With a sick feeling, Pell realized Boro's life surely hung in the balance—if they didn't take him in, he'd soon starve.

Boro dropped, scrabbling, to Pell's feet, begging piteously for Pell's forgiveness. Dismayed, Pell looked up at the other members of their newly formed tribe. He saw expressions ranging from mild distaste over the emotional outbursts, to the outright horror registered on Gia's face.

Pell wasn't sure whether Gia's dismay emanated from what Boro'd done to Pell—a story she probably hadn't heard—or from considering Boro's fate if Pell drove the starving boy out.

As Pell stood looking at the other members of his new tribe, he recognized that, whether they liked his decision or not, they'd leave Boro's fate in his hands.

But, even if they did leave Boro to whatever fate Pell decided, Pell realized, if he cast the boy out, he'd lose the admiration his new tribe had for him. Even worse, he'd lose whatever esteem Gia had for him.

Thinking about it more, he found he'd lose respect for himself if he drove Boro out. He bent and tried to lift Boro, "Oh, for spirit's sake! Boro, get up. I won't turn you away just because you didn't protest Roley's casting me out—*you* couldn't have kept me in the tribe anyway."

Gasping, Boro clasped his arms about Pell's thighs and thanked him repeatedly. Pell couldn't believe how small his old friend's wasted arms felt as they wrapped about him. He still felt some loathing of Boro for chanting "ginja" with the others, but decided he felt glad the boy's starvation wouldn't weigh on his conscience.

***

Though the volume of stores at Cold Springs had pretty much decided the tribe on staying there, Boro's tale now made the group start talking again about moving out of the area. Unfortunately, the boy's addition to the tribe posed a problem because he wasn't in very good condition for a move. It wasn't just his poor health, though they could ill afford to move the two invalids they already had, much less three. For one thing, Boro had no warm footwear. It was getting colder and colder and the boy had no warm clothing.

He'd made it this far by only traveling during the warmest part of the day. The rest of the time he'd spent dug into drifts of fallen leaves. The leaves at least insulated, and in some cases actually heated him through their decomposition.

The group decided they couldn't consider moving for a few days. Manute could make Boro some moccasins and some of the others could patch together a makeshift cloak for him.

The next day they fed Boro three moderate-sized meals. The abundance of food put some energy back into him. Manute made him a good pair of fur-lined winter shoes while everyone else contributed some labor to a cloak consisting of a patchwork of furs. It was ill-made, as they didn't want to cut the skins until Manute could work out a final cutting for a good coat. They just roughly stitched overlapping layers into an approximate shape. It didn't leave him good use of his arms, but it was thick and warm.

With the cloak finished, they were ready to leave the next day. Boro wouldn't move very fast, but neither would they, as each of the able-bodied tribespeople would pull one of the travois Deltin had taught them to make. The travois would be loaded with either stores or an invalid. At the new cave, they'd leave Falin and Boro to care for Agan and Panute.

Gia, Manute, Deltin, Donte, Pell, and Tando would hurry back to pack up more supplies. If the weather remained good, they'd make a third trip.

The morning they were going to leave, Tando brought up another problem. "From what Boro's said, the Aldans must know where we live. We're leaving a lot of important stores behind during this first trip." He looked around at the others, "What if Denit comes to raid us while we're gone? We still have a lot of important goods stored openly here in the cave, awaiting our second trip. We could lose tools and other things we really need—without even having a chance to defend our possessions!"

They all looked around at the things they hadn't room to pack for the trip. Not just food, but bundles of spear shafts, the smoking frame, stacks of leather and fur. Deltin said, "Is there a place nearby where we could hide this stuff? Perhaps not as good as the 'escape' sites where you've hidden the food. Just a place where they wouldn't find our tools."

After some discussion and a little argument, they began moving supplies to a couple of large crevices a little farther up Cold Springs Ravine from the cave. They crammed their goods into them, packing rocks and thorn brush in on top to conceal the hoards.

They left the food hidden under the floor of the cave where it was. It seemed unlikely Denit would think to dig up the floor. They also left quite a bit of food and firewood in the cave for him to steal. They'd decided they could afford to lose *some* food as long as it kept the Aldans from searching, and thus finding the rest of it.

***

Most everything had been moved and Pell was inside with Gia, Agan, Panute, Boro, and Falin, re-packing some things before they left. Tando, Deltin,

Manute, and Donte had climbed up the ravine to hide a final load of stores.

Pell heard a gratingly familiar voice calling out.

"Tando? You in there?" The voice broke as it spoke so that Pell wasn't sure of its intended tone—was it threatening? Querulous? Friendly? Broken or not, that voice belonged to Denit, there was no doubt in Pell's mind. Ginja raised her head, growling menacingly.

Saying, "Great spirit! That's Denit!" Pell grabbed his spear and ran over to peer out the flap covering the cave entrance. Ginja shouldered Pell's knees aside to look out herself, her growl turning into a low, vicious sounding snarl, hair standing up all along her back. Pell got a clear look, it *was* Denit!

Pell heard rattling as the others grabbed spears behind him. However, Pell desperately thought about how their three strongest hunters were all up the ravine! Denit was about thirty feet from the entrance to the cave, down at the foot of the little walkway leading up from the clearing.

Denit seemed thin, though not nearly as skeletal as Boro. Dirty, disheveled, and unkempt, Pell thought he looked like a dead animal's carcass. Pell remembered how difficult it had been for Denit's mother to get him to cut or braid his hair. His furs lay in ragged layers, looking like they hadn't been off his body for moons.

Roley stood behind Denit looking like he'd been chewing Pont's hemp. In fact, Pell thought he still had a wad of it in one cheek. The healer stood behind Denit too, as did Belk, Gontra, and Exen. Pell suddenly realized that with the loss of Pell, Tando, Bonat, and Boro, these six were all the hunters that remained in Roley's band.

Still, they had more hunters than the Cold Springs band. The huge, dominating Roley was, all by himself, a fearsome force. Pell found himself trembling, "Hello Denit. What do you want?" Pell felt pleased his own voice didn't break.

"Pell?"

"Yes."

"Doesn't Tando live here?"

"Yes."

"I want to talk to him."

"He'll be back soon." Pell certainly hoped so.

"Then I'll wait and talk to him when he gets back." Denit turned and began whispering to Pont.

Gia was looking out the other side of the flap. "Pell," she whispered, "is that all of their hunters?"

"Yes," he whispered back.

"Do you think they're here on a raid?"

"Yes… Maybe we should just give them some spirit meat?"

For a moment she didn't respond. Then she said, "Do you think if we gave them some, they'd leave? Then, if we hurried, we could finish moving before they came back for more."

"Maybe. But the more I think about it, the more I think it's pretty risky. If we gave them some, they'd probably decide we must have more. I think they'd just decide to attack us for whatever we might have left."

Denit turned away from the healer. "Hey Pell, is that sniveling whiner Boro with you?"

Pell glanced back and saw Boro, big-eyed and shaking. To Denit he said, "Boro's here, yes."

"You know, he wasn't any better at hunting than you were. Worse really, kept driving away all the game. Does Tando really think he can bring in enough meat to feed both you girls in wintertime?" Denit laughed at his own joke. A couple of the others snickered erratically with him.

Pell swallowed. He felt humiliated that he'd been insulted in such a fashion with Gia listening. He tried desperately to think of a witty response but nothing came to mind.

He couldn't bring himself to look toward Gia, especially while he knew he was blushing in embarrassment. "We've joined with another group now. We've got more hunters than just the three of us."

"Great! We had some really bad hunts when Boro was bringing us bad luck. Now that we're rid of him, we're planning a big fire drive hunt down in the valley to put away a big supply of meat just before winter's freeze. We need more 'good' hunters to do it well. Maybe Tando and your new hunters could join us. We'd split the meat with them."

Pell was afraid to say they didn't need any meat. That would *certainly* make them the target of a raid. "Well, maybe we could," Pell said, stalling for time. *Why aren't Tando and the others back yet?!*

Denit laughed. "Not 'we' Pell. Girls like you and Boro aren't what we need on this hunt. We want *hunters*." He laughed some more at his own wit, nudging Exen with an elbow.

Gontra looked over at Denit, "I know Boro was bringing bad luck Denit, but Pell could certainly help with a fire drive."

"Oh come on Gontra. You know he's just as worthless as Boro. He almost killed Tando in that last hunt."

"Tando must have forgiven him. He lives with him now."

Pont leaped in front of Gontra, slavering. "You *know* that's just because Tando thinks Pell 'fixed his wrist.' I've explained over and over that it was *my* intervention with the Spirit of the horses—whose horses we were hunting when Tando got hurt. *My intervention*, which eventually resulted in the healing of Tando's wrist!"

Denit snarled, "Yeah, Gontra, just because *Tando* believes Pell's rubbish, that doesn't mean you should too." The group fell to arguing among themselves in a confused rumble that Pell couldn't interpret.

"What can we do, Pell?"

Pell turned to see Gia looking at him fearfully. Why was she asking him? He wasn't the leader of their little band. He looked over at Agan and said, "Agan...?" but Agan was also looking at him wide-eyed.

Agan slowly said, "Our tribe didn't get into fights with others. I don't know what to do. I do know that when tribes fight, their hunters do the fighting, but with Tando, Manute, and Deltin gone, you're our only hunter. What do you suggest?"

I'm the hunter? Pell thought anxiously. They certainly couldn't win by brute strength alone... he knew he wasn't a good hunter much less a fighter. His father would have said to use a tool but what tool? They needed to outwit the others.

All of a sudden Pell remembered the trap he'd set up on the path to the cave moons ago! "Wait!" he said with excitement, moving to the other side of the cave entrance flap and peering out. Yes! He could still see the braided leather rope going up the side of the cliff. It looked okay, though he hadn't checked it for many hands of days. The leather might've deteriorated from being out in the weather. What about the smaller rope going up to the trigger brace? He could see it was intact, but it also might be rotting. He peered up the cliff. The net full of rocks that served as the counterweight to drive the trap looked okay. If the leather in it had rotted, the rocks probably would have fallen out.

Denit and the others were farther down the path than the location of the noose though, so there wasn't any point in trying it right now.

Pell stepped over to the trigger rope, "Boro! No, Gia! Here, hold this rope. Hold it as if it were our very lives. If I call out 'pull,' jerk on it with all your might." Gia, looking puzzled, took the rope and gave it a tentative tug. "No!" Pell shouted, "Sorry! I didn't mean to yell, but don't pull on it *until* I say! Then, pull *hard*." Lowering his voice, he said, "It's *very* important *not* to pull on it before I say." He moved over to peer back out the flap. The argument amongst the Aldans had petered out, but they were still talking amongst themselves and looking furtively toward the cave entrance.

Denit turned, "Pell, why don't you come on out and talk to us? You don't have to hide in your cave; we don't mean you any harm." A little snicker at the end of his words belied the friendly tone.

Pell took a deep breath and stepped just outside the flap. "What do you want to talk about? Aren't you just waiting for Tando and our other hunters?"

Though Pell didn't understand why, Denit's little group looked shocked. They were astonished by the vigorous, healthy appearance of the strapping young man who'd appeared at the entrance of the cave. After a moment's hesitation, Denit said in a calculating tone, "Oh, aren't your *other* hunters here either Pell? Is it *just* you?" Before Pell could think of a response, he continued, "Oh my, look at you Pell, Tando's been feeding his little wifey well hasn't he? Did you know we've decided that Tando must be mating with *you*, now that Tellgif's dead? We can't imagine why else he'd keep an outcast *girl* like you around." Denit nudged Exen and barked a laugh at his own humor.

The color rose in Pell's cheeks. With a sinking sensation, he realized that, without any fear of other hunters who *might've* been present in the cave, Denit and his band were shuffling forward a little, preparing to attack. Despite the queasiness in his stomach, Pell felt his rage building. Astonished at his own temerity, he heard himself say, "Well *now*, if Tando were that sort, why wouldn't he have mated with you, Denit? Maybe because you *smell* so bad?"

Denit flushed with anger and stepped forward, hefting his spear. The others moved forward behind him, but they stopped, staring at a spot just behind Pell. When Pell glanced back, he saw that Ginja had shouldered the flap aside. Hackles up, lips curled back in an ugly rictus, she stood just outside the cave entrance, snarling. Spittle dripped from her maw as she took a few stalking steps forward.

Denit turned to snap at Pont, "I *told* you he controlled the Wolf Spirit!"

Pont gaped momentarily, then pulled out one of his rattles, admonishing, "The wolf spirit will be on *our* side soon." He started one of his chants.

Pell felt hugely relieved that Ginja's appearance had stopped them for now, but his mind roiled. When would Tando and the others get back?

Could the healer really bring Ginja under his control? He looked down uncertainly at the animal. Now that the Aldans had stopped approaching, Ginja'd stopped moving forward herself.

Pell looked back to Denit and the others. With dismay, he saw they'd crept a little closer. He shifted his grip on his spear.

Should he call Boro out to stand with him? Or would they attack all the faster when they realized that he really didn't have anyone but Boro to back him up?

Pell saw they were approaching the area where the noose was buried in the dirt. *Where was it exactly?* He couldn't see it, nor remember its precise location! *How long would it take to work? Would it work at all? Why didn't I try it out?*

At the time, he hadn't wanted to carry all that rock back up after tripping a test run, but that seemed a weak excuse now. Spirits! At least he could have marked its location better. He stood on his toes peering for evidence of its whereabouts.

"What's the matter, Pell? Afraid of our feet?" Denit's jeering tone roiled Pell's stomach further.

Denit danced ahead a few steps and cast his spear! Dodging, Pell shouted, "Pull! Gia, pull! Now!" Then he thought with horror that Denit was all the way on the near side of the trap. He didn't think the others were in it yet. "No! Don't!" As if in slow motion, he saw the small rope snap tight against his wishes.

Snarling, Ginja leaped forward to meet Denit.

Denit's spear missed Pell by a handspan, struck the wall behind him and clattered back.

Pell raised his own spear, wondering whether to cast it or save it for fighting hand to hand.

The rope of the snare burst up out of the dirt of the trail, closer to the cave entrance than Pell had thought. Denit was in its reach but only his trailing leg!

The rope snapped up the inside of his leg and the noose sawed shut about his knee. Jerked upside down, Denit shot up the cliffside.

As Pell watched Denit's screaming, jouncing transit up the face of the cliff, his gaze encountered the net full of rocks descending just beyond Denit.

Afterward, Pell would recall the events in short, slow-motion segments:

The net burst open.

A swarm of rocks, each the size of a man's head, exploded forth.

Denit's ascent hesitated, and then Denit began to descend again, preceded by the bounding stones.

Pell's gaze swung down to encounter Denit's band.

Their faces gaped upward openmouthed—the hunters simultaneously realized that those small boulders were hurtling at them.

All the hunters but Roley began to scatter.

Roley, staring dazedly upward, the wad of hemp visible in his gaping mouth.

Roley, struck on the head by one of the rocks, fell as if clubbed to the ground by a giant.

Denit bounded away from the cliffside as he descended.

The rope caught on something above so Denit swung back to slam into the rock face with a sick thud.

As the stones struck the path, clouds of dust puffed up so Pell could hardly see.

His horror grew as a bounding rock struck one of the Aldans a glancing blow to the back and tossed him bodily from the path.

Ginja yelped and scurried back toward Pell.

As he stared at the carnage, Pell dimly perceived the others coming out of the cave behind him.

Agonized screams rose from within the dusty cloud hanging over the path. *What've I done?* Pell thought with dismay.

In his mind, he'd always pictured the trap snaring a small group of enemies and lifting them a short distance off the path. There they would hang, arms bound at their sides by the rope, helplessly watching his triumphant approach. They'd plead for mercy and readily agree to whatever conditions he set.

Instead, Pell rushed toward them, gorge rising in his throat. He came first to Roley, thrashing violently about on the path. Pell stopped, staring, but fearful to approach closely because of his dread of being struck by Roley's powerful, wildly-swinging limbs. Limbs that Pell had learned to fear during his years in the Aldans.

Not knowing what to do, Pell looked about and saw someone lying just off the path, gasping in obvious pain. He moved that way. Worried about a counterattack, he looked cautiously about for the others. He thought he saw Exen running away in the distance. Perhaps, through the clearing dust, he saw someone else lurking near the edge of the trail.

Pell looked down and saw Belk was the one lying at the edge of the path. Belk twisted in agony and gripped the right side of his back. He gasped for breath, but hadn't turned blue like others Pell had seen dying for lack of breath. Pell knelt beside him and said, "I'm sorry Belk. Spirits, I'm sorry! I didn't know this would happen! What can I do?"

Belk rolled his eyes, struggling for breath. Pell remembered having the wind driven from his chest by Denit when he was younger. Maybe a loss of wind was all that was wrong with Belk? People did get better from that. Pell looked up to see Gia and Boro standing near, eyes wide. Agan, Panute, and Falin stood just outside the cave, surveying the scene. Ginja leaned against Pell's leg, growling at the thrashing Roley. Gia said, "What spirit attacked them, Pell? How did you call it?"

At first, he wasn't sure what she meant; then he realized that she had no idea of her role in tripping the noose. He'd never explained it to anyone but Tando and Donte. "I'd set up a trap... outside the cave... in case we were attacked. The rope you pulled tripped it. I didn't mean for it to do *this*!"

"Trap?" she asked.

"Uh, yes, it's a... device to catch things. It's how we hunt. This one was only supposed to *catch* people... not to actually hurt them... but something went... went terribly wrong."

"Spirit! That was amazing!" Boro exclaimed. He, as opposed to Pell, obviously wasn't horrified by the outcome of events. "*You* did that?! Can you teach me how? Or do you need to be able to control the Wolf Spirit?"

Gia shook her head during Boro's questions, looked about, and interrupted. Gesturing at Belk and Roley, she said, "What should we do for these men?"

"I don't know. Belk," he said looking down at the injured man, "where are you hurting? Can we help?"

Belk rolled his eyes again, but this time managed to grunt an answer, "Get Pont!"

A voice over Pell's shoulder said, "No, don't ask for *Pont*! Pell's a better healer than Pont ever was Belk, ask *him* to take care of you."

Pell looked back. Gontra had come up just behind him! Running up the path behind Gontra were Tando, Donte, Manute, and Deltin—certainly a welcome sight.

Pell looked around, Where are the rest of the Aldans? With Gontra behind him, that meant that he now knew where, how many? He looked about, Roley, Belk, and Gontra by the path, Exen running. Where was Pont? Maybe in the bushes, that was five... Oh! And Denit hanging from the rope! Remembering Denit, Pell looked up, "Tando, Gontra, Boro, help me get Denit down!"

He went over to where Denit hung limply upside-down, above the path. Pell scrambled up onto Tando's shoulders and, pulling out his knife, cut the rope around Denit's thigh. With the others' help, he lowered Denit to the path. Once Denit was down, they all stared at him. His head lolled at an unnatural angle and his face had turned a dusky hue. At first, Pell hoped that the color only resulted from being hung upside down, but shortly it became obvious his color wasn't improving.

Gia knelt and put her ear to his chest. "He's not breathing... His heartbeat is weak. He'll die soon." She said this unhappily, but with the complete assurance of someone who felt certain of an outcome.

Pell said, "What can we do?!"

Gia looked up in puzzlement. "I don't know of anything, do you?"

"No! I'm not a healer! Maybe Agan knows of something? Some herb?"

"I'll ask, but I'm sure she doesn't." Gia rose and jogged up the path to her grandmother.

Tando was looking on with a puzzled expression. "Pell, why would you try to help Denit anyway?"

"I… I'm not sure… but we shouldn't just let him *die*, should we?" Pell said, eyes still following Gia as she ran.

Tando shrugged and curled his lip in disgust. "I would."

Boro, said in a venomous tone, "Yes! Why not? He'd watch *you* die with delight. He's never helped *anyone*. Denit only brings pain and misery!"

Pell knelt himself to listen to Denit's chest. Pushing aside some dirty furs and leaning his ear against Denit's ribs, he found himself looking past a few curly hairs at the other's feet. Yes, he could hear a heartbeat, no breathing, but an irregular, faint heartbeat. He looked up at Denit's face. It had turned even duskier than before.

Gia returned to say that Agan knew nothing that could be done to help someone who wasn't breathing, "But, remember when Falin wasn't breathing, hurting his leg helped. You could try that."

Pell quickly knelt and tried bending Denit's fingers back. That didn't help so he tried squeezing the bones together above the wrist.

Denit didn't squirm or take a breath so Pell looked hopefully up at Gia.

"When people have completely stopped breathing like him, they all die," she said simply, then turned to examine Roley and Belk again.

Not knowing what else to do, Pell pinched Denit's inner arm a few moments. There was no response, so he followed Gia to look at the other two. No longer thrashing, Roley now quivered rigidly.

Gia knelt feeling his bloody scalp, "His skull's broken here," she said. She looked up at Pell, "Does your bone setting trick work for skulls?" her clear gray eyes were curious.

"Uh… I don't think so. Only for bones that're shaped like sticks." He also knelt and examined Roley's bloody head. He felt a soft area in the hair. Just as Pell probed the soft area, Roley threw up, or at least he heaved up and his mouth filled with something that smelled like vomit.

"Oh no!" Gia exclaimed. She reached into his mouth to try to scoop the vomitus out but, like the rest of his muscles, his jaw had clenched rigidly shut. He heaved again, vomit spewing out through his nose. Shortly after that his breathing began to labor. Gia shook her head sadly. Saying, "This one will die soon as well," Gia turned to walk over to Belk.

Pell was aghast, thinking to himself about how Roley'd thrown up just after Pell touched the soft spot in his skull. Perhaps it was his fault if Roley died?

Well, of course it's my fault! I set the trap!

But somehow Pell thought that was different than killing him while trying to help him. He wondered if anyone else had noticed it happened when he was probing Roley's skull. Was it because he'd pressed in? He tugged uncertainly on Roley's hair over the area that had been crushed inward by the rock, trying to pull the crushed area of the skull back outward. Nothing good happened; in fact, Roley's breathing got more and more labored. Pell thought frantically there must be some way to help him breathe—but for the life of him, he didn't know what it would be.

He looked around for Gia. She knelt by Belk, probing at his back. Pell thought he should ask her again if anything could be done for Roley, but remembered she'd already checked with Agan and that they'd concluded nothing could be done for someone who wasn't breathing.

Pell looked back over at Denit who was now a dark dusky blue. Denit lay unmoving, open eyes staring up at the sky, head still twisted at the odd angle. He certainly looked much the same as other dead people Pell'd seen in the past. Durr'd looked that way when Pell found his body, ages ago. Though Durr hadn't had the blue coloration.

Roley continued to make little heaving motions as if trying to take a breath, but no air seemed to be passing in or out of his nose or mouth. Foul-smelling vomit surged in and out when he heaved, but that was all. Distantly, Pell noted Roley was turning blue as well. He thought to himself, Tando's not going to think very much of "Pell the healer" now! As he considered his impending loss of recognition, he wondered if he should feel grateful.

It'd be good if people didn't expect so much of him.

Deep inside though, he realized he liked having people respect him for something. Years of ridicule for his poor hunting skills had left him with a deep hunger for esteem. He dreaded losing it. After a moment, he mentally cursed himself for worrying about his impending loss of respect. *Roley and Denit are* dying *for the spirits' sake! I should be worrying about them.*

Gia called Pell over to inspect the huge bruise forming on Belk's right mid and lower back. "I think it's below his ribs. Do you think that he could have broken ribs anyway? If they are broken can you put them back in place? Ribs are shaped like sticks aren't they?"

Gia had been palpating the bruised area gently. She clearly expected Pell to feel it also, but Pell, fearing an event like the one that had occurred when he'd probed Roley's skull, couldn't bring himself to touch Belk. He looked carefully at the swollen, bruised area. Not yet black and blue, it appeared pink and had abrasions in the center of the area. Pell felt his own back. "Yes, I think it's just below his ribs. Anyway, my trick wouldn't work for ribs; I couldn't get a grip on them to straighten them out." He glanced back over at the stricken Roley, noting with despair that Roley appeared to have stopped his heaving attempts to breathe.

Gontra squatted down next to Belk. "Remember Belk, I said that we shouldn't try to attack Pell? I *told* you he controlled powerful spirits."

Belk grunted. "You only said it to me though."

"Yeah," he snorted disgustedly, "like Denit ever listened to anyone else anyway." He looked up, "Pell can you call again to the 'Trap' Spirit that sent those rocks down on us? Ask it to help Belk. Belk isn't your enemy. I swear it. He and I were only here because Denit told us we had to come."

Pell was startled once again by this misinterpretation. "It wasn't a spirit! It's only a trap. A trap is... is a tool... like a spear... or a basket. It does what you make it do. But I didn't mean for it to do *this*."

"Yes, well..." Gontra said bemusedly, "could you ask your *tool* to help Belk?"

In astonishment, a bewildered Pell looked over at Tando who, to his further consternation nodded, "I think you should. Belk's a good man. I'm sure he wouldn't have come raiding if Denit and Roley hadn't bullied him."

Pell's perplexity rose even higher. Did Tando believe in a "trap spirit" too? Or did he just think that Pell should go through the motions of calling on it to raise their standing in the Aldans' eyes? Maybe... maybe it wouldn't be too bad an idea for them to fear his control of "Spirits." Finally, Pell shrugged and said, "All right."

He stood up and in his deepest voice he called out, "Hayuuh, hayuuh, hayuuh, oh great Trap Spirit. Hayuuh, hayuuh, hayuuh, Belk is a good man. Belk is a friend of mine. Hayuuh, hayuuh, hayuuh, I didn't intend for you to strike Belk down. Hayuuh, hayuuh, hayuuh, please help Belk to get better. Hayuuh, hayuuh, hayuuh."

Pell sat back down feeling pleased with himself for sounding somewhat like Pont did during his ceremonies. Then he thought that, if Belk died anyway, calling on the "Trap Spirit" to raise their prestige was going to backfire.

Oh well, Belk had already been looking better before Pell called on the "Spirit." Maybe it would work out the way it did for Pont when he took credit for people who got better on their own.

But Pell felt embarrassed remembering how he'd despised Pont for using that tactic. A tactic Pell'd always thought was despicable. He grimaced at the violation of promises he'd made to himself.

Belk rolled over onto his hands and knees. He slowly stood up, holding his own back. "Thanks, Pell, it's feeling better already."

Astonished, Pell glanced up at the big noose hanging against the cliffside. *Could a Trap Spirit actually exist?*

Gia turned to Pell. "What should Belk do now?"

Pell was surprised again. Why was she asking him? Surely Gia knew more about these problems than he did. He looked around. Everyone was looking at him as if he knew what to do! "Um, I'm not sure, what would you suggest?"

"Hmm, well, Agan and I usually have someone who's been hurt lie down to rest. We could make him a willow-bark tea for the pain."

"Yes, yes, that's a really good idea. Why don't we take him back up to the cave and let him lie down?" Soon the group was headed back up to the cave. At the door, Tando stopped everyone, asking what to do about Denit and Roley, who by then were obviously dead. After conferring briefly, Agan detailed Gontra, Tando, Manute and Deltin to move the bodies across to the other side of the clearing. When she'd been making the assignment, Pell had thought surely he'd be assigned to this duty as well.

Pell felt tremendous relief at not being delegated to moving them. He didn't want to go near the bodies anymore.

Then Pell learned he hadn't been assigned to move the bodies because everyone seemed to think he was needed to care for Belk! Though he didn't have anything to offer, he was so relieved at not having to touch the dead that he refrained from saying anything.

But guilt surged through him again—after all, it was his fault they were dead! Morose he turned, "I should help with the bodies. I'll come back to check on Belk."

~~~

Pell went back out after the others, oblivious to the awed stares and whispers of those remaining in the cave. They weren't sure whether he was going to oversee the proper handling of the bodies, or perhaps intending to consign Denit and Roley's spirits to some dark place. However, in awe, they felt his intention to supervise the unpleasant task of handling the bodies must be another portent of his power.

***

After talking to the members of the Cold Springs tribe Agan decided to call off their move for now. The major danger they'd feared seemed to be gone. Tando made a brief detour to check part of the trap lines during his trip away from camp. He brought in a groundhog and a rabbit. The others shook their heads over his usual good luck with small game and settled in to cook it. Manute complained again about how he wanted to learn how to trap, but did it quietly so the two Aldans couldn't hear.

The mood threatened to become celebratory, but couldn't with Gontra and Belk of the decimated Aldans in their midst. Then Belk limped out to pass his urine and returned trembling in fear because it was a dark bloody red.

Pell feared he'd be expected to know what to do for this ailment as well, but Agan had apparently treated several people with blood in their urine in the past. She immediately began brewing large quantities of tea and urging him to drink as much of it as he could. This apparently helped. After drinking so much liquid, he soon began having to go out to pee frequently. As he did so, his urine became less bloody.

While they talked over their evening meal, the Cold Spring group's spirits were high now that their fears of being raided were eased. Gontra however, became morose. Partway through the meal, Pell looked up to see tears running down Gontra's face. He asked, "Are you sad that Denit and Roley died, Gontra?"

Tears continued to roll down Gontra's face and he simply stared into the fire. For a while, Pell thought he might not respond at all. Eventually, he did speak and when he started talking, the words just poured out, more than Pell had ever before heard at one time from the usually taciturn Gontra. "No. Denit, and even Roley, have been causing nothing but trouble since before you left. It's been getting worse and worse. But our tribe! We were down to just six hunters and were already having trouble getting enough meat. Now we have only four. Belk's hurt. Pont's *never* been any good as a hunter and my son Exen's young. I hope Exen will be a better hunter in a year or two, but Denit's been leading him astray for so long. A young hunter has to constantly practice his throwing to get to be any good and Exen doesn't practice at all. Certainly, I haven't been able to teach him much lately because of Denit's influence."

Pell felt embarrassed to realize that he rarely if ever practiced his own throwing. *I've got to start practicing more,* he thought.

Gontra continued, "We've got six women and four children to feed this winter and no one built up much fat this summer because of the poor hunting we've had under Denit. If we don't have a couple of lucky hunts soon, especially right before the frost, *many* of the Aldans'll die this winter.

I know your little tribe here's also too small and so you're facing the same thing." He stopped and looked around at them, "Though at least you've got some fat." He shook his head, "I've never been this close to winter and been so thin before. The women have done well storing grain and roots. Denit didn't affect them much, but you know we need meat or our people will get sick. I've lost children before in the winter, even when we had more food than we do this year. I can't bear to think about losing my little Tila. I thought she was old enough to survive, so I've let myself care about her too much.

"But, Tila's already thin at the *beginning* of the great cold. I'm afraid everyone's going to expect me to lead now that Denit and Roley are gone and I don't think I can solve these problems. But, even if I fear leading myself, I surely don't want Pont to lead. He's too addled from chewing his hemp. Maybe if Belk recovers, he can lead us, but I don't think Belk can lead hunts that'll find us enough meat for the winter either."

Gontra let out a great sigh, "I don't know what to do... I just don't know what to do... I don't know... For a while there I thought Denit had a good idea, asking Tando to rejoin us, especially when we heard you had other hunters here, maybe a couple of big hunts would've set us up.

But of course, Denit had to screw it all up and try to attack you instead of joining with you. He was sure you were hiding a bunch of that meat that doesn't rot. You know, like you were trading at the marketplace? I asked him how he thought you would have gotten so much meat and he didn't know, 'I just know they have it,' he'd say. I told him we should wait until Tando got back, but he wanted to have the meat already in our possession. 'Then Tando will *have* to join us,' he said.... Denit always wanted to do everything by fighting. Spirits... I hated him so!"

Gontra's long monologue had been delivered flatly. Almost, it seemed, without emotion. But for the tears that continued streaming down his face and the mild exclamation as he ran down at the end, he might have been recounting a sad story from years ago.

Several times, while Gontra was speaking, Pell glanced around to see how the others were taking it. Boro, like Pell himself, had been angry during the parts where Gontra thought it reasonable that they try to get

Tando to join the Aldans, presumably leaving Pell and Boro to fend for themselves. The others seemed upset that they, like Pell, hadn't thought about how their own good fortune in the death of Roley and Denit bode ill for the other members of the Aldans, especially the hapless women and children of the tribe.

People Pell had liked. Pell thought back on the mind-numbing grief that came every winter when one of the babes or children died. The same winter his father'd died; Pell's baby sister had also passed to the spirit world. Though to Pell, the significance of the baby's death paled in comparison to the agony he'd felt over his father's demise.

No one had said a word when Gontra abruptly shook himself and stood up. "I have to get back to the tribe. Pont's probably almost there already. He'll cause all kinds of trouble." He looked over at the sleeping Belk, "I'll come back and get Belk in a day or two."

Tando grabbed his arm, "You can't go now. It's dark. Sit back down—we'll make plans tonight. You can go in the morning." Tando and some of the others laughed nervously. Pell wondered if they thought Gontra might actually go—during the night when big cats prowled.

Gontra pulled himself free. "No. I need to go *now*. Pont'll be there soon. He'll tell Tonday and Lenta that Belk and I are dead along with Roley and Denit. Belk's kids too, they're old enough to understand. Thank the spirit that little Tila's too young. For that matter, he's probably been bending my boy Exen's mind the entire trip back. As if it wasn't bent enough from hanging around with Denit all the time. Just telling the truth to Roley's wives will be bad enough. Having *Pont* tell them will really make things ugly... I've got to go now." He was practically muttering by the end, his eyes darting about.

Pell was dumbfounded. Gontra really intended to go! "Gontra! You can't go! It's dark and there's no moon tonight! Stay tonight. I'll go with you tomorrow."

Gontra stared at Pell a moment, then his eyes dropped. He sat back down and said, "Okay."

Astonishment washed over Pell. When he'd told Gontra to stay, Pell had fully expected him to reject the idea, just as Gontra had when Tando told him to stay. In fact, as he thought about it, he realized he only told him to stay because he felt he should.

Not because he expected to be obeyed.

With dismay, Pell realized he didn't *want* to go with Gontra to the old cave. Especially, he thought, to tell everyone of the deaths of Roley and Denit. Certainly not when he'd been the one who'd killed them! Particularly Roley's wives, Fellax and Ontru. He didn't want to face the healer either. Nor Exen.

Why did Gontra obey me after rejecting Tando's pleas? How did I get myself into this?

He was still pondering these questions when he fell asleep much later that night. Was there a way to honorably get out of his promised trip? Maybe Gontra had acceded to his request to stay without really expecting Pell to go with him in the morning?

***

A hand on his shoulder startled Pell awake. It was still dark. He heard Gontra's whisper, "Pell. It'll be light soon. Let's go. I want to get there before Pont screws everything up."

Spirits! Pell thought, *He really does want me to go!*
"Okay, Gontra," he groaned, "give me a little time."

Pell built the fire up a little, balancing the waking of
the others against their joy at having a warm cave when
morning came. He began digging around for his
traveling supplies. Gontra followed him about the cave,
unable to help with Pell's preparations and pestering
him with whispered questions about why they couldn't
just *go*. Pell was alternately annoyed, and puzzled by
what seemed to him to be Gontra's childishness. Surely,
Gontra understood the value of planning and
preparation? As he thought on it, he recognized his old
memories of Gontra were of an impetuous man.

In fact, he supposed, the same could be said for
most of the men of the tribe. Their hunts had little
preparation, just a simple "let's go out and kill
something" decision that initiated the hunt. When they
found game, there would be a brief planning session
regarding the best way to surround and kill it. Pell
hadn't found that surprising when he lived with them,
but since he'd begun living on his own, he'd taken to
planning everything.

He'd had to, to have any chance of surviving.

Now, to his inner amusement, he recognized the
behavior of the Aldan adults seemed immature. Even
more, he was beginning to realize that he'd always
thought of the men in the Aldans as being… smart.
They'd certainly known more than Pell did as a child.
But now he was confronted with the fact that he just
didn't think Gontra was very bright.

Had the stress of the previous day's events reduced
Pell to a less accepting state? Or was Pell just now
assessing Gontra's intelligence from the vantage point a
period of separation had given him? It made him think

of the others, even those in his new tribe. Many of them had difficulty grasping Pell's ideas, even after he explained them repeatedly. Then, when they saw those ideas in action they often decided the outcomes were the result of magic or spirits, rather than simply the function of a new kind of tool.

Maybe they never had, and never would understand how Pell's tools and devices worked?

Gray light was filtering in from outside the door flap of the cave when Pell was finally ready. As he and Gontra stepped outside Gontra asked, "Why do you have these skins hanging over the mouth of the cave Pell? They keep you from seeing outside. If a big night cat was to creep up on you, you wouldn't even know it was there!"

"It keeps the wind out, Gontra. With the flap there, it stays warmer in the cave. Besides the big cats are afraid of fire. I don't think they'd try to come in because of the smell of smoke."

Pell looked Gontra over critically. It didn't look like he'd gotten much sleep during the night. There were gaps in his furs that must leave him cold. Especially Gontra's legs, they were nearly uncovered!

Pell stepped back into the cave and found an extra set of the winter leggings they'd learned about from Manute. Pell brought them out and tried to put them on Gontra. At first, Gontra didn't understand their function and said he didn't need them. Then, when Pell finally got them on him and he felt the warmth they provided, he pronounced them wonderful and effusively thanked Pell.

As they set out, Pell handed Gontra some spirit meat. Gontra took it, saying, "What's this?" He held it up to his nose to smell it. "Hey, is this meat?" He nibbled at it, "Oh, is it some of the 'meat that doesn't rot' they were talking about at the trading place?"

Pell said, "Yeah. Tando calls it 'spirit meat.'"

Gontra said, "Huh, I was *sure* you wouldn't have any left. I guess Denit was right that you still had some." Gontra consumed it hungrily. He looked astonished when Pell gave him some more. "Thanks, Pell." Sounding a little reluctant, he said, "You really should keep some for yourself."

Pell shrugged, "I've got plenty."

"Well, if you don't mind I'll just save this for Tonday and Tila. Especially poor little Tila. At least she's better off now that Denit's gone. He'd already been restricting the little ones' meat. Said they didn't need it as badly as the hunters did. The women either." Gontra turned to look searchingly at Pell, "I think they need it just as bad as we do. What do you believe?"

Pell found himself amused by the usually taciturn Gontra's rambling. First last night, now again this morning. "Yes," Pell said, "I think women and children need meat just as badly as hunters do. But you don't need to save that one for them. I have more in my pack."

"Really?! That's great!" Gontra said, getting it back out of his pouch and gnawing hungrily on the remainder of the tough piece of spirit meat. "Tando must be a really great hunter—like they were saying last night. He was always good, but I thought he was done for when you broke his wrist. The spirits you called on to fix his wrist must still live in it, helping with every throw of his spear." Gontra shook his head, "It almost makes me wish I'd broken my wrist instead of just a finger." A perplexed expression crossed his face. Pell could see it as they had finished wending their way down the narrow path out of Cold Springs Ravine and were now walking side by side out into the big valley. "I wonder if *I* throw better since you fixed my finger. Not that I've had much of a chance to throw a spear in those abortions that Denit called 'hunts'." He brightened, "Now that Denit's gone I'll bet I do better at hunting too, just like Tando."

Pell found himself irritated at the way that Gontra assumed that any successful hunting had been done by Tando, even if Gontra was ascribing Tando's successes to Pell.

All at once he realized that, before they'd decided to leave, he'd laid out a trap line up the small valley just to their left. In their hurry to pack up and get on their way he'd forgotten about it. "Gontra, I'm going to take a little detour here. I'll meet you at that lone tree up there when the sun's moved a fist. You can go down to the water there and see if you can spear a fish while you're waiting."

"No! Pell, we need to keep moving. If we keep up this pace we can make the whole trip by midafternoon."

"So it'll be dark when we get there," Pell shrugged, "you know the paths close to the cave like you know your own hand. This is important."

Gontra acquiesced, though in a surly fashion. Pell felt like he'd reacted like a child would if an adult told him to behave. Pell hiked up the little valley looking for the limestone marks he and Tando had been using to mark their trap lines.

The marking system had become necessary to keep them from losing trap sites, especially when one of them laid the traps out and the other one picked them up. Soon he was on the line and excitedly remembered he'd laid out one of the rope traps they used for large game.

The first trap was empty. The second had had something in it, but it'd been discovered by scavengers and there was little left but blood and disturbed earth. The third and fourth were also empty and the noose for the sixth had been knocked loose and hung limply off to one side of the path.

Pell's heart began to sink. He should re-join Gontra. He had to check the last one though; it had the large and valuable rope for the large animal trap and he wanted to take it with him.

~~~

Gontra was sitting at the edge of the river, spear in hand while he peered sullenly into the water. Pell threw the young boar down by his side.

Pell had found it recently snared and in good health. The noose was snug about its neck and it'd obviously struggled a while from the looks of the torn up dirt and foliage in the area. Trapped, panting and spraddle-legged; it almost seemed as if it was waiting for Pell's spear. It'd succumbed to his first thrust. Even better, its bristly coat didn't show noose marks that might give away Pell's departure from standard hunting techniques.

Pell had noiselessly padded up and Gontra had startled admirably when the boar thumped down at his side. "It's a good thing I'm not a lion Gontra, I'd be having you for dinner," he chuckled. "Instead, I brought you some food! Is having this boar to take to the Aldans worth a little delay?"

~~~

Gontra goggled quite satisfactorily at the boar. "Spirits, Pell. This'll be wonderful! We haven't had this much meat for hands of days! How did you kill this boar without other hunters to help you surround it?"

"I just had it hold still while I ran my spear through it," Pell said, reflecting that the jest was actually close to true.

They set about cleaning it. After putting the cleaned stomach, intestines, heart and liver in Pell's carry pack, they set out again with the boar itself draped around Gontra's neck. Despite Gontra's greater maturity, he tired quickly carrying the heavy boar. They took to trading it back and forth, with the other carrying the pack. Pell was surprised to realize he was carrying the boar farther and much more easily on his turns than Gontra was.

But then, Gontra hadn't been eating as well as Pell had.

At one point, as they stood face to face to shift the boar from Pell's shoulders to Gontra's, Pell realized that he was looking down on Gontra. *I'm taller than Gontra now*, he thought, shocked, though he knew he shouldn't be. After years of looking up at Gontra and considering him a big man, this was a sudden and startling insight into his own growth.

Despite Gontra's weariness, they made good time along the flats bordering the great river. By late afternoon they were in country familiar to Pell since it was near the Aldans' cave.

Huffing up a slope with the boar about his neck, Gontra turned to Pell and said, "Now, if you'd planned this better, you would have had this boar meet you here and I wouldn't be worn out from carrying it."

Pell laughed, thinking wistfully how nice it would be if he actually could summon animals to be killed wherever he wanted.

It was after dark, though just barely, when they arrived below the cave. The moon had risen, a brilliant auroch's horn shape in the sky. It cast an eerie glow over the landscape where its light struck, but ominous shadows lay elsewhere. They could see the light of the fire flickering inside the Aldans' cave when Gontra stopped and turned, letting the boar slide down off his shoulders to thump into the dirt at Pell's feet. "I think you should wait here, Pell. I don't want them to get hit with too much at once. I'll go on up and tell them Belk and I aren't dead."

They stood for a moment in silence. Pell could hear the women wailing in the cave. "Yeah, I think Pont's gotten them pretty worked up. Go on ahead. Call out when you want me to come on up." Pell sat down on the boar's carcass, thinking just how little he wanted to be amongst the people in the cave, especially once they knew he was the one who'd killed their hunters.

Gontra walked up the path a way then stopped. "Pell, come with me," he whispered, "I can't face Fellax and Ontru alone."

A cold dread seeped over Pell, but he climbed to his feet, hoisted the boar to his shoulders and started up the path behind Gontra.

Too soon came the sight of the pitiful group huddled about the fire, most of the women wailing. Pont, his back to Gontra and Pell, was gesturing animatedly, though Pell couldn't understand what he was saying. With some surprise, Pell observed they all had their furs about them, even though they were close around the fire. But then he remembered how cold the cave had always been in winter, even with a fire burning.

The fire had to be built near the entrance or it choked the cave with smoke, not having an exit hole like he'd built into the wall of the Cold Springs cave. The cave entrance was wide and couldn't be closed off the way the new cave could be with its flap of skins. Thus wind swirled freely through the cave, cooling everything not directly heated by the fire.

Pell looked at the scene and the people in it, thinking fondly of some, like Lessa, the healer's mate, and Lenta, Belk's woman, both of whom had been kind to him as a boy. He dreaded meeting again with Pont, or with Fellax, Roley's imperious first wife. For a moment he considered just tossing down the boar and leaving, but instead, he merely shuffled to a stop. Gontra turned and saw Pell falling back. With a hand gesture, he motioned Pell to keep coming. As Pell resumed moving, there was a shriek from the fireside.

Lenta rose, pointing to Gontra and saying, "Tonday, I, I... see Gontra's spirit!!"

Tonday burst to her feet, looking wildly about, face streaked with tears as Gontra stepped fully into the firelight. Gontra surveyed the scene, then said, "No, I'm not a spirit, I'm here!" He stepped forward, throwing his arms about Tonday. He reached out a hand to Exen.

Pont reacted almost angrily, "No! I saw you crushed by the rocks!" Somehow Pell wasn't surprised when, almost without taking a breath, Pont changed his tone completely to proclaim in sonorous tones, "Never have my pleas to the spirit world been answered so quickly. Gontra! Back from the dead! How do you feel?!"

Gontra didn't respond at first. For a moment Pell feared Gontra would go along with the healer's preposterous claims, the way he had when Pont claimed the spirits reduced Gontra's finger dislocation. Instead, Gontra took a deep breath and turned on the healer. "No! You didn't 'see' me crushed. You were running away like a frightened doe!" He turned to the others. "Our Medicine Man didn't even check on the rest of us to see who was hurt, or who might need help. Instead, he ran back here as fast as his crooked little legs would carry him."

Pell winced. An insult about the healer's short bowed legs hadn't been uttered aloud since Pont's childhood, though Pell'd heard they'd been a common source of taunts back then.

No one would have dared the *Medicine Man's* wrath.

Gontra continued, "*Pell*, who we'd gone to attack... *Pell* was the one who came to help us. He came to heal us from our injuries, injuries inflicted by rocks the Trap Spirit cast down on us. Rocks which the Trap Spirit cast upon us when Pell asked it to protect him from us. While our own healer scurried into a crack like a lizard, Pell, who's become known as a great bonesetter in his region, Pell came to our aid." Gontra's voice broke with emotion, "Pell," he rasped, "came to help those who'd been about to steal his tiny tribe's food."

Pell missed Gontra's next words in his consternation over the continuance of the "Trap Spirit" explanation of what had happened. Hadn't Gontra been listening when he explained that the trap was only a device? Then he remembered acceding to requests that he pray to the "Trap Spirit." He was brought back to the present by the women's cries, "Us? Did the others survive? How are the others? Where are Roley and Denit? Is Belk okay as well?"

Gontra looked about wildly a moment, making shushing motions with his hands. He looked back over his shoulder toward Pell and the group discerned Pell as a shadowy figure. Gontra gravely said, "Belk survived but he's been hurt. The Trap Spirit took the lives of Roley and Denit in payment for their attempt to attack Pell."

Lenta leaped to her feet, apparently thinking the figure in the shadows was Belk. She ran towards Pell, shrieking Belk's name as she ran. Pell stepped forward into the light so that she'd be able to see he wasn't Belk. The group about the fire was startled at the apparition before them. They recognized Pell's face, but, because of his tremendous summer growth spurt, Pell was far bigger than they remembered. In fact, larger than anyone in their tribe except the massive Roley. The boar draped over his shoulders like a huge cowl markedly emphasized this startling first impression. Having initially surged forward, they now drew back and shrank in on themselves, some gasping in fear.

Pell, having spent his life in subjugation to these people, felt stunned by their frightened expressions. He could, however, see they were thin and hungry looking—appallingly so. In response to his recognition of their hunger, and in hopes of influencing their opinions positively, he swung the boar down off of his shoulders and carried it to them. He said, "We brought food."

The eyes of the group flashed up and down, from Pell to the boar and back again. Gontra thundered over their murmurings, "*Pell*, brought you that boar—after hunting it down, *by himself,* in just an hour or two. He's become a *mighty* hunter, a powerful bonesetter, and, *the Shaman of the Trap Spirit!*"

Several of the group about the fire prostrated themselves before him. Pell started back, then knelt, urging them back to their feet. "Lenta, get up, I'm sorry, I didn't mean for Belk to get hurt... I think he's going to be okay," he whispered, grasping her arm and urging her to her feet and back to the heat of the fire.

He couldn't quite bring himself to say he hadn't meant for Denit or Roley to be hurt, but he did help Ontru, Roley's lesser wife, back to her feet. He saw that Fellax, Roley's first wife, remained on the far side of the fire, eyes fixed on him with a fierce and angry glare. There would be no prostration from Fellax he suspected. He looked around at the children, who looked fearful, and the women, who ranged in expression from awe, to fear, to hate. Exen glowered at him from across the fire, where was the healer?

All at once Pont struck Pell from behind! The healer pounced from Pell's right rear quarter, wrapping his left arm about Pell's neck and surging around with his right to thrust a wicked flint knife at Pell's chest! The world moved slowly as Pell's own right hand flashed out to block, then grasp the healer's forearm. Pell felt distantly surprised when the knife's approach stopped. He easily forced it away.

Pell mused to himself that Pont must really have weakened from lack of food. He'd always been much stronger than Pell. Pell grasped Pont's choking left forearm with his own left hand, pulling it away, not easily—but again, he felt astounded that it was possible. The struggling healer's legs beat a tattoo about Pell's waist and Pell staggered about while the others looked on in horror. Gontra had stepped toward the fighters as if to intervene, then, realizing Exen looked as if he were about to help Pont, turned instead to confront his own son.

Then Ginja burst out of the dark, knocking Pell and the healer to the ground beside the fire. As they bowled apart, Ginja leaped onto Pont, snarling, slavering and as the healer rolled away, attacked the medicine man's throat. Somewhat to his own wonderment Pell found himself exclaiming, "No! Ginja! No!" His own hate for the healer and deep-set wish to see Pont dead came second to his lifelong understanding that the tribe needed every man it had. Nonetheless, Pell kept his grasp on the wrist of Pont's knife hand, preferring Ginja kill the healer rather than see that knife buried in his best friend's furry coat.

After a moment Ginja, still snarling, slowly backed away and Pell looked up into the ashen faces surrounding the fire—faces cowering fearfully away. The healer grasped his neck with one hand, trying to stanch the flow of blood from several bite wounds as Pell wrested the knife from his hand. Having wrenched Pont's knife free, Pell slowly stood, panting, wondering if Pont had another knife hidden about him somewhere. Pont cowered a moment, fully expecting the knife to fall on him, then the healer groveled at Pell's feet, begging for his life.

Pell paused, not even having considered using the knife on Pont when he'd first wrenched it from the man's grasp. Now Pell considered the healer's lifelong vindictiveness. If Pell let him live this time, wouldn't Pont simply knife Pell by surprise some other day? Wouldn't it really be better to have Pont gone so Pell could live without worry—even if it was a hardship for the others? Others who'd, after all, cast him out to fend for himself? For a moment the knife rose, nearly of its own accord, then Lessa was there, on her knees, clinging to Pell's right arm, begging for her man's life.

And Pell remembered Lessa's many kindnesses when Pell'd been a child. His arm slowly, slowly dropped.

He looked into Lessa's fearful eyes, "I must sleep here tonight, if I let Pont live, how can I be sure he won't knife me in my sleep?"

In a craven display that turned Pell's stomach, Pont began shrieking his purity of thought and future deed. But Lessa, staring clearly into Pell's eyes, simply said, "Tie him up."

Pell was startled. He'd never seen anyone tied, though he'd heard of it. "I wouldn't know how."

Gontra stepped over and said, "I can tie him. I've seen it done."

Pell looked at Pont, considering, "What if someone cuts him loose in the night?"

Gontra pondered a moment, then, "We'll place him at the back of the cave. You and I'll sleep between him and the others. Anyone going to help him would have to step over us. If we lay dry twigs around him, they'll snap if someone does manage to step over us." He looked down at the sniveling Pont, considering for a moment. He looked back up, "On the other hand, you're probably right. Better kill him now. We can't do this every night." Gontra reached for his own knife.

Pell stopped Gontra with a hand on his arm, "No. I'll be gone tomorrow night."

At this statement, Gontra's eyes flashed a look of dismay, but he called for thongs and set about tying up the healer. As he worked, he demonstrated the knots for Pell, first tying Pont's hands behind him. Gontra dragged Pont to his feet and marched him to the back of the cave. There he forced him to the ground and began tying his feet together. He tied each of Pont's bonds to pieces of firewood, small enough that the healer could move them, but large enough that moving them would take effort and make noise. They laid dry twigs and grasses about Pont and placed bedding of grass and furs for Gontra and Pell between Pont and the rest of the Aldans.

Meanwhile, the women had eagerly set about butchering the boar and preparing a feast. Pell had eaten some of his smoked meat just before he and Gontra arrived. Not wanting to incur any obligation by partaking in the feast, he pled weariness and lay down in his place in front of Pont so he could sleep.

Despite his pleas, he thought he wouldn't be able to sleep after the excitement of the day's events. After asking permission, Lessa brought Pont some of the food and fed it to him, though neither of them spoke.

The next thing he knew, Pell woke, freezing cold, as dawn broke outside.

He checked to be sure that Pont was still securely bound, then stepped around Gontra and went out to empty his bladder. The sky was clear, the last stars were fading and it was bitingly cold. He stamped his feet, passed his water and came back in to stoke the fire. He sat before it, trying to warm back up and decided to leave as soon as he could decently get away.

He couldn't help thinking morbidly of all the problems the Aldans' little tribe faced, all the worse for the loss of two of its hunters. He wanted to get away and back to his own, simpler problems. He'd leave them the spirit meat he'd brought and perhaps he could send some more meat with Belk when Belk had recovered enough to make the trip?

For now, Pell just wanted to get away. In fact, his feet were nearly warm. Perhaps he could get out before they woke up and not even have to be reminded of their despair when they woke and set about the new day. He set about assembling his things.

He was nearly packed and ready to go when Gontra woke and saw him getting ready. "No, Pell, don't go! Tonday! Exen! Ontru! Lenta! Pell's getting ready to leave!" The others bolted up out of their own sleeping nests, exclaiming in dismay. Soon the entire camp was up, even the crying children, disturbed by the adult's emotional displays. Pell's heart filled with despair as they began to beg him to stay. One of the women cried, "The *children* will starve without your help."

Others joined in, "We don't have enough hunters."

"The hunting's been so bad."

"We talked until late last night. We want you to be our new leader now that Roley's dead."

"We know you're a great hunter and a mighty shaman."

"Please, save us."

"Please?" Pell looked over at Pont, whose sullen glare told him that he certainly couldn't remain safely with the Aldans while the healer still lived. Though Roley's second wife, Ontru, was pleading for Pell to stay, he could see hate remained in Fellax's eyes. He turned to Lessa as she kept begging him to stay, saying, "Look, Lessa, look deep into the heart of your husband, Pont. Can you truly tell me that I'll be welcome, or even safe here?"

Lessa looked over at Pont, then turned and looked out to the horizon, biting her lip. A tear formed and rolled down her cheek, but she said nothing.

He looked over them all, catching each one's eye in turn, "I have to go. I'm not welcomed here by some and, truth be to tell, I love my new home and my *new* tribe. When Belk's well enough to travel, we'll send some meat back with him. Some of our 'spirit meat that doesn't rot' so that you'll have something for when your hunts don't work out. Maybe, without Denit leading your hunts your luck will improve."

"No! Then take us with you. Let us join your tribe. We'll do *whatever* you say."

Pell shook his head, "I'm not the leader of my new tribe. I've learned many things from our leader, Agan, and an important one is that she can lead because of her wisdom, not because of others' dread the way Roley did. Agan's an old woman, but she's wise and therefore mighty. So it wouldn't be up to me to decide whether you could join us. It's not even up to Agan. She'd consult with everyone in our tribe before she decided."

Gontra stared at Pell incredulously, "Pell, I've seen the way they look at you there. If *you* asked, they'd take us. They'd do *anything* you asked."

Taken aback, Pell considered. *Could Gontra be right?* He shook his head, "Even if that was true Gontra, I wouldn't ask the members of my tribe to make an exception to their rules for me." He looked around at all of the Aldans' hopeful faces, thinking quickly. "I'll put the question to them when I return. In the meantime, I'll stay two days and hunt for you. I'll also teach you how to make your cave warmer."

"Can you teach us to make the spirit meat?"

"Uhhh... no, that's our tribe's secret. I'd have to ask the others before I could teach you that. But I *will* ask them." Pell thought to himself with some irritation that it was his idea—he should be able to teach the secret if he wanted. But, Tando thought the smoking process was a very important secret and—Tando was very important to Pell, so...

Pell spent an hour planning out a mud wattle closure for the cave's wide opening. He looked at the cave opening and laid it out. Then he took members of the tribe out and showed them the kind of staves, sticks, and grasses they'd need to collect. He found some good mud at the stream's edge and organized others to carry skins of it up to the cave.

That done, he borrowed some thongs and a hand axe and set out to lay some snares. He said he was going hunting and, when he did, Gontra and Exen wanted to come. He didn't want them along, first because he didn't want his image as a great hunter tarnished and second, because he wanted them to contribute labor to the improvement of the cave. Under Roley, the hunters had lolled about watching the women and children doing laborious chores. Pell felt that, since he'd been doing such chores himself, it'd do the hunters of his old tribe some good to do such work as well.

He tried to deter them by explaining that his hunting technique required him to be alone to be successful. They got excited and wanted to learn this new technique, but he insisted that today they needed him to bring back some food. Also, to close off the cave opening, the others in the cave needed their strong backs. He promised to show them some other time.

As he walked about, setting snares, he thought of his dilemma with one mind and with another saw his old homeland around the Aldans' cave in another light. He'd come to think of this area as "different" than his new home because he'd had so little success while hunting the region when he was a boy. He snorted to realize that he thought of himself as a "boy" back then, even though it was only a Spring, Summer and Fall ago. So much had happened that it seemed as if it were ages ago. Now he saw that this region had all the same kinds of wildlife he regularly saw at Cold Springs.

He saw the rabbit runs in the brambles and set snares in them. He *noticed* the game paths now, though they must have been there before. He used his traveling rope and the rope which had caught the boar to drape nooses across two places where game paths narrowed next to sturdy trees. He saw root vegetables, including the kind of plants that he'd never seen before digging them up accidentally at Cold Springs.

He'd discovered those roots when he was digging up every kind of plant hoping to find something edible— because he didn't know what the root vegetable plants actually looked like. A large number of such plants grew in one area. The parts of the plants that were above the ground were withered, but he saw no evidence any of the roots had been dug up. He realized that the women of his old tribe just didn't recognize that this plant had an edible bulb, any more than he'd known about that particular root before being cast out. He dug up an armload of the root vegetables to take back.

When he neared the cave, he saw there was a large pile of staves and smaller sticks beside the entrance of the cave as well as mud and dried grass. It didn't look like enough to wattle the opening though, and so he was angered to see everyone sitting about the fire. He realized that they didn't know how much would be needed. He should have told them what to do next anyway.

But Spirits! They should be out trying to hunt or gather if they didn't have anything else to do! Were they just *waiting* for *him* to bring them food?! He thought back on old times and became aware that his old tribe spent little time trying to improve their lot, or stock up for winter. If there wasn't an immediate need, i.e. an empty stomach, they simply lay around relaxing. The women did try to stock up on root vegetables and grain for winter and the men would have a big hunt around the time of the expected first frost, but otherwise little thought or planning addressed the future. Perhaps the better situation his little tribe at Cold Springs had was more due to hard work than good luck?

"Hey, it's Pell," called Gontra as he walked up.

Pell stopped before the fire and set down his armload of root vegetables. Exen snickered, "Look what the mighty hunter killed! Roots!" He burst into a laugh.

Pell's face darkened as he stood back up. He walked around the group, many of whom, even the women, were also smirking at this evidence of a man doing a woman's job. He bent, swept his traveling gear into his carrying sling and stood, throwing it back over his shoulder. His gaze swept over the group, now looking apprehensive and uncomfortable. As they focused a moment on Exen, Pell's eyes dripped contempt. He stepped back around them and headed out of the cave.

Gontra leaped to his feet. "Pell! No! Don't leave! We're sorry! Please! We need you!" But Pell stalked out of the cave and down the path towards his new home.

Exen stood as well, but only to grasp his father's elbow and say, "Come on Gontra, let him go, we don't need him."

Gontra struck a backhanded blow that sent Exen flying into the gaggle of women behind him. He turned on his son and shouted, "You... you are going to *starve* this winter without his help. Look at him! Is he skinny and wasted like you? No! He's been *eating*, and eating well! The Spirits themselves are on Pell's side! I've seen what the spirits do to those, like Denit and Roley, who don't respect him. He knows things you desperately need to learn. Now get your ass down the hill, apologize to him, beg his forgiveness, and urge him to return... or... or... I'll cast you out of this tribe myself! My own son or not, I swear I'll cast you out for the harm you've just done all of us!

Pell was far enough down the path in his rage that he heard Gontra yelling, but not the substance of his words. When he heard someone running down the path behind him, he looked to see who came. Seeing Exen, he gathered himself to resist an assault. He was horrified when Exen fell to his knees, begging Pell to return. His heart remained hard as others came down the path behind Exen, also pleading. However, when several of the children ran up, sobbing piteously, to throw their arms around his legs as well, his heart melted. Eventually, he turned to climb back up to the cave again.

However, after returning to the cave he remained angry enough that he drove them relentlessly for the remainder of the day. It'd warmed enough to make it a good day for building the wall to close down the cave opening.

He set some of the Aldans to cutting more poles and scooping more mud, some to digging a little trench for the bottoms of the poles, others to stacking the poles in place and lashing them together. When most of the staves were in place he set groups to slathering on the mud, small sticks and straw.

The stones that contained the fire were moved over beneath an upsloping part of the cave roof. This upsloping area rose to their new wall, where they left a hole at the top of the wall so the smoke could exit.

Some of the women were put to work stitching together a heavy drape of old skins to cover the entrance.

Pell took the time to explain to each of them, including the men, what the leaves of the new root vegetables looked like and how to find them. When the new wall was nearing completion, he sent a small party out to find some. He especially enjoyed telling Exen to join the group of "root hunters."

Pell also enjoyed driving Pont as hard as possible. Initially, he'd been angry when he saw the healer was untied, but Gontra explained that he thought that the healer should work just as hard as all the rest of them.

At the outset, Pont had sullenly tried to refuse some task Pell assigned him as too menial, but before Pell had a chance to react to Pont's insolence, Gontra'd cuffed the medicine man to the ground, threatening to cast him out or kill him immediately.

Lying on the ground, Pont had tried to bluster and threaten as in the past, "Gontra, you can't treat your Medicine Man this way. Who's going to care for you when you're ill?"

"Pell will," Gontra rasped out in a barely contained fury. "He's a far better healer than you ever dreamed of being."

Pell wanted to protest that he wasn't a healer, just a bonesetter, but he kept his peace.

Still lying on the ground Pont made some finger motions at Gontra and began to chant. Though Pell had no respect for Pont, he still felt a chill run up his spine at the thought of Pont casting his spells. Gontra, however, wasn't intimidated. He stepped forward, delivering a huge roundhouse kick to Pont's ribs that left him gasping for breath. "Chant around that, you boar's turd! Try it again and I'll cut your throat." Shaking his head he muttered, "I should've done it last night."

It took Pont a while to recover, but since then he'd complied immediately with Pell's every demand. Pell made a point from then on to assign him the most menial tasks he could think of. Pell pitched in and worked alongside the Aldans, though carefully far from the healer, wanting to provide no opportunities for an attack or even an "accident."

Pell's excellent physical condition allowed him to work easily, even after the others all felt exhausted. They began to watch him with more and more awe. Soon the wall and door were in place. The cave was darker and somewhat smokier, but already much warmer. The others noticed the difference even before it was finished, exclaiming in delight. Pell showed them how to use a brand from the fire to see when they needed to go into the darker areas of the cave.

They finished the hard day's work with a feast composed of more of the boar from the day before and roasted versions of the new root vegetables Pell had brought them.

While they ate Pell found himself giving them a little philosophy lesson about his concept that *everyone* should know how to gather and everyone should understand hunting and cooking well enough to do a little if pressed. When the men protested that the women couldn't possibly have the strength for hunting, Pell pointed out that they could still act as beaters, driving animals toward the men. The Aldans would certainly need such tactics in their decimated tribe.

He also reminded them that not all animals were large and dangerous. "*If* I teach you my new methods for hunting, you'll find that they work as well or better for small animals. Women can employ these new methods just as well as the men. A small tribe like yours, one with few men, should appreciate these changes. You certainly shouldn't resist them."

After eating, conversation sprang up around the fire. First, talk of old times, then plans for the future. Ginja, sitting at Pell's side as he fed her bits of roast pork drew questions about how Pell controlled her and how he communicated with the Great Wolf Spirit. Pell found himself almost constantly suppressing mistaken notions about the animal.

The Aldans' conversation about the future seemed to contain *some* hope. A little optimism instilled by a long hard day of work in which everyone had pitched in and something of significance had been accomplished.

As the tribe prepared for sleep, Gontra tied Pont up despite his protests. Initially, they were protests of his innocent intentions, then of his importance. Finally, it degenerated to threats of what his magic would do to those who dared restrain him. Pell worried that Gontra might buckle under the threats as so many had in the past, but Gontra continued unfazed, reminding him of his earlier threat. "Pont, you go ahead, start a spell on me. Just like I promised before, I'll cut your throat before you finish."

Pell wondered what was to keep Pont from cursing Gontra during the night while he was asleep, but apparently, Gontra didn't think such a thing was possible with Pont's hands tied behind his back.

Hobbled and led to the back of the cave, Pont shot Pell a venomous glance that chilled his blood.

When Ginja lay down to sleep her warm body was in direct contact with Pell's legs. He found her presence reassuring.

The next morning Pell awakened feeling good. He secretly delighted in rousting the others—obviously sore from the previous day's hard labor. He told them he was going hunting again, but he expected them to be working while he was gone.

When they protested he castigated them for their laziness. "You *tell* me you're worried about surviving the winter. You whine about how hungry you'll be and cry about the children who might starve. Yet, you lie around as if you were a bunch of fat pigs. If you're fat, fine, but then don't ask for *my* help. If you're starving, work like you're hungry."

He set them to gathering firewood and, after criticizing Exen's party of the day before for only bringing back a few of the new root vegetables, sent out more digging parties.

He explained his theory of dryness and air circulation as regarded the rotting of food and had some of the Aldans begin weaving shallower baskets for storing food.

He even put the children to work, restacking the root vegetables and turning the grain that the Aldans had stored that summer, admonishing them to make sure any moist areas dried out.

When he set out to check his traps with Ginja bounding at his side, Pell was in a banner mood. It was a brisk winter-fall morning and their breath puffed out before them. There was a little frost on the ground, but he felt warm with his thick new moccasins, furs, and leggings. He even felt as if most of his old tribe members might survive the winter, with a few gifts of "magic meat" and some coaching on some of Pell's new ideas.

He'd been worried the traps might not yield much so late in the fall. Hunting had always been hard late in the year except for the occasional bounty from big herds migrating through on the high plains above the cave.

Sometimes they could be trapped in a location where a herd could be driven over a steep edge into one of the ravines. Usually, several of the big animals broke their legs on the steep slopes and could be killed easily. If the winter freeze had already occurred, or occurred soon thereafter, the meat could keep almost the entire winter.

Of course, Pell had no experience trapping in late fall, but he'd feared the success rate would fall off drastically as some species began to hibernate and fewer animals were out and about. Thus he felt gratified to find a rabbit in his very first snare. The next several were empty but then he found that he'd snared three squirrels who'd used the previous warm afternoon to try to collect a few more nuts for winter.

Best of all, one of the two large nooses he'd set up from his traveling rope had a young deer in it. The deer had broken its own neck trying to get away. Pell didn't even have to spear it. Finding it difficult to carry all the animal bounty at once, he stopped to clean all five animals, then put the heart, liver and smaller animals inside the deer's abdominal cavity.

At first, he thought he'd sling the deer over his shoulders like he'd carried the young boar, but realized this would turn the deer so the small animals could fall out. Remembering the travois they'd planned to use for the move at Cold Springs, he cut two poles and tied the deer between them. *This is easy*, he thought as he started back, dragging the poles behind him on a game trail.

Pell was almost back to the cave when he thought to stop and stick his spear between the deer's ribs in order to support his "hunting" story. He struck the smaller animals with rocks, thinking to himself that he'd never even heard of someone managing to hit even two squirrels in a single day.

As he rounded the bend into the little valley below the cave, Ginja began a low, rumbling growl. She turned to look back down the path behind them. Pell was dismayed to see one of the big cats following the scent of the deer's blood on their trail. He knew he should leave the meat and run, but thinking of the hungry people in the camp, he couldn't bring himself to give up the deer.

Trotting down the path, still pulling the travois, Pell called out, "Gontra! Bring fire! Hurry!" He was pleased his voice didn't break, but a glance back showed him the lion had stopped following the scent trail and picked him up visually.

It loped after him a moment, then stopped to roar. Pell's heart pounded in his throat, but he kept running, reasoning that, if it attacked, it would initially pounce on the deer. If he had to, he could always leave the deer to the lion at that point.

He really wanted to have his spear in his hand though, and he couldn't, not with both hands already dragging poles. The spear was stuck into the bonds holding the deer in place. Another quick look back assured him the spear remained close to hand.

Unfortunately, the big cat's ground eating lope quickly brought it close. Pell dropped the travois poles, grabbed his spear and stepped back.

Ginja, snarling and snapping, hackles raised, backed slowly alongside him.

The lion stopped to let out another roar, then eyes on Pell and Ginja, lowered its head to snuffle at the deer.

Pell thought of casting his spear, but was afraid to give it up.

He picked up a rock and threw it, but missed. However, there were plenty of rocks available. He picked up a handful and began throwing them, calling out to Gontra again and again.

He was surprised to realize his aim *had* gotten better! He hit the big cat a couple of times making it snarl, looking about, but not recognizing Pell as the source of its pain.

A couple more strikes and it threw its head back and roared, apparently hoping to drive the irritant away. Pell managed to hit it just about every time it lowered its head to feed, though it'd managed to tear away a couple of mouthfuls. After a hard strike to its nose, it leaped back, slashing about with fangs and paws.

Finally, in a fury, it charged toward Pell and Ginja. However, once they scurried back, it returned to the carcass it'd claimed and didn't want to give up.

Thinking that he must not be within hearing distance Pell decided he should go to get Gontra. Perhaps he could get back with fire in time to drive the lion away before the entire deer had been consumed.

As he turned to go Gontra and Tando rounded the bend, each carrying burning brands in their hands. "Pell! What do you need fire for?"

"Quickly!" Pell pointed. "We've got to drive the lion away. It's eating our deer," Pell ripped up a big armful of dry grass from beside the trail and held one end to Tando's brand. As it started to burn he trotted back toward the lion.

They looked where he was headed, focusing on the big cat for the first time. "Great Spirit Pell, look out! Look out!"

"Come on! Lions are afraid of fire. Start some more grass burning so we can drive it away."

~~~

Gontra and Tando thought Pell'd lost his mind. Nonetheless, they also ripped up some dry grass, lit it with their brands and started warily after Pell.

Pell approached the big cat, yelling and waving the flaming grass at it. He bent to light the dried grass that stood beside the trail.

The lion eyed the flames warily. After a few moments, it bent and, grasping the deer's hindquarter in its jaws began to back away. The travois poles, still bound to the deer, promptly snagged between a tree on one side of the trail and some rocks on the other, anchoring it firmly.

Pell stalked toward the lion, waving flaming bundles of grass in both hands. The grass burned his right hand and he threw what was left toward the cat, stopping to tear up more. Unfortunately, when he threw it, the bundle of grass flew apart without really threatening the big cat.

Tando lit another big bundle of burning grass for Pell. This time, when he approached with the flaming bundle, the lion finally gave up and loped away.

Gontra stood about twenty paces back. Tando a little closer, both goggle-eyed. "I can't believe it! You chased a *lion* away from its kill?"

"No, I chased a lion away from *my* kill," Pell said, sticking his spear back under the bindings and picking up the travois poles again.

As Pell turned to start back to the cave, Gontra began a stream of questions. "How'd you kill the deer? How'd you think of the travois idea? What made you think you'd be able to chase a lion away from the carcass?"

Tando said little, but he was obviously deep in thought.

Pondering answers, Pell looked ahead. His eyes lit with delight, Gia stood up the trail a little way, her eyes shining.

As he got closer, she ran up and threw her arms around him. "Oh, Pell! Chasing lions?" she said unbelievingly. "What if it'd attacked you?"

Overcome with emotion, Pell bent slowly to set the travois poles down, then stood to put his arms around Gia. She hadn't let go, even while he was lowering the poles. Powerful feelings washed back and forth over him. For a moment, he felt swamped with his relief at escaping the big cat, his wonder that Gia was holding him, and his dismay that the lion might have killed him and he'd have missed this moment.

Pell whispered, "I'm sorry Gia."

She looked up at him with tears in her eyes. In a choked voice she said, "Oh, Pell, I know you've hardly noticed me. Even so... I, I... I don't know what I'd do without you. I barely have the courage to talk to you, but I still dream of being your mate. If I can't be your mate, I still want to live where you live. I don't know if I could've gone on living if that lion had killed you." She pushed her head against his chest and clutched him to her, hard.

Pell's ears were ringing and he felt a little dizzy. *She, wanted him*? He said nothing for a moment as his eyes rimmed with tears, "Gia, I haven't been able to tell you… any of my feelings truly… since first I saw you at the trading place … I never dreamed that you might want me the way I want you. I'd be honored… *so* honored… to share your life and be your mate."

She wrapped her arms around his neck and pulled his head down to hers.

After a pause, in a small voice, Pell said, "I promise not to chase any more lions." Gia stifled a little giggle against his neck.

Gontra cleared his throat. When Pell'd blinked his own eyes clear and looked over, Tando's eyes were moist and Gontra was staring off into the distance. Gontra said conversationally, "Um, maybe we should get this deer back up to the cave before the lion comes back? I could drag the poles for you."

Pell found himself walking up the trail behind the travois, a firebrand in one hand and Gia wrapped under the other arm. Chills and goosebumps ran over his body, as he continued to be wracked by powerful emotions. Pulling the travois, Gontra was just in front. Tando walked on the other side of Gia.

Pell asked Tando and Gia why they'd come to the Aldan's cave.

Tando said he'd come back with Belk, who was better, but didn't seem fit to travel alone. "For some reason, Gia felt like she had to come along too," he said, winking at Gia, who punched him lightly on the arm. "She had a lot of reasons, 'The children might be sick, Belk might get worse, I'd like to see that area,' but if you ask me, she just wanted to see a certain young man…"

Gia ducked her head. "Yes," she whispered, "it's true."

"Besides," Tando continued, "I thought the Aldans might need some help from some of your new ideas. Knowing how pigheaded I've been about not sharing your ideas and how honorable you've been to me, I was afraid you might not feel free to tell them some of the methods that, after all, were really yours. So, I came to tell you to teach the Aldans whatever you wanted, if *you* thought it was the right thing to do."

He shrugged, "Maybe we should swear them to be our sister tribe and ask them to keep the secrets too." He shook his head sadly. "But now that I've seen them, I know they won't live through the winter without your help and your crazy tricks."

Gontra was beside himself with joy and apprehension, "*Will* you teach us, Pell? Tando says it's okay with him, but that it's actually up to you. Will you?"

Pell pondered his answer. In view of his hate/fear relationship with Pont and his dislike of Exen and Fellax, the decision didn't seem to be as simple as he'd thought it would be—at least before Tando had set him free to decide for himself.

As if he were looking directly into Pell's mind, Gontra said, "I know you're probably still worrying about Pont. Wondering how you could live around him, even for the brief time you'd need to teach us some of these things.

Right? But Pont solved that problem himself this morning! He said that he and 'his people' were going to leave because they didn't want to stay here with me as the leader, doing whatever *you* said. I think he thought a lot of the others would go with him, but even Lessa refused. When it came right down to it, it turned out 'his people' were Pont and Fellax. He and Fellax did pack up and leave. He says he's got a friend who's the medicine man in the Oppo tribe. They're going to go join them."

Pell's mind whirled. The only person left in the Aldans that Pell had a problem with was Exen. He didn't want to complain to Gontra about Gontra's own son. Pell was torn between feeling that the right thing to do was to teach the Aldans and still wanting somehow to teach Exen a lesson. Before he'd decided anything they got close enough to the cave that people saw them. The Aldans poured out to surround them and the deer, sparing him the need to answer right away.

It was apparent that Gontra considered the entire episode with the lion to be nothing less than a miracle. He started describing the events he'd just witnessed, heavily embellishing the story. Pell's answers to Gontra's questions about the lion attack became almost unrecognizable. At first, Pell felt embarrassed by the attention, then flattered by everyone's awe, then embarrassed again.

That he'd killed a deer by himself amazed the Aldans. But they just couldn't accept the fact that he hadn't run when the lion appeared. They also couldn't believe the wolf had stayed with him to face a lion. Pell could see the awe in all the faces except Exen's. Exen, on the other hand, showed first anger, then grudging respect, then jealousy, and finally anger again.

Pell, embarrassed by all the attention, started trying to get them back to work on his projects, preparing food storage, completing the flap to close of the cave opening, etc. This attempt was derailed when Ontru, who'd begun to move the deer carcass in order to start preparing it to be roasted, discovered the rabbit and three squirrels in its abdominal cavity. Astonishment flared anew. "You killed a deer, a rabbit and three squirrels in *one* hunting trip?!"

Pell shrugged, "Sometimes you get lucky."

Gontra guffawed, "That is waayy beyond luck, Pell. Hey Exen, what do you think of our mighty 'root hunter' now?! Maybe, after he teaches you how to hunt root vegetables, you *might* be able to learn how to hunt animals like this, eh?"

There was no answer and Pell looked out of the corner of his eye at Exen, expecting to again see hate or anger in his eyes. Instead, he saw Exen staring in awe at the deer, rabbit, and squirrels. Exen's eyes shifted to Pell, still with undisguised amazement in them, then they dropped to the ground in shame. He shuffled his feet a moment then slowly made his way over to Pell. He stood a few heartbeats, staring at Pell's feet. "I'm sorry," his voice was almost a whisper, nonetheless it carried well in the sudden dead silence that pervaded the cave. "I'm sorry for the terrible things I've said... I'm sorry for the times when I took Denit's side against you, especially... after you fixed my father's finger. And I'd be grateful for the rest of my life if you taught me how to hunt like that."

Pell felt his face flush, and he snorted. "First... First, you've got to do a better job of hunting roots you know."

A flush of embarrassment rose on Exen's face, but he looked up into Pell's eyes and then in a strong voice, one that resounded around the cave, he said, "I'd be proud, forever proud, to one day tell people that the *Bonesetter* taught me to hunt roots."

The End

**Hope you liked the book!
If you'd like to read more, try**
Bonesetter 2 -winter-

**To find other books by the author try
Laury.Dahners.com/stories.html**

Author's Afterword

This is a comment on the "science" in this science fiction novel (many would consider this story to be "prehistoric fiction," but as an important part of this story is the discovery of "new to them" technology, I think it also fits into science fiction). I've always been partial to science fiction that posed a "what if" question. Bonesetter poses "maybe" and "how" kinds of questions.

Maybe some ancient artifacts that have small slits or holes in them, have them not for decoration, but because peering through a pinhole corrects vision defects such as near-sightedness.

Most prehistoric stories focus on hunting, but it may be that snares were terribly important, but just aren't typically made of materials like flint that survive for archaeologists to find.

How did wolves become domesticated into the dogs we know today?

Primitive tribes do have people who work as bonesetters, how did the first one learn his trade?

Preserving food had to have been a huge advancement for primitive people, how did they figure out how to do it?

Acknowledgments

I would like to acknowledge the editing and advice of Gail Gilman, Jack Gilman, Nora Dahners, Lotta Bangs, and Jan Mattei, each of whom significantly improved this story.

Made in the USA
Middletown, DE
14 March 2023